CONT
UN_ _ _ _ _ _ _

A collection of tales from David Court

Author Illustration: Rees Finlay

David Court

Contents May Unsettle

Cover artwork by David Court

Edited by Lance Fling

Contents

David Court

Foreword by M.F. Wahl

HELLO THERE, dear reader. You've made a wise choice by picking up this copy of Contents May Unsettle Not just because of the exercise (I suggest you buy a few copies if you really want to maximize these benefits), but also because you've cracked the cover of something I believe to be truly special.

In my travels, I've written for the (now defunct) Mash Stories, written book reviews for the highly regarded Dread Central, fancied myself the Editor-in-Chief of an ill-fated horror-art and short-story anthology magazine, and bested the angry red mountains of notifications spewing from my digital inbox, stuffed with work from various writers I have had the pleasure of knowing. Suffice to say, I have read a great many works by a great many writers. Of these, products of both known and unknown writerly personalities, David's work stood out to me from the first story of his I read.

We first met under the umbrella of a small micro-press publisher, both doing our best, learning how to put our own writing out into the world. Although I had read a few pieces of flash fiction he had written for the publisher's blog, the first proper story I read of his was *Microcosm, Macrocosm* (thoughtfully included in this collection). It was as I read this story, that it dawned upon me how absolutely talented David is (just don't tell him I said so). His work evoked memories of many a "Year's Best Sci-Fi" anthologies, packed full of big names and big ideas, the likes of which many writers aspire to reach.

Foreword by M.F. Wahl

Just to be sure David wasn't a one-hit-wonder, and to keep a close eye on the competition, of course, I offered my (probably unsolicited) input on the story and expressed my desire to read more of his delightful work. Since then, it has been my distinct pleasure not only to get to know David, eventually considering him be a good friend, but also to witness the birth of the collection you now hold in your hand.

What strikes me most about David's work is his stunning knack for writing in a way that absorbs the reader. Despite the many varied settings in which he has allowed his imagination free rein, from sea to shining star, he has managed to tie them all together with an often sardonic and sometimes scathing critique of the human condition that is oh so, David. Good art tells us a story about ourselves, it entertains, amuses, and above all else, it resonates deep within us, leaving an indelible mark.

When reading the stories in this collection, it's easy to see the influence of shows such as The Twilight Zone, The Outer Limits, or Creepshow. It is also just as easy to draw parallels between his writing and some of the greats, such as H.P. Lovecraft, Clark Ashton Smith, Ray Bradbury, or Kurt Vonnegut. It shouldn't, then, be surprising to discover the often thought- provoking nature of the collection. It asks many questions of us, pushing us to reconsider the views we hold dearest and, of course, leaves the answers in the hands of the readers.

In spite of the dark and heady themes that run through these stories, there is one thing that stands above all else, *this collection is damn fun*. David never misses a chance inject his trademark wit and humor, nor does he shy away from hard hitting subjects, which brand of pork scratchings is most delicious (Boarwell's, of course), what to do when grandma thoughtfully gifts you a pair of socks for Christmas, or how best to make mashed potatoes.

David Court

It has been said there is nothing so frightening as a blank page. Perhaps, I think, whoever first said this hadn't actually read much, as there surely is nothing truly so frightening as man's imagination. I suspect David's quill has rarely been held by a hand unsteadied by fear of a blank page but perhaps, after he has darkened it with his words, he has given pause—if only to marvel at his sheer (and sometimes evil) genius.

There is one caveat you should heed as you flip through the pages of this book: David is something of a warlock. He has the uncanny ability to use his words to cast a spell upon the reader that is nearly impossible to break until you have reached the final word. Know that it is likely your sense time will be affected, making you late for various appointments, such as bedtime. Your friends and family may become worried about you, as the external world melts away, leaving your social media feeds empty of your political thoughts and pictures of your cat. So too, may your snacks be suddenly attracted to your clothing, seeming to leap from your lips, barely noticed as you are unable to peel your eyes away from the page for even a second.

If you, brave wanderer, should dare to venture further, take comfort in the fact that this book is worth your while and won't eventually make for a handy doorstop (unlike all that exercise equipment). And, if my word isn't good enough for you, person I don't know, it may entice you to be aware that this collection has been fully endorsed by the great Rod Serling ('s ethereal being). In fact, he loved it so much he agreed to cameo.

Never stop reading,

M.F. Wahl

Introduction

WELCOME TO my new collection, and most welcome you are, too. From *The Shadow Cast by the World* through to *Forever and Ever, Armageddon*, a brief detour via *Scenes of Mild Peril*, and here we all are!

Thanks to my two partners in writing crime – Lance Fling and M.F. Wahl. Between the two of them they have four eyes and two brains I couldn't be without, and they're a pair of good friends (and awesome people, to boot) whose opinions and enthusiasm keep me writing.

Infinite thanks also to Emma and Matty-Bob at Burdizzo Books, two of the best writers, publishers and finest specimens of people you could hope to meet.

Also, much love to George Bastow; word wrangler *par excellence*, poet, and old head on terrifyingly young shoulders.

Anyway, I hope you enjoy the selection of tales presented here. They're a varied bunch (poems, science fiction and horror stories, and one attempt at erotic horror. You'll recognise that one because it has the word 'erection' in it. Twice.)

David Court
April 2021

David Court

Entanglement

THEY WERE ALL huddled up in those icy trenches, coats pulled tight, Ushanka-hats pulled low, no man able to recognise his neighbour.

It was Maxim's accusatory tone that roused Artem, even over the howling violent winds. It was delivered in a tone even colder than the ice plains that surrounded them in every direction.

"*Zjelob!* You damned half-wit, Artem. You've left the Madsen cartridges behind".

Artem pulled his collar down, looking desperately about himself. He could hear his fellow soldiers cursing him, even with their words muffled through the warmth of their jackets. He was *sure* he'd still had the bulky bag of ammunition with him when he'd leapt for cover into the trench.

Old Orlov was up first, scrambling up the ladder and slowly poking his head up over the trench's edge. With a wordless gesture to Artem, the boy handed him his binoculars.

"Maxim's right," Orlov said, turning to face the rest of the men, "Borscht-for-brains has left the bag in the town."

A collective sigh echoed from the men, along with a few more choice insults. The embarrassment did little to add colour to Artem's frozen pale face.

"It was an accident!" he cried, trying to placate the frustrated soldiers. He remembered it clearly; they'd rested for a moment in the abandoned town on the outskirts of Galicia. Volkov, ever

Entanglement

the connoisseur of architecture, had stepped out into the open to admire the beauty of a synagogue. Unlike the rest of the town, it was mostly intact – Volkov joked that God had apparently seen fit to shield it from the recent shelling and cannon fire.

The shooting started and Volkov had gone down missing half of his head, and that's when everything became a little hazy. Old Orlov, sprinting so fast his face had gone as red as the borscht he so loved, was screaming at them to run back to the trench they'd only just left. Artem had put down the bag to collect his rifle and – *hadn't picked the bag back up.*

"A mistake, eh? That's what your *matushka* said when she saw your baby head popping out from between her milky thighs," laughed Orlov, dropping back into the trench. "You'll have to go and fetch it."

"And face that sniper again? The game isn't worth the candles."

Maxim, the huge rifleman, stepped into the fray. He leaned over Artem, glowering down at him. Only his piercing angry blue eyes were visible in the gap between his collar and the brow of his Ushanka. He undid the top buttons of his greatcoat, freeing both a fine red beard and his snarling mouth.

"How many people have you killed, Artem?"

Artem looked nervously about, shivering from both the cold and the sheer fear he felt in this goliath's presence. He tried to stammer an answer, his mouth suddenly painfully dry.

"I'll rephrase that, Artem. How many *Germans* have you killed? You've probably killed a handful of fellow Russian troops just through your own incompetence."

Artem looked over to Lebedev for support. Lebedev and he were the youngest and most inexperienced in their squad, and, as such, were often the subject of humour and derision amongst their fellow soldiers.

"Lebedev, you saw me kill those two Germans, right? Back at Galicia?"

Lebedev, seemingly as similarly disappointed in Artem as his colleagues, simply shook his head and looked away.

David Court

Maxim stepped over and picked up his Madsen light machine gun. It would have dwarfed any of the other soldiers, but in his huge hands, Maxim made it look like any other rifle.

"*Svetovid* here-" he said, cradling the barrel of the gun as though he were caressing a long-lost lover, "Svetovid here has killed more than four dozen Germans."

No matter how hard he tried, Artem struggled to formulate words. The vowels atrophied in his mouth, reduced to nothing but cold air by the time he went to say them. With each step Maxim took toward him, Artem was forced to take one back.

"There's not a man in this trench who'd argue that you're more important than Svetovid."

Artem's back was now against the trench wall, but that didn't stop Maxim leaning in even closer. Their faces were almost touching, and Artem could feel the anger radiating from his skin, melting the ice around them.

"And you see, the problem is - the *big* problem that we *all* have is that you've left Svetovid's dinner back in the village."

Maxim stood back; arms folded.

Artem, sensing how badly this was all going, looked around his fellow soldiers in a last-ditch attempt to appeal to their conscience. They all seemed reluctant to meet his gaze, turning their attention back to their cigarettes or to their own shuffling feet.

"My friends, to go back is a suicide mission. Surely, we can make do with the ammo that we have? Is it truly worth it, to risk a human life for a bag of cartridges?"

Orlov was once again at the top of his ladder, peering over the edge of the trench. He took a glove off, licked his index finger and held it to the wind, nodding quietly to himself.

"Don't waste any time breaking into a sprint once you get over the top," he instructed, an eyebrow raised. "By my

Entanglement

reckoning, you'll have about thirty seconds before he starts shooting at you. Forty, tops."

The old man moved aside so Artem could use the ladder. "Why is that, Orlov?"

Artem was at the top, ready to go, before Orlov gave his answer, barely hiding his amusement.

"He'll be so surprised that the Russians breed idiots who run directly towards snipers, that he won't be able to hold his rifle straight through laughing. Now, fuck off and get that ammo."

Time moves at a distinctly different pace when you're fearing every moment will be your last, but by Artem's reckoning, the old bastard was out by about twenty seconds. The kill-hungry sniper in the village didn't waste any time opening fire.

What Artem lacked in speed of thought, his legs more than made up for. Even his fellow soldiers, watching the silhouette of their companion dwindling into the distance, had to admire the boy's pluck and speed.

Orlov now wished he'd opened a book, opening a wager into how far the boy would get.

There was a knack to running across the snowy plains, one that Artem had learned over many months while becoming skilled in the art of retreating. You didn't want to run too fast, or you'd risk tripping. Run too slowly, and you might as well stand still. Learning the lay of the land was also critical – encounter ice, a deep patch of virgin snow, or a low clump of barbed wire - and you'd be a goner.

Run in a straight line, and you were a sniper's dream – shortly to be nothing but another scratched notch in his gun stock.

Artem could feel the displaced air from each bullet as it passed him by, pelted with rock and snow from every near miss. He winced with the noisy whip-crack of each and every shot.

There was a flash from the easterly tower of the synagogue at the village's corner for each shot made, the tell-tale sign of the sniper's location, now given up any pretence at hiding.

His lungs were burning, a warm pain growing to engulf each of his legs. Fearing his feet would give way, he began running to the only cover between here and the village, a building reduced to a single sturdy wall, scarred with twisted and scorched rebar.

The sniper, spotting his targets sudden change of course, increased his rate of fire. Artem found himself screaming, a cry of pain and determination.

He threw himself behind the concrete remnants of the fortification, rolling to an undignified halt in the snow and mud. A last shot rang out, pebbles of cement ricocheting off the cold earth. The sniper, realising the futility of trying to shoot through solid concrete, ceased firing.

Lebedev, despite his earlier apparent lack of concern, was the one nagging at Orlov the most about Artem's progress across the battlefield. They all had their own binoculars, mind, but it seemed stupid for more than one of them to risk sticking their head over the edge of the trench. The frustrated sniper might be looking for a *fresh* target.

"Has he made it, Orlov? Is he still alive?"

Orlov turned and looked down on the massed soldiers.

"Remarkably, yes. The boy appears to be as fast as he is foolish," smiled Orlov, "He's not at the village yet, but there's only a short while to go, and he's having a rest behind some cover. The *sooksin* might actually do it."

Maxim punched the air in celebration, and the other troops turned to look at him, surprised by his sudden uncharacteristic bout of compassion.

Entanglement

"It's my ammo I'm concerned about," he said, sheepishly. "I'm more bothered about that than I am the boy. If he doesn't get it, we're sending Lebedev over the top next."

Orlov was rarely given to optimism, but even he was beginning to think the boy could make it. It was only when he heard the rotors of the German Albatros D.III aircraft pass overhead that he realised the poor boy was doomed.

Artem heard it too, the familiar drone of an aircraft engine. He'd guessed it was a D.III before he even turned to see its approach, this particular aircraft becoming more and more commonplace every day the longer this war lasted. The Germans seemed to be able to build them quicker than the Imperial Russian Air Service could shoot them down.

They were fast, manoeuvrable – custom-built for ground-attacks. Especially against unarmoured seventeen-year-olds with nowhere to run.

He sat with his back to the wall, facing the oncoming plane. The pilot was now beginning his attack run, and it would only be a few moments before the double Spandau machine guns would begin to spit molten death.

Artem unslung his Fedorov Avtomat rifle from his back, squinting down the barrel as he levelled it towards the approaching plane. The ground in front of him erupted into flame, a deadly wall of bullets drawing closer.

Artem screamed in defiance as his finger squeezed on the trigger, firing a desperate burst of rifle fire at the oncoming D.III, closing his eyes as he waited for his inevitable doom. Let braver men than him face death down.

David Court

Orlov watched incredulously as the wing of the Albatros began to cough out plumes of thick black smoke, levelling up from its descent and veering sharply right. By the time the aircraft had crashed into the sniper's synagogue tower, all the men were up their ladders and watching the scene unfold.

The plane, now a flaming pyre of scattered metal, fell to the foot of the tower. Most of the tower, a huge chunk of brickwork lost to the initial collision, collapsed on top of it. Grey smoke belched skywards, releasing a thin layer of dust that coloured the surrounding ice and snow. Flames licked around the base of the tower for a few moments, before they were extinguished by the settling rubble.

Within moments, they were all running to Artem across the ice plains, screaming and whooping like excitable children. Even Maxim, a man not given to shows of emotion, was cheering.

Artem was still bewildered as they surrounded him, staggering around glassy-eyed, clutching on to his rifle like a walking stick. He was covered in a layer of grey dust that coated both skin and uniform, the white of his staring eyes shining through. A giggle from him became hysteric laughter, a joyous expulsion of disbelief and relief, his white teeth gleaming in the failing light.

"Artem, the grey ghost" quipped Orlov, slapping the young boy heartily on the back, "We all saw you do it this time. The man who killed two Germans at once!"

Maxim scooped up the bag of Madsen ammunition, whispering a quiet Russian prayer to himself.

The German troops had, not surprisingly, cleared everything edible or drinkable from the bar before they'd moved on. The beer and wine barrels that they couldn't carry, they'd rather

Entanglement

selfishly taken an axe to. A king's ransom of wine and ale were now just overlapping stains of dried sediment and dust on the cellar floor.

However, the bar seemed like as good a place as any to relax and to celebrate Artem's minor miracle. If you ignored the broken windows and the smashed tables and chairs, the place had a certain coarse charm.

Orlov had a hipflask of potato vodka, and they were passing it around amongst themselves. Maxim handed the tiny metal flask to Lebedev, but he refused it.

"You seem agitated, my young friend," said Maxim, passing the flask back to Orlov.

"We were ordered to wait in the trenches for our reinforcements," said the boy, ever a stickler for the rules. He looked to Artem. Ordinarily, Artem would have agreed – but for now, he was revelling in the attention, feeling like one of the men for once. Much as how Artem had had no support from Lebedev earlier, Lebedev found himself receiving none now.

"You worry too much, Lebedev."

"I came to serve my country, not to carouse in a ruined alehouse."

Without another word, the young man collected his rifle and marched out. Nobody tried to argue with him further, or to follow him.

"There'll be sacramental wine in the synagogue, surely?" asked Orlov. He'd had the lion's share of the vodka, rightfully claiming owner's rights, and having drunk on a starving stomach, was by now quite well-oiled.

Maxim, hoisting his rifle over his shoulders and picking up the bag of ammunition, sneered at the old man.

"You damn heathen, Orlov. The Jews don't do communion."

Artem would never have ordinarily corrected the man-mountain that was Maxim, but recent events (and a bellyful of vodka) had imparted upon him an uncharacteristic boldness.

"They do Passover, though. They might have wine for that."

Artem hadn't seen Orlov move as fast since he'd been running, under fire, for that trench. Maxim and Artem ran out to the street in pursuit, but the old man was almost at the synagogue.

He was struggling with the thick wooden doors, but two rounds of fire from his Avtomat rifle, one after the other, reduced the handles to blackened splinters. With a strength belying his weather-worn frame, Orlov kicked open the remnants of the doors and was inside.

"Be careful, old man!" screamed Maxim, trying his best to keep up with Artem and hoping the old man would hear him over his enthusiasm. "The rest of that tower looks fit to fall."

As they stepped inside the darkened room, the damage was apparent. A corner of the room had collapsed, the early evening light shining through a jagged hole in the ceiling, a pyramid of brickwork lying scattered beneath it.

The stairs to the tower were similarly damaged, the stairwell filled with the remnants of the tower above. The only place Orlov could have gone was to the crypt, a tiled spiral staircase leading down to its depths.

Artem spotted the man first, a corpse whose bottom half was lost to the rubble, crushed beyond recognition. A Scharfschützen-Gewehr rifle lay at arm's reach from the body, dropped as its owner had been crushed by the collapsed ceiling. It was a sniper's weapon, like – presumably – the one wielded by the soldier's dead companion in the tower above.

They both recognised the uniform, as they'd been fighting these soldiers since Galicia. These were German allies from the Ukrainian Galician Army – The *UHA*.

Entanglement

"*Zhydivs'kyy Kurin'* UHA", said Maxim, leaning down to the body. The dead boy looked no older than Artem, blank staring eyes that hadn't seen much of life.

"Eh?"

"Jewish battalion of the UHA," he said, snapping a pendant from the boy's neck and handing it to Artem. It was blood and mud-spattered gold, the familiar six-pointed figure of a Star of David.

"Look at this," said Maxim, turning the boys head one way, and then the other. There was a small length of fabric pushed into each of the boy's ears, each a makeshift earplug.

Maxim and Artem looked at each other, nonplussed.

"Perhaps he'd grown tired of the sound of shelling," said Maxim, placing the boy's head gently down and closing his eyes with his fingers.

"They were a long way from their front," mused Artem, turning the jewellery over in his hand.

"Just what I was thinking, Artem. And why post two soldiers in a synagogue in an abandoned town?"

A shriek from the crypt halted their musings; not a cry of distress, but an exclamation of delight from their elderly drunkard colleague-at-arms.

The two men descended the stairs to find an overjoyed Orlov standing over a freshly opened small wooden crate. In the candlelight of the crypt, they could see the bottles of wine neatly nestled inside.

"*Ypa!*" Orlov declared, pulling out a bottle and holding it to the candlelight. "We've hit the mother-lode, my good friends!"

Maxim had picked up one of the candles and was wandering around the hall. It had been adapted into makeshift living quarters; two canvas bedrolls lay unfurled on the floor, a well-thumbed copy of the Hebrew *Tanakh* lying on one of them. He held the candle up to a passage that led from the main hall, the light from it flickering on the corridor's tiled floor.

"Maxim, Orlov," urged Artem, "We should be making our way back soon. Or else every one of us except Lebedev will be court-martialled."

"The boy is right," said Maxim, merrily picking up two of the bottles and placing them into his ammo bag, "Get the last of the wine, and let's get back."

Orlov picked up the three remaining bottles, dropping one into each of the two long pockets on his greatcoat. The third he threw to Artem, smiling at the boy as he pocketed his prize.

"Much as it would be nice to drink this wine down here in comfort, I guess you are right, Maxim."

It had grown dark by the time they emerged into the main entrance, the cold evening winds already blowing through the splintered door frame of the synagogue.

"It looks to be better tonight," moaned Orlov, "It's a shame we can't stay in that dry cellar."

"Be off with you." Tired with the old man's lethargy, Maxim virtually pushed the old man out of the synagogue. "You've at least got some wine to warm your old bones in the trenches."

Artem placed the Star of David pendant back in the cold open hands of the dead UHA soldier and made a silent wish. Not a prayer for the boy's soul, mind, but a wish that Artem would be spared a similar fate. It was only as he stepped through the shattered exit that he noticed the writing, masses of scrawled chalked Hebrew text adorning the inside of what remained of both doors.

The trip back was slower than Artem would have liked. Darkness had settled quickly and now the only light they had was from a flickering lantern Maxim had taken from the synagogue, the growing wind threatening to extinguish it. It

Entanglement

didn't help that Orlov kept regularly insisting on taking a few sips of wine for his nerves, and as a result his drunkenness kept lurching him away from the group. Artem and Maxim were having to take it in turns to hold the old man by the shoulder, both keeping him standing upright and frustratedly correcting his course when necessary.

The evening was particularly cruel, the wind biting colder and stronger than it had in a long time. The pinpricks of light from Lebedev's trench were drawing closer, but painfully slowly.

They had to walk in a huddle, as close to Maxim's wavering sphere of light as they could. Even then, they'd have to keep stopping to avoid the obstacles they only saw when they were virtually on top of them.

A whistle sounded from the trench, two shrill pips from Lebedev. His fingers struggling with the cold, Artem pulled the whistle from around his neck and responded in kind.

The lantern suddenly arced through the air, landing on a snowbank a dozen feet or so away from the three soldiers. Miraculously, it had stayed alight.

"What the hell are you doing, Maxim?"

The giant sounded panicked, pulling Artem and Orlov closer to him. The old man was now muttering away to himself, barely coherent.

"It wasn't me, Artem. It was as though something grabbed it!"

With fingers trembling through cold and fear, Artem unslung his rifle. Pointing it into the darkness, however, didn't fill him with any confidence.

The weight of Orlov, once resting against Artem's shoulder, had now shifted. The old man was staggering away from him, and in just a few steps had vanished from sight into the all-encompassing darkness.

"Don't move, Orlov!" screamed Artem, moving to where the old man had stood but finding him gone. He could hear him in the near distance, muttering away to himself drunkenly, but the whistling winds had picked up and were already hiding him.

"Artem?" came Maxim's voice, further away than the boy had expected. "Are you there, Artem?"

"I'm here, my friend. Stay where you are." Artem called, taken aback by the fear in Maxim's voice. He'd never known him scared.

"I'm not moving an inch, Artem. Orlov?"

Bizarrely, Maxim sounded further away than ever before.

"I've lost him. Can you see him?"

"I can't see *anything*, Artem. Only the light from the lantern."

Artem looked about himself, realising he'd lost his bearings. The light from the trench had gone, and all that the boy could see was the dull glow of the lantern light a few dozen feet away.

"ORLOV!" screamed Artem, knowing it to be a futile gesture before the word had even left his lips.

"Come to the lantern!" yelled Maxim, his voice already fading.

Artem began the walk to the light, every step cautious and considered. As the tip of a boot would brush against the rusted metal of barbed wire, he'd slowly alter his course. As his foot would come to rest on the sheer flatness of black ice, he'd do the same.

Like a blind man with his stick, he edged forwards.

He pulled his coat tight against him as the cold winds became strong enough to pick up the loose snow, pounding him with ice-cold pellets.

It was only when he felt himself pulled forwards and inside the warmth of Maxim's greatcoat that he dared to properly breathe. The two men stood there, huddled together for warmth, rooted to the spot. When their legs gave out, they fell to their knees. When their knees resigned, they slumped back to back.

Entanglement

The lantern died at first light, the tiny flame spluttering out just as the sun began to emerge over the battlefield.

Tired and cold, Artem opened his eyes. He felt Maxim groan, the giant's muscles shifting against Artem's back as he, too, stirred.

Under the dim light of the sun, their surroundings looked bleached of colour. Everything was tinged with a dull monochrome, colour only slowly creeping back into the world as the sun inched higher.

With protesting muscles, Artem slowly got to his feet. They'd wandered further off the beaten path than Artem had feared, finding themselves in a patch of barren wasteland dotted with puddles of sheet ice and scattered patches of vicious looking barbed wire.

How they'd blundered through it unscathed was nothing short of a miracle.

Two crows broke the silence, noisily announcing their presence to the world as they spiralled overhead.

Orlov was a few feet away from them, lying on his back. Artem feared him dead but the old man suddenly coughed in his sleep, turning to lie on his side and snoring noisily. In one of his hands, he was gripping on to an empty wine bottle with whitened knuckles. There was a length of barbed wire hooked around the toe of one of his boots. The old goat had no doubt tripped against it, but – miraculously – had avoided landing on it and cutting himself to shreds.

Maxim stood up, stretching his tree-trunk like limbs and yawning noisily.

"I can see the trench," he proudly announced to Artem, pointing at it with his gloved finger. They'd gotten closer than Artem had hoped. "Wake the old man and let's go home."

"Orlov!" shouted Artem. The old man stirred briefly, rambling under his breath, before closing his eyes even tighter and settling down again with a contented smile.

David Court

Artem stretched his arms and rubbed at his eyes, tired and desperate for one of Lebedev's strong cups of coffee back at the trench.

"Come on, old man" he said, approaching him.

The length of barbed wire around the old man's boot suddenly burst into life, snaking around his right leg. It wound loosely around his ankle and his thigh, emerging like a hungry root from the cold earth. Orlov shifted slightly in his sleep, oblivious to the barbed wire coiling around the entirety of his leg, the cruel barbs sliding loosely across the trousers of the old man's uniform. Artem froze on the spot, unable to comprehend what he'd just seen. The wire was clearly moving slowly, rippling as though alive, a blade of grass in the wind.

"Come on, you *bydlo*" said Maxim, appearing at Artem's side. "I want to get off this damn -".

He stopped in his tracks as he saw the barbed wire wrapped around the old man's right leg.

"What the hell? How'd you get so tangled up, you old fuck?"

He took a step closer, presumably looking to untangle his colleague. As he approached, more of the wire tore free of the ground, wrapping around Orlov's leg like a constrictor snake. This time it dug in, innumerable barbed hooks tightening and digging into Orlov.

He woke up with a pained scream, sitting up with a start, his fingers instinctively clawing at his leg. He pulled his hands back, each of them now reduced to damp scarlet gloves, strands of jagged skin hanging from each.

The more Orlov screamed, the more he writhed. The more he writhed, the tighter the wire squeezed. The leg itself was now barely visible, hidden under a swelling mass of glistening red wire.

Orlov's screaming subsided, now wracking sobs that shook his body. He looked at the two men, eyes glistening with tears. They could only watch on impotently as Orlov pleaded with them, crying for help.

Entanglement

He suddenly jerked on the spot, arms briefly flailing, one eye twisting violently out of place in the socket, the pupil replaced by white. A single word came from his newly blood-filled mouth, a sole resigned utterance.

"Oh."

The wire suddenly retracted back into the earth, unravelling at a terrifying speed. As the massed blades around his leg span away, they garrotted, they cut and tore. Every moment saw another layer of skin and flesh flayed, matter reduced to a spray of blood and meat. The air around them became filled with a fine scarlet mist, the smell of burning flesh and bone causing Artem and Maxim to violently gag. Orlov thrashed as he died, the force of the thing jerking him like a marionette.

As the last of the wire vanished from sight, all that remained of Orlov's right leg were a few thin shards of bone, splayed strands of gristle, the rest of the leg lying liquefied beneath it. The old man slumped back, dead.

The whistle from Lebedev sounded, shrill and clear. Artem and Maxim couldn't respond, both frozen with terror to the spot. Both men were covered with a thin layer of their dead friend, staring at his still-twitching corpse.

"A new German weapon. That must be it. That must be it" muttered Maxim, struggling to convince himself. He began to stagger backwards, unsteady on his feet.

Artem was forced to get behind him, placing his arm around the man's waist to bring him to a halt.

"We need to go *that* way", said Artem, pointing back to the trench. There was a relatively clear path between here and there. They could be back with Lebedev within twenty minutes, if they could keep their heads.

They'd become so used to the use of barbed wire on the battlefields that they'd become blind to it, almost treating it as part of the scenery. Now it was as much an enemy as the Germans – and it was ubiquitous, *everywhere.*

Maxim seemed reluctant to move forward, pointing about himself desperately, a thousand-yard stare in his wide eyes.

"The wire – it's *everywhere,*" he stammered.

"There are gaps, Maxim. We can make it, if we stick together. If we don't do anything foolish."

Maxim said the thing that Artem didn't want to hear – it was a truth that he knew, but he felt if he heard the words said, then it would sap all their will.

"It came up through the *ground*, Artem. Nowhere is safe."

"Still, we must try."

Artem took that first step forward, and Maxim dutifully followed. Their roles had been reversed; Maxim was typically the stoic one, but as a man, he'd been firmly grounded. Now his tentative hold on what he knew to be real had been challenged, and it had all but defeated him already.

The two men were careful to tread lightly, cautious of the thing that lurked both beneath and about them.

Lebedev's whistle sounded again, and Artem pulled out his own to respond.

"Are you sure that's wise?" he asked, nervously. "To announce our position?"

Artem nodded in agreement. Maxim's apprehension was indeed justified. It would only be a short while before Lebedev could see them, anyway.

Artem had spotted it first but was reluctant to voice his concerns out loud. Maxim, however, was under no such qualms.

The path had seemed clear from the start – a relatively straight course back to the safety of the trenches. However, the scenery was shifting in front of them. The patches of barbed wire

Entanglement

were *moving,* moving so slowly as to almost be imperceptible, but moving, nonetheless.

They'd made a few minor course deviations that should have been unnecessary, given their original course. Maxim had vocalised their concerns best of all, as the truth had dawned on him.

"It's herding us."

The giant was right. They were now standing at the edges of a small frozen lake, banks of barbed wire now hemming them in to both the left and the right. They could go back, but they both sensed they'd only end up being walled in.

It was like a game – if you stood still and watched the wire, it would not move. However, you sensed the wire that you *couldn't* see was slowly moving elsewhere.

They could only go forward.

"The ice here is thick," reassured Artem. "I think it'll take our weight."

"Yours maybe, *myshka*. Mine, I am not so sure."

"I'll go first, then. Follow me – I'll be keeping to the edges as much as I can. The ice will be thicker there."

Artem stepped onto the frozen waters, keeping his soles as flat as possible. There was crunching underfoot, but it was just compacted snow.

Having taken a few tentative steps forward, he looked behind him. Maxim crossed himself, before daring to step onto the ice.

The snow had become melted the further they travelled, the white frosting on the lake now a reflective blue and white sheen. The slightest of cracks now sounded beneath them as they travelled, but they were halfway now.

The only sound from Maxim had been the giant talking to himself as he concentrated on each step he made, but he suddenly piped up and spoke aloud.

"What do you think it is, Artem?"

"I don't know, Maxim. A monster, I think. Something just as evil as this war, anyway."

"We've never spoken much, boy. Are you a man of faith?"

David Court

Artem knew that Maxim was, and unashamed of it. He was forever praying, and it seemed to have seen him through this war so far.

"I am not, Maxim. My family were, but it's not for me."

"Not to worry, young *Tovarishch*. I am big enough to have prayers for us both."

Artem suddenly felt uneven, as though his balance had shifted. He swayed unsteadily, thinking for a moment the ice was tilting – but then it became apparent. The ice was not moving, but there was something visible *moving beneath it*.

"Maxim!" he turned to scream at his colleague, "There is something under the ice – we need to move!"

Artem sprinted a few steps, ignoring the unnerving cracking beneath his feet. He turned to check that Maxim was still following, but he was not.

"Maxim!"

Maxim was just standing there, staring at Artem. The ice beneath his feet was darkening, a growing pool spreading out like a red ink spot across blotting paper. Thin cracks spread out from that same spot as a growing spider's web, hairline fractures creeping across the ice.

Artem stopped in his tracks, and urged his friend to move, to take just a single step forward.

Water was welling in the corners of the giant's eyes – flowing salty tears became stained with red, rivulets of blood pouring down Maxim's face.

His skin was moving, bulging in parts.

A pained voice came from the giant, a sorry, strangled gargle.

"It's moving inside me, Artem."

His skin cracked as the barbs inside him slid through his soft flesh, his body bulging and contorting as those self-same razor tips slid around and between organs.

The thing had erupted from the ice beneath him, boring up through his legs and into the rest of him. Artem suspected it was

Entanglement

only the thing inside him keeping the giant standing. The entire surface of his skin was shifting now, peeling apart as raw strips.

"It hurts, Artem."

A moment of silence as he just stood there, swaying.

"It wants you to know that it *hurts*."

Maxim erupted as a cloud of razors burst from within the soldier's ruined form, barbed tentacles hurtling out from his pulped corpse.

Artem could hear the wire scraping across the ice behind him as he ran, a thrashing, expanding cloud of blades. He could feel the ice cracking beneath his feet, the displacement of air behind him as the wire desperately grabbed out for him.   He lunged for the far side of the lake, scrambling up the shallow snowbank. He slowly got to his feet, sighing with a bitter disappointment as he faced the huge wall of barb wire that blocked his path, towering above him.

The writhing mass extended a few tentacles of rusted steel towards him, the barbs along their surfaces flexing and contracting like cat's claws.

It was a futile gesture, but Artem unslung his rifle. Squeezing the trigger, he opened fire on the mass, squinting from the light of the flashes erupting across the thing's surface. Broken wire healed as he watched, severed links now reattached.

As a final, frustrated, last act of defiance, he threw the exhausted rifle at the wall of razor wire, watching as the wire wrenched and crushed it, reducing the weapon into shards of metal and splinters of wood.

The tentacles took him, grabbing him by his limbs and by the waist. He tried to turn away, but they held his head in place, prying his eyes open.

Artem was forced to endure every step of being dragged into the whirring, thrashing blades.

David Court

Lebedev peered through the mist of the battlefield, still unable to see his companions. He whistled again though, and moments later, they dutifully answered.

"Thank God," he muttered, lifting the binoculars to his eyes.

And then he saw him. A single figure, out there in the swirling mists. Slowly, they drew closer. They had their hat pulled down; their coat pulled tight.

It had to be Artem, having neither the bulk nor the gait of Maxim or Orlov.

Lebedev clambered up the ladder to meet him, and the two stood face to face.

"Where are the others?" he asked, panicked. "What happened to them?"

The coat was pulled back, and the hat fell away. The thing that had been Artem was just a hollow pale shell, a writhing puppet with holes where its eyes had been, a forced rictus grin on the flayed, stretched skin of its face.

It was only then that the bulk behind it shifted into view; a mountain of barbed wire, a thick metal tendril extending from the bulk and into Artem's back, wielding him like a mockery of a glove puppet.

Like a river, the mass flowed over and through Lebedev, filling him, filling the trenches, flowing like a red, rusted tide.

"It's a protective ward," said the soldier, his hands carefully tracing each of the words written inside the ruined doors of the synagogue.

"I didn't know you knew Hebrew," came the response. There was an element of mockery there, his companion caring little for superstition.

"I'm a scholar, of sorts. It's a hobby."

"What does it say?"

"Something about a golem."

Entanglement

"What, the *Juden* monsters of clay or mud?"

"A common misreading of the myth. It can be any inanimate object."

"Are they words for a spell? To conjure it?"

"No, to keep it *in*."

The soldier peered closer at the writing as his fingers continued to move over the last of the words. He whispered them to himself, knowing his companion would care little.

"*It will plead to escape, but you must be deaf to its cries.*"

His friend lit up a cigarette, striking his match against the rough stone of the synagogue wall. He took one last look at the writing on the doors.

"It's just magic and superstition, my friend. You can't win a war with that."

His colleague stood up, scratching at his moustache in the way he did whenever he was deep in thought.

"I wouldn't be so sure," he mused. "There might be more to this kind of thing that we like to believe. Never underestimate the truth hiding behind myth."

"You've been out of Bavaria too long, Adolf. The sooner we get both back the better."

The two men stepped out of the synagogue, tightening their coats against the wind.

And so, it remains. It flows through the trenches like blood through tributaries, and it burrows underground as a worm through earth. Discarded fragments of it itself it sloughs and sheds, just enough to trip or ensnare the unwary.

And when it does not move, it waits.

And when it does not wait, it moves.

ISOL-8

GREG MADE MUMBLING noises through his mouthful of food, waving his finger in the air to gesture that he'd thought of something appropriate to say. There were a few moments of awkward silence as he hurriedly chewed on the last of the disk of flavoured cardboard this place dared to call a chicken burger.

I'd hoped it was both worth the wait and suitably profound. It was neither.

"Do you know who didn't break out as a writer until he was fif-"

"Raymond Chandler," I interrupted. "Raymond fucking Chandler. Everybody always brings up Raymond Chandler. Do you know what the difference is between me and Raymond Chandler?" I asked, hoping Greg would understand it wasn't a question I expected him to answer. "Raymond Chandler wrote The Big Sleep. The book that frequently pops up in *The Best Books of All Time Ever* lists. I've written – sorry, am *writing* – a shitty Science Fiction satire that I'll struggle to give away."

"For all you know, Chandler might have thought The Big Sleep was shit when *he* was writing it."

"He might have, but we'll never know. And anyway, he was unemployed at the time, probably living off his oil company executive retirement fund. I'm working full time and struggling to find the time to write even a couple of hundred lousy words a night."

"You could always take up..."

I gave Greg the *look*. It was a look I'd only ever given him once before, one reserved for very special occasions.

We were fifteen at the time, both of us plastered with enough acne to form a complex dot-to-dot picture of the French Riviera. We'd both joined the school Dungeons and Dragons society a few months previous, because we'd heard a rumour that a girl had joined.

This was patently untrue. Turns out that Justin Bailiss had just gotten into Megadeth and was now easily mistaken for a girl from the back.

Our intrepid band had been questing for nigh on two months. We'd slain the Dread Banshee of Gil'morath and had bested the Bloodling assassins of the Night Quorum. Now we were at our journey's end and facing our nemesis, the Necromancer of Rockvale. Everybody except for Greg – who'd been diverted by a nearby treasure chest – and had been paralysed with a foul enchantment. Here, in the fantasy realms of the Eighth Vale, Greg was the mighty (yet easily distracted) Rugarth the Barbarian.

We'd scoured three dungeons searching for the one weapon that could defeat the Necromancer – *his true name*. All Greg had to do was shout it out loud, rendering the foul Mage's magic useless and making him vulnerable to mortal weapons. Our team could then happily hack him up, grab a big recognisable piece of mage cadaver each, and claim the bounty on it in our homelands.

"I shout the Necromancers name," declared Greg, triumphantly.

All eyes fell on him.

David Court

"What name do you shout?" asked the Dungeon Master, already turning the scenario manual to the victory page.

The name was written on all our character sheets, in large heavy pencil. We were all mouthing it silently in Greg's direction, willing him on.

Greg glanced at his character sheet, nodded sagely at us – and then gave the name of an inconsequential non-player-character we'd met two scenarios back.

"Are you sure that's the name you want to say out loud?" asked the incredulous Dungeon Master, trying to spare all our lives. Greg, suddenly panicked, looked at me.

I gave him the *look*.

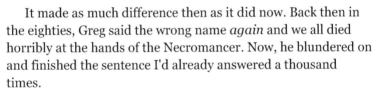

It made as much difference then as it did now. Back then in the eighties, Greg said the wrong name *again* and we all died horribly at the hands of the Necromancer. Now, he blundered on and finished the sentence I'd already answered a thousand times.

"You could always take up the writing full time."

"And what am I going to eat? Rejection slips? I'll be too busy using those to heat my freezing house. Or to pile against the door to stop the bailiffs getting in."

Oh, to be able to clone myself. I was sure that if I could just spend an extra two or three hours a day on the novel, I'd get enough momentum to properly finish it. Problem was, those extra two or three hours were taken up by everything else that wasn't work.

I needed a miracle.

And, inadvertently, Greg had the solution.

ISOL-8

The next evening saw the two of us sitting in the snug of the Albarossa Arms, putting the world to rights over two pints of *Ale Hydra*. Greg suddenly remembered something, grabbing a crumpled piece of paper from his bag and handing it to me with the enthusiasm of a puppy dropping a ball at his master's feet.

"It was on the office noticeboard. It's the answer to all your problems," he proudly announced. Unless the paper was a crinkly cheque for several million pounds, I sincerely doubted that.

I carefully unfolded the A4 sheet, which had been subjected to the hidden torments lying in the bottom of Greg's work bag. An assortment of crumbs, dirt and fluff fell from their respective paper-fold prisons.

I blinked at the gaudy, haphazard clipart, forcing myself to squint past the font choice. I could feel Greg staring at me as I read the first couple of lines. It appeared to be some nonsense about a clinical trial taking place for a product called ISOL-8. It sounded quite promising at the start – a means of relaxing and extending your free time – but by line three it had gotten into the realms of science fiction.

"It's some kind of con," I said, trying to hand him the sheet of paper back. He refused it.

"Why? It sounded spot on to me."

"For one, it's written in Comic Sans. That doesn't scream credibility to me. It's a font basically weaponised to irritate anybody with an IQ higher than their shoe size. And I fail to see how sticking myself in virtual reality is going to make–"

I traced my finger along a line of text on the sheet, reading it aloud in a nerdy voice.

"–your waking hours markedly more productive, whilst having no detrimental effects on the other aspects of your life."

"That sounds great though, right?"

"Also, completely impossible."

"You could always go along."

"You're not coming along yourself?"

David Court

"Strictly limited numbers, mate, and I can't really think of any reason I'd need it for – I'm not short of free time. And I thought you'd enjoy finding how it's a huge con and it is giving you something to take the piss out of me about."

"You honestly think I'm that shallow, that I'd go solely to have ammo to wind you up over?"

"If you'd just like to fill in the name badge and this questionnaire, we can see whether you're appropriate for the trial."

Despite the fact she'd gone through the process a hundred times since I'd joined the queue – smile, hand over the questionnaire and a blank name badge, deliver the line – her enthusiasm hadn't faltered in the slightest. Her smile looked *almost* genuine.

I was tempted to make up a false silly name for the name badge ("Ivor E. Towers") but chickened out last minute. I also answered the questionnaire with more honesty than I'd originally intended. For what I still suspected was a con, everybody was so bloody nice and sincere.

The questions were *mostly* straightforward enough; how many hours did I work, how much free time did I have outside of work hours, hobbies, phobias? I handed it in and the receptionist – still infectiously enthusiastic and happy – placed it on a shelf of other completed entries behind her.

"There are some drinks and snacks next door, if you'd like to go through" she said, gesturing to a door which I'd seen a fair few people enter and leave, "and we'll call you through if you're chosen."

I still wasn't entirely convinced this wasn't a front for Scientology recruitment, but I'd at least deprive them of a sizeable quantity of hobnobs and herbal teas. That'd hit them where it hurts.

ISOL-8

Being British, once laden with tea and chocolate digestives, I naturally gravitated to the part of the room that was furthest away from anybody else. We Brits have an unerring knack of being able to mathematically calculate the optimum position in any location that will keep us as far away as possible from other human beings. There's a certain irony in finding that skill in a culture genetically predisposed from birth to stand next to each other in queues as often as possible.

I'd barely managed to finish my third mini-pack of biscuits when they called my name, ushering me through into a small theatre with no more than two-dozen seats. A small projector was shining the ISOL-8 logo onto a screen that took up the far wall of the room. A small white wooden lectern sat in front of it.

I'd just begun the preliminary calculations of working out where to sit that wouldn't put me near any strangers, but the choice was taken out of my hands as I was led to a seat bearing a sheet of A4 paper with my name handwritten on it in thick black marker pen.

One by one, people filed into the room: male, female, black, white, young, old. When the last of the seats were filled, a tall imposing figure stepped into the room. She was about my age, albeit a good head taller, and carried herself with an air of authority. She walked over to the lectern, and stood behind it, surveying the room.

I swear her eyes lingered on me more than they did anybody else in the room.

"I'm Doctor Suzanne Levy," she declared, "and you have all been chosen, should you wish to take part, for the first United Kingdom trials of ISOL-8."

The lighting in the room dimmed as the logo faded from the screen and was replaced by a cartoon of a man sitting in a cubicle in an office.

"In the bustle of twenty-first century life," a calming yet authoritative voice announced through a variety of speakers set into the ceiling, "it's becoming increasingly difficult to master that work/life balance."

I recognised but couldn't quite place the voice.

"Impending deadlines, too many commitments... they all add up."

As the voice spoke, the screen showed speeded-up footage of the man in the cubicle waking up, having his breakfast, going to work, sitting in a cubicle with an ever-growing In tray, going home, going to bed – this was repeating over and over, the orchestral soundtrack becoming increasingly discordant.

By the twentieth-or-so loop, the pile of paper in the man's In-tray was as tall as he was, teetering precariously. The soundtrack suddenly stopped as the man screamed.

"But now, designed for frenetic twenty-first century lifestyles, we have the solution."

It was *Terence Stamp*, that's who it was. That gave this whole set-up an air of believability. I bet he didn't come cheap.

The man was suddenly alone in a blank white space, the grey watermark of the ISOL-8 logo fading in behind him. Grass appeared at his feet, and he sat on it and smiled. A butterfly flitted about, lazily.

"ISOL-8."

The cartoon was replaced by video footage showing a young woman in a doctor's office. The doctor was going through some papers with her, and the two were smiling. The legend who had played Zod in the awesome Superman 2, and Chancellor Valorum in the considerably less awesome Phantom Menace, continued his narration.

"With a simple and painless – and reversible – procedure, the ISOL-8 port is wired into your nervous system."

The young woman was now at home, sitting alone on a comfortable armchair in one of those sitting rooms you see on television that are too tidy to have ever been lived in. She was holding a small white plastic glowing snub-nosed pyramid in the palm of one of her hands – the pyramid had the ISOL-8 logo etched in black on every surface and a single black button on the top.

ISOL-8

"And when you want some time just to yourself, you're just a button press away."

The woman's surroundings faded into whiteness, and she was standing in an empty void.

Here was Terence again; "This is *your* place. As empty or as fill as you see fit, a virtual realm for you and you alone. With inexpensive In-realm transactions, you can customize it as you see fit. It's completely removed from the real world – there'll be no distractions from phone calls, emails – your realm is utterly remote."

The woman's surroundings shifted, from a tranquil looking forest, to an exotic desert oasis, to a medieval banqueting hall. The woman turned slowly on the spot, eyes closed, smiling.

"It's a place for relaxing, for reflecting – for spending as long as you like in. And the beauty is..."

The image shifted back to the woman in her sitting room, slowly opening her eyes, visibly relaxed.

"When you return to the real world, only seconds have passed."

The screen now showed the white pyramid rotating slowly on the spot, the ISOL-8 logo prominent. The orchestral music moved to a swell, and Terence had the last words before the screen switched off and the lighting in the theatre came back up.

"ISOL 8: Tune in to *you*."

One of Doctor Levy's aides was handing out brochures to those assembled. It looked like an expensive lifestyle magazine, full of sickeningly pretentious inspiration quotes in white italics. Still, I had to admit to being intrigued.

"Are there any questions?" she asked, and an array of hands shot skywards. I was a little astonished to see that mine was one of them.

She turned to face me, squinting over the top of her thin-framed spectacles to read my name badge. She pronounced it correctly first time, which was somewhat of a surprise.

"How can you spend as long as you like in there?" I asked, intrigued by the technology. "How does that work?"

David Court

"The human mind," she began, as though reciting from a memorized script, "when not burdened by all that messy and cumbersome bodily control, is an incredibly powerful processor. Because it's a direct neural interface, your brain is processing information thousands of times quicker than it ordinarily would. The figure varies slightly between people, but on average you'll get eight hours in ISOL-8 per second of real time."

That was met by a flurry of impressed murmurs. I noticed a few hands go down, all presumably from people who'd had the exact same question I'd had.

"The video mentioned micro-transactions," asked another. "How much does this all cost?"

That was exactly the sort of cynical question *I* should have asked.

"This is a local trial, so the ISOL-8 equipment is free. You'll need to go to one of our designated private hospitals for the surgery, but that'll be subsidized. The brochure details the prices of the customization options available to you, but they're all easily affordable micro-transactions. Most of the basic options are free, anyhow, but you can have the ISOL-8 up and running exactly as you'd like it for the price of a couple of cups of good coffee."

"What does the surgery entail?"

"It's a minor procedure that will take about twenty minutes to complete. A nanofilament will be inserted into the nape of your neck, and that'll be connected to a small metallic tattoo that'll act as the wireless interface. There will be some residual bruising, but no more discomfort than that. It's the sort of thing you could do in your lunch break."

"What about fatigue? Won't you just get exhausted by potentially adding so many hours to your day?"

"One of the key points of ISOL-8 is that, when you're in your realm, your brain thinks that you're asleep. You could spend ten hours in there but when you come out, you'll be completely relaxed. When we say free time, we genuinely mean that it's *free*."

My mind was abuzz with the possibilities. I could finally get that book finished. My realm could be my writing domain – I wouldn't even need any micro-transactions to customize it. A table, a chair, and a typewriter or word processor would be all I needed. The fewer distractions, the better.

My customary cynicism was oddly disengaged, incapable of preventing me from staring firmly into the gaping maw of this particular gift horse. Apart from a brief sarcastic comment about the length of the hefty Terms and Conditions document that was briefly scanned before being signed, they had me hook, line, and sinker. Even the ordinarily terrifying medical disclaimer documents were completed with nary an alarm bell going off.

My singular focus was on that virtual writing retreat.

Greg and I had been sitting in the bar of the Albarossa in silence for a good half an hour - me lost in thought, him stuck on the crossword – before he broke the silence.

"You can thank me any time you like, you know" said Greg through a mouthful of Guinness foam.

I stared back at him, quizzically. *Thank him for what?*

"For telling you about ISOL-8," he interjected, clearly recognizing the confused look on my face.

"Oh, I probably would have heard about it anyway. Something like this will be *huge*."

He went back to nursing his drink, muttering something under his breath. I looked down at my barely touched lager, realising that I didn't really feel like drinking after all. I was too excited about the potential of ISOL-8, and I'd been thinking about it all night.

"I'm going to make a move," I said, standing up and collecting my things. "I'm with the doctors first thing before I go to work. I'll let you know how it goes."

Greg gave a half-hearted wave goodbye and staggered over to the jukebox, fumbling with a handful of small change.

The process was, as Doctor Levy had promised, painless. I'd always toyed with the idea of getting a tattoo – I'd just never imagined that my first ever one would be a nanofilament-laden corporate logo. After the process was complete, I was handed a surprisingly lightweight polythene sealed and logoed white box that contained my customized ISOL-8 unit.

Work dragged on that day; such was my excitement at getting the unit home to try it out. Sitting in my kitchen, I carefully opened the box and removed the white pyramid from its polystyrene cocoon, placing it on the counter. The only other things in the box were a USB cable for charging the device, and a small quick-start guide.

"Your device is fully charged and ready to use!" it proudly boasted. A small unnecessary series of iconic diagrams showed a man – the same cartoon figure from the promotional video – sitting in a comfortable chair and pressing the button on the pyramids flat top.

I carried the small device through to my sitting room, placing it on the wide arm of my favourite chair. Sitting back and settling against the shifting black leather, I pressed the button. The pyramid shone with a strobing inner light and an impressive transition effect saw a rectangle of white in the centre of my vision grow until it surrounded me.

The velvety tones of Terence Stamp welcomed me to ISOL-8.

ISOL-8

The void; an infinite white plane of uniform whiteness, as vacant and as empty as a politician's promise. The experience was slightly disconcerting – I had physical form, but, despite the nothingness, I was not falling. I was simply *suspended* there.

I could see the reason for the questionnaires now – this would be *hell* for an agoraphobic.

A grid of icons suddenly rushed towards me with the velocity of a subway train, screeching to a sudden halt mere inches from me. Each icon was a flag, and Terence urged me to choose one for my chosen language setting.

Craning my neck to look at the array of options provided, I reluctantly chose the American flag in the absence of a Union Jack. As I stared at it, it merrily rotated for a few moments before the icons whooshed away into the infinite distance as quickly as they'd arrived.

The next series of options talked me through connecting my ISOL-8 account to PayPal, and Terence Stamp sounded almost giddy with excitement in letting me know everything had been connected correctly, and that I was free to proceed.

I looked down at my physical form, a basic humanoid wireframe shape, the same colour as the world that surrounded me, only visible because of the thick black outline that surrounded me. I remembered from the brochure, that the customization options didn't only extend to my bottle universe but also to my own crude avatar.

It was too empty here. I had to create *something*. I wonder if this is how God felt, in those early days – although in this case, the team at ISOL-8 had created light *for* me.

The neural interface worked like a charm. I only had to think of terrain customization and a list of options appeared on a panel that floated in front of me. Some were free, but the price increased accordingly the more elaborate and interesting they got.

I started simple, choosing a grass floor template. Even something as straightforward as this had a list of tweaks and options (grass colour, length, something called RealFeel™ that added a couple of pounds to the price), but I chose the default.

Upon selecting it, an infinite plane of grass extended as far as the eye could see in every direction. I was suspended in space no longer, now standing on the grass, which I could actually *feel* against my polygon toes.

I crouched down to examine it more closely, finding a repeated pattern of small pixelated green blades. I tentatively extended a wireframe finger and could feel the touch of each, rubbery and smooth.

I spent a few moments walking, feeling the physical (albeit slightly unreal) sensation of movement and the grass beneath my feet. It felt as though I could walk as far as I wanted in any direction, and the landscape would remain unchanged.

From the array of skyscapes available (including the skies of alien or fictional worlds), I opted for a simple (and more importantly, *free*) Earth sky, ticking the option for real-time day/night transitions. The evening sky appeared, a beautiful shade of black and dark blue gradients pin-picked by vivid white stars.

Now, mostly immersed in darkness, with barely adequate lighting coming from the aforementioned stars and a brilliant white crescent moon, I selected and erected a streetlamp. It looked somewhat out of place, something that would have been more at home on a roadside and not on a grass plain, but it served its purpose, bathing the area around me in a warm luminescence. It didn't really fit in with the minimalistic theme I'd accidentally given the place, but it was free.

I then choose a simple building, a rectangular flat-roofed block with a door and windows. I opted for a warm red brick skin for my little construct, wandering around its walls and brushing my fingers against the coarse clay and mortar.

I stepped inside, flicking the light switch just inside the door. I spent the next half hour decorating this empty chamber, first lining the brick walls some plain wallpaper and placing a dark

ISOL-8

brown thick carpet beneath my feet. I set a single table in the rooms centre, and then looked through the menus for a suitable tool on which to continue my masterpiece.

Despite the free word processors available, I spent the lofty sum of seventy-nine pence on an antique typewriter. It was a beautiful silver and black thing, possessing a greater level of detail and realism than anything else that populated my tiny world, me included.

The record player I set in the corner of the room was free, but the music was not. I was assured from the menu that when the ISOL-8 software went properly live, I'd be able to link it to my Spotify account, but the time being, I'd have to purchase music separately. It was a limited selection, but luckily adequate.

I chose *Bitches Brew* by Miles Davis, the same album I used to accompany my writing at home. In some weird way, it felt like the link between that reality and this one, a potent nexus to keep me grounded. As the haunting strains of *Pharaoh's Dance* filled the room, I smiled at this little dominion I'd created.

Another seventy-nine pence were spent on a decent leather office chair. Even though I doubted it was possible to get back strain from a virtual world, it seemed like a worthwhile investment.

It was only as I sat on it, pulling myself closer to the typewriter (and the pile of paper that came with it), I came across my first hurdle.

In the real world, I'd written sixty or so pages of *Nova's Gambit*, my would-be/impending science fiction epic. And for every page of the novel, there were three pages of scribbled handwritten notes.

How the fuck would I get them *here*?

A quick call to a very patient gentleman at ISOL-8 Customer Service next morning talked me through the process (He said his name was David, but he spoke with a thick Indian accent, so I doubted the honesty of that statement). There was a small fee to open what they called a "Shared Document Account" – these micro-transactions were certainly adding up – but it would be possible to upload documents from the real world into to a folder I could access from my ISOL-8 realm. The more money I spent, the larger the potential storage space of the shared folder.

Despite my promises to myself that I wouldn't allow ISOL-8 to interfere with my day job, much of that morning was spent scanning in my notes and manuscript on my works equipment, hiding my activities from the prying eyes of my inquisitive boss (who'd already been asking me questions about my new tattoo).

I couldn't finish work quickly enough, wolfing down my evening meal with such ferocity that I could feel the pains of indigestion even in my virtual realm. My manuscript and notes were there waiting for me upon my arrival, and the ground-breaking jazz of Miles Davis accompanied me through a productive three and a half thousand words of story.

As I've said previously, I'm a Science fiction writer, but was now using technology that was almost beyond the realms of anything I'd even *considered* possible.

If I were writing about this kind of tech in a short story or novel, now would be the point I'd start dropping hints about how there was a sinister side to it. Perhaps ISOL-8 were using their apparent benevolence as a cover to harvest people's brainwaves, or to use the hardware for some devious identity theft scenario.

Perhaps the protagonist (me, in this case) would start encountering previously unexpected side-effects from use of the ISOL-8 equipment. Perhaps I'd become addicted, ending up as a gibbering wreck unable to distinguish the real world from the virtual one.

ISOL-8

Perhaps my employer would start to notice a change in my personality, an obsessive or short-tempered side to me. I'd be fired, and I'd retreat to my virtual realm, becoming ever more separated from reality.

Maybe I'd encounter another being in that empty realm, an electronic ghost of somebody whose physical form had died, and they'd become trapped in that digital limbo. Or even worse, I'd gone insane believing that there *was* a ghost in there.

The real world, as it turned out, even with this fancy gizmo, remained equally as mundane. As with most corporations, the most ominous aspect to ISOL-8 was their love for money – resulting in a somewhat lengthier credit card bill for me than usual, with an array of assorted seventy-nine pence transactions dotted throughout.

And one ninety-nine pence one. I'd fancied a nicer carpet.

I'd banked a fiver's worth of profit on the Quiz Machine when Greg appeared behind me, jabbing at the button wrongly declaring Geri Halliwell to be a member of All Saints and losing me the lot.

"Sorry, mate" he half-heartedly apologized, handing me my three quarters of a pint of lager. It looked like he'd spilled most of it between here and the bar.

As we sat ourselves down, he opened his pack of Boarwell's Pork Scratchings and laid it splayed on the table like some manner of porcine sacrifice, spilling most of the contents on the floor. Unphased, he leaned into me conspiratorially.

"So, when are you going to introduce me to this ISOL-8 lot, then?"

"It's a closed trial, Greg. I don't think it works like that."

"Tina in Reprographics says they've opened it up. She signed up Bill from Procurement, and he's having the surgery tomorrow."

David Court

Come to mention it, there had been something in the ISOL-8 newsletter about introducing friends. Truth be told, I hadn't paid it that much attention.

"What would you use ISOL-8 for?"

It'd be *wasted* on him. Within twenty minutes, his ISOL-8 realm would be a gaudy mess of mismatched architecture and pop-up boxes. And, knowing his self-control, he'd have spent his month's wages on In-realm tat by the end of the first week, and *I'd* have to buy all the drinks.

"I've always fancied re-learning the guitar, but I've never had the time. Or the space to practice. It'd be *perfect* for that."

"*Re-learn*? That implies you knew how to play it in the first place. I saw your first band back in the early nineties, remember? You sounded like a game loading on the ZX Spectrum. I'd stick to the triangle, mate."

Greg sat back in his chair; brow furrowed. He shook his head as though he'd thought of something to say but had then decided against it. However, just as he started to relax, he blurted it out regardless.

"Do you know what, mate? Fuck you. Fuck *you*. Don't forget who it was who told you about ISOL-8, and here you are, not wanting to do the same back."

Greg occasionally got a bee in his bonnet but didn't usually need much placating to see reason.

"Oh, come on now, mate. You just got me a flyer from the office noticeboard. Hardly a herculean effort."

Far from calming down, Greg got to his feet.

"Don't call me *mate*, mate. I'm the one who has to listen to all your shitty ideas and read through your equally shitty stories. You know, the ones where you told me to be honest, until I told you anything I didn't like about them, and you told me that was because the ideas had gone over my head. All I've ever gotten back from you is fucking sarcasm and arrogance."

"Oh, fuck off, Greg. You told me you liked reading them."

ISOL-8

"Only because you fucking flounce off if I tell you otherwise. So what if I was a shitty musician? You were a shitty writer too, but I helped you. And you won't even do me the same bastard favour back."

He turned on his heels and headed back towards the bar.

Prick. He'd soon come back when he realised he'd left his Pork Scratchings.

Any time soon.

Any... time... now.

Fuck it, I'd have them.

The real world became a means to earn money, refuel myself and empty my bowels. Without that annoying prick Greg and his obsession with going to the pub and socialising, I threw myself into finishing the novel. As ISOL-8 grew more popular, the default transaction price rose from seventy-nine pence to eighty-nine pence, but it was still a (literal) small price to pay.

I'd spent some money on improving the landscape outside my ISOL-8 "house". It was nice to have a break from the writing and wander along the new babbling stream I'd had installed, watching the Koi Carp frolic beneath the lapping waters (with realistic Tru2Life Liquid Physics™).

Between chapters, I'd often stare into the distance at my adapted Mount Rushmore. All but one of the faces were characters from Nova's Gambit, Washington's head replaced with my own sixty-foot-tall gurning mush.

I'd taken to using the skies above the house as a scratch pad for my notes – a new feature they'd introduced that I'd initially childishly abused by having "FUCK GREG" plastered up there in a font size big enough to render each letter the size of a small moon.

I'd written it in Comic Sans. It seemed appropriate.

David Court

With perfect timing, I'd written "THE END" just as the last track – *Sanctuary* – drew to a triumphant close on Bitches Brew.

It was complete. All one hundred and eighty thousand words of it. From first draft, to finished manuscript – hundreds of man hours of work in my ISOL-8 realm taking up just a few minutes of my life in the real world.

I couldn't have been happier with it. With all this time, I'd perfected it. Every line of dialogue was snappy and critical to the plot, every single moment was carefully balanced and integral to the story.

It was, truth be told, fucking great.

I'd keep my ISOL-8 realm, I decided. The subscription was cheap enough to keep going, and I'd be needing it for the inevitable sequels. The publishers would be squabbling over this one, I had no doubt.

Only the shared folder didn't seem to have an "Upload" option. There didn't seem to be a way to get this hefty document back into the real world.

That nice man from Customer Services would help.

I'd once experimented with my ISOL-8 environmental settings by temporarily shifting the location of my realm to their equivalent of the Antarctic. That environmental shift had lasted an entire eighteen seconds before I'd selected "undo". It was fucking freezing, and I was feeling that same way now.

It was Martin on the phone this time, a thick accented Pakistani.

"It's all in the Terms and Conditions, sir. ISOL-8 is designed as a relaxing environment for contemplation, and it clearly states in both paragraphs one-one-nine-two and two-two-oh-four that it's not to be used for creative endeavours."

"Yeah, yeah, I got that much. But let's just say that I *did* use it for creative endeavours."

"Page one hundred and sixty-two; your brainwaves pass through our proprietary ISOL-8 software. Any creative works created using our bespoke toolset are the intellectual property of the ISOL-8 Corporation."

"But I wrote a *book*."

"I'm afraid it's our book now, sir. You did agree to our terms and conditions that explicitly stated that."

"I can remember what I wrote. I'll just do it again in the real world."

There was a moment of silence from Martin, thoughtful contemplation before he delivered that chilling, calculated line.

"We'll sue, sir. I'm afraid it's our book now."

Short of launching a tirade of obscenities at the cool-as-a-cucumber "Martin", I was suddenly lost for words. And the irony of having lost my *actual* words to ISOL-8 was not lost on me.

"But... they're all my ideas. Everything in it. Years of work. This is so unfair. You can't suddenly say they're yours because of a hidden clause buried away in a nine hundred-page document."

"We can, sir. That's precisely what I'm doing. And it was mentioned four times, and the document in question is only eight hundred and seventy-eight pages in length."

"But... there'll be other writers. Poets. Artists. Musicians. Loads of others who have spent hundreds of hours inside ISOL-8 creating *stuff*."

"I hope not for their sakes, sir. If they are, they're breaking their terms and conditions."

"You... you can't do this. I'm the writer. It's all mine. I had *sequels* planned. Is there nothing you can do to help me?"

There was a pause, as though Martin was leafing through his *Bumper Corporate Guide to Being an Obnoxious Wanker* for the precise entry explaining how he could be as cutting as he possibly could.

David Court

"As a goodwill gesture, sir, we'll refund your last month of transactions. It's the least we can do."

You've got that right, Martin. *You've got that right.*

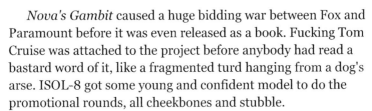

Nova's Gambit caused a huge bidding war between Fox and Paramount before it was even released as a book. Fucking Tom Cruise was attached to the project before anybody had read a bastard word of it, like a fragmented turd hanging from a dog's arse. ISOL-8 got some young and confident model to do the promotional rounds, all cheekbones and stubble.

To add insult to injury, the fake name they gave him was an anagram of mine.

The film has its premiere tonight, and the bastards at ISOL-8 have – as a complimentary gesture and final parting *Fuck You* - sent me two tickets. There are rumours they're expanding ISOL-8 in the next couple of weeks for a secondary market; they're going to sell it to old wealthy people as a virtual retirement home, so they can live on for the equivalent of *centuries*.

There's some small solace in that I'm not the only creative that ISOL-8 screwed over – misery loves company, after all – but it turned out that none of us had a leg to stand on. That one checkbox – "I have read, understood and accept all the conditions" – fucked us all royally. They lost a lot of creatives from their user base that way, but they've already demonstrated that ISOL-8 can make money for them in a lot of other ways. Turns out they've been *just* as creative.

The irony was that they'd earned enough money from our works combined to afford all the lawyers they wanted to protect *them* from *us*. Possibly a few judges and politicians along the way, as well. And their lawyers probably used ISOL-8 themselves to spend all the time they needed making any case against them *watertight*.

ISOL-8

If I was a cynical man, I'd suspect that that was their ploy all along.

I'm sitting there, cradling the tickets in my hands, wondering where it all went wrong.

There's at least *one* thing I can correct.

Greg answers the phone after a couple of rings, and I can hear him jabbing at his phone's buttons randomly, shouting at nothing. Eventually, he sorts it out.

"Long time, mate" he says, calmer than I could have hoped.

"It has been. Too long." I reply, genuinely happy that we're talking again. "I've got some tickets for that *Nova's Gambit* film, mate. Fancy joining me?"

"That'd be great. Pub after?"

"Pub after."

"ISOL-8" was featured on Episode 550 of the Sci-fi podcast StarShipSofa.

David Court

The Necronomnomnomicon

A THOUSAND SHIPS are shipwrecked, adrift on stygian shores,
Their billowing sails all stripped and gone, but he'll need a thousand more,
Until he's all the white ones, they're the ones he needs the most
To sew them in the costume of a thousand-foot-high ghost

He didn't eat the sailors, he left them all to drown,
He's saving space for candy which he'll greedily gulp down,
In his house at R'lyeh, dread Cthulhu is dead keen,
To go out trick-or-treating on this special Halloween.

Shub-Niggurath is coming too, he's dressing as a bat.
If Hastur's mum will let him out, he will be wearing that
Flat-headed outfit he insists is one of Frankenstein.
"That's the doctors name", they all maintain – Hastur's so asinine.

Yog-Sothoth can't come tonight, he's feeling rather peaky,
Stabbed by some investigators, that made him somewhat leaky,
Curse his vulnerability to that damned enchanted sword,
He's at the local hospital, stuck in Charles Dexter Ward.

The Necronomnomnomicon

It's a rare old treat for Elder Gods, this special celebration.
Herbert West's prepared the drinks, a special green libation
"With qualities", he proudly boasts, "of great rejuvenation".
(Presented in a punch-bowl full of green illumination).

And if that band of Elder Gods end up upon your street
And you are faced with that grave choice, I urge you to say
"Treat".
Be sure to be insistent as you won't be asked again –
A trick from Cthulhu and his pals can render men insane.

Halloween ends; Our Elder Gods are all clutching at their chests
To shed this heartburn and bellyache will take a lengthy rest.
Cavernous bellies full of jellies, candies, chocolate, cake and pie
That, which is now full of sweets, can now eternal lie.

Power Trip

THE WORST THING about it? Dan's perfect green eyes were the last to go. The sensible part of Brigitte knew he'd have been dead way before then, more than likely a victim of ventricular fibrillation as the current passed through his heart. If that hadn't killed him, the shock from his flesh burning would surely have done the trick.

But even at the end, as Brigitte was forced to leave him, dragged away by her colleagues, she'd taken one last glance back. Perfect, undamaged white orbs glared back at her from a smoking and jerking husk, and Brigitte was convinced there was still life in those staring pupils.

The expression in those eyes.

Pleading for her help, or begging for death? Moments later, Dan's blackened shell had burst into flame, rendering both redundant. Brigitte was deaf to the cries of her colleagues as eager hands grabbed and pulled her away.

The lives of Brigitte and her office colleagues had been, temporarily at least, spared quite by chance. A networked game of Quake – one of the few games that would run on the underpowered office computers – had dragged on longer than expected. Ordinarily, this wouldn't have been an issue, but it had been determined that tea and coffee duties for the whole of the next month would be determined by who scored the least *frags*. With something of such importance on the line, it wasn't unexpected that Brigitte, Eric, Dan and Clive found themselves late and having to sneak into the meeting room, mingling with the assembled crowds at the edge of the room, as though they'd been there all along.

Eric had, as ever, beaten them all soundly. Clive had narrowly come last, managing to snatch defeat from the jaws of victory in an attempted sneak attack on Brigitte. It wasn't an ideal result, as Clive's tea and coffee-making skills were somewhat lacking. *A good cup of tea*, Dan had once insisted, *should have the colour of the skin of He-man*. Clive's were a closer match to Skeletor.

Dick Elswood, owner of Stimulus Laboratories and their top-level boss, was in full flow. All the department managers were standing behind him, pretending their level best to appear captivated by every eloquently enunciated word that spilled from his moustached lips.

A slideshow unfolded on a large monitor behind him, showing detailed animations of radar dishes swivelling into position and satellites in geo-synchronous orbits neatly aligning themselves. Some bombastic and inspiring music was playing in the background, loud enough to hear but not loud enough that you could make out the tune or for it to drown out Dick.

"...and, of course, none of this would be possible without the boffins from Tesla Lab," Elswood smiled, gesturing to a group standing in front of the stage. "So, without further ado, let's switch it on."

Tesla lab. Always bloody Tesla lab. And nobody used the phrase 'boffins' anymore. This was the twenty-first century, for frag's sake.

Stimulus Laboratories was, ultimately, a think-tank. A privately funded organization, it housed dozens of individual groups of scientists and technicians, all of whom were beavering away at any number of unconnected secret projects. Other than the odd rumour, many of them didn't even know who their colleagues *were*, let alone what they were working on.

So, having mostly ignored every part about the meeting email other than what time to attend, Brigitte and her small team had no idea what was going on.

Elswood, away from the microphone now, stood on the edge of the stage holding a champagne flute aloft. He began to gesture at the assembled crowds and the managers behind him to raise their glasses too.

"That's not fair!" moaned Clive, never usually one to miss out on a freebie. "They've all got glasses!"

"They were all here ten minutes ago, Clive," smirked Brigitte. "During which time, you'd been busy throwing yourself off the edge of the Quake map with a misplaced rocket jump."

Eric laughed, and it was only then they noticed he'd somehow managed to be holding a full glass of champagne in his hand. Clive was about to ask him where he got it from when Elswood began the countdown from three.

Brigitte and her team had no idea what everybody else in the room – themselves included – were counting down *to*. Sometimes, it's just easier to go along with the crowd. Right on cue, timed to match the over-exuberantly bellowed "Zero", the lights briefly flickered and dimmed.

There were a few moments of silence, followed by some murmurings from some of the assembled crowd. A shower of sparks exploded from the stage, and the room was plunged into sudden and complete darkness. The general vibe of anticipation quickly transformed into confusion and mild panic.

"Everybody stand still!" Elswood could be heard shouting above the general bewildered hubbub. "No need to panic – the emergency lighting should kick in at any mom-"

Brigitte clearly remembered two things happening at the same moment. The emergency lighting, as Elswood had reassured, *did* burst into illumination. So, however, did poor

Power Trip

Dick. Jerking around on the stage like a marionette in a typhoon, violent blue flames exploded from his every orifice. Despite his fierce thrashing, his limbs violently twisting with enough force to snap bone, he staggered about in front of the crowd, somehow managing to remain upright.

Those who'd considered panicking whilst immersed in darkness had now decided, not unreasonably, to fully commit themselves to it. It was clear from the general shouting, screaming, and hollering that a great deal of the assembled crowd was tempted to join them in blind terror as well.

Still Dick stumbled around on stage, his vacant sockets and open mouth glowing bright blue from an inner light. His blazer was appropriately beginning to catch fire, flickers of orange and yellow flame appearing around the collar and lapels. It was disappointing, but not unexpected that none of upper management were trying to help him. All they could do, it would appear, was attempt to stay out of the way of his flailing, flaming grip.

Sensing the mood of the room, Brigitte and the crew had begun to make their way towards the exit doors.

Dick's limbs suddenly jerked out straight, like a man crucified. White-hot bolts of lightning leapt from the fingertips of this electric messiah, arcing like phosphorous-bright wildfire through the assembled management. Like a poorly rehearsed boy band, they jerked and writhed as the electricity coursed through them. What remained of Dick was finally engulfed in a brief inferno that sputtered and faded as his ashen corpse collapsed in on itself.

Brigitte could feel the hairs of her neck and the backs of her hands stand up on end as unnatural energies surged around the room. Fingers of lightning shot from person to person, felling each as they hit, an ever-growing deadly radius approaching them from the direction of the stage.

They'd fallen through the doors, screaming survivors at their heels. The aroma of freshly painted and polished lecture theatre had been overridden by the acrid stench of charcoal and the sulphurous reek of smouldering keratin. Only a handful of them had escaped from the room, the remainder presumably electrocuted and draped over each other in a smoking pile of corpses.

Blindly, they'd ran. In any direction away from that hall, but somehow instinct and perhaps something more had kept them together and, as one, they found themselves back in their lab, puffing and gasping for breath as they collapsed against the walls.

This was a refuge of sorts. As Software and Hardware support, they were afforded a certain level of privacy. After all, nobody sane would dare venture down here, lest they be blindsided in a flurry of unintelligible jargon.

The usual identikit corporate posters found dotted throughout the remainder of Stimulus Labs weren't to be found down here. There wasn't a motivational one-sheet with some supposedly inspiring photograph of scenery (with an insipid empowering quote) in sight. The only posters down here were ones of vintage computer games or some in-joke you'd need a degree in computer science to comprehend, and a master's degree to get.

They stood there in silence for the longest time, heavy and laboured breathing being replaced by gentle sobbing from all of them, except Eric. He simply stood there, calm and quiet, staring intently at his empty champagne glass, as though it held the answer to everything.

And then Dan, level-headed Dan, always calm in a crisis, suddenly rose to his feet. There was a look of determination in his face, that familiar expression that always appeared just as the rest of the team were panicking over the most recent high-priority work-related crisis.

He strode over to his desk and picked up the phone, holding the receiver to his ear. After taking a deep breath, his index finger flashed towards the speed-dial button.

Power Trip

A jagged, witches' claw of white lightning leapt from the earpiece and engulfed Dan's head before spiralling around the rest of his shuddering form. The phone, reduced to a misshapen mass of molten juniper-green plastic, fell from his jerking grip.

And that was how they'd lost Dan. Ironic that the one amongst their number who'd made a career out of being management material, but never being promoted, had met their fate.

Even huddled in the confines of the IT storeroom with the door closed, they could still smell him – that sharp tinge of ozone and copper. It was Clive who broke the silence.

"Does anybody know what Tesla Labs were actually *doing?*"

"I'd heard from Janine in Reprographics that they were doing experiments in sustainable energy," muttered Brigitte, staring at the floor and refusing to make eye contact. "Harvesting the electricity present in humid air, something about the ions in charged water in the atmosphere. *Hygroelectricity*, she called it."

Clive looked at her, quizzically, somewhat annoyed that she couldn't see his expression.

"Janine from *Reprographics*? The woman who does our copying and faxing?"

"She's got a photographic memory," answered Brigitte, still concentrating on one patch of the floor. "She's wasted in that job."

Eric was still holding his wine glass, temporarily baffled by the concept that anybody still faxed anything these days. Something suddenly sprung into his cavernous, impenetrable mind, joining the party of restless neurons.

"I think that was Faraday team," he proudly announced, placing the glass carefully down on one of sturdy metal racks that lined the wall of the room. "I play squash with Shaun from

Franklin Labs, which is next door to Tesla. He said that they were building something to pick up alien radio signals, weird orbital power fluctuations or something."

Clive and Brigitte stared at him, incredulously.

"Shaun *is* mostly full of shit, though."

Tutting loudly in that unique way that only agitated Brits are capable of, Clive reached into his jeans pocket and pulled out his mobile phone. Brigitte's eyes widened in panic and in a single impressive move, she lunged towards him, striking his hand with enough force that the tiny device spiralled out of his grasp. It bounced twice against the metal shelving units and landed on the floor face down. Clive threw his arms up in the air.

"What did you do that for?"

"You saw what happened to Dan!"

"If it *is* the electricity that's screwed up, it's a mobile phone. It's not connected to anything. And I doubt there's enough power in a mobile phone battery to electrocute a grown man."

He shook his head and crouched down to pick up the device.

Eric piped up, his tone dry and emotionless.

"The desk phones in the room back there run off power provided from a USB-C cable. There's not enough power going through *that* to electrocute a grown man."

Clive's hand halted, his open trembling fingers hovering over the mobile phone.

Eric took the change from out of his pocket and began to arrange it on the metal shelf in front of him, piles of smallest coins to largest. He looked down at Clive, frozen there like a statue.

"But you know. Tell Dan that. You be my guest."

Clive looked at Eric, and then back to the tiny, innocuous looking phone. Treating the tiny device with the reverence and fear one might give to an unexploded WWII bomb, he slowly stood up and backed away.

It suddenly rang, the synthesizer tones of the theme from Knight Rider filling the tiny storeroom. Clive and Brigitte nearly

Power Trip

leapt out of their skins, whereas Eric barely batted an eyelid, placing the last of his twenty-pence pieces onto his currency piles.

"You might want to answer that," he deadpanned.

Clive signalled to Brigitte to pick it up, a gesture that was countered by a less polite one from her reminding him that it was *his* phone. After a few moments of hesitation, he gritted his teeth and picked up the device. Tentative fingers swiped against the cracked screen to switch it to speaker phone, and he hurriedly placed it down on a nearby shelf, eager to be rid of it.

He leaned in as close as he dared.

"Hello?"

The faint sound of static could be heard through the mobile device's tinny speaker, white noise that rapidly fluctuated in volume. There were sounds behind the shifting frequencies, the distant murmur of voices straining to be heard.

Suddenly one sounded, as clear as day through the garbled crackles. The voice of Dick Elswood, barked and emotionless.

"*Coming*"

Even Eric joined the others in shrieking when the small device suddenly flipped itself into the air, the screen exploding in a shower of sparks. By the time the chunks of it had landed back on the shelf, every piece of it had melted into fused blobs of plastic and wire. Each tiny fragment momentarily arced with white crackles of power, before falling silent and fizzling away into ash.

Clive, his voice cracked, pointed a shaking finger at where the phone had sat.

"You heard that! You all heard that!"

Eric, ever the optimist, nodded.

"Yeah, somebody is coming to rescue us."

"No, whatever killed everybody out there is coming for us," countered Clive, the pessimist – The Yin to Eric's Yang. They were the same at work. Every bug was an insurmountable issue for the eternal worrier Clive, and merely a challenge to the infinitely more pragmatic Eric.

David Court

Brigitte felt compelled to speak.

"Look, something crazy is happening with the electricity, I'll grant you that. But what's out there that you're so scared of?"

"I... I think I know what's happening here," announced Clive, his tone suddenly serious and utterly sincere. "I've encountered it before. Vengeful ghosts, out to kill us. Matter can't be destroyed, right? Even when you're dead. They're controlling – no, they *are* the electricity. Come to wreak jealous retribution on the living."

Brigitte didn't know where to start. She raised a finger in the air as though to speak but had to compose herself again. No, the words simply refused to form. Eventually, she managed to spit them out, hardly believing what she found herself saying.

"You've encountered this before, Clive?"

"Nineteen eighty-three. Advanced Dungeons and Dragons. *Into the Necromancer's Necropolis*."

Eric rolled his eyes skywards.

"This is ridiculous. We've shut ourselves inside a store cupboard. We have no idea what's going on out there, and we can't survive by eating..."

He gestured wildly at the few occupied shelves "...trackballs, 28.8k modems, acoustic couplers and dust."

Brigitte stepped over to him and placed a hand on his shoulder. She'd intended it to be reassuring, but it honestly came across as more than a little clingy.

"You don't know what's out there."

"There's an old saying. Fortune favours the bold. I guess I'm about to find out."

"But, Eric..."

"That was Captain Benjamin Sisko, Deep Space Nine, Season six, and episode six. *Sacrifice of Angels*. I don't care what's out there. Sentient alien energy, harnessed forces beyond mortal understanding, I can't just stop in here. If Dan was here, he'd have a plan. The least I can do is try to fetch help."

Power Trip

A confident hand pulled the door slightly ajar. The smell of Dan drifted languidly through the gap.

"...or it could be electrical ghosts, Eric."

"I'm not even *entertaining* that thought, Clive" were the last words he said before the door was closed and he was gone.

If there was a hypothetical list called *"Colleagues you'd want to be stuck in a store cupboard with in the event of a potential apocalypse"*, Clive would be very low on said list. Possibly even behind Nigel from the front desk, whose hobbies seemed to mostly revolve around Live Roleplaying and smelling of slightly-off soup.

The ridiculous sentient electrical ghost hypothesis, poor as it was, was the best thing he'd brought to the table. Brigitte was trying to do the British thing of panicking in relative silence, but Clive was incapable of doing even that. The time he wasn't pacing around muttering to himself – doing that annoying thing where you weren't sure whether he was trying to get your attention or not – he was drumming his fingers irritatingly on the shelves. He'd learned that each shelf, dependent on its thickness and load, produced a slightly different sound when tapped.

Much to Brigitte's irritation, he seemed to be trying to compose a finger-tip version of The Imperial March by trial and error.

Tap tap tap tap taptap tap taptap
Tap tap tap tap taptap tap taptap
Tap taptaptap tap taptaptaptap tap tap
She should have gone with Eric.

David Court

The sudden noise from outside roused her from a not-unpleasant daydream in which she was force-feeding Clive dismantled shelving rods. She sat upright and saw a similarly roused Clive sitting across from her, blinking his eyes wildly. They both hurriedly clambered to their feet, grabbing what was nearest to hand; Brigitte, a bulky toner cartridge and Clive, an old laptop.

"Eric?"

Brigitte received no reply, save the sound of wooden table legs squeaking against laminated flooring.

"What are you doing?!" whispered an incredulous Clive as Brigitte stepped towards the door, raising the toner cartridge like an unwieldy powder-filled club.

"It could be Eric!"

"If it is, he knows where we are!"

She realised her hand was trembling as she turned the door handle, pulling the door open a fraction to peer through. Clive, realizing his plaintive cries were being ignored, suddenly fell quiet and backed into the shadows behind one of the shelves.

She saw Dan first, a blackened corpse draped across the wall. His skin was desiccated and cracked, and it looked as though any contact would reduce what remained of him to a pile of ash. Eric stumbled into view in the office, his back to her. His scalp was mostly bare, his thick, auburn hair reduced to sparse clumps dotted across a scorched dome. His shirt was similarly blackened. Long, streaked marks traced across pinstripe blue lines. She went to call his name again, but something stopped her. He was standing between two desks, holding himself upright by holding onto each. He looked unsteady, as though he might fall at any moment.

Suddenly, he released his grip and stood, swaying and trying to retain his balance. It was like watching a child taking those first, unaided steps. An unsure left leg moved forward, and his body weight shifted to match it. Slowly he faltered forwards, feet dragging along the ground.

Power Trip

Brigitte had to remember to breathe again, watching him with a sense of growing unease. Eric stopped and began to slowly turn, jerky movements spinning him gradually on the spot.

Little by little, he turned to face her. His eyes were gone, replaced by charred, dark cavities. The burns across his back continued across his front, a patchwork of brown and black smears crudely dotting his stumbling form. The absence of eyes wasn't the worst thing – that would be the crooked grimace across his mouth. Eric looked inordinately *pleased* with himself.

He began to shuffle towards Brigitte, his grin widening with every awkward movement. His jaw began to shift awkwardly, his mouth opening and closing like a landed fish. Weird sounds were emerging, like those from a singer warming up by doing vocal training – drawn-out guttural vowel noises and bizarre clicks contorted from his throat.

And then a word, a tentative "Hello", the word drawn out and more awkward than it had ever sounded. And then repeated, as though Eric were testing it, feeling how the word felt as it passed over his dried and scorched lips through his blackened soot-stained teeth.

Brigitte whimpered a mostly unintelligible response, fear freezing her to the spot. With a strength of will she hadn't exhibited since the last Laboratory Christmas party had had a free bar, she pulled the door closed and flicked the latch.

She staggered, jolting in fright as her back brushed against the wall. A gentle arrhythmic tapping sounded against the outside of the metal storeroom door, like water dripping onto tiles. Clive stepped out from the shadows and joined Brigitte, placing a reassuring hand on her shoulder.

"It's Eric," she stuttered in a half-sob, leaning into him. "But it's *not* Eric."

Brigitte would even have preferred Clive's awful rendition of his tapped Star Wars theme medley to the noises that came from beyond the room now. They both listened, paralysed, as Eric spoke to them through the door.

At first, he'd just repeated the word "Hello". Different volumes and with varying inflection – even different languages and accents. Not-Eric had posed it as a query, declared it as a greeting, even announced it as a fact.

There had been silence for a while, and Brigitte and Clive had half-considered opening the door and making a run for it, but Not-Eric had soon piped up again, this time with an enhanced repertoire. He stumbled over some of the words, repeating the odd one over and over to himself, but with every passing moment, he was becoming more verbose.

He'd started with an apology. Like a talking thesaurus, he'd said sorry in more ways with more words than Brigitte knew could be used to express remorse. At times, it felt as though he were talking to them, at others like he was addressing only himself.

After the first few hours, Clive had retreated to the seclusion of the dark shadows in the corner of the room. He'd placed his fingers firmly in his ears and was rocking back and forth, all the time murmuring to himself with his eyes tightly closed.

There'd been a string of random words then, as though Not-Eric were still trying to determine how they sounded, like a translator working out the rules behind the syntax. This was interrupted loudly by one word, clear as a bell – not in the atonal voice she'd listened to for the past few hours, but clearly that of Eric.

"*Brigitte*".

It was the voice of the Eric that she knew. He gave her name that French *twang* that made it sound way more exotic than it was. She'd always mocked him, but secretly adored it. Brigitte stood up and leant against the door, imagining Eric doing the same on the other side. She pressed her palms against the warm

Power Trip

metal. She glanced over to Clive, whose rocking silhouette remained oblivious.

"Eric?"

"Accident – it was an *accident*. You are conductive skin-bags of water, and our earlier attempts at communication were... *flawed etiquette.*"

Flawed etiquette was a bit of an understatement, thought Brigitte. Flawed is swearing when you didn't mean to. Flawed is picking up the wrong spoon for dessert. The phrase somehow didn't seem to adequately cover barbequing most of the upper, middle, and lower management.

There was something Brigitte had to ask, despite knowing she wasn't keen on hearing the answer.

"What are you?"

"I...we ...don't know. That knowledge will return, in time."

At least he hadn't said electrical ghosts. That didn't mean that could be ruled *out*, but the options were still open.

"What do you plan on doing with us?"

"What do *you* plan on doing, Brigitte?"

"I don't want you to kill me, like you did with Eric."

"Our first contact was flawed, as were our later attempts. But we have improved. All of Eric is not lost – we don't want to harm *you* at all. We just want you to join us."

"So, it's an invasion?"

"It has taken more of your chronology than we would have liked, but we've mastered control of your energies now. The power that drives you all, the energies in the air itself, all bend to our whim. We could kill you both now, if we so wished. Electrify the oxygen in your lungs, boil the blood in your veins. You're really quite, quite vulnerable as a species. But enough energy has been lost today."

"That sounds like a threat."

"If you stay in there, you'll starve. Now that's *not* a threat, but an inherent weakness in your physiology. Come out."

Not-Eric was right. Even if they wanted to, they couldn't fight.

David Court

She took one last look at Clive, who seemed to have drifted off to sleep, his fingers still wedged firmly in his ears. Brigitte sighed and flicked the latch, slowly opening the door.

Not-Eric stood there facing her. He was no longer swaying but seemed to have mastered the act of standing up straight. His empty sockets glared at her, his head cocked at an angle. His straight lips raised into a smile.

She looked back to the storeroom as Not-Eric placed his burnt hand on her shoulder.

"He'll come in his own time. Leave him."

She walked, guided, through the empty corridors of the laboratories. There was something in the air, she could feel it, some sense of anticipation. Or, as the scientist in her couldn't help but remind her, it could have just been down to the ionization of the air particles.

She glanced at the main meeting room as they walked past. The corpses had all been tidied away. The smell of burnt flesh remained, but even that was fading with every step. Whenever she slowed, Not-Eric would slow as well. She was being directed, but not *rushed*.

The first glimpse she got of outside was from the windows in the stairwell. The evening sky shifted between iridescent purples, oranges and blues, the clouds themselves burning with a fierce inner light. The air around her grew heavier with every floor she ascended, uncomfortably so as they arrived at the roof. She was forced to gulp in larger breaths of air each time and Not-Eric sensed her concern.

"That will pass," he reassured her.

There were others on the roof, standing on the edge of the balcony and staring at the heavens. Some were charred and damaged, like Not-Eric, others were like Brigitte, seemingly untouched. A few of them were seated in a circle on the slate-chip flooring and they smiled at Not-Eric and Brigitte as they stepped past.

Power Trip

"What happens now?" she asked, staring out at the blinking lights of the surrounding city.

"Whatever you like," replied Not-Eric. "You're part of us already, whether you want to be or not. And you'll never know – or care – whether you made the decision voluntarily. The thoughts in your head are just neurons firing over the surface of your brain. Just another form of energy that we can manipulate."

She looked back at him, not concerned.

"But you probably don't care," he said, before turning to look at the skies.

He was right. Here, surrounded by this beauty, she couldn't for the life of her work out what all the fuss was about. Everything – the clouds, the lights in the city, the thoughts in her head – it was just so much energy, after all. They were all just so insignificant in the scheme of things but, paradoxically, *crucial*. It was only fair that everybody should feel like this, hear this electrical sermon. The Power Stations would be their cathedrals, the pylons their churches. This word needed to be spread, and the growing masses in the building and soon, the city, would all know the good news.

It looked like it was going to rain. Or at least thunder, anyway.

"Power Trip" was first published in "Sparks", the electricity themed horror anthology from Burdizzo Books.

David Court

Brother, can you spare a Paradigm?

THERE ARE ELEVEN people in this bar, and three of them are me. Hell of an icebreaker, ain't it? If I ever get around to writing my memoirs, it'll all be fully explained there. For now, just take it that a messy encounter with the fabled Albarossa Crystal in an old case ended up creating several duplicates of yours truly. Blackstone Senior had asked me to put them out of their misery, but it reeked a little too much of suicide for me. As it was, I called in a few favours and got their memories "altered" and still, to this day, our paths sometimes cross. A bit of the old Blackstone magic and they don't recognize each other, or more importantly, *me*.

All three of us regularly gravitate here for the same reason, but only I know what that reason *is*.

The *Toot Suite* is one of a handful of jazz bars in Manhattan, and you'd be hard pressed to tell one from the other. They're all dark basements with inadequate lighting and overpriced liquor, filled with cigarette smoke so thick you half expect the hound of the Baskervilles to emerge. There's a difference here though, and she's on stage right now.

Before you look at her, just listen. That's a helluva voice, ain't it? I used to think Scat was nonsense, just a bunch of messed-up syllables and wordless vocables – that was, until her.

Brother, can you spare a Paradigm?

Cassandra Solomon.

Listen. Properly listen, I mean. Breathe it in, like you would a cigarette. You go in any other jazz club and you'd have to strain to hear over the chatter and clinking of glasses. There's an appropriate reverence here, and everybody stays shut up for her. She's the Queen, and we're nothing more than her oh-so-loyal subjects.

You can make out words, if you listen hard enough. *Feel* them, pressing against your heart. That's *poetry*, man - poetry from a soul deeper than the Atlantic. That's a voice that's properly lived – from somebody who's had their heart lifted up into the sun as many times as it's been shattered like ice.

Now look.

Admittedly, she's a sight to behold. That shimmering blue dress that moves like the night, that long black hair, that pearlescent white skin pierced by bright red lipstick, those gams that just don't know *when* to stop – but that ain't the first thing you notice, is it?

Be honest, you expected somebody older, didn't you? She's young, but with an old soul. She's the kind of person to make you believe reincarnation is the real deal, that anybody with a voice like that must have lived a dozen lifetimes.

Her bass player has chops at the best of times, but tonight he's smokin' more than the salmon that hangs glassy-eyed in the fishmongers next door. They're riffing off each other as the song builds to its close, the tempo raised up a notch and the crowd captivated by every moment, nodding their heads, tapping their feet, or both.

The musicians fall silent as Cassandra holds on to that one last note like a drowning woman clinging on for life. You can feel it against your skin, hugging your bones.

As she stops singing, the room remains deathly quiet for a single beat. Then, there's applause so noisy and enthusiastic, you'll swear the room was filled with four times as many people.

David Court

She steps gracefully from the stage and is handed a bunch of flowers by an eager fan. She acknowledges him with a wink and a smile, and purposefully strides towards me. I read the situation, the look in her eyes, the speed of her steps, the suddenly serious expression on her face.

She'll lean in and ask me to meet her backstage. "Alone", she'll insist, her voice tinged with worry and concern. She'll step past me, her fingertips brushing against my shoulder for a moment longer than is comfortable for either of us, and she'll quickly vanish. Her perfume will linger in the air long after she's gone.

My predictions are, as to be expected, accurate. Unless I'm very much mistaken – and I'm not – her perfume's *Joy* by Jean Patou.

I know full well that she'll wait for me, so I savor the rest of my Bullshot while the next band sets up. The beefiness of the broth threatens to – but doesn't quite – overwhelm the heat from the vodka, cayenne, and Tabasco, and it goes down easier than a five-dollar whore. They've just started playing as I approach the ape guarding the backstage area. I know he's already been warned of my arrival, and he steps aside to let me in without so much as a grunted "good evening".

Right, this is as good a moment as we'll get, so there are two things we need to get clear at this stage.

I know you're there and listening to me. Blackstone Senior let me in on this whole cosmic charade thing and that we're being watched from forces unseen, so I'm just being polite in explaining the situation to you as best I can.

Secondly, within a short while, you'll be wondering why I seem to know so much about what is going to happen before it actually happens. It may make me come across as a little smug or over-confident, but that's not the case.

Brother, can you spare a Paradigm?

I'm what Blackstone nicknamed a *Vorticist*.

A clever little part of my subconscious sees the patterns in things – the patterns in *everything*. You might think everything you do is down to your own free will, but it turns out the universe is just one big machine – you're a tiny little clockwork cog in this vast contraption, and everything you've done or will do has all been carefully planned out in advance.

"That's bull," you're thinking. "I'll just do something unpredictable."

I've seen it all. Turns out, you were *always* going to react that way.

Mind-fuck, ain't it?

So, I'm gifted – or *cursed*, you might argue – with being able to see these patterns. Sometimes minutes' worth, sometimes hours. It sounds great, but it fucks with you on a daily basis.

Imagine sitting down at the theatre, or for a movie or piece of music, and you already know exactly what you're in for. You already know how every bite of that Porterhouse steak or that expensive wine is gonna taste.

That's why I always end up here in the *Toot Suite* Jazz club, and probably why my doppelgangers do too. Blackstone informs me that the gift didn't pass over to them when they were unexpectedly created, but instinct keeps guiding them back.

Turns out my "talent" has a blind spot when it comes to improvised jazz.

I can't read or predict it. Every chord progression is a revelation, every modal harmony and plucked or hammered note a unique pleasure. I can lose myself in the musical journey, temporarily freed from the burden of this precognition. And the discordant chaos when the musicians "free blow" and ignore the chord changes, improvising as they see fit: it's nothing short of bliss. And improvised Jazz doesn't come any better than at the *Toot Suite*.

David Court

I knock on the door, already knowing it'll be opened just after the second knock. It's the club owner, a sour kraut named Max who made a tidy profit from WWII and built his name in the village as a property owner. Both the man and his temper are notoriously short, and I remember him breaking the fingers of a musician who cheekily addressed him as "Jazz Hans". Poor schmuck couldn't play his instrument for two months. Max argued he could barely play it before.

Max looks me up and down – mostly up, due to his diminished stature – before leaving the room and leaving us alone. Cassandra has her back to me, but stares at my reflection in the mirror. I'm looking forward to the way she's about to say my name, the words seductively lingering on her lips as though she's trying to seduce me. The hint of a Southern accent she's been tryin' to disguise that occasionally slips through.

"Rick Bannerette."

She turns to face me, extending a slender hand. My acumen reveals to me that the kiss I'd intended to plant on the back of her porcelain white hand gets me nothing but a vicious glare, so I change tack and gently shake it instead.

"The name I got stencilled on my door is backwards, but I think that's what it says. What can I do for the Manhattan Queen of Jazz?"

"Josef tells me you've got a penchant for dealing with unusual cases, Mr. Bannerette."

Josef works the bar here, a giant of a man and a relative of Max. I got him out of a fix a couple of months back when the ghost of a dead Josef from a sideways reality decided to start hauntin' him through mirrors.

"It's been known. Let's get a drink and you can tell me all about it. I'm guessing a lady like yourself is fond of..."

She'll smile and... what? I'm suddenly overwhelmed by a flood of images, a surge of shattered fractals. They're hanging in the air like shards of broken mirror, each with a different suspended image of Cassandra within. She's in a variety of

Brother, can you spare a Paradigm?

different dressing rooms, in an assortment of different outfits. I hear a chorus of her voice requesting a hundred different drinks: *champagne, white wine spritzer, bourbon, single malt, red wine.* This is different from the blissful void I get when listening to the jazz – here I'm seeing *every* possibility, *all* eventualities.

A myriad of assorted Cassandras dash to help me, some supporting me, some too late to stop my fall. Just as I think I can't cope with the torrent of sights and sounds assaulting my senses, everything settles again into just a single, solitary paradigm.

Her arms are around me, and Jean Patou's *Joy* rouses me like smelling salts. I blink and try and regain some sense of dignity, blinded though I am to what lies ahead. It's all I can do to concentrate on the here and now, let alone beyond that.

"Are you okay, Rick?"

"I am. Just a little dizzy, is all."

Within moments, I'm seated and there's a glass of water in my hand. I typically only drink water when it's in the form of frozen cubes floating in a glass of rye, but today I'll make an exception. I've been feeling run down recently, and I'm hoping this empty feeling will pass. Time to at least try to get back into character.

"Thank you. So, what's your problem?"

She rummaged around in her handbag, pulling out an assortment of varied makeups and packs of Juicy Fruit.

"I don't know how scared I should be, Mr Bannerette. Everywhere I go, I keep finding these. Somebody keeps sending them through my mailbox, leaving them in my dressing room. I throw them in the trash, new ones appear."

Suddenly, her eyes lit up with recognition, and she pulled a card from the dim recesses of her seemingly infinite bag. It was the size of a playing card with a dull, matte black back. I held out my hand for it, only now noticing my trembling fingers.

David Court

Even with my precognition on the fritz, I felt a sense of dread. Perhaps it was just a lifetime's worth of instinct, but I was loath to turn the card over and look at the face.

At first, I thought it a spiral, but with a closer look, it was a pattern of concentric circles. A pattern of jagged black and grey teeth, a trick of the eye giving it the illusion of movement. There was a solid black sphere set at the centre, like the staring pupil of a monstrous eye set against that two-tone iris.

I recognize it instantly. I've spent so much of my life literally ahead of myself, that I sometimes to forget to look *back*. The card falls from my fingers, gently fluttering on the floor, and my heart sinks with it.

It's a *trap*. I was cursed the moment I laid eyes on that damned thing, and, thanks to my power, my mind's eye saw it. It's a trap I'd fallen into before it was even sprung, and before I could do anything to protect myself from its power.

Same as how you'd get if you stared at a bright light for too long, the negative afterimage on the card is imprinted on my retina. In all honesty, I'd never intended for this to be an origin story, but certain elements have now become critical. I was little more than a kid at the time – off with Blackstone on one of his crazy adventures. "The Case of the Pilfered Participle", it came to be known as in his journals. Presumably that rolled off the pen easier than "The Case Where Your Kid Sidekick Ends up Staring into The Heart of Infinity and Getting Crazy Precognitive Powers".

I remember it as though it were yesterday. It was the day when Blackstone learned the hard way that if you insist a kid doesn't do something, he's going to go and do it. I heard he had a kid of his own after our escapades – followed him into the magic game.

You're familiar with the Nietzsche quote, something like "If you stare into the abyss, the abyss stares back at you"? I'd always assumed that the abyss was a metaphor – turned out that it was an *actual* abyss, somewhere deep in Chang Tang in Tibet. The

Brother, can you spare a Paradigm?

ancient grimoires called it *God's Eye*, but the locals had another term for it - *God's Sphincter*. Anyways, despite the advice of my highly trained and educated mentor, I stared right down there – and something stared back at me; a brilliant white eye, glaring at me from the heart of the multiverse.

And in that pattern, I saw the inverse of the pattern on the card, which ended up imprinting on my soul and turning me – in Blackstone's words – into a Vorticist.

They've led me right here, like a rookie. They've taken advantage of my three weaknesses – jazz, bars, and pretty ladies – to rid me of my powers and leave me exposed and vulnerable. After years of trying, they've finally mastered the replication of the pattern of the anti-abyss and switched off my gift.

"Get out of here!" I scream at Cassandra. She doesn't need telling twice, as scared of my sudden outburst as anything else I might be warning her about. I heard him before I saw him, the grinding of machinery and the pounding of pistons accompanying his arrival.

If you ever go anywhere real remote, miles away from people and their incessant chattering and motor cars, just *listen*. If you're lucky, and the wind is right, you might hear them. The gentle whoosh of pressurised air or steam coming from pneumatic machinery, the tick-tocking of cogs pushing cogs pushing cogs. These are the sounds of the quantum machineries that power reality, the perpetual motion machines that will never stop as they operate to infinitesimal precision, driving the universe and everything in it.

When he arrives, that fragile membrane that separated us from those infernal machines is peeled back slightly. I know who I'm dealing with now – there's only one foe I know who knows of the source of my powers, the only one who would have even stood a fighting chance of capturing the exact precision needed for the anti-abyss to nullify them.

David Court

There was that oh-so-familiar sense of synaesthesia that I'm used to from our previous encounters, as I'm gagging from the acrid scent of him screaming my name in defiance. He unfolded in front of me like an idea given detail, suddenly standing there as a series of small black and white geometric cubes approximating a human form.

The Futurist.

We'd met before, but I'd always had the upper hand. Despite his aggressive and unpredictable nature, his "smear of violence" as he called it, I could read him like a book. An abstract pop-up book, admittedly, but a book, nonetheless. He couldn't defeat an opponent who could predict his every move, and I'd been a constant thorn in his minimalist side.

Hence the trap.

"How does it feel?" he bellows. His voice is always disconcerting, accompanied, as it was, by an invisible atonal choir. "How does it feel to be stuck in the here and now?"

He didn't even give me chance to answer. Reality rippled around him like an ill-fitting swimsuit, and we are suddenly both elsewhen and elsewhere. This is his realm; a vast, monochrome, grid-scored landscape. In all honesty, I was relieved he'd moved our conflict to a different plane – anything to remove the risk of innocent bystanders being caught up, transformed into Dadaist concepts – or worse.

I throw a punch, but he cheekily alters the laws of physics before it gets anywhere near him. Any momentum my fist had is lost, and my knuckles simply brush against him. His own retaliation is swift and brutal – I'm suddenly standing about three feet away, two pints of blood down. He's kept that where I was, and I briefly see it suspended there in a rough humanoid shape, before it splashes across the flat ground.

The battle has hardly begun and – thanks to the blood-loss – I felt myself growing faint. For his next trick, he undid the tonsillectomy I had a year or so back; the infected tissue was suddenly there at the back of my gullet, inflated and sore. I could

Brother, can you spare a Paradigm?

barely breathe, clutching at my throat. Any protective wards I had that would have served me, I was now incapable of reciting.

The synaesthesia is back, and I can feel the barbed touch of his gloating laughter against my fingertips.

Think, Rick, think.

A zen-like moment of tranquillity passes over me as the answer becomes clear. Trying to ignore his triumphant bellowing, I closed my eyes tight and concentrated. The negative image on the card is still there, a faint afterimage burned across the surface of my retina. And a negative of a negative is...

The image from the abyss is there, faint, but humming with potential power. Before the afterimage faded and was gone for good, I called on the last of its reserves.

I can see the Futurist's next attack, signposted in front of me as clearly as if I were watching it unfold on a cinema screen – the potential killing blow. A skilled feint sees him miss me, several important nerve points exposed and vulnerable. With the few moments I have to spare, a self-taught move from an amalgam of several schools of martial artistry sees the Futurist at my mercy.

It's not one to kill, but it *is* one that hurts. He's still screaming as reality deposits us back in the dressing room, everything temporarily paralysed by my attack except for his mouth, tongue, and vocal cords. I chose that specific attack for a very specific reason.

He's a considerably less imposing foe, stripped of his reality-altering powers. Less imposing still after I retrieve Dorothy – my trusty Smith & Wesson 29 - from my jacket pocket and plug his head with a cylinder full of .44 Magnum rounds.

I don't need any powers of precognition to know what his head will look like after that.

Josef and Max are at the door, stopping Cassandra in her tracks so she doesn't have to see what's left of my arch-nemesis. My throat is healed, the tonsillectomy restored.

David Court

"You won't be getting no more of those calling cards," I reassure her on the way past. She doesn't look particularly comforted.

"What do we tell the police, Mr. Bannerette?" asked Josef, dumbfounded. "What if they need to speak to you?"

"Tell them I'm on the next flight to Tibet, Josef," I smile.

"Brother, can you spare a paradigm?" was first published in "Visions from the Void", the op-art inspired anthology from Burdizzo Books.

The Strangest Thing has happened

THE STRANGEST THING has happened in the
PrimeGen Research Station
as a lifetime's worth of study, enquiry, and investigation
looks like it may just finally be coming to fruition
to the glee of every gathered engineer, scientist, and logician.

Their detractors now stay silent, for they have been proved
wrong
By the pluck and bloody-mindedness of this assembled throng
who, even after failure, remained faithful to the cause.
The type when asked, "Why do it?" simply answer, "Just
because."

The alarm that roused them all's switched off,
to stop their ears from aching.
A science experiment one- hundred- million
long years in the making.
Trembling claws the size of moons rub tired, sun-sized eyes.
The assembled scientists gather round as the defrosted sample
dries

And there it is; a perfect sphere, devoid of imperfection

David Court

A tiny ball of textured green and glistening blue reflection
Assembled voices "oooh" and "aaaah" in self-congratulation
and empty wine glasses are refilled, all primed for celebration.

Sample EAR-7H hangs there, a flawless gleaming jewel.
The research head stares beaming and announces,
"Scientists, you'll
Be remembered for this breakthrough, long after you've all
gone."
He speaks too soon, an alarm sounds –
something has gone wrong.

A blackened tiny oil-like speck appears there on the crust
And tendrils of it grow and spread much to their disgust
Corruption's quick and total, and they're past the time for panic.
The tiny living fractal flaws both viral and organic.

Without a word it's taken, a hastily sketched proposal
that EAR-7H's a failure, fit only for disposal.
Into the stasis chamber, this experiment is done.
It floats with other failures round a tiny yellow sun.

A success in all other regards; aesthetic and tectonic.
EAR-7H would be perfect, if not for the life upon it.

Our Elegant Decay

"**I**T'S LIKE THIS**, Gemma - at the end of the day, there's simply no growth in botany." If anybody other than Doctor Randwick had uttered those lines, they would have seen the inherent humour in that statement. However, Randwick – head of the faculty and therefore, unfortunately, my boss – was as humourless as he was short and as short as he was dull.

"If you look up the word 'uninteresting' in a dictionary," one of my colleagues had once remarked, "you'll find a picture of Doctor Randwick". I remember countering with the fact that I thought you would only find *half* a picture of the esteemed Doctor, the poor artist would have long since given up through boredom trying to accurately capture the tedious little man's overly generic features.

The Doctor and I had never seen eye to eye, either literally *or* figuratively. He was one of those archaic dinosaurs of education, a man who felt – and made no secret of the fact – that he didn't think science was any place for women. Even after all these years, the odious little turd still refused to call me by my title.

"What about our pharmaceutical contracts?"

"Our contact at Rejuvenon informed me last Friday that they won't be renewing our contract. They've finally got wise to the fact that it's a lot cheaper to outsource their plant research to a bunch of Guatemalan kids who live on the edge of the jungle rather than go to the expense of shipping the plants over here."

"But what about Grainger Biotech?"

He gave a snort of derision, shaking his head. Classic Randwick condescension. I considered whether it'd be better to stab him repeatedly in the eyes with my pencil, or simply to embed a weeding trowel in his forehead.

"Grainger? They're tiny. Their yearly budget would barely stretch to cover a hydroponic lamp. Without big Pharma, we can't justify the expense of four staff. We're simply going to have to let you and Margaret go."

I knew it. I fucking *knew* it. I'd been trying to rationalise my recent bouts of paranoia as being a side effect of my fondness for Class A hallucinogens, but it turns out it was entirely justified. Sometimes the bastards *are* out to get you.

"And meanwhile, Todd and Charles keep their jobs?"

"Doctors Hale and Brooker, yes. They'll be back at the start of next term."

I went to say something but thought better of it. I knew from experience that anything I said in anger would only give Doctor Randwick ammunition. I'd been unfortunate enough to overhear the triumvirate of twats once when they believed they were alone in the lab. Each of them was taking turns to do a poor falsetto sing-song impersonation of my voice and repeating some of the grievances I'd discussed with them previously. They were like the Three Stooges without the charm.

Like a cop handing in her badge and gun, I ripped my laboratory lanyard from my neck and threw it onto Randwick's desk. We glared at each other for a few moments before I stormed over to the door in silence.

The locked door.

My dramatic exit was somewhat lessened by the fact I had to skulk back to his desk and gingerly retrieve my lanyard. My face reddened like an *Amanita muscaria* mushroom as I swiped the card hanging from it and left the room, trying to hold back the tears.

Randwick couldn't resist a last parting shot as I walked out. "Happy holidays, Gemma."

I slammed the car door shut behind me and slumped deep into the leather seat, half willing myself to sink into it and be lost forever. Glancing around to check the carpark was empty, I released a primal scream which felt as though it had been building up within me for the better part of a decade. I followed that with a few satisfying minutes of hammering my fists across the steering wheel, pretending it was Randwick's smug little face.

Aaaaand relax.

Sitting next to me in the passenger seat was the meagre pile of belongings I'd amassed during my thirteen years of botanical work. The box was mostly filled with research books, ones that I'd purchased with my own money, so was *damned* if they'd get to keep them – but there were a few personal trinkets scattered about. There was an assortment of pictures of my husband – some of just him, but most were of both of us.

I picked up the pile of photographs, subconsciously shuffling them into chronological sequence before I'd realised what I was doing. Looking at the first one, I thought how young we both were. It was a picture from the days before I'd even started working at the research centre, when there was still a noticeable light in my eyes. I flicked through the rest.

Rather than provoking whimsical nostalgia, they were a sobering slideshow of the aging process.

With each new photograph, and with every passing year, my posture visibly changed. I'd never really noticed it before, but I appeared shorter and more crouched in every one, as though the pressure of life was crushing me. Those weren't wrinkles appearing on my face, but cracks – stress fissures from an unseen but ever-present burden.

Daniel, however, had barely changed. Oh, the odd grey hair had sprung into existence, elegantly seasoning that dark, thick crop with salt and pepper, but he looked as carefree and as youthful as he ever had. In the early photographs, I looked like his wife, in the later pictures I looked more like an older sister. If I could picture the photographs to come, I could well see myself looking like his mother.

That was what was missing from the photographs, missing from our *lives*. *Motherhood.* In one of the pictures, those snapshots of our lives, a new life should have appeared. Cradled in our arms at first, then peering from the plush confines of a pram. Later, sitting on one of our shoulders. Forever growing older, taller. Our son, or our daughter.

Had we been trying for a child from the very first photograph, or did it just feel that way? The two of us had both been through so many inconclusive tests over those years. Daniel would head off to the clinic for the umpteenth time, quipping that he was "wanking for science," but the joke was stale now and became less humorous with every mention.

Moreover, despite putting on a brave face and trying to sound genuinely excited when another childhood friend announced their pregnancy, the words were beginning to stick in my craw. The well-rehearsed congratulatory phrases were a hollow cover for laments that cursed our misfortune.

A plant's primary botanical function is to reproduce. If unable to carry out that simplest, most ancient, and basic of biological roles, it renders its entire purpose moot. As time went on, I felt the same. Once, when we were both young, it had been a nagging doubt. Now, it was an emergency. There was a *time limit.*

A chipped mug sat at the bottom of the box, bearing a black and white cartoon of a partying mushroom exclaiming, "*I'm a Fungi*" in a hideous Comic Sans font. Daniel had given it to me as a gift on the evening of my first day in the lab. It had been irrecoverably tannin-stained for so long it now served better as a penholder than a drinking vessel, but it conjured up memories of happier days. I went to pick it up but as I lifted it, the handle broke away. The earthenware crumbled away like fine powder in my hand. I dropped the handle into the box and drove home.

Daniel was laying back on the sofa as I walked in from the kitchen, his face illuminated by the screen of the mobile phone from which he could never drag himself away. Our evenings had long ago deteriorated into me trying and failing to make conversation as he eagerly replied to every bleep and ping from that bloody electronic ball and chain.

"Work," was the one word reply I invariably got whenever I asked who was texting or emailing him. He made me feel like a mushroom myself, keeping me in the dark and feeding me nothing but shit.

"You never know, this might be the best thing that could have happened to us," I said, standing in the doorway.

He looked up from his phone at me, an eyebrow raised. He looked more distracted than interested.

"Huh?"

"We always complained that maternity leave at the lab was rubbish. Now I can look for a job that doesn't have a policy created for the dark ages. Ready for when, you know, the IVF works."

"Cool. Yeah."

His eyes went back to his phone.

I had to find another job right away – Daniel's wage was reasonable but wouldn't cover the expensive In Vitro Fertilisation procedures for which we'd been forced to fork out.

"I'm going to work in the greenhouse for a little while. Give me a shout if you need me."

David Court

"Uh-huh"

I knew that sound. That non-committal grunt that meant he either wasn't listening or didn't care. Fine. There was no point in trying to break an uncomfortable silence we both wanted.

Even though warm and humid, the air in the greenhouse was still less heavy and oppressive seeming than that of the house. I decided against listening to any music, content with the background noises of the greenhouse, the humming of hydroponic lamps, the gentle trickling of the water filtration system, and the buzzing of tiny insects.

I swear that on a quiet day, if you listen hard enough, you can hear the plants growing. They emit the faintest sound, a barely audible noise that resembles that of stretching rubber.

I checked in on each of the plants that occupied the containers lining each of the walls, coming to the Laughing Cap mushrooms last. Over the last couple of weeks, the *Gymnopilus junonius* had developed from a dull brown to a glorious orange, their dry and scaly surfaces pocked with the occasional blue bruise. A couple of the caps dominated the container they were in, so I plucked them out, taking great care not to disturb the rusty orange spores that dusted their rings. The water on the small camping stove was boiling up nicely as I dropped in chunks of the yellow-orange flesh, then eagerly watched them as they turned green in the blistering liquid. I had boiled up a larger quantity of water than I ordinarily would (purely because of the somewhat large size of the mushrooms), so I dropped in three teabags rather than two for good measure. Each vanished into the water, the tiny perforated bags spiralling down to their doom in the increasingly murky liquid.

Fifteen minutes later, I was leaning back in a deck chair, holding the mug of tea in both hands, and letting the steam from the brew moisturise every pore in my face. I closed my eyes and

Our Elegant Decay

breathed it in deeply before taking a sip. Sometimes I would add honey to cover the distinctive fungal undertones, but not today.

A less experienced and more timid drug user would probably have considered the ingestion of this amount of the hallucinogen *Psilocybin* a little foolhardy, especially after the kind of day I'd had. However, as somewhat of a psychotropic connoisseur, I couldn't see the problem. I'd spent so much of my working life looking over my shoulder that the worst a little drug-fuelled paranoia could do would be to add a little variety, and as for hallucinations? Today, I relished them.

Eventually, the plastic arms on the cheap deck chair began to undulate and shift, molten globules of wax-like material dripping off onto the floor. They hissed where they landed, the concrete floor dissolving at the touch. The glass panes in the walls, clearly not wishing to feel left out, started to do the same – each oozing slowly to the ground, pooling in large reflective puddles around me. Stars danced within each tiny lake.

I'd left the remnants of the "*I'm a Fungi*" mug teetering precariously on the corner of a shelf. I'd thrown away the handle but couldn't bear to part with the rest of it. Behind it, the Eastern Poison Ivy plant - *Toxicodendron radicans* – suddenly started to grow at a phenomenal rate. Bright green vines laden with almond-shaped leaves began to creep across the walls and carefully wrapped tightly around the mug before dragging it into the mass of vegetation. The cartoon of the partying mushroom opened its eyes in wide horror for one fleeting moment before it vanished within the green morass.

I closed my eyes, relaxing to the sound of my own heartbeat that now filled the room like the sound of tribal drums. It only seemed appropriate in the jungle in which I now found myself, the vines of ivy wrapping around my ankles and spiralling upwards. With my eyes still closed, I rode out the sensation, relaxing into it. The vines constricted around my wrists and then, ultimately, around my throat. I was not scared.

It was several hours later when I awoke from the trip into a world of darkness; Daniel having switched all the lights off around me. He tolerated this one vice, and we rarely spoke of it. In my stumbling to get out of the greenhouse, my foot connected with the remnants of the mug and inadvertently kicked it against the wall. It shattered as it connected, meeting the same fate as its decayed handle.

Despite sharing a bed, these days we only ever slept alone. I vaguely remembered hearing some murmurings from him as he left for work, but it was nearing lunchtime when I finally stirred from a sleep punctuated with the oddest dreams – most of them derived from the false memories caused by the previous evening's heroic dose of psilocybin.

Even in that confused state, I knew that I wouldn't last long if I allowed myself to sink into a drugged stupor every evening. Without the nine-to-five of my day job, I needed something to give my life some formal structure. Job-hunting could wait until after the weekend, but before then, I needed to do *something*.

Crap-filled corners of the house that had lain dormant since we moved in almost two decades ago, experienced the overdue fury of the vacuum cleaner. Surfaces almost inch-thick with twenty years-worth of dried skin and grease, were made to shine like a star gone Supernova.

The misnomered "Important Documents" folder whose primary role had been to prop a bedroom door was prised open. I half expected angry spirits to spring forth, a little like the end of Raiders of The Lost Ark.

Utility bills from companies that no longer existed were collected and shredded. When I was done, I had enough confetti for one of those mass weddings that the Moonies throw every now and then.

One must never underestimate the doggedness of a cleaner, or their determination to bring light into every nook and crevasse. Like Bindweed – *Convolvulus arvensis* – they'll get

Our Elegant Decay

everywhere. Their uncaring tendrils reaching into places forbidden, inaccessible, or rarely visited.

What had at first appeared like just a pile of old jumpers and sweatshirts in the bottom of Daniel's wardrobe were ideal candidates for the charity shop run I had planned.

I didnt expect the dull *thud* when I'd lifted them off the floor, as a cheap and ancient mobile bounced off the bedroom carpet.

It was a mobile from the days back before smartphones, when a single battery charge could last a whole week. From those halcyon days when people used cameras to take photographs, arrived at appointments on time, and still sent birthday cards to one another.

My astonishment at holding this ancient piece of technology faded as I explored further. The address book held just a single name and number, and the lengthy call history showed nothing but phone calls to and from this stranger "Andrea," the owner of that unknown set of digits.

It was the text messages, though, that changed everything. With each one-hundred-and-sixty-character monochromatic missive, a controlled explosion ripped through the already frayed foundations of our marriage.

The blatant affair between the conspirators was bad enough, with Daniel saying romantic or sexual things in those messages that he hadn't said to me in a decade. However, there were worse revelations to come. The fact that the two of them had openly mocked my desire for children, and, finally, the thermonuclear explosion that vaporized everything – Daniel had undergone a secret vasectomy some six years previous.

My legs buckled beneath me, as though somebody had just kicked me in the back of the knees. I fell to the carpet, crying. A message – jet-black against illuminated bright orange – stared at me from the phone that lay in front of me.

I can't leave her, the stoic martyr bemoaned, *I think she'd hurt herself.*

"Close, but no cigar," was the immediate thought that sprang to mind.

David Court

When Andrea opened the door to me, I remained silent. In all honesty, I was just interested to hear what she had to say. I knew damn well she'd recognise me because they'd slept in our bed and my accusing photo would have been staring down at her from the wall. I wonder if they'd turned it around as they fucked, or had simply left me hanging there as an impotent sentinel?

Ha, impotent. Poor choice of words.

It was as though the neurons in her brain couldn't fire sufficiently to put words in her mouth. She was still standing there, her wide eyes gaping and wordless mouth flapping, when I leaned forward and pushed her.

I'd done it with rather more force than I'd anticipated, and the back of her head cracked noisily against her tacky marble telephone table. The abrupt streak of red suddenly looked out of place against the blue Stilton-like surface. I'd never hurt anybody in my life before – it had felt natural – *easy,* even. I was surprised that I felt more upset by the mess I'd made of the table than the mess I'd made of Andrea. I stepped inside and pulled the door closed behind me as I stared down at her twitching form.

I had prepared a deadly syringe of Water Hemlock root – *Cicuta virosa* – but now it looked like it might not be necessary. That was quite the pool of blood sprouting beneath her shaking head, an ever-growing Mandelbrot pattern of scarlet. One eye was glaring at me, the other was bloodshot, dislodged, and staring at the wall. For a moment, it looked as though I might need the syringe after all, but then the shaking stopped, and she suddenly shouted "Five!" at a space behind me before falling still and silent.

Outside of aphids and the odd vine weevil, I'd never killed before. I was rather surprised at how easy it had been. I'd hoped that *my* final words on this Earth would be somewhat more profound. In fact, I was already planning them.

The Bee Orchid - *Ophrys apifera* – is a remarkable plant. Instead of doing the typical plant-like thing of hoping that a bee will just happen to pop by, the Bee Orchid is slightly more proactive. It grows a flower that looks (and smells) just like a female bee. Your friendly, short-sighted, neighbourhood bee drops in for a quick fumble, is coated in the flowers discharge, and flies off – pollenating all.

Matching her smell was easy enough – Andrea was a big fan of a brand of perfume that she had shipped in by the gallon. Seriously, there were industrial drums of the stuff on her bedroom shelves. *Eau de Adulteress*. It was overwhelming, tacky, and cheap, much like the décor she'd filled her house with.

I found three sad-looking emaciated moth orchids – *Phalaenopsis* – in her bedroom. Despite being low-maintenance house plants, they'd been neglected to such an extent that they were beyond saving. If I'd felt any guilt whatsoever over Andrea, every trace of it was evaporated as I consigned the emaciated husk of each plant to the bin.

Andrea's looks were, as fate would have it, easy to match as well. She was a similar height and build to me, and even her hairstyle wasn't that dissimilar to mine. In fact, I found it somewhat offensive and bewildering that Daniel chose to have an affair with somebody so strikingly alike.

I'd read enough of her SMS messages to know how to comfortably disguise myself as her. She had an endearing habit of attempting admirably long words that she couldn't spell, and occasionally lapsed into text speech like a ten-year-old from a decade ago.

David Court

I thought a plaintive text message from the damsel in distress to Daniel would work. Some bullshit about how all the fuses had blown in the house and how he *simply* had to come straight from work. If he got there quickly enough, the fuses won't be *all* that'd get blown that night... That last bit was a bit self-indulgent, but it amused me a little to know that I managed to message something far wittier than Andrea could ever have managed.

For a moment, it looked as though he wouldn't bite, but then my phone bleeped into life with the usual text from him to say there was a problem at work he'd have to deal with and he would be late coming home. I thought back at how many of those I'd received over the years, never doubting his word for a moment. I imagined the maggot had it saved as a *template*. Then, within seconds, the horny fucker had sent a text to Andrea's phone saying he was on the way.

I knew from their lengthy communications that he'd had a key for some time, and that he would let himself in. He was calling Andrea's name as he stepped into the darkened hallway (both body and blood-soaked rug long since removed). I coughed loudly, having never heard her voice so I could formulate a passable impersonation, and he stepped into the front room. All he'd have seen was my naked silhouette, highlighted from the streetlights through the curtains behind me.

Slowly approaching, he called out, "Rea, where do you keep your fuse box?" In that single query, there were as many words as he'd said to me in a week. The blue-tinged streetlight from behind me reflected well enough off his skin that there was no chance of me missing his head with the cricket bat. No great utterances from him as he went down, no random numbers inexplicably blurted out. Just a simple, heavy, inelegant *thud*.

Our Elegant Decay

Administration at the lab was, and always had been, *terrible.* Even though I'd lost a dozen access key-cards, they never changed a single code with any of the new cards they'd given me. My recent spate of tidiness had uncovered five of the buggers; each a little faded, scratched, and scarred, but guaranteed still to work.

Conveniently, the greenhouse was right in the centre of the doughnut of buildings that formed the Science Faculty. The poorly paid and demoralised caretaker never did anything more than a cursory scout around the circumference, so I knew we could remain completely undisturbed for weeks. I had *plans.*

Andrea was easy to drag in, a literal dead weight. Daniel showed brief signs of stirring as I accidentally knocked his head against the doorframe, but thankfully remained unconscious. I was slightly relieved; it was the first sign of movement he'd had since Andrea's house, and I was worried for a while I'd inflicted more harm to him than I'd intended. It was important that he was alive for the next step.

I tipped my holdall out onto the greenhouse floor, a variety of sealed plastic tubs clattering out. The syringe case was at the very bottom, underneath several soil-filled containers.

I took a syringe from the case and held it up to the light, studying the contents: a viscous, yellow-tinged liquid swimming with tiny fragments colliding against each other. I'd dabbled with a weaker cocktail of the fungi *Panaelous cyanescens*, *Psilocybe azurescens*, *Pluteus cyanopus,* and *Mycena cyanorrhiza* as a recreational drug in the past but had never dared to risk a concentration such as this.

David Court

My first experience of it had made for one hell of a weekend. It provoked an overwhelming sense of euphoria coupled with a torpor that made movement difficult, if not possible. I felt so disassociated from my corporeal form that any form of physical activity felt utterly *futile*.

I prepared Daniel first, carefully setting up the large industrial nutrient drip with the equipment I'd borrowed from the medical labs. He was still unconscious but shifted uncomfortably each time the scalpel dug into his skin to peel it back. I flinched every time his body jerked, but he remained thankfully comatose.

It was more difficult having to do it to myself. The hefty dose of regular Psilocybin masked some of the pain, but not all. Through my drug-addled senses, I couldn't help but think that my patches of skinless flesh looked like raw tuna steak. That thought made it slightly easier to push the spores and seeds into it.

Eventually, we were both ready. I had prepared the room by shovelling soil from the greenhouse trays into a corner and now sat down next to Daniel. A separate drip fed us both, and the banks of hydroponic lamps were set to full burst. I'd already checked and double-checked the automated sprinkler system and with a final injection of a particularly high dose of a special fungal cocktail I'd prepared, the process could begin.

I stared at the syringe in my hands, suddenly aware of the enormity of the situation. These motions were the last I would ever make, all going well.

Taking a deep breath, I plunged the needle-tip into my arm. It felt like liquid magma as it went in, a warmth flooded through my veins, soon to become roots and tributaries.

Our Elegant Decay

The alteration to my perception of time was not unexpected but was, as always, a delight to behold. In one moment, I could watch the flowers and fungus slowly grow, hours speeding by like minutes, and at other moments, the seconds crept at such a pace that I could observe the individual vibrations of the wings of a fly as it kept its tiny and fragile frame aloft.

I was so heavily drugged that I was unable to make the slightest of movements, even to crane my head, and I remained blissfully unaware of the passage of actual time. If I could have run the experiment again, I would have placed a digital clock with a calendar in my field of view. There wouldn't be another opportunity.

The spray of water on my face with each cycle of the sprinklers woke me, reminding me where and who I was. If I closed my eyes, it sounded like rainfall.

I noted that physical movement was impossible now. As expected, the toxic cocktail had acted as a neuromuscular paralytic and had probably done irreparable damage to my nervous system.

I *think* it was on the third day that Daniel awoke, after what seemed like hours of blinking, followed by him slowly opening his eyes. How must I have looked to him then? I'd deliberately chosen different strains of fungi and plants for each of us. By the painful act of moving my eyes down, feeling like at least twenty minutes of hard work by my reckoning, I could see dull brown floret tips of fungal growths dotting both our forearms. His own peeled cheek had begun to blossom with the lemon yellow *Leucocoprinus birnbaumii*, their fungal hoods taking shape as they gained structural integrity.

I had carefully sat Andrea's corpse between us and scattered her body with water and a variety of mosses and fungi. Her open eyes were quite distracting, at the time forcing me to place a dampened cloth shroud over her face.

Daniel started making the most terrible noises at some stage. With hindsight, I would have removed his tongue or at least have used it as a handy source of moisture for some controlled fungal development. It seems so obvious now. He was still paralysed, but fully cognizant, and I must have looked quite the horror by then, forced, as he was, to stare at me.

He was quite beautiful with a dazzling display of mushrooms and toadstools erupting in vibrant clusters from the flesh on his chest, face, and arms, vivid with poisonous and exotic reds and yellows. The Colorado Blue Columbine flower – *Aquilegia caerulea* – had begun to emerge from his wounds, shrouded in dried and congealed red, making him more attractive in the act of dying than he'd been in years. His eyes were fixed open, the beginnings of a beautiful crop of brilliant white sunburst toadstools erupting from the corner of one.

Despite a yearning for self-destruction through drug abuse, none of my scientific knowledge had left me. In the end, my timing had been perfect. As the last of the drips drained, I could feel the plants and fungus within me. Some, as designed, had grown to face the sun whereas others had retreated, sinking deeper into me.

Daniel, Andrea, and I were all connected – tendrils of moss and patches of vegetation engulfed us and much of the floor around us. I could feel as somebody approached. The gentle vibration in a hundred stamen, the ripples across countless leaves. Daniel had passed on, the light vanishing from his eyes long before the fungal growth had hidden them. The final hiss that left his constricted throat was accompanied by the chorus of the gentle sound of the ventilation system.

It was Doctor Randwick who opened the door. I was filled with a sense of disappointment when I realised he wasn't accompanied by Doctors Pace and Brooker, but it would still do. His expression was the same as the one Andrea gave me when she found me on her doorstep, but more exaggerated.

Our Elegant Decay

He staggered inside, horrified. The smell must have hit him first, one to which I'd grown used to. A beautiful fungus I had a soft spot for, and had grown on Andrea's corpse, was the Stinkhorn – *Phallaceae* – and had a stench that resembled decomposing meat. Mind you, Andrea had been decomposing for some weeks now, so it'd probably be hard to tell the difference.

His foot brushed against what was left of Daniel, bursting a fragile membrane containing a billion eager spores. As the air filled with the seed of my husband, Randwick, his mouth agape with surprise, couldn't help but breathe in huge mouthfuls of the stuff. He staggered towards the window, disrupting more spore containers in his clumsy stumbling. He threw open the window and clouds of spores were propelled out into the glorious sunshine.

It hurt to smile, but I forced one out with two words, just as the vines constricted around my heart and moss smothered my brain.

""Our children."

"Our Elegant Decay" was first published in the Issue 1 of the Stitched Smile Magazine, published by Stitched Smile.

David Court

At the River's Brink

*S*AINT FRANCIS OF ASSISI *then*, thought Meister Irmesch as his gnarled and weathered hands delved deep into his robe, thin and frail fingertips quickly locating the appropriate talisman. It seemed the better choice – who better to protect him in these woods than the saint of nature and animals? He clenched his fist around the charm and slowly removed his hands from his pockets, muttering a silent prayer in the hope that he had indeed picked the correct one.

If he hadn't, he'd certainly have doomed himself. The thing that stared at him from behind the trees – the thing whose bright and demonic red eyes were locked on his own – was undoubtedly a Skogsrå. Experience told him that he was safe for as long as they made eye contact – it would only be when he looked away, even if only for an instant, that it would be upon him – a frenzied dervish of razor teeth and poisonous bark-sharpened claws.

Irmesch cursed both his stupidity and his over-confidence – The evidence of the creature had been right in front of him from the moment that he'd entered the woods. To Irmesch's credit, he'd noticed the carefully placed stone cairns and the lack of birdsong, but to his folly he'd thought the beast long gone.

His eyes, tired from staring, began to ache. Each blink seemed longer than the last, and he could hear the fiend purr in anticipation. *Lord, grant me strength.*

At the River's Brink

Without warning, Irmesch stepped forward purposefully, right arm outstretched. He opened his mouth to speak as his fist unclenched, the talisman dropping and dangling from the chain that he'd wrapped around his wrist. The *right* talisman.

"Oh, Divine master!" he exclaimed, defiant, resolute, "Grant that I may not so much seek to be consoled as to console!"

The creature did not flinch or move from the shadows but simply stared back, scarlet eyes narrowing to vicious slits. Irmesch could sense the beast's confusion – this was clearly a creature used to its prey turning their back on it and fleeing.

The creature thinks me a frail old man, thought Irmesch, barely breaking his stride. *But I am armoured by the Lord our God.*

"To be understood as to understand!" he continued, "To be loved as to love!"

The eyes lowered in the darkness. *The beast crouches to pounce*, thought Irmesch.

"For it is in giving that we *receive!*"

With that last syllable and a flick of the wrist, the talisman was flung towards the beast. Arcing through the air between them, it landed at the feet of the creature. As the talisman burst into light, Irmesch caught a glimpse of it – a vile, corrupted thing, ancient and diseased – before he was forced to shield his eyes from the brilliance. The creature, briefly trapped in the light, erupted into a violent cacophony of shrieks and howls.

Irmesch's tone was quieter now, more subdued, as he stopped in his tracks and dropped to one knee. He calmly unsheathed his sword and crossed himself with his other hand. With his head bowed and eyes tightly closed, he prepared himself.

"It is in pardoning that we are pardoned; It is in dying to self that we are born to eternal life."

With the power of the talisman exhausted, the beast, blinded and angry, leapt at Irmesch. A roar of frustrated rage grew louder and closer until the old priest, as patient as he was skilled, stood up and thrust his blade forwards.

David Court

The howl stopped abruptly. Irmesch opened his eyes to see the beast impaled on his blade, the light already fading from the eyes of the blighted thing. With a single tug, the blade was pulled free and the Skogsrå slumped onto the sodden earth, an oily black ichor pouring from the creature's single wound. Irmesch stared down at the beast – a rough approximation of a human shape with unnaturally long limbs and pronounced features, as though drawn by a simpleton or a child. Pearlescent, membrane-thin, light blue skin scored with thin grey veins slowly pulsed and throbbed as the thing breathed its last.

Irmesch mused as he wiped his blade clean – the creature was a juvenile, barely a few days old. It had clearly been given life by the presence of the evil that haunted the towns and villages along the banks of the Weser River, the same evil that Irmesch sought to cleanse. The carcass of the pony he'd encountered upstream was probably the beast's first kill. Thanks to Irmesch and his faithful blade, it was also its last.

Normality had temporarily returned to the woods with the slaying of the beast – pleasant bird song returned to the trees, albeit tentatively at first, and massed patches of dappled sunlight began to filter through the thick foliage. Despite the task at hand that weighed heavy on him, his own mood lightened for a favourable stretch of the journey, and Irmesch found himself whistling along with the birds, content with Gods' grace.

That was to be only a fleeting respite though – as Irmesch approached the town, the atmosphere became more ominous, grey clouds gathering overhead as a dread chill began to wend its way through the trees. Even the noise of the distant river seemed muted and slowed, as though the very current dragged itself laboriously towards the town, loathe to approach it.

At the River's Brink

This town was much like Brevörde, which was much like Pegestorf before it. All were modest sized and humble settlements that relied on the neighbouring river for their trade, and there was a time when the river Weser would have been abundant with boats – either those of fisherman or merchants transporting their wares both up and downstream.

That was in the days before the plague.

The two guards on the town gate, both uncaring, let Meister Irmesch in with nary a nod. As a man of the cloth who was clearly dressed and carried himself as such, Irmesch had come to expect a certain amount of leniency in his travels, but never had he witnessed such complacency. That same apathy extended to the citizens within the town walls – a languor hung in the air, something Irmesch found unnerving but had regrettably become used to. There was one clear difference here though, one he noticed when he strained to listen for any sign. On every street in Brevörde and Pegestorf, you could hear it – a remorseful keening, a tortured lament for the dead. There was no such sound here – perhaps this time, by the grace of almighty God, he'd arrived in time.

A meagre collection of mostly bare market stalls lay scattered around the town square, their attendants silent and morose. Irmesch approached a fishmonger who barely looked up from his measly stock and, upon asking for directions to the mayor's abode, was answered wordlessly with a single dispirited finger pointing up the hill.

Irmesch, having arrived at the top of the mound, leaned against the wall of the Mayors house. *Doing the Lord's good work is the solace of the young*, he thought to himself with a smile. Long gone was the day he'd have tramped up the hill with nary a pause. He took a few moments to capture his breath before knocking on the heavy oaken door, which was met with no response. A second knock a few moments later had the same result. After the third knock - one loud enough to wake the dead – was also unanswered, Irmesch begrudgingly began the walk downhill back to the town square.

He spied an individual beginning the walk uphill – from his fine green robes and chain of office, it was clearly the mayor. He was a ruddy faced individual, stout and short. Irmesch sat on a rock that lay beside the path and waited for him and, as the individual drew near, stood up and held out a hand in greeting.

The mayor took it and shook it half-heartedly, seemingly distracted by something. Irmesch introduced himself.

"Good afternoon, Mayor Bulstrich. I am Meister Irmesch, loyal servant of the church. I am here on a matter of some import and would seek an audience."

The mayor grunted a response and looked around himself before acknowledging the priest.

"Bulstrich retired, and his timing was impeccable for him and miserable for me. I'm Mayor Schade. Walk with me, Meister."

The clouds over them began to break and sunlight returned as they began the walk back to the house. The mayor muttered something under his breath before turning to Irmesch.

"What brings a representative of the church to our gates?" he asked, his tone sharp and accusatory, "Come to raise our taxes for another church in Hanover, or are you just here for the sightseeing?"

"Mister Mayor," retaliated Irmesch, well used to dealing with men such as this, "My visit here is nothing to do with the arranged tithe, but..."

"That's good. Because we have nothing for you. We've been dying on our arse here for the past week, and our prayers didn't help."

Irmesch could tell from the man's demeanour he had yet more to say, so the two walked in silence for a few moments.

"Rats, priest. Rats. A plague of them. Like something from the bible. Razing our fields, using our storerooms and basements as their larders, growing plump from our fish and our grain and our chickens. Where was your church then?"

They were now standing outside the house and the Mayor fumbled inside a pocket for his keys. With plump and shaking fingers, he unlocked the door and stepped inside, gesturing for the Meister to enter. Irmesch followed the man into the kitchen by which time the mayor had already retrieved a large ceramic flagon from a shelf and was pouring himself a generous amount of red wine. Glass in hand, the portly man pulled back a chair and slumped into it, the weight of the world seemingly balanced on his shoulders.

"I'd offer you some wine, priest, but this is all I have."

Irmesch sat in a chair across the table from Schade and leaned forward to speak, eyes narrowed.

"I've seen this plague before. I've followed it down the river. At Brevörde and Pegestorf too, but I was too late. I am here in pursuit of a great evil. The woods around are teeming with the forces of darkness, all drawn out from their pits like worms emerging from the mud when the rains fall."

The Mayor looked concerned, as though something in the holy man's words had struck a chord with him. As he spoke, he seemed incapable of looking Irmesch in the eye, staring down at the wine in his cup as he slowly swirled the remnants about.

"We've... lost people. Runners sent to Brevörde haven't returned. We've heard nothing from outside these walls. We'd thought them delayed, but now you speak of it... There has been a mood... an *atmosphere*. I'd put the malaise down to the rats."

Irmesch stood up and walked over to the window, pulling the shutters aside and letting the sunlight flood in. He looked down the hill.

"I walked through these gates", he muttered, staring in the direction of the gatehouse. "And no-one raised a hand or a sword to stop me. There is an individual – *the one who travels* – who would seek to enter this place. We had sent *laity* to give warning, but they must have perished in the woods. You must give instruction and give it soon. Ingress to this town must be prevented."

Schade's face, despite his reddened complexion, grew unnaturally pale.

"And what... what do we know of this one who travels?"

Irmesch slowly turned around and looked down at the Mayor, his manner cold and portentous.

"He appears slightly different to each man, woman, and child. To some, he is a youth. To others, an old man. But for all, he is dressed in cloth of many colours and a brimless felt cap. And carries nought but a pipe."

The Mayor, his expression suddenly crestfallen, looked down into his drink.

"I must confess, Meister, that we have had dealings with this man. He gained entrance before nightfall yesterday and offered to rid the town of its rat problem."

Irmesch slammed his fists down on the table, causing the Mayor to jump and his glass to spill.

"Where is this man now? Take me to him!"

"Driven out of the town not an hour back", cowered Mayor Schade, "Upon completion of his duties, he'd tripled the price first promised, outright refusing to take the original fee. I sent the swindler on his way without a single *pfennig*, and good riddance!"

"We must act quickly", shouted the priest, a renewed vigour in his eyes. "Or Hamelin will share the fate of its neighbours!"

"Where in God's name are we *going*?" implored Schade, hurriedly ushered out of the house by Irmesch as they traipsed out into the crisp early evening air. The old priest was striding purposefully down the hill and the Mayor almost fell over his own feet trying to keep up.

At the River's Brink

"I've seen the aftermath of this twice before, and I'll be damned if I have to witness it a third time." Irmesch spat, seemingly trying to convince himself of this as much as the Mayor.

"Seen *what*?"

"In Brevörde they offered him all the guilders for which he'd asked, but he still did it anyway. In Pegestorf they did the same as you when he doubled his fee. Kicked him out. He did the same deed to them also."

Irmesch waved at two guards at the foot of the hill and gestured that they walk up to meet them.

"Do *what*, Meister?"

"He took their children. With the music from that confounded pipe of his. They emerged from their houses in a trance-like state, much as the rats had done. They followed him to God only knows where. Except for the lame that could not dance and the deaf that could not hear, they were all taken."

"Their *children*? Did the people of Brevörde and Pegestorf stand idly by and do naught?"

"From all accounts, they were frozen to the spot. The same glamour that caused their children to skip and dance their way after that accursed piper froze the adults in place. They could do nothing but watch. The piper passed amongst them, unhindered."

The two guards were with them now, awaiting instruction. They looked more like poorly dressed civilians than soldiers, thought Irmesch, with their ill-fitting armour and poor discipline. The Mayor went to speak but Irmesch interrupted him, barking instructions.

"Get the other guards and tell all the parents. Secure all the children. Tie them down, barricade their doors, whatever it takes – something is coming for them, and when it does, we will all be powerless to fight it."

The confused guards looked at the Mayor for confirmation, who nodded back at them.

David Court

"Do as the priest says. Get all the rope and timber you need from the storerooms."

Schade glared at them, throwing his hands in the air.

"What are you waiting for?" he cried, "Ring the bells! Tell everyone!"

The guards looked at each other for a brief moment before sprinting back down the hill, armour plates clanking noisily with each stride. Irmesch and Schade hurried after the two.

The clanging of the town bells in the main square saw guards gather and the townsfolk roused from their torpor. With barked instructions from the Mayor, soldiers and civilians alike gathered rope and wood and began to make their way to the houses. Irmesch gathered stragglers and tried to explain as best he could what was going on, urging people to go to the town square and aid the masses gathered there.

It was then that Irmesch heard it, even above the clamour of the townsfolk and the cacophony of the bells. A series of light tones, easily mistaken at first as wind, then becoming chaotic and discordant and gradually escalating into a recognizable tune. Irmesch knew the tune from somewhere but couldn't quite place it.

It was only when it grew louder, drowning out all other sound, that he recognised it. It was the lullaby sang to him by *mama*, an old folk song from her youth that he'd never heard sung by another in all his long years.

"Sleep speedily, leave off crying,
May you sleep till morning, dear man's son,
    For the child breaks, flowers blue and red,
    On the morrow sends."

As beautiful as it was haunting, Irmesch was overwhelmed by nostalgia. Oblivious to the world around him, he struggled to contain the raw emotions that began to fill his very being.

At the River's Brink

Emotions within him that, as a Meister, the Church urged him to suppress. Tears filled his eyes, both screwed tightly shut. He found himself humming along, quietly at first, but then louder as the memories returned. He could feel her warm touch against him, the smell of the honeysuckle from their garden on her skin, her comforting words calming him and sending him off to a peaceful sleep...

No.

His eyes sprung open.

There was a brief sense of bewilderment as Irmesch struggled to remember where he was and what he was supposed to be doing, before the horrors of reality came flooding back. One of the townsfolk - an old gentleman in his twilight years – was standing in front of him, eyes closed and hands gesticulating wildly as though in dance, albeit with feet locked in place. His old and withered lips silently mouthed the words of a song that only he could hear.

Irmesch looked about – everybody in sight, soldier and townsperson alike, were transfixed by the same glamour. Some sang loudly to themselves, some simply rocked and swayed rhythmically. All were rooted to the spot with eyes closed or wide open and staring jubilantly at the heavens. The haunting pipe music continued to play. Irmesch noted that everybody in sight was dancing or swaying at a different rhythm and tempo, presumably all lost in their own variant of the tune.

The young began to slowly emerge, shrugging off half-tied knots, crouching to pass through partially boarded windows and doors. A young girl being held by her transfixed and oblivious mother wriggled free of her flimsy grip and dropped to the ground. She turned briefly to look at Irmesch, her eyes blank white, before picking herself up and joining the line of children.

Irmesch, despite being the only one around who could see what was going on, found himself incapable of movement. The muscles in his legs simply failed to respond, each feeling like heavy stone that had been fused with the very earth itself.

David Court

It was then that Irmesch saw him, at the head of the line of children. A young man with delicate elfin features, clad from neck to toe in a multi-coloured jacket. From the stories, Irmesch had thought the clothes of the piper to be made from different coloured cloth but that wasn't the case – the jacket glistened like oil in a puddle, shimmering with a myriad of different colours and hues as the fading sunlight struck it at different angles.

The line of the young children measured two score now, all staring ahead with blank eyes, their feet shuffling in a slow march as they followed the piper. Irmesch tried to move again, but it was in vain. He began to shout and scream at the townsfolk, hoping to rouse them from the witchcraft that bound them. The only reaction came from the piper himself, cocking his head towards the source of the sound. With a few great strides, he was soon standing in front of Irmesch and towering over him.

"So, you're the one they sent to stop me..." he spat as he leaned towards Irmesch, his face uncomfortably close to that of the priest. "It must be said," he hissed through gritted teeth filed into razor sharp points, "that I'd expected somebody... younger."

"We will stop your evil," retaliated Irmesch, his tone one of angry defiance.

"Mine is a tune that cannot be stopped," smiled the Piper, "yet you are welcome to try."

The piper's face changed as Irmesch stared back, youthful features becoming corrupted, inhuman – blackened scarred horns forced their way through the piper's forehead, twisting in on themselves.

"Then the rumours were true!" gasped Irmesch, "You truly are the Devil. Not a lord of the dance, but the *Lord of the flies*."

The piper smiled, his face softening again into the youthful features they'd been mere moments before.

"My song is older than that, priest."

With a spring in his step, he skipped back to the children. Irmesch could do nothing but watch as he led his captives –

At the River's Brink

twice as many as there had been before – on a slow but steady march towards the edge of the village, heading towards the hills that lay outside Hamelin. The only child left behind was lame, crawling desperately along the ground and clawing at the earth, his walking stick discarded.

God grant me strength, thought Irmesch, fighting to resist the glamour with every inch of his being and the entirety of his long-held faith. *Your humble earthly servant needs your strength and aid.* The strain was almost too much to bear as his muscles burned with the exertion, but with every prayer muttered, feeling began to return. At first just a warmth spreading from his feet, but then the feeling of fire in his legs as muscles were reawakened. With sheer strength of will, he managed to push one foot in front of the other. *The Holy Spirit is flowing through my veins like fire*, rejoiced Irmesch, now standing upright, the witchcraft's hold over him vanquished.

Trying to shake any of the townsfolk out of their fantasy – or more appropriately, their *pipe dream* – met with no success. Even one he managed to push off his feet simply continued his dance from where he lay on the earth, tracing trails and whorls in the dirt as his limbs dragged across the dry soil.

Irmesch, his legs still pained, staggered towards the direction in which the piper had led the hapless transfixed children, following the sound of the pipes which was now growing more distant with every passing moment. With his sword now in hand, he stumbled in the direction of the hills. He found himself having to rely on propping himself up against a fence or wall less and less with every passing minute.

He broke into a sprint for that final stretch, alarmed that the pipe sounds were fading faster than he could keep up with. It felt as though his heart and lungs were filling with magma, every step a fresh new agony. He found himself on the crest of a hill, exhausted beyond belief, to see the last of the line of children crouching as they made their way into a cave in the base of a chalk-white rock wall. The sound of the pipes echoed from within the caverns beyond, fading now. Irmesch threw himself

David Court

forwards, half running and half falling towards the cave, mostly momentum carrying his exhausted form forwards now.

Knowing the futility of his actions before the words had even left his throat, he screamed in desperation at the last child to come back. She briefly looked back at him with tiny blank white eyes before vanishing into the darkness. As her form faded from view, a terrible rending sound filled the air, rock grinding against rock. Irmesch watched incredulously as the rock around the edge of the cave entrance expanded and grew, fingers of white stone wrapping and knotting around each other until it was as though there never was an entrance at all in the white chalkstone cliff wall.

Irmesch fell against it, hammering on it and screaming aloud in frustration. The rock was as thick as it had ever been, immovable and impassable.

The last note of the piper faded into silence, replaced by a new harrowing sound as the spell was broken.

The sobbing of the distraught from Hamelin.

"We are more fortunate than those in Brevörde and Pegestorf," shouted Irmesch as he led the townsfolk through the hills, "in that we know where our children have been taken."

At his instruction, the menfolk had picked up any tools they had to hand. A phalanx of angry townsfolk followed closely behind the priest, armed with shovels, pickaxes, mallets and hammers – whatever tools had been to hand when Irmesch had rallied them together.

Arriving at the white chalkstone wall, Irmesch gestured to where the cavern entrance had been. Without a word, the largest of the townsfolk broke from the group, those without hammers grabbing one from their colleagues. White rock splintered beneath a barrage of hammer blows, revealing nothing but more rock. All the townsfolk joined in now, attacking the cliff face with

At the River's Brink

a violent ferocity. Irmesch helped in the only way he could, reciting a prayer for counsel.

The men's enthusiasm drained as their actions appeared to be for nothing – the rock of the wall was simply too thick, and their actions seemingly insignificant.

That was until one of the men whooped with excitement as a blow from his pickaxe caused a huge section to crumble into pebbles and white powder, revealing a man-sized cavern leading deep into the rock. Eager to deliver judgement and to recover their lost children, the men began to noisily gather in front of the cavern, pushing each other out of the way in order to be the first to gain entrance. Irmesch suddenly stood up and roared at them to stop, and they turned as one to face him.

"As a Servant of God, I will enter first," he stated in a tone that indicated that this wasn't a matter up for argument. "You can all follow me. Let us both find your children and deliver God's wrath."

The tunnels were narrow, but not impassable. Although it soon became clear that it would be very easy to get lost, as one could barely walk two dozen steps before reaching another junction, both paths leading deeper into the cliff. The chalk walls of the tunnel glittered with lantern light, veins of white crystal flickering in the darkness. On occasion, one of the men would call out the name of his child, but they all remained unanswered. The robes of Irmesch and the clothes of the men were gradually becoming ripped and torn and stained powder-white from some of the sharp outcrops of stone that lined the walls of the naturally formed passageways.

Irmesch raised a hand, bidding his followers halt. The cavern opened out into a larger chamber – an island surrounded by black freezing cold waters, stalagmites glinting in the light. A gentle breeze echoed through this grotto, a cool wind from the outside world. What concerned Irmesch though was the figure that lay in front of him – the Piper, motionless and laid back, the pipe gripped firmly in his right hand.

The few men crowded behind Irmesch who could see what he saw struggled to get past him, eager to seek vengeance. Irmesch was pushed aside in the squabble, falling to his knees in the melee.

"No!" he implored, tasting blood from a recent wound at the corner of his mouth. "If you kill him now, you may never find what he's done with your children!"

Common sense ruled, and they saw the wisdom in staying their hand. One of them helped Irmesch back to his feet. He glared at them and made his way to the sleeping form of the Piper, bending down and pulling the pipe from his grip. Instantly, he recoiled at the touch. It felt warm and writhed in his grasp, serpentine and malevolent. He threw it as far away from him as he could, and heard it splash down into the cold waters that surrounded them. He wiped his hands on his robes, anything to remove the memory of that touch.

"Take him back to the town!" cried Irmesch. "He'll answer to God for his crimes there!"

Without hesitation, the Piper was lifted off the ground and carried back through the network of tunnels. And if whilst being carried he should hit his head off the walls of the tunnel, it was merely an unfortunate accident – an unfortunate accident that befell the piper a dozen times, at least. He remained still throughout – breathing, yet seemingly unconscious.

With a third bucket of tepid stream water tipped over him, the tightly bound piper was woken. Even then his eyes were half open, the fiend seemingly exhausted. He looked about himself, bewildered and confused. Irmesch glared down at him whilst Schade paced up and down. Some of the townsfolk were waiting nervously outside, with the remainder scouring the caverns seeking their children.

The piper's robes were dull now, all iridescence faded. He looked far from youthful, this old and frail man that sat tied to a chair in front of them.

"If you tell us where you put the children, this could all end now," said Irmesch calmly, "Grant these parents some mercy, here, at the end."

"Here at the end, Priest? I think you'll find it is *their* end and not my own."

Irmesch held the crucifix in his hand and contemplated its weight, trying to ignore the venomous tone of their captive. In a single moment the crucifix was held inches away from the face of the piper, who did not flinch.

"In the name of the Lord our Father, you tell us where the children are! Or I will drag those words from your bleeding remains!"

The corner of the piper's mouth turned up in a faint mockery of a smile.

"Do your God's worst, priest."

The word 'priest' was bitterly spat out with utter disdain.

Irmesch unsheathed his blade and watched the lantern light reflect from the polished surface. The piper merely glared at him as he leaned in closer. Irmesch had seen the like before, and knew this stoicism would, with a slice, be banished.

Schade turned away before the screams started – He'd never had much of a stomach for the sight of blood.

"He did not confess, even at the end." said Irmesch to the gathered crowds outside the guardhouse. The pipers ruined corpse, covered with a blood-soaked cloth, was carried out by the largest of the town guards and placed on a pyre that the townsfolk had built. Irmesch felt no satisfaction as he watched the things body burn, knowing that but a short distance away parents were crying as they searched dark tunnels for children that might never be found.

An overwrought Schade had found him lodgings for the night – one of the disused guard houses. Too cold for habitation in winter, but pleasant enough on a spring evening such as this. As he sat in the candlelight he poured himself a glass of red wine from the flagon that had been left for him – even God would forgive him, a man of the cloth, for having a drink on a night such as this.

What a day it had been. Even though he had hunted and killed his prey, he felt no satisfaction. If he hadn't been slowed by the Skogsrå, if he'd only arrived a few hours earlier, this could all have been very different.

Truth be told, his emotions were still raw after that fleeting memory of his mother, the one that had kept him transfixed whilst the children were stolen from under their noses. The ability the piper had seemingly had to tap into their memories, all their weaknesses exposed.

"Sleep speedily, leave off crying,
May you sleep till morning, dear man's son,
For the child breaks, flowers blue and red,
On the morrow sends."

As he finished the last note, he lifted the glass, and thought of his mother. He gulped deeply from the red wine, spitting it over the floor when he heard the words spoken from the shadows in the corner.

"Priest."

The Piper stepped from the shadows, his coat once again a vibrant tapestry of colour. Panicked, Irmesch went to scream for help, but his voice was hollow – just a rasping hiss.

"As long as the tune sounds, the piper lives on."

He threw his arms wide in a mockery of the crucifixion and whistled the same tune that Irmesch had begun.

At the River's Brink

"But this piper needs an instrument" he smiled, nimbly leaping onto the bed just as the floor became carpeted with a living mass of fur and tails – a swarm of rats, a pipe being carried amongst the mass.

"Thank you, my children" chirped the Piper, delicately picking up the flute and rising it to his lips. "Music is so important, don't you think? If played well and at the right time, it can be truly... *transformative*."

"This tune, priest," he said, smiling now, "is just for you."

A new tune from the pipe now, one so loud that Irmesch wondered why nobody else heard it – distressed at why nobody was coming to help him.

A twist in his gut, one that caused Irmesch to collapse to his knees, the rats neatly clearing a space for him as he fell. He leant forward on his hands to try and stand back up, but they refused to take his weight. His body was suddenly wracked with agony, bones twisting, warping, knotting, and shrinking. The last of his sanity snapped as thick black hair exploded from the bloodied skin of his flesh-stripped arms, his fingers merging into sharpened claws. The piper loomed over him, a giant now.

He cradled the large old black rat in his hands, stroking the fur on the back of his neck to calm his agitated squeaking. He stared into the black eyes of the rodent, only a primitive instinctive intelligence locked within there now.

"Come, my children. To the next town" said the piper, skipping out of the guardhouse.

The swarm followed, always drawn to the call of the piper.

David Court

Microcosm, Macrocosm

I **DREAM OF** the sea. In the interest of full disclosure, I feel that it's only honest of me to let you know that these dreams aren't memories. The only sea I've ever seen in real life - from a safe distance, I'd hasten to add - was a polluted burning black lake of sludge that sluggishly bubbled and hissed against the rocks, a toxic morass that caused my Geiger counter to click like a brittle-boned octogenarian falling down the stairs.

The sea of my dreams is the one from old movies and photographs. From the time when things used to live in it, those halcyon days when the ocean still ebbed and flowed in tides.

You could *swim* in it - can you believe that? Contact with it wouldn't burn, choke, or blind. In my dreams, I'm standing in it with the cool water lapping around my ankles. I'm out there alone, watching the sunset. Now you can't even look at the sky without powerful photo-chromatic lenses, and even then, the pollution-clogged clouds burn so brightly it's hard to tell them apart from the sun itself.

I've been away for so long. Is there a sea left at all now, or has it - like the experts warned - burned away into the atmosphere?

The human brain is an incredible piece of technology. Not only am I vividly dreaming about something that I've never personally experienced, but I'm also defying the contents of at least a dozen research papers written by people much smarter and infinitely more verbose than myself.

Microcosm, Macrocosm

They all conclude the same thing, but they're all clearly wrong.

They say you can't dream in cryogenic suspension.

Brain activity is slowed to such an extent, they all say, *that the electro-chemical reactions that we call thoughts simply cannot and do not happen.*

Yet here I am. Admittedly I only dream shortly before waking and my time here will be fleeting, but everything I am experiencing now flouts scientific logic. The waters are warm and the currents gentle. The temperate wind that brushes past me is tinged with the scent of salt. If only those scientists could be standing with me now.

Scratch that thought. Scientists here with me now would be a terrible idea. They'd be complaining about the fresh air and insisting I fill out all manner of questionnaires. I know scientists all too well. They tend to be a terrible buzzkill.

The feeling of weightlessness hits me sooner than I'd expected, and I'm forced to adjust to the feelings of nausea as my reluctant and protesting consciousness is pulled back into my waking body.

Somebody once told me - and I have no idea how much truth there is in this - that after a woman gives birth the brain generates such a heady cocktail of endorphins she effectively forgets the detail of quite how painful the whole squeezing-out-a-baby process was. If it didn't, she'd never even consider giving birth again.

That's the brain attempting to do the right thing for the continued survival of our species. The irony is that if it hadn't bothered, Earth might not have such a chronic overpopulation problem.

If that whole chemical release thing is true, Cryo-sleep is exactly like that. Any minute now, a panel in my cryogenic cradle will slide silently open and a needle will inject me with a bucketful of happy juice. Until that moment though, I'm reminded again why I hate cryogenic sleep.

For one, it suddenly hurts to *live*. The body you've been thrust back into just aches everywhere. Oh, the Cradle has tried damn hard to massage your sleeping limbs and keep your muscles from atrophying away, but it still hurts. Every beat of your waking heart sends a pulse of dull pain throughout your entire system as warmth and movement slowly oozes back into dead digits.

Never again. This is the last time. It all just hurts *too much*.

But with a gentle hiss, there it is. A series of hypodermic needles are inserted into strategic points and flood me with joyous, blissful warmth. I'm momentarily riding a wave of euphoria, the thoughts in my head unable to properly formulate as the agony of the last five minutes is suddenly forgotten.

I lie there for a few moments and flex and relax my arms and hands, wincing as they crack noisily. The scientist in me reminds me that the noise is only air bubbles in the joints being released, but that doesn't make the sensation any less unpleasant. It sounds like ice cracking.

With a pneumatic hiss, the Cryo-coffin slides open and the cold air from outside rushes in. Goosebumps form on my exposed skin and my teeth begin to chatter involuntarily.

Every time. Every single time.

I open my mouth to speak, but nothing comes out of it except a hoarse croak - a painful and sore expulsion of wounded air. I cough painfully - dislodging a years' worth of mucous from my throat - and try again, the words escaping me this time as a throaty rasp.

"Matron!"

I'm about to speak again when the familiar ping from the intercom indicates she's heard me. There I am, gendering the automated computer system again - something I've tried very

Microcosm, Macrocosm

hard never to do. *Just because they gave it a female name*, I've argued with the rest of the crew, *it doesn't make it female*.

Matron; Monitoring by Autonomous Transmission/Reception Organic Network. I know what you're thinking. The brains behind that *definitely* came up with the acronym before they came up with what it stood for. As a phrase, it's laboured, unwieldy, and barely does justice to the sophisticated ship-wide artificial intelligence it represents.

I saw the core of it once, just as it was being installed into the computer network that would house and preserve it. A tightly woven bundle of lower primate brains suspended in a jelly so dark red it looked like raspberry.

"Good morning, Doctor Hatten, and congratulations."

There's just that tiny noticeable delay between the words Doctor and Hatten, like the slight pause you get on your satellite navigation system. That faintest of discrepancies in the voice that reminds you she's not real.

It's not real. Not she. IT'S not real.

They're nearly all female. Almost every artificial intelligence I've ever encountered on every space station or ship, that is. The experts would tell you that's because the human brain is weirdly coded to respond to female voices better, but that doesn't remove the overwhelming sensation you get of being nagged at.

I'm briefly confused as to why she's congratulated me before the fog of Cryo-sleep clears and I remember. It is indeed a very *special* day. Albeit one, as ever, with a frosty start.

"I told you last time just before I went to sleep. I couldn't have been more precise - You need to switch the heating on the day before you wake me up and leave it on for twenty-four hours."

She's silent for a few moments. I try to fool myself that's because I've got her bang to rights, but truth be told I know she's only quiet because she's formulating an inevitably terse yet accurate response from her vast knowledgebase.

"The radius of the nearest celestial body is two thousand four hundred kilometres, giving it a day length of approximately one thousand three hundred and ninety-three hours. The heating was switched on last August and kept on for twenty hours, just as you instructed."

Two months ago. I swear she - *it* - does it just to wind me up. I lift myself out of the cryogenic capsule and wrap my exposed arms around myself in a futile attempt to warm myself up. Legs that haven't worked as legs for the longest time wobble precariously, but against all odds manage the not unimpressive feat of keeping me upright.

Ten minutes later and I'm dressed and slightly warmer. I decide to wear my lab-coat, more for the sense of occasion than anything else. I get one of the automated vending machines to make me a coffee and I hold it tightly between my chilled fingers as I make my way through the ship.

"Matron?"

A bleep. It's listening.

"How's the ship?"

The word ship almost seems laughable now. With a fucked navigation system and no means of manual control, we're more like a crash waiting to happen.

"Systems are optimal. There was a minor collision with a meteoroid ninety-eight days ago, but automated reparation systems repaired the damage sustained to Corridor Seventy-Nine. It didn't seem important enough to wake you ahead of your requested date."

"Is it still accessible?"

"Yes, Doctor Hatten. A momentary hole in the right wall was sealed within one hundred and eighteen seconds. Minimal loss of life."

Minimal loss of life? I'm briefly concerned before realisation dawns, aided by my newly awakened olfactory senses. I smell it before I see it. The problem with waking up in a dead spacecraft is that the air decontamination and filtration systems take a while to kick in, and for a short while you're stuck with every stagnant smell that's been lingering whilst you've been asleep.

Microcosm, Macrocosm

In this case, the enduring odour of small piles of varying sized lumps of excrement against the walls of the corridor. Some are small and marble sized, others long like a cigar. From black to brown to beige. An entire spectrum of shit.

Minimal loss of life. That'd be the cats then.

Like a high-tech Noah's ark, some boffin back on Earth had had the bright idea of bringing two cats along. And the even brighter idea of transporting them - to save space - in the same cryogenic chamber. Turns out that if you defrost them - as I'd done by accident - they're considerably livelier than humans are when they come around. Especially if the female one is in heat. As luck would have it, I'd managed to capture the male, but the now pregnant female had eluded me. And in this maze of a ship, she could have been *anywhere*. And, as I should have predicted, her offspring have been busy doing what cats do best the whole time I've been asleep. Shitting, pissing, fighting, and fucking.

Cats are creatures of instinct. When one desperate cat feels the need to relieve himself against the wall of the corridor, all the other cats take that as a sign that it's okay to do the same.

And then, after a while, you just end up with a whole corridor of shit. Which, if it wasn't real, would be a marvellous metaphor for something.

I walk past it, gagging from the acrid aroma. It's all I can do to avoid vomiting there and then. I guess at least that would add some variety of colour to the piles and puddles of organic waste lining the floor.

I'm at the end of the corridor when I see it looking at me. It's a tiny black thing, wide blue eyes almost as big as the thing's face. What a sight I must be to this tiny little kitten - the first human he's ever seen.

It tentatively pads towards me, a scrawny pipe-cleaner tail pointing towards the ceiling. The only sound that escapes its tiny mouth is a meow almost too high-pitched to hear. It stops when it gets close, sitting down on the spot and staring up at me.

I kneel slowly, trying not to startle the thing. I gently put my hands around its frail little waist and lift it to my face. He's a brave little one. If something twenty times my size decided to pick me up, I'd do more than just look cute and stare doe-eyed at my captor.

The light vanishes from its eyes the very moment I tighten my grip. Fragile bones less than a fortnight old offer little to no resistance from my strength. That little new life is snuffed out in less time than it takes to breathe in and out. I drop the limb body at my feet, and something splinters inside it. Other eyes glaring at me from the shadows, bright green and pearlescent blue, blink and vanish.

What? Was that too much? Would it have been better if I'd just tickled the thing under its chin and put it down, smiling as it scampered merrily off? If it makes you feel better, imagine I did that. Imagine I did exactly that. And remember what your sensibilities made me do.

Will the other cats see it as a warning? Or are they so feral that their once-sibling is now merely regarded as fur-coated food? Tempted as I am to see how they react, I walk on. There are more pressing matters to deal with today.

Incidentally, I think I may have gone insane. Killing a kitten in cold blood doesn't even cause the slightest increase in my pulse rate, which is surely indicative of some manner of sociopathic trait. As is this need to narrate my every activity to an imaginary third party, just as I'm doing now. I don't say this for sympathy - It's just something I've come to terms with.

Whether it's my hurried walking or Matron finally having mastered the environmental controls for the ship, I'm soon warming up nicely. I remove my lab coat and throw it over my shoulders, my pace increasing.

I slow as I approach the mess hall, though. My brain fogs, memories addled by cryogenic suspension. Things that only happened days ago to me feel so distant, having happened years ago in what we laughably call *the real world*. The memories become clearer as I step inside, like an image gaining clarity through the white noise static of a damaged view-screen.

Microcosm, Macrocosm

The memory of that meeting suddenly overwhelms me. Captain Kulkarni had done one of the few things he was any good at – he'd called a meeting.

"I guess you're wondering why I summoned you all," growled a clearly distressed Kulkarni.

He's folding and unfolding his cap, I noted. *He only ever does that when he's angry or nervous.* I hoped it was the latter, having been at the rough end of his temper before. His standard issue baseball cap, once neatly embroidered with the name of the ship, wasn't holding up well under the stress. The fabric was splitting under the pressure of the man's twisting, fat fingers. I'd never made any secret of the fact that the man repulsed me - as tall as he was wide, he's living proof that both the mental and physical standards required for space travellers had dropped dramatically.

"You've been reading too much Agatha Christie again?" quipped Doctor Menzies. She looked to me for confirmation, fully aware that I'd be the only other person in the room who got the joke. I ignored her, and she emitted a short, nervous laugh.

I glanced around the room. Whatever the reason for the meeting, it must have been important – the heads of nearly every department and division were present. Corporal Bostrom met my gaze with the only expression he seemed capable of – utter derision. I'll admit to not liking most of the crew, but Bostrom I *loathed*. He was a violent bully who took every possible opportunity to belittle me, preferably in earshot of as many other crew members as possible. I looked away.

"The suspense is killing us, captain." I sighed, annoyed to have been pulled away from my research. Kulkarni shot me an evil glance, but I simply stared back, unimpressed. He looked down to his ruined cap before continuing. I noted that he was making eye contact with everybody except for me as he spoke.

David Court

"I'm not sure how to say this, but there's been a... problem. Our trajectory is incorrect, and we're not going to make landfall on Krueger-B."

I went cold. Having been involved with this colonisation project since the very outset, I knew exactly what he meant. The assembled crew laughed and tutted amongst themselves and were about to ask the captain a whole bunch of questions I already knew the answers to.

Almost in a daze, I staggered towards the door. Menzies went to stop me, but I brushed her away, only my forward momentum keeping me from falling flat on my face.

The problem was the United Pan-American Starship *Concordance* wasn't your traditional spacecraft. It was like the rockets of old, pointed in the right direction and let rip. Space that would have been ordinarily taken up by a bridge and navigation systems were crammed full of frozen colonists all looking for a better life, all of which had paid a pretty penny for the privilege. Stacked high, wide, and deep.

For as long as I can remember, the budget for research into space travel lay somewhere in the federal priority list between stationery and the budget for those little plastic things that fit into desks to keep cables tidy. Typically, it was only when it was all too late - when the last of the polar icecaps became small enough to fit comfortably into a glass of gin - that they decided to do something about it.

Terraforming - the art of transforming inhospitable alien landscapes into something more suitable for humans - had failed. Noxious unbreathable atmospheres simply became noxious, unbreathable, and flammable. Experiments into faster than light transportation that would have allowed us to search other galaxies for life-sustaining planets had failed. I dread to think of the number of dogs, chimps and square-jawed pilots that had been flattened to a single point of singularity whilst trialling all manner of dodgy experimental propulsion systems. If I'd have been a religious man, I could have sworn it was God's way of telling humanity "Look, guys. You've fucked up what I gave you. Don't think you're going to go running off elsewhere to fuck anything else up too."

Concordance was the last hope. From all the thousands of probes they'd sent randomly cartwheeling off into the cosmos, only one had anything positive to report. Just one. Dozens of thousands of planets surveyed, and that single blue-green sphere was all they found. It looked like the universe itself was trying as hard as it could not to let us leave, and I couldn't blame it.

Krueger-B, they'd named it. Whether that was the surname of the guy lucky enough to flick through the reams of probe logs for that day - or whether somebody was just a huge fan of that old vid-flick *Nightmare on Elm Street* - I'll never know. It had breathable atmosphere, oceans, and a conveniently orbiting moon to give those oceans tides. A virtual copy of Earth, albeit one less fucked up because it didn't have any advanced primates shitting all over the surface whilst stabbing each other in the face.

The technology to build the craft and launch it was funded by those willing to pay to leave Earth. As the planet was a rapidly heating piece of rock on which you could count the number of surviving species of plants and animals on the fingers of two hands without needing your thumbs, it wasn't a difficult decision for the rich to make.

Boil or freeze. Albeit, freeze temporarily.

So, off we went. Launched into the void of space with a minimal crew in charge of a hold full of tycoons, world leaders, sporting legends. and reality TV stars. The plan was that we'd land, stick a pretty little flag in it and call it something witty like "Earth Two" or "New Earth" and that'd be that. Here's your new home, ladies and gentlemen.

My role in all this? I trained as a behavioural scientist, learned in the systematic analysis of human behaviour through control and observation. I was on board to study the psychological effect of humans colonising a new planet and being stranded countless light years from home, as well as act as ship counsellor.

Even though I'd stormed out of the mess hall, my studies into the crew members meant I could predict with reasonable accuracy what was unfolding in there right now. This was my curse.

Menzies, even though I'd snubbed her, would be insisting that somebody come and fetch me. The two of us were the only crew on board with academic backgrounds, and her personality was such that she constantly needed emotional reinforcement. For some reason, she felt safer around me, feeling - somewhat accurately - that the remainder of the crew distrusted scientists.

Captain Kulkarni would have ignored her, asking the room if anybody had any questions. He'd be secretly glad that I wasn't there.

Brown, the Chief Technician, would have gone white. Just like Kulkarni, he'd be - no pun intended - aware of the gravity of the situation. What it meant for all of us is that the UPS Concordance would just keep hurtling into the dark unknown, the computer systems designed to slow and land it never firing. Brown and I don't get on – the reasons elude me now - but I can't deny that the man is smart. He'll be running through every possible way to resolve this situation, each of them coming up blank. Any attempt to alter the flight path of the Concordance would be futile – we simply don't know where we're *supposed* to be going. That was all supposed to be taken care of back on Earth.

McGuigan, Brown's young assistant, would wonder why everybody looked so crestfallen. Even when he'd had it explained to him, he wouldn't understand. He'd just look around the room doing that annoying gaping mouth thing he does when lost in thought, looking for all the world like a landed fish - albeit blessed with a fraction of the intelligence. Either that, or he'd turn up late having got lost on his way.

Microcosm, Macrocosm

Corporal Bostrom, our military representative, would already be planning on how he could effectively and secretly steal the one-man escape shuttle - the only steerable thing on the whole ship - and find some quiet semi-hospitable rock on which to spend the rest of his days.

The other few - most of them so inoffensive and inconsequential I couldn't even bring myself to remember their names anymore - would be doing that typical human thing of being either angry or upset. Or rapidly fluctuating between a combination of the two.

Truth be told, we were *fucked*. Oh, sure, the ship was stocked with adequate life support and the vast hold contained enough equipment, medicine, and food to last us for our entire lifetime providing we didn't wake up too many food and oxygen greedy colonists. That said though, I didn't fancy spending the rest of my days in these anonymous grey corridors accompanied by such a dull group of boorish clods. My whole purpose for being on this ship - and therefore my whole purpose for *existing* - had been snuffed out.

I resolved then to go back to my quarters and drink the whiskey I'd been reserving for landfall. And the gin. And the wine.

But first I had an escape pod to sabotage.

But that was then, this is now. The mess hall lay empty as those bottles now, the ghosts fading as quickly as the memory arose. Most of the cupboards are ajar and empty, drawers opened, and contents picked clean by resourceful cats. Empty potted beef and jerky pouches lie scattered across every surface.

The refrigeration units, however, were safe. The cats would need opposable thumbs to be able to unlock them and I haven't been asleep *nearly* long enough for them to progress any further along that evolutionary path.

David Court

The dull mustard light inside *plink-plink-plinks* into life as I stare into the interior, grabbing a handful of flat-packed ship rations.

I don't bother to look at what I'm grabbing. I've long since learned that the fish flavours are indistinguishable from the meat flavours, which in turn are identical to the vegetable ones. Regardless of colour, smell, or *supposed* flavour, they all taste like chicken and have the texture of densely packed Styrofoam.

Still, the packs are full of essential vitamins and minerals and are essential eating after any cryogenic sleep lasting more than a few months. The cats seem to be attracted to the smell - God knows why. They smell like a yeast infection.

I'd happily kill for some cake. It's a special day, and I think I *deserve* some cake. *I should teach myself to bake.* I suspect I never will.

The long-since-used tap causes a hollow echo to reverberate through the walls as pressure is restored to the ship's vast storage tanks. I fill two flasks with water and clip them on my belt next to my portable voice recorder.

A makeshift engineering crate left in one of the corridors makes an effective trap. I make my way to the rear of the ship. By tactical wafting of the pungent food sticks, it's easy to tempt the younger and more naïve cats towards me - the older ones are warier, having encountered me in the past or tasted the food sticks for themselves. By the time I reach the engineering deck, I've got eight of the little buggers angrily meowing and pleading to be set free.

It's as I near my destination I realise that there's a spring in my step and I catch myself humming a tune. I *never* hum. I can't place it at first, but then it comes flooding back from the dim recesses of my subconscious - it's the chorus to an annoyingly catchy pop track that hung around at the top of the charts for a few months before we launched. I think the singer of it - an androgynous prepubescent whose name I can't recall - is one of the frozen would-be colonists in the Cryo-compartment.

Microcosm, Macrocosm

Christ, what was his name? Stretch, Skritch or Scootch, or something similarly inane. I'll try and remember to check the manifest after I'm done here, before I finish for the day. I'm half tempted to wake him up from cryogenic sleep just so I can punch him in the throat. It's a special day – I owe myself a treat.

And then I find myself standing in front of it, the door to the outer hold. I'm *excited*. I told you earlier – today is a very special day – and beyond that thick steel door is my special reward. My well-deserved gift to myself. (Note to self: Possible narcissistic tendencies).

Just like Kulkarni, the bulkhead is large, thick, and nondescript. I carefully set the engineering crate down and ignore the plaintive mewling as I log onto the console inset into the wall.

I'm relieved to see that structural integrity is still sound. If the hold was ruptured in any way, it'd put a stop to this bold experiment. After I'd found cats in the inner hold last time, I was worried that there might have been some damage. As it was, they'd probably snuck in with me as I'd gone through the door or through a hidden vent too small for humans. Sneaky little bastards. Still, they've probably paid the price for that.

I key in my passcode ("openSe5ame" – I'm nothing if not a traditionalist) and the door slides open, metal scraping against metal as long- dormant, dust-coated cogs grind into life. I pick up the crate and walk in, closing the door behind me.

"Matron", I yell.

The reassuring *ping*. It's somewhat of a relief that her systems extend to down here - an unfortunately aimed stream of cat piss had briefly cut off the connection last time and I was forced to repair it, and I've never been all that practical. Still, it proved my makeshift jury-rigged fix still worked.

"Yes, Doctor Hatten?"

"I'm going to head up to the viewing platform. Can you check that the force fields are still active?"

David Court

I'm loathe to open the inner door unless she - *it* - answers in the affirmative. I want to make sure there are no nasty surprises waiting for me.

"Affirmative, Doctor Hatten. The force fields are still fully operational."

I smile to myself as I open the inner door and begin the long walk up the stairs that lead to the platform. The smell gets worse with every visit, and with every step. The aroma of blood, excrement, and sweat - a heady combination and unfortunately the one thing that force-fields can't prevent getting through.

The lights flicker to life on the bank of consoles on the observation platform as I step onto it. I peer over the edge at the expanse of the inner hold, cloaked in darkness. The kittens don't make a noise as I gently place the container down.

I hadn't even considered the time of day as I'd ventured up here. I'd set the lighting in the hold to automatically give twelve hours of light followed by twelve of darkness, something to roughly simulate daylight. Turns out my calculations must have been slightly offset, because I'd expected it to be lit up.

Still, I chuckle to myself, am I not God here? I enter a command into one of the consoles and the hold lights up slowly, sectors of it flickering one by one into illumination.

Let there be light.

I instinctively duck as something from below - from something down in the hold - hurtles towards my face, sparking into fireworks as it hits the force-field. It's reduced to so much atomised carbon now, but for a moment it looked like an arrow or a makeshift spear.

Cursing myself for flinching even though perfectly well protected, I look down into the hold towards the source of the projectile, catching a glimpse of him darting back behind the landscape of cargo crates.

Corporal Bostrom, naked and smeared with his own filth, appears to have fashioned some manner of crude yet effective bow and arrow. Before he ducked back into cover, I could make out some manner of symbol carved or painted onto his chest - the split circle that is the Greek character for Theta.

Interesting. The vast hold is split into a large three by four grid of twelve chambers, each clearly indicated by a Greek symbol; Alpha through Mu. I hadn't expected territorialism to kick in to such an extent or for a little while yet, but it looks as though Bostrom - through the clear markings on his body - is visibly showing his affiliation with the Theta Quadrant.

From all my studies, the regression of Bostrom was always the least of the surprises. The man was basically a Neanderthal in a pressed uniform anyway, so that apple didn't need to fall far from the tree.

Apples. Why did I have to think of apples? Oh, for some fruit. Food with some *colour*.

I sit down at the main console and place both of my flasks on the table. I pour myself a glass of water and lean back into the comfortable leather chair, studying the various environmental monitors. It's at times like this I regret having barricaded myself into my quarters and having drunk all of the remaining alcohol on the ship on the evening we'd all heard the bad news - a glass of '36 Sauvignon Blanc would be an absolute treat right now.

Time to do my job. With skilled fingers and muscle memory like a concert pianist, I tap a sequence of keys on the console to show me closed circuit camera footage from around the hold. I'm dictating my notes aloud as I do so, storing them for my research.

McGuigan is first, in the Alpha Quadrant. I must admit that with every one of these sessions, he's the one who surprises me the most. I'd not expected him to last the first month but what he lacked in common sense and smarts, he more than made up for with youth, brute force, and ingenuity.

Despite their cumbersome bulk, McGuigan and his companions managed to push some of the cargo containers together near the start of the experiment to effectively build themselves a secure walled compound. There's only one way in, which is currently being guarded by one of his lackeys who is armed with a large spiked stick. He's a brute of an individual, all muscle and a labyrinth of scar tissue. I eventually find McGuigan himself in one of the cargo containers that he's adapted into makeshift living quarters. Until the image is brightened, the audio feed of grunts suggests that he's currently involved in some manner of physical conflict. It's only when the image clears that I can see he's being noisily fellated by two of his harem.

Rather than the emaciated forms I'd expected to see, all three are looking well. Some cursory evidence of malnutrition, but the pot bellies on each of them indicate that they're certainly finding food from somewhere. Even with my strong stomach though, I'm finding it distasteful to look at any of them for any length of period. It's not this crude display of sexual coupling that interests me (although I must admit to being *slightly* intrigued by how McGuigan uses this method to show his dominance over his "pack") but the pile of bones lying next to the filth-streaked threesome.

As expected, some are small. Some, however, are too large to be from the frozen animals located in a few of the crates. My knowledge of human physiology is somewhat limited, but from the scattered stack I recognise a femur, sternum, tibia, and fibula.

The meat has been stripped from the bone. I'd expected cannibalism to occur, just not so soon. I snigger when I spot the worn-out baseball cap of Captain Kulkarni lying tangled amongst the strewn carcasses - I can only presume the man was more palatable in death than he ever was in life.

It was during my final ever drunken haze on that fateful night that it came to me.

I stood there naked, the remains of several bottles of contraband spirits scattered about me like the corpses of my

Microcosm, Macrocosm

enemies. I pressed myself tightly against the cool plasti-steel glass of the window, drunkenly willing myself to phase through it and drift off into space.

The inky void was a darkness mostly unblemished by sun or star, an infinite panorama of nothingness. An oblivion into which we were plummeting headlong, unable to slow or stop our descent.

It was either Springsteen or Nietzsche who'd once said, "When you gaze long into the abyss, the abyss gazes also into you". I'd never understood what he'd meant until that moment.

The prospect of a life - or more precisely, *existence* - surrounded by those people without even the prospect of alcohol to help me cope with them was simply too much. I pulled myself away from the window, my warm skin making a pleasing *schlep* sound as it gently peeled away.

One single glassful of alcohol remained; a gin so expensive that I felt guilty in gulping it down as opposed to savouring it. I stumbled over to my bedside cabinet and pulled out a pill bottle, my drunken fingers barely able to hold it. A whole ten minutes of dedicated effort saw the childproof cap removed, and I poured the tablets into my mouth. A last glorious slug of gin and every painkiller was swallowed.

It was time to kill the pain of this pitiful existence.

I slumped back against the wall, sliding to the floor, the glass falling out of my grip and rolling towards the door. The artificial light of my quarters refracted pleasantly from it as it moved, casting bright spots and streaks of light onto the dull walls.

My head swam as the glass jerked into life, suddenly righting itself. Tiny eyes etched onto it blinked open, and tiny glass limbs began to emerge. With a white-toothed smile, it skipped across the floor towards me.

"I don't think the painkillers are having any effect," I slurred to my jolly little translucent companion. His smile quickly sank into a concerned expression.

"I think I may have made a terrible mistake," I shouted way too loudly as the walls began to melt and warp like heated plastic, exposing the blackness of space. I dug my fingernails into the tiled floor, desperately trying to keep myself from spinning off into the cosmos.

According to my bedside chronometer, I'd been unconscious for nearly five hours. I'd been woken by the loud grumbles from my stomach and had opened my eyes to see said stomach's evacuated contents lying pooled on the floor around me. Mostly liquid, with the odd lump of organic matter speckled with tiny undissolved white tablets.

I slowly got to my feet, steadying myself against the wall. The room was spinning wildly, my seriously deteriorated sense of balance struggling to cope.

And then it hit me, a single solitary purpose detonating in my consciousness.

I've dealt with the clinically insane before. Despite what some doctors would have you believe, there is rarely a single determining factor that causes a mental breakdown. It's a succession of tiny events, a drip feed that gradually erodes the layers of sanity. It's like a cliff face being worn down by centuries of erosion, one day eventually collapsing into the ocean.

If I'm to be honest, I think this is the moment when the last vestiges of my sanity left me. With hindsight, it's easy to see now. Perhaps the painkillers did something to my brain, or it was just something that was always going to happen.

I now had precisely zero alcohol remaining, but I'd gained a raison d'être. In the grand scheme of things, it seemed like a fair exchange.

Microcosm, Macrocosm

By the next morning, I'd formulated a dozen plans in my head, all increasingly complex and convoluted scenarios to convince every crew member to make their way into the hold.

In the end, I achieved my aim through a combination of cunning and doing the bloody obvious. I simply stood on the same viewing platform I'm on now and put out a call on the intercom for all crew members to meet me in the hold.

It was as simple as that.

It's amazing how easy it is to get the attention of a bored person whose very reason for existence has been removed. Within ten minutes I had all but three of the crew in the hold. That would suffice. Without a word, I retraced my steps and sealed both the inner and outer hold doors behind me.

I'd remotely opened a few of the cargo containers; Food, drink, seeds, medicine and hydroponic equipment. I'd also set a time-lock on some of the others to open at specified periods over the coming days and weeks. I'm not a *monster*.

I drugged and dropped two of the remaining three off the viewing platform. I didn't even bother to look to see whether they'd survived the fall. With the third, I was slightly overzealous in the headlock. Her corpse was dumped into the hold as well.

The great advantage (and curse) of having spent most of a lifetime studying human behaviour and psychology is that I'm sure I know what you're thinking. You're thinking I'm a monster. Inhuman.

I can't blame you. From all the evidence, you're probably right.

It wasn't always this way, though. I'd stepped onto the *Concordance* with an enthusiasm as boundless as my naivety. The *Concordance* project was genuinely exciting, and back then all the crew were similarly inspired. My initial pre-Landfall duties were straightforward enough – to observe the crew's behaviour and mental well-being. In the depths of space and forced to both live and work in such a confined area, it's easy for an individual to slip into depression or develop some manner of psychosis.

I noticed subtle changes in my behaviour less than four weeks into our journey. Everybody had been so keen at first, buoyed and overwhelmed by the huge leaving party they'd thrown us. But then following that immense high, reality brings you crashing back down to earth.

Whereas space travel seems exciting at first, after a short while even the infinite majesties of the endless universe become *just another place that you're forced to work in*. In my regular duties of ships counsellor, all the crew would confide in me. Each of them would come to me, convinced that they were the only person on the ship who'd grown to hate deep space. I'd smile and nod, give them some leaflets on cognitive behavioural therapy and various self-help techniques, and send them on their merry way.

You'd have thought me feeling the same way as them would have helped me sympathise with their plight, but if anything, it made me start to loathe them. None of them hated space *nearly* as much as I'd come to, and they didn't have to put up with a succession of people you reviled all complaining about *exactly* the same thing.

Hindsight is a wonderful thing. Turns out that the problem was I'd spent so long watching the others, I hadn't noted the gradual change in my own mental state. And, the mental wellbeing of the crew being somewhat of a low priority with the people back home, there's nobody to watch out for me.

Physician, heal thyself, as they say. Except this physician is beyond healing now.

In some alternate reality, there's a version of me living happily on Krueger-B. I'm a friendly and welcoming face to the colonists, happily putting the final touches to my third uniquely insightful research paper. A document so important, so revolutionary, that it may well have changed the face of psychotherapy as we knew it.

As it turns out, you're stuck with the variant of me that snapped. You get the one that crushes kittens and talks to himself whilst living out some manner of God fantasy with a few dozen crew members as his playthings.

Shit happens.

There's a school of thought in a type of behavioural psychology I trained in that promotes complete non-interference - one should simply observe, never influence. But, however incurably insane I might be - and that's a possibility I can't discount - I know full well that what is happening here has gone beyond a mere experiment and has become a means of satisfying my sick desires.

And, holding that thought, I flick a switch next to the console and the emergency sirens burst into noisy life. The viewing platform can be raised and lowered, and the alarm exists to warn those below of its descent - however, I'm not planning on taking the platform anywhere. I just want everybody to know that I'm here.

I see Bostrom first, his wild eyes fixated on me from the shadows. He prepares an arrow in anticipation, levelling it at my head. He doesn't fire it though, indicating that he's finally remembered the force-field.

McGuigan and one of his lackeys are next, tentatively stepping onto the edge of the hold. They're both armed. McGuigan spots Bostrom across the hold and his face contorts into a vicious snarl.

Other crew members begin to appear, some on their own, some in groups of two or three. All of them warily keep their distance from the others. Some are clothed - dressed in rough rags or the tattered and filthy remnants of their old uniforms - whereas others are naked.

I wave a disapproving finger at Bostrom and sit down, safely out of his line of sight. With the flick of another switch, I disengage the force-field, listening as the background hum of the generator fizzes and crackles before fading into a silence only interrupted by the snarls and growls from the people below.

I train the monitor on the chamber, panning it back to take in the whole scene. About a dozen crew are visible, none of them daring to set foot in the exposed centre of the hold. Most look as I'd expected - feral, gaunt, unkempt.

I open the lid of the engineering crate and look inside. Sixteen wide blue-green eyes stare back up at me.

Seriously, this isn't going to be nice. If it helps, just imagine I'm talking about rats. Horrible, mangy, diseased rats for whom death would be a blissful relief. All piercing eyes and yellowing spittle-flecked fangs - fairer to put them out of their misery, really.

In fact, why are you sure it wasn't always rats? After all, what's more likely? A ship full of rats, or a ship full of cute kittens? I hate to be all unreliable narrator here but come on.

It's also really quite revealing – and more than a little damning - that you appear to be bothered about the kittens than you are about those poor crewmembers.

A tortoiseshell one is the first to try and make a break for it, clambering up the sides of the crate. The others just sit there, shell-shocked. I pinch the scruff of its neck and lift it to my face where it tries to bat me with tiny claws. A single well-timed swing, extension of my arm, and a release gives the tiny thing a nigh-on perfect trajectory carrying it over the edge of the viewing platform and down into the hold.

To the things' credit, it lands on its feet. That'll be one of its nine lives gone. Some of the bolder, larger members of the crew begin to advance towards it slowly, crouching down as they do so. Their frenzied eyes flick nervously between it and their competitors.

Kittens two and three find their way into the hold as well, one thrown overarm and one thrown underarm to give the whole event a little variety. Neither are as lucky with their landing as the first, who has by now easily scurried off to safety away from the grasping, long-nailed hands of the crew. The two others are grabbed by crew members who retreat to the safety of the edge, holding their prizes close to then.

Now the crew have an idea of what is going on, the remaining five are thrown unceremoniously into the hold. I have little to do now other than sit back and watch the resulting massacre. One of the thinnest and clearly more desperate of the assembled crew scurries forward and grabs two cats, one in each thin-fingered hand. He tries to dart back into the maze of packing crates but two of the crew slam into him, sending him sprawling across the floor. He lies on his back holding onto the cats, reluctant to let them go but unable to get back up to his feet. He pushes himself backwards along the ground when the two are upon him again, leaping on him as a team and tearing at him.

All this time, the only noises I can hear are rasping grunts and screams. Everyone seems to have lost either the ability - or the inclination - to use their native tongue. Even when the poor sod on the ground is forced to let go of the cats to try to defend himself, pulling his arms up around him and struggling to get into the foetal position, the attacks don't stop. He's screaming out in agony, a piercing shriek that unnerves even me. One of the two attackers - a female toilet attendant, if memory serves - bites tightly down on the flesh above his eye and wrenches her head back, tearing a huge chunk of skin away. The other attacker is scrabbling desperately away at his victim's chest like a dog digging in the sand, broken and overgrown yellow fingernails scraping away skin, and then flesh and muscle. The screams fade shortly after, now replaced by a liquid burbling from ruined lungs.

David Court

The scene in the centre of the hold is just as interesting - two of the other five kittens have scurried away to safety. One of the male crew members is trying to stand between the immobile cats and the growing crowd, darting left and right whilst threateningly swiping his clawed hands at the thin air that separates them.

Bostrom leaps into the crowd, brandishing his bow and arrow. The cry that emits from his lips sounded almost human, like a combination of swear words spoken too quickly and loudly.

The crew members start to slowly back off, all of them visibly terrified by both the man and his weapon. He'd be screwed if they rushed him, but self-preservation is a strong influence, and no one wants to be the first one with an arrow in them.

He slowly approaches the three kittens, all the time pointing the drawn bow at everybody who hesitates to get out of his way. He crouches down in front of the three tiny bodies, but the situation begins to dawn on him, realisation further furrowing his already crumpled brow. He can't pick up the kittens without putting down the bow.

You can almost smell the neurons firing as the cogs of his intelligence begin to slowly turn. He draws himself up to his full height again and, standing in front of the bodies, starts to kick them backwards. Their tiny forms are propelled along the floor, limply rolling into place.

He's got them halfway across the floor of the hold - directing them back to where he emerged, presumably to take them back to some secreted den - when somebody makes a play. It's Scarface who was guarding the makeshift compound earlier on, pushed into the clearing by McGuigan himself. Bostrom angrily barks at the interloper, but he appears undaunted. Armed still with his spike-laden stick, McGuigan's lackey darts left and right, keeping his distance but clearly taunting his rival.

With a cry of frustrated rage, the twang of a bow sounds as the crudely carved arrow is let loose, piercing Scar through the

Microcosm, Macrocosm

eye. The hold falls silent as McGuigan's minion stands there for a few moments looking confused, thick torrents of scarlet pouring from the fresh wound of his ruined eye and socket. His knees give way beneath him and he stumbles forward, collapsing and remaining motionless. McGuigan gives an anguished yell before abruptly stopping, desperate not to show weakness.

Bostrom scoops up the two kittens nearest to him, turns and runs. A few of the other crew members take chase, screaming wildly, but he's had too much of a head start. A fleet-footed scrawny female comes in and grabs the last unattended kitten and dashes back to the relative safety of the hold.

The crowd disperses, making their way back to their own quadrants of the hold. Two corpses remain, blood neatly pooling on the metal floor around them. The wounds on the one killed by the two attackers are vicious - both the face and much of the upper torso have been brutally scraped away, exposed shiny, reddened bone gleaming in the artificial lighting. McGuigan's lackeys – now outnumbering those crew members who haven't slunk back into the shadows – drag both bodies back in the direction of their makeshift encampment. I predict the pile of meat-stripped bones I saw there will grow in height over the next few days. Waste not, want not.

The spectacle is over and I pour myself another glass of water. I continue my studies, toggling through the vast array of cameras set up in all the quadrants of the hold. I see empty makeshift camps drenched in blood and gore, along with teams of roving cannibals who now dwell in the areas of the hold where the lights have long since failed to work. I see the tiniest of dents in the walls along with charred panels where they've tried – and failed – to escape. I see the ruined and failed barricades of attempts at civilised society, and the hanging corpses of the few who simply did not wish to participate in my bold experiment.

David Court

I'm somewhat relieved to see that the population in the hold has remained *relatively* stable since my last visit. In the past, I've been forced to defrost colonists to make up the numbers. It's hard work but can be thoroughly entertaining. To do it properly, however, requires a little bit of forethought.

A favourite trick of mine is to unfreeze them and let them wake up naturally in one of the quieter sections of the ship. With a bit of imagination, it's possible to convince them that everybody on the ship except for them has been killed by a vicious alien let loose on the *Concordance*. Some scattered corpses, "help me" written in blood on a wall, that sort of thing.

By the time they've found their third strategically placed PDA with panicked audio-logs on them (My acting and frenzied screaming has got considerably better over the years) and they're *shitting* themselves. And then drug 'em, arm 'em, wake 'em, and dump 'em in the hold, and then they can look after themselves.

I reckon that that singer Stretch/Skritch/Scootch would have had a coronary by the *second* audio-log. Let's put that to the test next time.

After I've punched him in the throat, obviously.

It's as I'm preparing to conclude my studies for the day - as I'm absentmindedly flicking through the hundreds of closed-circuit television channels - when I find her.

It's only the glint from the metal of her spectacles that attracts my attention at all. Wooden and metal panels alike have been used to construct a wall, albeit one with an opening almost too easy to miss. Even by carefully angling the camera, it's only possible to make out a few details.

Doctor Menzies is alive and well. From what I can make out, her small den is lined with a stockpile of food containers. She must have been carefully rationing them, living for all this time

Microcosm, Macrocosm

from the virtually non-perishable contents. She's in a makeshift bed reading a book by the faint light from a small portable lighting rig.

Fascinating. She's escaped the fate of her colleagues. For one, she's still alive which is miracle enough in itself, but she's also retained her intelligence.

Would that I could dare venture down there and speak to her, perhaps formulate some manner of questionnaire with which I could glean all manner of useful research data. The glistening red, barbed pole at her bedside, however, implies she might not be that receptive to my company.

I sit there for a few moments in silence, ruminating, before switching off the console. As it powers down, the electrical hum fades and is replaced by the distant shrieks, grunts, and growls from my makeshift colony.

Maybe next time.

The cats continue to avoid me as I walk back to the cryogenic chambers. I remove my clothes, carefully folding them up and placing them on the allocated shelf.

"Matron?"

Ping.

"Yes, Doctor Hatten?"

"How many years has it been now?"

"Additional detail required."

"How many years since we've been doing this? Me waking up for a day at a time and doing my experiments?"

"Fourteen years, Doctor Hatten."

Fourteen years. And every time brings fresh new surprises.

"Matron?"

"Yes, Doctor Hatten?"

David Court

"I want you to set the heating to come on one Earth day before you wake me up next time. That's one standard Earth day of twenty-four hours. Twenty-four Earth hours."

"Understood."

"Right, I'm ready."

My cryogenic capsule slides noiselessly open, the comforting blue interior light flicking on. I lower myself into it, preparing myself for the cryogenic process. For one moment, I suddenly realise I can't remember whether I switched the force field back on or not. Still, too late to worry about it now. Even if I had, I doubt that they could get through the outer bulkhead and into the rest of the ship, even in force.

Probably.

The capsule begins to close.

"See you in three hundred and sixty-four days, Matron."

"Goodnight, Doctor Hatten. Sleep well. And happy birthday."

I dream of the sea.

Hastur La Vista, Baby

IT WAS IMPORTANT to have *principles*, thought Martha. George Orwell went to fight in the Spanish Civil War because of sympathies for their Republican movement, and Muhammad Ali was arrested and stripped of his boxing title because of his refusal to be conscripted into the U.S. Military during the Vietnam War.

Martha refused to buy products or services from any shop that used the Comic Sans font in their logo or publicity material.

But, as Infant:Inside were the only business within a hundred miles offering the particular baby scanning services she was after, this was clearly one principle she'd have to temporarily shelve.

She tried to ignore the cursing and swearing coming from the back room as she picked up a glossy brochure from the pile sitting on the waiting room table. She spent a few moments staring in disbelief at the company name on the front, which she still couldn't quite believe wasn't some kind of joke. Even though written in a bright cyan Comic Sans font, it still didn't stop the word looking – and even sounding - like Infanticide.

Another cry of frustration from the back office was followed by the sound of somebody kicking some furniture. A tirade of swearing burst forth, turning the air bluer than the company logo.

David Court

He'd seemed like such a quiet young man when he'd performed the ultrasound. Admittedly he'd barely seemed old enough to tie his shoelaces, let alone operate expensive diagnostic imaging hardware, but he was friendly enough.

"Who's the best guy in the building?" he'd quipped. "The ultrasound guy." It was a joke older than he was, but it had achieved its aim and put her at ease.

The sound of electronic hardware being firmly shaken could now be heard from behind the closed door, followed by the sound of two voices. They were arguing with each other in that type of way you do when you don't want anybody to hear, but you both defeat the object by each having to raise your voice to put your point across.

"You tell her," said one. "No, you," said the other.

Martha wondered whether it was a mistake coming here at all.

Some women were simply custom-built right out of the box to be perfect mothers. That seemed to apply to every single woman in the Antenatal clinic except Martha. They were all exuding that radiant glow and aura of natural calm, whereas Martha simply looked permanently unwell. They all had their loving husbands and doting boyfriends with them, and Martha sat there alone. The term was "one -night stand" but, to be fair, it was an evening in which Martha hadn't been doing a great deal of standing.

Martha wasn't the sort of person to go to nightclubs on her own. And yet, that one evening, she'd felt compelled. The same compulsion that saw her down an entire bottle of Prosecco and end up bringing some stranger back to her flat. He was tall, dark and handsome. She *thinks*.

Ordinarily, she'd have been put off by the font choice on the leaflets that the rep handed around the clinic, but something intrigued her. "A 3D model of your unborn child!!!" it proudly declared with an excess of exclamation marks. "For a special reduced price!!!"

The man-child sheepishly emerged from the back office, reluctant to make eye contact. He stumbled forward as though abruptly pushed forward by his colleague and crashed into the counter.

"There's... been a slight problem and I'm afraid we won't be able to provide the 3D modelling service for you at this moment in time."

Martha looked up at him.

"Oh?"

"If you'd like to... erm... bring your cash card over, we'll refund you the money."

Martha got to her feet, the weight of her belly feeling heavier than ever.

"If there's a problem with the printer, I don't mind waiting. I heard you swearing at it."

"Not a problem with the printer as *such*."

"What do you mean 'as such'?"

The boy went bright red, looking back over his shoulder at the closed back office door as though it would offer salvation. He looked at Martha, back at the door, back at Martha. His mouth opened and closed but intelligible words refused to form.

The door opened and an older man stepped through, placing his hand on the boy's shoulder. She took him to be the manager, an assumption borne out by the Comic Sans "Manager" badge clipped to his shirt.

"Ma'am," he said authoritatively. "My young colleague isn't entirely correct. It's *sort* of a problem with the printer. A restriction of the technology."

David Court

"I'm not sure I understand. What do you mean by restriction?"

"These 3D printers, you see. They're bound, as we are, by certain well-established guidelines of causality and physics. They're simply not designed to print out anything that doesn't adhere to the traditional rules of Euclidean geometry."

"Nuclearidian...?"

"Euclidean. Look, it says so in the book."

He placed a well-thumbed and coffee stained photocopied manual in front of her, pointing out a paragraph. It looked to be a troubleshooting page, and his finger was pointing at a particular question.

"Can my Saishomatsui 3D Printer be used to create shapes that do not adhere to the standard rules of space/time geometry?"

"No. Please refer to the operating manual."

Martha cradled the hot cup of tea in her hands. Tea traditionally solved *everything*, but even she struggled to see how infused leaves could make this any better. Even Oolong, she suspected, would struggle.

She stared blankly down at the handful of printouts the manager had placed on the waiting room table in front of her, the ultrasound scans of her unborn child.

In the first static-filled image, she thought she could make out a tiny hand. In the second, some tiny toes. The third, an infinite vista of impossible structures. The fourth, the utter insignificance of man in an uncaring and unknowable universe.

But the father – he'd been tall, dark, and handsome. At the time, she'd thought those protuberances were dreadlocks. Tall, dark, handsome – and squamous. Possibly squamous. Eldritch at the very least.

Hastur La Vista, Baby

She looked up at the sorry face of the manager who was still patting her on the shoulder in the manner one might reassure a dying dog.

"Can you answer me one question at least? Is it a boy or a girl?"

"Yes, I can certainly answer that."

"Well, is it a boy or a girl?"

"No. No, it isn't."

David Court

All Our Heroes are Gone

T ***HERE IS VISION*** *of sorts now, albeit fragmented. Tessellated lenses view the same scene from a myriad of angles. Muscles dotted around a dozen locations burn as they heal, their only links coming as searing pulses of agony that wash over him like the tide. Thoughts stretch out impotently, unable to cohere. There was something missing.*

The sign had once been bright blue, cheerily declaring "Leaving KANSAS. Come again". Now it was stained brown with rust, Gimmick's atrophied corpse chained around one of its equally rusted metal struts. The bright red leather of his costume hung from his body in thin-sliced strands, his face and body mutilated beyond comprehension.

Dot had liked Gimmick. He'd always been very good to her, bringing her trinkets and keepsakes to add to her own little Rogue's Gallery. He wasn't much older than her and had only just graduated from being a sidekick himself, so the lad had a certain amount of empathy for the girl.

She'd feared the worst as she'd been heading out of the city, having come across the scattered remains of Gimmick's little robot companions. They'd been crushed underfoot or smashed

All Our Heroes are Gone

by fists and weaponry, presumably having met their fate trying –
and failing – to save their master.

Out of a sense of decency, and because it felt *right*, Dot had
tried her best to close the eyes of the bodies she'd encountered in
her exodus from the Consortium headquarters, gently closing
their eyelids with trembling fingers. She could grant no such
mercy to Gimmick though, his eyes burned away and reduced to
narrow, scorched tunnels.

The best of them had already fallen.

The Evangelist had been thought immortal but had proved to
be anything but. They'd dragged his tortured form to the Capitol
City News Network and televised his murder across the world,
ripping his wings away from him with wire cutters and
chainsaws, before dousing him with kerosene and setting him
alight. He hung there flailing for a good twenty or so minutes
before finally expiring, his frenzied dying shrieks on every radio
and television channel.

They'd cornered the Nightgaunt in his own lair, taking turns
on him with baseball bats and cudgels. They'd dragged his
corpse around the city streets for the rest of the night, tied to the
back of his car. There was pretty much nothing left of him when
they'd finally stopped and set the vehicle alight, the Capitol
Cities Obsidian Defender of the Night reduced to little more
than bloodied gristle and rags. His sidekick had been similarly
beaten, left dying spread-eagled across the huge signal light on
the roof of Police Headquarters. A grisly dying silhouette,
shining on the clouds for all in the city to see.

There were rumours that Pariah had defected, betraying all
the heroes. Manolith, strongest but the kindest and gentlest of
them all had refused to believe it, until Pariah had proudly
boasted as such on the evening news. "I'm tired of being the butt
of the jokes of this super team," he'd gloated, "The Consortium
dies tonight. You *all* die tonight."

That had been exactly one week ago. The darkest of days, to
herald the dark days to follow.

David Court

Dot had been dreaming of green hills and glorious sunshine when the shrill tones of the Consortium alarm had woken her with a start. The klaxon had suddenly ceased, trailing off with a discordant whine as though broken, the noise replaced by pounding footsteps from the corridor beyond her dormitory.

She rubbed at her eyes, still only half-awake, confused by the cacophony erupting outside. Heavy fists beat against her dorm door, and a familiar voice called her name. With one mighty punch, the door burst open and Manolith stood there, his stocky, distinctive silhouette lit by the strobing emergency lighting of the corridor beyond.

"Dot!" he cried, visibly relieved. With one bounding step, the gentle goliath was at her bedside, sweeping her up with his giant arms and brushing her pigtails aside to look at her face. Manolith looked as though he'd been hewn from solid granite, all jagged angles, but really his skin was softer to the touch, like a thick leather carapace.

Manolith gave the best hugs.

"What's happening?" Dot had asked, still not fully awake.

"I think Pariah gave them the base codes," Manolith explained, carrying her out of the room into the corridor that pulsed with light. "I'm going to get you to safety."

Emergency lights pulsed across the walls of the lengthy corridor; a passage that led around the circumference of this floor that held the Consortium's dormitory rooms. The portraits that lined the walls were a Who's Who of the world's greatest heroes, a roster that had started back before even Manolith was born.

Over the heavy thudding of Manolith's huge feet, she could hear it now; the sounds of distant conflict – magic batons colliding with alien steel, cosmic rays deflecting off armoured shields, fists meeting jaws.

All Our Heroes are Gone

There was a blur of movement from the corridor ahead of them, and Headway appeared, decelerating from superspeed. He was wounded, with a huge, jagged gash from forehead to chin. Spots and streaks of blood were dotted and smeared across the contours of his frictionless white uniform

"We've lost the Atrium!" he stammered; the panic evident in his voice. Dot had never seen Headway even as much as scared before. Now he was hysterical and crying.

"No sign of The Utopian?" asked Manolith, holding Dot that little bit tighter.

"None," wept Headway, "The fucker's left us to it."

"Language!" tutted Manolith, polite even given the current circumstances. "We need to regroup. If the Atrium falls, they'll have access to-"

A beam of black light from the far end of the corridor struck Headway, and the force of the blast knocked him off his feet. He lay on the ground, writhing about as he clutched at the thick black membrane that clung to his face, suffocating him.

"That sounds like my cue," came a sneering English voice from the corridor. "If the Atrium falls, they'll have access to all the superweapons and gadgets that have been confiscated over the years."

Headway was a blur now, vibrating at superspeed trying – and failing – to free himself. Manolith went to help his old friend, but a searing beam missed him by inches. Manolith's shoulders sank. He knew he probably couldn't save Headway, but he could at least try to save Dot.

"Nimbus's Weather-manipulation belt. Mindbomb's Armageddon Dice. Code Red's Ultra-gauntlets. And that's not even the really juicy Black Mausoleum shit."

Manolith turned to face the source of it, already recognising the voice as one of Nightgaunt's old nemeses.

The Viscount. Standing there clad in a suit of the Ultra-Technician's Power Armour, wielding a Kolqanon Imperium Element rifle. "I must say what a fuckin' delight this all is, being spared from having to listen to Headway's witty banter for once.

Let's just savour this unique moment, shall we, mates?" he boasted.

Headway was panicking now, grasping hands desperately trying to pull the molten matter from his face. Choking beneath the foul, clinging substance, his movements were becoming quicker and more erratic.

Manolith reached out a hand, but another well-aimed beam missed him by inches.

"You'll leave him to die, Manolith. And then we'll see what other settings this weapon has to use on you - *and* your pretty little girlfriend."

Manolith lifted Dot in front of him with his huge hands, staring at her with bright blue eyes that filled with milky-white tears. He leaned in closer and whispered, his voice breaking.

"I'm going to do something, Dot. I'm going to drop you, and you're going to dash behind my legs. You know where to go then. Do you understand?"

Dot nodded, fighting back the tears. Manolith smiled, nodded, and let her go.

With a speed that betrayed his huge bulk, he stepped over her, thumping his fists together. The corridor walls and floor shook with the force of his defiance, a lightning whip-crack resonating through the narrow chamber.

Dot scurried up from her knees up to her feet, running in the opposite direction down the corridor. In her initial tentative steps, she felt the flash warmth of a dozen blasts, all of them blocked by Manolith's monstrous form. A few haphazard sparks from one of the blasts landed on her pigtails, forcing her to hurriedly pat them out as she ran.

Still running, she turned back. The Viscount was hitting her friend with blast after blast from his alien rifle, but Manolith remained standing steadfast. He may as well have been rooted in the ground for all the effect they were having on him, the blasts dissipating against his mighty form.

All Our Heroes are Gone

For a second, it looked as though he might triumph but in those last moments, the instant before Dot reached the door, she looked back, and saw they had begun taking their toll.

"Run!" he mouthed; his face contorted with agony. The Viscount had been joined by his colleagues, all attacking Manolith at the same time with a variety of superpowers. His rock-like skin was cracking, hairline fissures rippling across his body like the lines separating jigsaw pieces. Heat vision, ice blasts, and projectiles were taking their toll. Golden magma was beginning to pour from opened wounds, scars appearing like strips of brilliant neon. Headway had stopped struggling now, dead on the floor, next to his dying colleague.

She slammed the bulkhead closed behind her, the heavy metal door drowning out the remainder of Manolith's anguished scream.

In the dull red glow of emergency lighting, she navigated the maze of engineering corridors. It would flicker occasionally as a muffled explosion sounded elsewhere within the Consortium headquarters. Her journey was far from silent, accompanied by the intercom-borne cackles of super-villains and defiant howls of released prisoners.

By the time she'd arrived at the emergency Trans/Mat chambers, most of the pre-set destination locations were already highlighted in blood red. All those places – all those allies – *gone*; The Idaho Justice Concordance – deceased. The Maine Offenders – wiped out. The South Carolina Lancers – missing, presumed dead.

She watched in powerless horror as the icon for their last deep space refuge, Asteroid 253 Mathilde, flickered from green to red. That was the last of their bases, headquarters, and safehouses from a long, long list. The only one that remained active was The Utopian's secret lair, showing in a glowing amber. That meant it hadn't been taken over or destroyed but had simply been deactivated at source. The Utopian himself must have severed the connection.

But *why*?

A sequence of random bleeps began firing out from the central console, the lights around the periphery of the Trans/Mat pad cycling into life.

Somebody – or something - was going to materialize *here*. With the console running under emergency power, it was impossible to tell from where. Had the teleportation coordinates been compromised along with the details of their base's security measures?

A shimmering silhouette formed on the pad, a kaleidoscope of crackling fractals forming a human shape as the mysterious traveller's atomic structure was slowly reassembled. It was a standard humanoid shape, no indication of their identity.

Dot grabbed a half-charged shock baton from a rack on the wall, waiting for the visitor to fully form.

The room suddenly rocked with a powerful explosion, one that shook the walls. It sounded bigger and more powerful than the others and could only have come from a catastrophic breach in one of the hydro-reactors that provided emergency power for the base.

The Trans/Mat pad went dark, every light across it simultaneously fading. In the brief second before the room was plunged into complete darkness, save for the blue glow emanating from her shock baton, Dot saw the shocked face of the hero Array atop a mass of warped, bloated, and twisted flesh.

An inhuman shriek filled the air, tailing off with a painful sounding death rattle. The Trans/Mat, switched off mid-flow, had attempted to do what it could with the matter it had gathered, failing miserably in reassembling a standard human form from the corrupted data it had. Presumably, the same had happened to the half of Array still stuck on Asteroid 253 Mathilde.

All Our Heroes are Gone

He'd died twice.

She'd been forced to escape from the base the old-fashioned way, crawling through the water inlet pipes that led to the nearby reservoir of Waconda Lake. As she emerged out into the freezing night air, she didn't know what was making her shake more – the cold or sheer fear. She'd promised herself t she wouldn't look back, but the tears welled in her eyes as she looked up at the towering edifice of the Consortium Headquarters. It had once been a mighty beacon, towering over every surrounding structure. Now it was little more than a gargantuan mausoleum. As she waded through the silt banks to take cover in the heavy grassland, the skies above her were lit up in a myriad of colours and explosions.

Hopelessly outclassed and outnumbered heroes fought against overwhelming numbers; eye beams, lasers, bullets, and missiles tracing multi-coloured paths through the pitch-black night. The villains toyed with them as a cat would taunt a mouse, sometimes allowing them to escape to a certain distance before luring them back in. More than one hero fell into the waters of the lake, either dead already or exhausted and fit for nothing but drowning. Flaming bodies hurtled to the ground like a meteor shower.

Yet, where was The Utopian?

The Utopian was the first of them all, the inspiration for a thousand costumed heroes. He'd fled here from a dying world, determined not to see the same fate happen to his new adopted home of Earth. He was the smartest, the fastest, the strongest.

And supposedly, the *bravest*.

Where was he? He could have stopped them with a modicum of effort – indeed, just his very *presence* was enough to make supervillains surrender themselves to the authorities. Dot had met him once, when he'd visited the Consortium headquarters during one of those regular team-ups that seemed to happen every few months or so.

He'd crouched down to her level and took her hand in his. This was a hand capable of levelling mountains, of stopping *comets* – and yet his touch was as gentle as anything she'd ever known. He'd looked her in the eyes, and her into his – cyan-splashed orbs that had seen civilizations born and destroyed, the lava-filled interiors of worlds, and the freezing depths of space – and, at that very moment, it felt as *nothing* could ever be wrong.

She needed to get to Colorado and find him. If not to confirm his unlikely defeat, then to dare ask him why he did not help. That was her promise to Manolith's legacy.

He can see properly now at least, the image of one solid piece as opposed to fragmented components, flickering on and off. Something feels wrong though, out of place. Like a rogue-coloured brick in a uniformly-coloured Lego house, or a battery placed the wrong way into a slot. Thoughts still feel like spaghetti, like he's controlling everything through an overly sensitive remote control. Wearing mittens. And a blindfold.

She'd wandered through deserted, rubble-strewn streets. The Viscount, who seemed to have adopted the role of spokesman – perhaps leader - of this villainous revolt, had declared a curfew. Booming and crackling loudspeakers warned that anybody seen in the open after nightfall was fair game, a plaything for the monsters that leapt between buildings, hurtled at superspeed through the streets, or dominated the skies.

She'd been trained in how to stick to the shadows, how to remain unseen, but there were those who were not so lucky. She'd seen innocents plucked from the streets, flown to the edge of the atmosphere to have their arms ripped off and left to plummet. She'd seen others slammed at near-light speeds into the sides of buildings, living beings reduced to a stain, sentience into sediment.

After what had seemed like an eternity of cowering and slow travel, she'd met a team of sidekicks cowering in an old fairground just outside Sharon Springs and had shared food with them; they'd dined on Twinkies, cold frankfurters, and Coke made from so much syrup it made them all cough.

The young and frightened teen known as Velocipede had been Headway's sidekick. When asked if Dot had known of his fate, she'd told the boy he'd died with honour. She knew from the look on the kid's face that it would have destroyed him had he known his idol had died suffocating.

"There are kind-hearted lies, and self-serving lies," Manolith had once explained, "The former can be a hero's tool, the latter has no place in a utility belt."

They'd outright refused to travel with her to Colorado. A few days before, she'd have been sickened with their cowardice. Now they'd all been through a similar hell, she could see their point. They filled her rucksack with as much food as would fit, presumably in some way to assuage their guilt. She shrugged and left.

It was some time the next day that their foes stayed true to form and did something they excelled at.

They *gloated*.

Every piece of technology capable of receiving a signal – be it television, radio, drive-by cinema, laptop, or tablet – began to broadcast the exact same thing. On top of that, the armoured Kill drones of the supervillain Scourge were acting as mobile speakers, soaring through the streets as they bellowed their vile propaganda. As if terrified that a single fragment of hope remained in the soul of any of the mortal survivors, the villains had set about destroying that with pinpoint laser accuracy.

Not all the heroes had been killed outright. Some – *many* – had been captured. The devices all broadcast one single show, running twenty-four hours a day. Even if you tried to avoid seeing it, the booming amplified sounds that filled the air meant you couldn't avoid *hearing* it. Screams and endless commentary. Commentary delivered through smirks and giggles in gleeful, graphic detail. Whenever the show had a temporary break, they'd play *Africa* by Toto on repeat. She'd liked that song once.

As Dot tried to sleep, covering her eyes and cowering in the ruined basements of buildings incinerated by haphazard pyrokinesis, or long-abandoned "safe" houses, the contents of the shows would haunt her dreams.

They'd tortured her heroes, one by one.

Sh'aard, the Crystalline Venusian, the most thoughtful and serene of them all, had been subjected to precisely engineered aural blasts. He made sounds that no mortal being should make as his crystal form was carefully cracked open from the inside, internal organs shifting painfully but still functioning. It was like taking a scalpel to a *soul*. He screamed for a death that never came.

They'd subverted the powers of Minutiae the Shrinking Man, sticking him in a tiny metal cell and making it so he was growing by a fraction of an inch every hour. It was almost worse not to see what was happening to him, the only evidence of his torment a speaker that broadcast his every agonized shriek as he grew and grew against unshifting, ungiving walls.

Extendor was being wrapped around a rack, his elongated limbs stretched transparent-thin like liquorice laces. His larynx and vocal cords were stretched too thinly for him to vocalise the pain he was in, his mile-long maw gaping helplessly.

Kostanza, Magus Majestic, was left in a chamber as the plaything for the various demons he'd conjured and sacrificed over his career, all of whom had had thousands of years to conjure up the most painful tortures imaginable, even by demonic standards.

After a while, she'd managed to drown the memories of those noises out, imagining music to help her sleep. It was part of an extensive suite of mental exercises that Manolith had trained her in, a mantra to keep her sane, to keep her rested.

But, despite that, she sat bolt upright one night, soaked in sweat. At first, Dot thought she'd imagined it, but there it was again.

The pained groans of Manolith, distinctive and clear.

"Alright, mates! As a very special treat for all you VTV fans," boasted The Viscount, clearly delighted with himself, "all the way from the Consortium Headquarters, we have a very special guest. A Rock Star, you might say. The Guardian Golem. The Concrete Conqueror. The one and only... Manolith the Immortal."

She rummaged in her backpack for the cheap electronic tablet she'd found in a hardware store off Interstate 70. The very moment it was switched on, the electric trickery of the villainous consortium took it over, hijacking the operating system.

The Viscount, clad in a dark grey pinstripe suit, stood over the wracked form of Manolith. Her old friend's eyes were dark and sunken, no evidence of the brightness and vitality that once burned there. His rock-like form was scored with molten scars, blackened and scorched.

Dot had witnessed Manolith's incredible powers of healing on multiple occasions but had thought even him defeated by The Viscount back at the base. She'd seen his powers in person after he'd been nearly killed in combat once, severed limbs reattaching themselves to his bulk and burst eyeballs inflating like tiny white balloons until like new.

But something wasn't right here. The guttural noises that Manolith made barely sounded human. He was reacting like a wounded and scared animal, flinching and backing away from The Viscount as the supervillain stared down at him.

David Court

She'd seen her mentor like this once before. It was imperative that she found The Utopian as soon as possible.

"As you know, our obelisk-esque wanker has extensive healing powers."

The Viscount reached into the inside of his Infinity Jacket and pulled out an obscenely large and bulky industrial bolt gun, waving it in the air like a cowboy.

"So, this particular show should just run –"

The barrel was pressed against the side of Manolith's head, and the trigger squeezed. There was a dull *thud* and a squeal of pain from Manolith as he recoiled, the metal bolt embedded in his skull, glowing ichor pouring from the wound.

"–and run–"

Another bolt fired into the dark tunnels of one of Manolith's eyes. Another pained shriek.

"–and *run.*"

Thud. Thud. Thud. *Thud. Thud. Thud.*

Three long days and nights followed, with little to differentiate them. Nimbus, his weather control powers restored from his no-longer-confiscated belt, had made the heavens a mass of turbulent grey and black clouds, lightning erupting with violent fury and striking the streets below. The streets themselves were a maelstrom of hurricanes and hailstorms, both capable of flaying the skin from the unwary. The only small blessing was that the howling of the wind drowned out the torture broadcasts.

The weather settled at night though, as a bored or exhausted Nimbus returned to his lair to rest. Every day saw more heroes captured, adding to the roster of victims. Their captors gleefully read a list of those who had perished at the hands of over-enthusiastic torturers or had died whilst trying to escape.

All Our Heroes are Gone

The Viscount seemed to take a particular delight in tormenting Manolith, dedicating much of the evening to his suffering. He'd work on him for uncomfortably long periods, before allowing the tortured hero to regenerate for a moment – and then beginning the cruelty anew.

He'd describe the impending tortures in great detail, before singing songs to himself or cracking jokes, as he severed Manolith's limbs with Alzo Rán's flechette whip or pounded his skull flat with Lady Leviathan's gravitic hammer.

It was at dawn the next day when she saw it; The World's Wonder View tower. Built in the twenties, this sixty-five-foot tall, decrepit tower once housed a museum of curiosities. Now it was wind-swept and barely standing - yet it stood atop the secret lair of The Utopian. When it was made, the promoters boasted that it was possible to see six states from the top. To think of all the visitors this tourist attraction must have had, every one of them blissfully ignorant to the secret base that sat beneath them. With the current weather, even if you dared to clamber up its creaking rusting heights, you'd struggle to see much of even surrounding Genoa.

Now she was here, on the verge of meeting her idol – hell, *everybody's* idol – she realised how nervous she was. It was fear and adrenaline that had driven her here, and she hadn't even considered arriving in one piece to fulfil the promise she'd made herself back at the Consortium Headquarters.

Suddenly, Dot was sent reeling, hurled onto the dirt track underfoot. Rabid whooping faded into the distance, vanishing into the clouds. The warm, coppery tang of blood trickled from her cheek into her mouth, and she pressed her hand against a fresh and jagged wound on the side of her face. She went to clamber to her feet but the whooping re-emerged, drawing closer at incredible speeds. She was suddenly yanked forward by something that had grabbed hold of her pigtails and tried to yank them out by the roots.

One tiny angry hand held her face down whilst the other pulled at her hair, tiny frenzied clawed fingers scrabbling against her scalp. Whatever it was, it was laughing manically and hovering above her. She threw her arms back to try and push it away, but it vanished as quickly as it had emerged.

Spots of blood hit the ground, trickling from her wounded scalp. She was frozen to the spot, not daring to move for fear of the vicious little thing – or *things* - coming back.

As if on cue, two sets of laughter now, directly in both ears. Hands grabbed each of her shoulders, jerking her upright like a marionette. There were metal things on each side of her, warped robotic homunculi flying with vibrating razor wings that moved at a blur.

One of them spat at her and pushed her head so it was facing forwards and not at it or its twisted kin.

Pariah stood between her and the tower, his black cape billowing about him, living tendrils of blacker-than-black fabric writhing and twisting either in the wind or of their own devices. The silver mask he wore had been crudely sprayed black, untouched patches dotting its harshly-angled contours.

"Dot!" he exclaimed, a twisted malevolence to his tone. He looked – and sounded – like a corrupted version of his former self. All colour had been stripped from his costume, which was now just a uniform blackness. His long, thin fingers now looked more like tendrils than digits, clawing at the air between them.

"Do you think Manolith will recognise you?" he gloated, as she was carried closer to him, so close now she could feel the heat from the breath that hissed from his mask's vents. "Do you think he'll react at *all* when Dreadnought drowns you in a water prison in front of him?"

Dot tried to turn her face away from his, anything to avoid breathing in those noxious fumes, but her head was forced back into place.

"Why did you do it, Pariah?" she sobbed, "Manolith was your friend. Why did you betray him – why did you betray us *all*?"

She could feel the intake of breath as he prepared to speak, just before his masked head vanished with an abrupt flash of

All Our Heroes are Gone

light. Steam hissed from the cauterized stump of Pariah's now-unburdened neck, his jerking corpse falling into the billowing masses of his cloak. Two more flashes over each of Dot's shoulders and she tumbled to the ground, no longer being held aloft. The tiny molten fragments of all that remained of the mech-homunculi landed next to her in two neat little piles. A further flash engulfed his sentient cloak, which shrivelled and shrieked until it was quickly reduced to smouldering embers.

"Got no time for thish," slurred The Utopian as he landed in front of her, his eyes still glowing from the use of his Inferno vision. One arm hung limply at his side, the other was clutching for dear life onto an open bottle of a clear liquid. She could smell the alcohol on his breath as he towered over her.

"You're *drunk*?"

"Did Manolith teesh you those detective schkills?" he asked, floating slowly off in the direction of the tower, his altitude drifting up and down erratically. She followed behind, brushing tiny metal fragments from her shoulders.

He passed through the base of the tower, vanishing from sight. Slowly she approached the same spot, and found her fingers passing through what looked like solid matter. With a deep breath and a single step forward, she was in The Utopian's secret lair.

The same clear bottles were scattered across the floors and console, some intact, but many of them smashed. The room smelt faintly of acetone. The Utopian hovered above his throne that sat at the centre of the room for a few seconds, and simply fell into it. The bottle remained firmly in his grip, however.

Dot stepped her way over the assorted glassware and approached him.

"With everything that's happening, I can't believe you've been drinking."

"With everythin' thass happening, I carn believe you're *not*," he sputtered, taking a hefty swig from the bottle. With a flailing arm, he gestured around the room.

David Court

"Do you know how mush effort it takes for me to get drunk?" he asked, interrupting Dot before she could protest. "I have a super *conschtitushion*, for fuck's shake. This is pretty mush my entire lair's collection of medical alcohol. It wasn't a deshision I made lightly."

There was a bank of monitors suspended from the ceiling, each of them showing a news network from a different country. The ones that weren't reduced to static were showing the proceedings or aftermath from the villains run amok; buildings reduced to rubble, freeways wrenched open like a children's construction set, oceans ablaze. The Utopian was staring at them, glassy-eyed.

Dot stood at his side, staring up at the same displays. The world was dying.

"You could have stopped all this, you know?"

She heard the bottle shatter, the hand that held it – a hand that could condense coal to diamonds – suddenly balled into a fist. She turned to face The Utopian to see the steam rise from his eyelids, welling tears evaporating from the heat of barely restrained Inferno vision. He closed his eyes tight, and Dot could see a nova of light erupting behind each eyelid. The Utopian shifted in his seat, then drunkenly fell forward, landing on his hands and knees.

As he knelt there, fists balled on the floor, the tiles cracked beneath him, spider web lines coursing across the rest of the room. The air felt heavy, as though it could crush her, and there was suddenly a pain behind her eyes, a pressure in her lungs. The monitors exploded, glass raining down on the room like fine crystalline hailstones. The rushing of blood in her ears sounded like the ocean, rushing in and threatening to drown her.

Just when she felt as though she could stand it no longer, it stopped.

The Utopian slowly got to his feet, brushing the glass and tile fragments from his navy-blue cape. He slowly opened his eyes, the intense inferno now replaced by the twinkling of light blue.

All Our Heroes are Gone

He seemed sober, as though he'd burned the alcohol from his system by sheer will alone.

"I'm scared."

Despite his origins, she'd never thought of The Utopian as anything but human. However, those two words from him sounded more alien than anything she'd ever heard. She stood in front of him, defiantly staring up at him.

"But you're The Utopian. You're what scares the *bad* guys."

"When I arrived here, Dot, a certain quantity of an element from my doomed home world arrived here with me. The unique qualities of your world – your gravity, your proximity to the sun - gives me incredible powers, but exposure to the radiation from Element X renders me weaker. I'm made *vulnerable*."

"But–"

"Most of the element is kept in safekeeping on our Asteroid 253 Mathilde stronghold, and a little of it here. But my foes somehow got hold of a small quantity of it from where I'd arrived on your world, and used it against me."

He walked forward to one of the consoles and placed his hands on it, leaning forward as though staring intently at its blank display.

"I nearly *died*, Dot. I only survived thanks to my foes squabbling over who got to kill me and a sheer stroke of luck. Now our enemies have got their hands on the entire *supply* of Element X. What chance do I stand?"

Dot picked up one of the bottles, sniffing the clear liquid within before placing it carefully back upright on the floor. She took a deep breath, collected her thoughts, and stared at the despondent hero.

"Are you fucking *kidding me*?"

The Utopian, brow furrowed, turned his head to face her.

"I've travelled across two states to come here, and I don't have any superpowers. Do you think Headway cried himself to sleep in his base each night because he worried about getting killed? Do you think Synergy thought twice about helping somebody out because she was worried she might get hurt?"

"But... but you don't understand. My powers are lessened, and I..."

"What, so you can only leap buildings of *moderate* height with a single bound? You can only change the course of *less* mightier rivers?"

"But I can be *killed!*"

"I've journeyed here, fully aware that I could be killed at any moment. All your colleagues, the ones without your world-shattering powers, they risked *everything* to do what they did."

The Utopian stared back at her, open mouthed. There was nothing he could say.

"I think that's what made them heroes."

Dot turned, walking back towards the hidden entrance. She muttered her parting line, fully aware that The Utopian would have heard it crystal clear with his super-hearing.

"But I think all the heroes are gone now."

He'd learned that if he concentrated on the other place, he could forget this was happening to him. It still hurt, but the pain was manageable – as though dulled. That's not to say it wasn't complete agony still, but he felt he could survive this. He had to survive this.

Dot had no idea where she was going to go, but she'd see where this straight line took her. Like the sidekicks she'd met back in Kansas, there had to be other heroes out there. Perhaps enough of them to even form a resistance, taking back Earth a town, a state, a country, a continent at a time.

She'd gotten as far as the edge of Genoa when she heard him land behind her, the whooshing of his cape in the dawn winds.

"How can I help?"

All Our Heroes are Gone

She turned to face The Utopian and smiled.

The Consortium Headquarters had been mostly picked clean, as a pack of vultures would strip the last meat from dry bones. She'd felt The Utopian's fear as they'd approached it, hugging him tightly as he flew as quietly and low as he could. Now they stood in its once majestic halls, and realized they were alone. Their foes hadn't seen fit to place any guards here, clearly sensing there to be little remaining of any value.

They'd certainly gone to work on the place. It was as though the villains had taken a very special kind of delight in destroying what this place represented, as though every wall and ceiling destroyed was a hero being slain.

The Hall of the Fallen was the worst; it was supposed to be a sacred and peaceful place where their dead were laid to eternal rest, but evil had since visited. Bodies had been exhumed; bones scattered across the floor. Even the mighty Titanic, who in life had been the size of a large truck, had been unearthed, his huge bones shattered and burned. Gravestones and mausoleums had been similarly desecrated, daubed with excrement and blasphemous obscenities.

She had to steady herself when she stood where Manolith had first fallen, the waves of emotion battering against her like a flood against a weakening dam. Headway's corpse, the mouth and nose of the skull still coated with that foul black membrane, had been torn to shreds.

The Utopian stood in one of the doorways, facing in the other direction. Dot realised it was as though he couldn't face what he'd allowed to happen. For all his super-powers, his conscience was seemingly atrophied. Where some might see stoicism, she saw only cowardice.

After a few moments, she joined him, tugging at his arm.

"Did you get what you came for?"

David Court

"I did," she said, composing herself. "Let's go back."

The Utopian had been quiet on the flight back, lost in thought. He was that distracted, he almost flew over his lair. It took Dot yelling him at him to bring him to his senses, causing him to promptly turn and plummet towards the ground, stopping mere inches away.

He didn't speak until much later that evening, emerging from his study having changed from his costume until something that more resembled ceremonial robes.

"Are you hungry? You must be hungry."

"I am, yes," she replied, realising she hadn't eaten any proper food for several days.

The Utopian that stood in front of her now was awkward, nervous – a far cry from the Alpha hero she was used to. It felt as though he was uncomfortable with human interaction, fear having reverted him to a different person altogether.

"Soup," he announced, "I think we have soup. Do you eat soup?"

She thought of asking him what kind, but truth be told, she didn't care. She simply nodded, and The Utopian scurried off towards the kitchen. She stood up and followed him.

"You've changed. I've never seen you in anything but the costume."

"That costume, as you call it, is battle armour from my home world. You must *earn* it, pass a rite of passage. Through my inaction, I've shamed myself. I cannot, with a clear conscience, wear it again."

If Manolith were here, he'd have known what to say. He'd have placed his mighty rock-like arms around The Utopian and delivered some morale-boosting speech about how heroes fall to rise, or something. Something inspirational that would have lightened the mood in the room and strengthened the broken heroes resolve. Dot, however, remained silent. Manolith wasn't here. And he wasn't here because The Utopian did *nothing* except for retreat to his lair and lock his doors to a dying world.

If she did have a speech within her, she didn't feel that The Utopian deserved it.

She watched as he fumbled around in his cupboards, muttering away to himself as he rifled through the jars and tins until he found something suitable. There was a bowl of fruit on a counter, and Dot reached for a shiny apple-sized sphere, the blood-red surface dotted with seeds like those on a strawberry.

There was a blur of motion as it vanished from her hands, The Utopian appearing with it back where he'd just stood.

"I wouldn't eat that," he smiled, the most emotion she'd seen out of him in hours, "It's a G'arthian Firepit pepper. About nine million Scoville units' worth of heat. It'd probably shut down your nervous system. Put you into a coma, at the very least."

The Utopian took a bite from it, beads of sweat forming on his brow.

"Yeah, that's hot."

He placed the chunk of uneaten pepper down on his kitchen counter, the scarlet juices from it staining the marble surface. He turned his attention to the can of soup in his hands, his eyes glowing a brilliant yellow. Moments later, with his other hand, he peeled away the metal lid with the ease of somebody removing wrapping paper, before pouring the boiling contents into a ceramic bowl.

They'd sat in silence as Dot finished her soup. She watched him as she ate, The Utopian still lost in thought. It'd seem odd to call what he was doing a thousand-yard stare, given as these were eyes capable of seeing the detail on items on distant worlds.

"I'm going to go to the Sinister Stronghold," she said, placing her spoon into the empty soup bowl. The Utopian slowly turned his head to look at, an incredulous expression on his face.

"That's not going to happen. They'll kill you."

David Court

"Something Pariah said to me before you turned his head into a Roman candle. I don't think they will. Not straightaway, anyway."

"Well, they'll certainly kill *me*. I've beaten every one of them at some stage. They *hate* me."

"You don't need to come in with me. I just need your help getting me there."

"And if I refuse?"

"Then I walk there. And you know I'm stubborn enough to do exactly that."

The Utopian sighed, rubbing his forehead with his hands. This alien warrior, once scourge of a thousand worlds, knew this was a fight he couldn't possibly win.

"Tomorrow at dawn, then. We both need our rest for what's to come."

He'd clearly planned ahead, blocking his bedroom from the inside. Unlike Dot though, The Utopian had forgotten the contents of his armoury - the weapons and lethal trinkets he'd confiscated from all manner of would-be Earth Dictators and despots.

She hoped she was pointing the Tormentor's Agoniser Rifle in the right direction and that she'd adjusted the settings correctly (and that the recoil wouldn't break her arm), she squeezed hard on the over-sized trigger. The door to The Utopian's bedchambers exploded out into a shower of rock, settling into plumes of coughed up dust.

He was already dying as she approached him, the Element X sediment visible in the rest of the water left in his bedside glass, shimmering like gold leaf in the subdued lighting of the room. He'd poisoned himself with the only thing he knew could kill him.

All Our Heroes are Gone

His skin had tightened around his face, aging him as she watched. His eyes were dull, the black veins of the Element X radiation poisoning having already blinded him.

She took his hand, shaking her head. His fingers were thin and weak and just the gentle pressure of her hand on his had caused a violent series of purple and black bruises to erupt across them.

"Why?" she sobbed.

His lips narrowly parted as he fought for breath, blind eyes staring blankly at her. A hoarse whisper hissed from his throat like air from a puncture, too quiet to hear. She leant in closer.

"Scared," he whispered.

His hand went limp in hers, his head slumping back and the skin across his face began to dry and crack. The petrification seemed oddly apt.

"Aw fuck," came a familiar voice from behind her. "I wanted to shit down that wanker's throat."

She turned to face The Viscount.

"I see from outside that you did for Pariah then. Only fair, I guess. Probably a good job too. He betrayed you lot, so he clearly wasn't one to be trusted."

"How did you –"

"Pariah had been following you since Kansas. We've let a few of you sidekicks off the leash to see if you'd lead us to your chicken-shit bosses, and a few of you came up trumps. Looks like he couldn't hold back any longer, but it all worked out in the end. I had people following *him,* see."

He picked up the Agoniser rifle she'd left in the doorway, stepping towards the foot of the bed. Dot could hear movement outside the room, furniture being smashed by The Viscount's numerous colleagues.

"Oh, sunshine," he said, staring at the Utopian, "What am I going to do with that shitload of Element X I've got now?"

David Court

She wasn't familiar with the supervillain who was carrying her, a huge lizard creature with pterodactyl-like wings who seemed to communicate solely by hissing and screeching. As the reptile held her tight, her skin scraped against his rough scales, causing her to wince with every flap of his vast, leathery wings.

The Viscount and his colleagues were heading back to their Stronghold in considerably more luxurious style, all four of them occupants of an invisible flying vehicle they'd presumably stolen earlier. The air around them shimmered with the vague displacement of their imperceptible craft.

They'd used one of the more powerful weapons from The Utopian's Arsenal on the World's Wonder View tower and the hidden base, reducing it and its deceased occupant into a magma-filled crater.

They'd been kind to her, considering. Apex Predator had offered to kill her quickly and painlessly, but The Viscount had ordered that no harm was to come to Dot. He'd made it explicit that anything that happened to her would happen two-fold to the person who harmed her. Coyote had quipped about how that threat would work if they ripped both of Dot's eyes out, to which The Viscount simply shot him dead. ("Tired of the little whining bastard, anyhow.")

That put a hasty stop to any further discussions vis-à-vis Dot's wellbeing.

The Sinister Stronghold was a hive of activity, villains arriving and departing without interruption or hindrance. As Dot was lowered into the courtyard of the imposing fortress, she watched as heroes were being deposited in cages. They'd widened their grasp to include heroes from other countries now;

All Our Heroes are Gone

Ashigaru and Bushido from Japan, Cairn and Tor from England, Canada's Absolution and The Void, Ireland's Changeling.

The sidekicks she'd encountered in Kansas were in cages here too, staring mournfully through their electrified bars, their usefulness out in the open presumably exhausted.

Gila Monster's sharp claws suddenly dug into her back, a stark reminder that Dot was a prisoner here too, and she was frog-marched into the heart of the fortress.

She remained as calm as she could. Her instincts had seen her right so far; she was relying on two things, both of which had so far come to pass.

The Viscount was waiting for her in the corridor, changed from his pinstripe suit into a pink-smeared butcher's apron on top of equally blood-spattered orange overalls.

"It's like a family reunion this, innit?" he smirked through stained yellow teeth. He pulled open a thick-set wooden door as she approached, beckoning her to enter.

"In you pop, love."

He leaned in close as she walked past, forcing her to brush against him. She flinched, convinced she'd heard him mutter something vile to her under his breath. She'd heard rumours of his depravity before. The door was closed and locked behind her, a series of thick metal bolts sliding noisily into place.

They stood in a large empty room, the floor of which had been covered in a thin layer of straw. It was dirty with soil and excrement, and seemingly hadn't been refreshed in weeks. The wall behind The Viscount was adorned with an assortment of vicious looking weaponry ranging from the archaic (medieval maces and cudgels) to the fantastic (disintegration rifles and vicious looking chainsaw/sword hybrids). It was guarded by Zeitgeist, one of The Viscount's closest lackeys, a terrifyingly armed android with a temperamental anger module. He stared Dot up and down, almost defying her to go for one of the weapons to give him just the excuse he'd need.

The Viscount, having spotted Dot looking at the weapons, stood between them and her, leaning in close.

David Court

"Did you ever wonder how we managed to win, love?" he whispered, conspiratorially, as though letting her in on a long-forbidden secret.

"Because of Pariah's betrayal", she spat back, "Without help you'd never have –"

"Oh, he *helped*", he interjected, "but there's more to it than that. One day it just... dawned on me. Popped into me noggin, just like that."

Dot stared defiantly back. He was clearly going to continue, regardless of whether she wanted to hear the answer or not.

"The magician Kostanza thought it was because we'd all become possessed, making us more evil and cunning than usual. BrainForce surmised sommat similar – that we'd all been taken over by a vastly superior alien intelligence."

He pulled a remote control from his apron pocket and pressed a button. Mechanisms clicked into place and a wooden door at the far edge of the room slid upwards, revealing a dark chamber beyond, in which shifted a bulky silhouette.

"That's all bollocks, mind."

The silhouette sniffed the air and pulled its way out of the room with huge bulky hands, shuffling on all fours towards Dot and The Viscount. As it drew closer, she recognised the huge form of Manolith. The eyes were blank and dead, no recognition there. His body bore the pained and tell-tale marks of a thousand healed injuries.

"We *won* because you fuckers have rules you play by. Rules that we used to play by, too. It was like a game; you'd catch us robbing a bank and you'd beat us up. Not too hard, mind. You'd then throw us in the slammer. Our mates would break us out, and we'd all repeat the cycle. Rinse and repeat. Rinse and repeat."

Manolith loomed in closer, but there was fear in his eyes. He recognised The Viscount, and he recognised the weapons. A bank of lights flickered into life in the ceiling, revealing a vast array of mounted television cameras.

All Our Heroes are Gone

"You see, this one day, I thought, *Fuck the rules*. And I told everybody else to fuck the rules too."

The Viscount wandered to the weapons rack, studying his options with an uncharacteristic moment of quiet contemplation. He had the expression of a man choosing wine from a list, looking for that precise, appropriate choice.

He nodded towards an oversized four-barrelled shotgun, crudely painted flames marking the handle. Zeitgeist handed it to him with a delicate gesture, nodding as he did so.

"And, turns out, that was all we fuckin' well needed. Should have done it years ago."

He gritted his teeth, cocked the shotgun, and strode towards the cowering form of Manolith.

"No!" screamed Dot, dashing in front of The Viscount, tears streaming down her face.

As he leant in closer to her, her hands went into her pockets.

"Villains always fail," Manolith had once told her, "because they always do two things. They always gloat, and without fail they're over-confident. That's the final lesson I can teach you."

She reached into her pocket and grabbed a damp piece of matter, scooping it and throwing it at the trembling form of Manolith in one single, practiced motion.

The Viscount watched at the tumbling chunk of organ spiralled through the air, splashing against and sticking to Manolith's craggy forehead.

"What the fuck was that?" he shrieked, levelling the four metal tubes of the shotgun at Dot's smiling face.

"A big chunk of frontal lobe, I'd guess. Looks like you didn't scoop all of the bits of him up back at the Consortium Headquarters."

The piece of pinkish-white matter slid like a snake towards Manolith's ear canal, vanishing as though it had been neatly hoovered up by the dark void.

David Court

The last piece of the jigsaw snapping satisfyingly into place. The delighted expression of the safecracker, upon hearing the click of that final tumbler. The last coloured edge aligning neatly with its brethren on a Rubik's Cube.

He was complete.

Synapses fire a twenty-one-gun salute, neurons excitedly reuniting with old, forgotten friends. He's like a rebooted computer, everything slowly switching on. He sees Dot, The Viscount, and Zeitgeist.

The connectivity floods through him, like a river flowing down long tried out tributaries. He's in control again, flexing those powerful hands, feeling the warmth on his spine as atrophied nerves reignite.

The Viscount looked panicked, levelling the gun at Dot, and then at Manolith - and then back to Dot.

"What have you fucking done, love? What the *fuck* have you done?"

He was panicked, genuinely lost as to his next action. The Viscount looked over to a similar bewildered Zeitgeist, his silicon brain struggling to calculate an appropriate response.

In an instant, The Viscount decided. If in doubt, kill something. He moved the shotgun barrel to point at the girl.

A huge grey hand lunged towards him, grabbing the man's head between a monolithic thumb and forefinger. With a simple squeeze, it was popped away with the technical efficiency with which one might remove a troublesome spot. His body twitched, before lying still.

Zeitgeist's front opened, an array of projectile and laser launchers sprouting forth from the mechanoids chest cavity. Manolith was upon him, pounding him to scrap metal before a single shot could be fired.

All Our Heroes are Gone

Manolith indeed possessed incredible powers of healing. But he could only heal what was *there*.

He craned his head to look at Dot, a light restored to his eyes. "Fuck the rules," he bellowed.

"Fuck the rules," she smiled back, stroking the leathery contours of his face.

They were outnumbered, but they had the element of surprise. They'd taken Manolith out before, but it had been long planned. And together, the two of them were *smart*.

Free the heroes. Together they'd take the Stronghold, the town, the state, the country, the continent.

The world.

Dot had had a tune on her mind for the past few days, but only now dared sing it, clambering onto Manolith's mighty shoulders, studying her new shotgun.

"I could while away the hours..."

His fists were poised, ready to smash through the wooden door that led out to the rest of the Stronghold.

"Ready?" he said, turning to look at her, an arched smile on his face.

"Ready".

David Court

Shadow and Substance

I'D GOT THE ART of getting ready and leaving the house down to a fine art now. My routine was occasionally thrown out of kilter on the rare occasion that he was lurking somewhere inside the house – more often than not outside my bedroom door or nonchalantly smoking in my kitchen - but I was both pleased and relieved to say that on that day of all days that that hadn't been the case.

I was running slightly late, truth be told, having hit that 'Snooze' button once too often. I hadn't slept well the night before - I'd caught him sitting on the foot of my bed when I went to finally turn in and I'd had had to shoo him out. He'd tried to start one of those portentous sentences of his, but I'd kicked him out of the house before he could deliver his ominous soliloquy. He'd started again whilst standing out on the drive, but I'd slammed the double-glazed windows shut before I could make out any of it. He'd carried on regardless to a non-existent audience, his words thankfully muffled and inaudible through two panes of thick glass. Even with the curtains drawn, I couldn't help but occasionally peer out at him, shaking my head as I watched him mouth empty words to nobody in particular.

After that it was mostly a heady combination of angry adrenaline and fearful trepidation that had kept me tossing and turning fitfully. Sometimes it was more terrifying *not* hearing

Shadow and Substance

what he had to say – that fear of the unknown, those thoughts that reverberate around the lecture theatre of your skull in the dead of night. Christ... Listen to me... I'm starting to *sound* like him now.

I was determined not to be late for the appointment, no matter what. I'd felt I'd had no option other than to go private when my usually sensitive GP had finally started to give me that look that confirmed he believed that I was insane, and decent private psychiatrists aren't cheap. I flung open my front door and – luckily for both of us – he was nowhere to be seen. With the foul mood I was in I'd have just elbowed him out of the way mid-monologue anyway.

It had been raining overnight and the weather was as grey as one of his suits and as bleak as my mood. I'd lost my umbrella a few days ago when I'd thrown it at him in a fit of pique and naively hadn't seen fit to replace it yet, so I was half-drowned by the time I'd arrived at the bus stop.

The one thing you have appreciate about my situation is that it's impossible to let your guard down for a single moment. He could suddenly appear at any instant, seemingly from nowhere, giving me no choice but either try to ignore him or simply to run. My options on the bus, trapped in that metal shell, would be even more limited – I've lost count of the amount of times when he'd unexpectedly been sitting behind me and I've been forced to leap out at the next stop. On top of everything else, he was costing me a *fortune* in taxi and bus fares.

Oh, I'd tried ignoring him, but it was next to impossible – some of the things he says can ruin your whole day. No wonder I'm a nervous wreck. Confronting him is pointless too – he just keeps talking, almost as though he's oblivious to your presence.

I'm not a violent man but a few days ago - at the end of my tether and pushed beyond any reasonable person's breaking point - I had finally snapped. With a cry of impotent frustration, I'd pushed him into the path of an oncoming taxi. After the bulky black cab had bounced over him, I stared down at the broken corpse that lay on the road, limbs splayed out at

David Court

impossible angles. A thick muddy tyre-track had ruined both the man and his usually impeccable suit. He stared back at me with vacant accusing eyes.

That was the end of that, I thought. My mood was buoyant for the rest of the day and there'd been a spring in my step. Normality was at last restored. I was just starting to finally feel good about life when I opened my shed that evening and there he was, leaning against my rusted wheelbarrow. Upon seeing me his mouth opened and he carried on speaking from exactly where he'd been interrupted, as though he'd been sitting there in the musty compost-scented darkness just waiting for his opportunity. Completely unharmed, completely unperturbed. I'd slammed the shed door closed and ran into the house, screaming.

The bus pulled up, and I cursed as a displaced puddle splashed over my clean shoes and roused me from my reverie. After confusing the driver by only half getting onto it and glancing nervously around, I finally committed myself to showing my pass. Despite the bottom floor of the bus being mostly empty, I stood. It was safer that way. Easier to make a quick getaway.

Arriving unhindered, the luxurious foyer of my new psychiatrist's office certainly showed why I had to get a bank loan in order to afford just a meagre handful of appointments. There was an elaborately abstract water feature occupying much of the room that would probably have cost me the best part of a year's wages. Any artistic merit it possessed was instantly nullified by the fact that the sound of trickling water from it just made me want to go to the toilet.

Other than the receptionist, I was the only person there, thank God. It would have been typical for him to have been waiting here for me when I'd stepped in. She smiled at me as I walked towards her, but it felt forced – it was disingenuous, a rictus grin. Working alongside that water feature, she must either be deaf or have a bladder of steel. She gestured silently

Shadow and Substance

towards a black leather sofa in front of which sat a marble table, bare except for a neat pile of magazines.

The leather squeaked noisily as I cautiously lowered my weight onto it. I perched awkwardly on the edge of the chair, wary that if I sat back, I'd collapse into it and struggle to get back up.

I glanced up at the receptionist who was now studying her perfectly manicured nails with the focused glare of a master safecracker. It only dawned on me then that she hadn't even taken my name, which probably meant I was the only appointment for the day.

I flicked absent-mindedly through the magazines on the table. This wasn't the kind of place where you'd find the Readers Digest or glossy gossip magazines – these were all aspirational catalogues with powerful single word names. Each was the sort of periodical that would have a twelve-page spread dedicated to expensive sports cars that they'd only ever made six of.

The receptionist called my name in a sing-song voice and gestured towards the corridor. I lifted myself off the sofa and awkwardly stumbled past her. I hoped she wouldn't notice the wet patches on the sofa I'd left behind from my rain-sodden jeans.

It was only when I was walking up the long wooden corridor to Doctor Matheson's office that my heart sank. *He* was waiting there ahead of me just outside the door, a freshly lit cigarette between his fingers. His permanent monochrome appearance - which I was almost getting used to now - was a sharp contrast to the plush velvet red curtains behind him. For some odd reason it always offended me that he blatantly ignored enclosed workspace non-smoking regulations.

Looking right through me, he went to speak. I raised an angry finger, a gesture more for me than for him, and threw open the door. A few words escaped his mouth before I slammed the door closed behind me, blocking him out.

"Imagine if you wi..."

David Court

It was then I was grateful for the luxury of these offices. The stupidly expensive, elaborately carved thick oak door I'd closed behind me drowned his words out completely as I slumped back against it.

Doctor Matheson, a true professional, barely blinked an eye at my antics. That said, the coarse thickness of his ginger eyebrows meant he could have had his eyes firmly shut and I probably wouldn't have noticed.

"As nice a door as that is to lean against," he quipped, gesturing to the red leather armchair in front of him, "perhaps you'd find a chair more comfortable?"

I looked at the chair and then back to the door, studying around the ornate handle - paying particular attention to the keyhole.

"Do you have the key for this?" I asked, nervously, "I don't want to be interrupted."

Doctor Matheson calmly poured a tea for himself and another for me. The silver teapot clanked noisily as he placed it onto the tray.

"Is he out there now?" he asked, sliding a delicate china cup across the table to me, "Did you see him?"

I'd heard that question from doctors before, but always in a patronizing tone of disbelief - of contempt, mockery and half-amusement. Matheson sounded genuine and absolutely sincere and reassuringly not in a way that felt like he was trying to humour me. This was so refreshing after the bad experiences I'd had in the past.

"I'm here to help," he said, getting to his feet and taking a few steps towards me. I went cold with what he said next.

"Let him in."

My heart froze. I'd spent so long trying to escape from him that the very act seemed alien to me. What would he do? What would he *say?*

Matheson must have sensed my apprehension. His voice grew quieter and calmer.

Shadow and Substance

"He can't hurt you with me here," he assured me, "Let him in."

My hand clutched around the handle and slowly turned it, my glance occasionally going back to Matheson who was simply smiling and nodding reassuringly. I could feel the mechanism inside the door click as the latch opened and, when the handle could turn no further, I slowly opened the door.

He was still there, his cigarette barely touched. It was though, when he was not being observed, time had remained suspended for him. I leapt back as he suddenly strode towards the door, a determined expression on his face. He neatly stepped into the room, refusing to acknowledge either of us. Staring at a fixed point in the far wall as though performing to an imaginary audience, he took a drag from his cigarette and began to speak.

"What fragile mysteries can be found lurking within the darkest realms of the human psyche? This seemingly ordinary psychiatrist's office, workplace of the well-meaning Doctor Ray Matheson, may well be the conduit used to unlock secrets that would be best *kept* secret. Secrets that are best kept... within the Twilight Zone."

Rod Serling, or rather a perfect greyscale facsimile of him (grey 3/2 sack suit, satin tie, white oxford spread collar shirt) stepped out of the room, job done. I slowly pushed the door closed behind him, my hands sweaty, my knuckles a pale white. It gave a satisfying click as it shut.

"Was he there?" asked Matheson, a gold-nibbed fountain pen poised above a notepad that had seemingly appeared from nowhere.

I bit my upper lip and nodded.

"And has he gone now?"

I nodded again.

He patted the armchair in front of him.

"Come and take a seat. Let's talk about him."

I slowly lowered myself down into the comfortable leather of the armchair, relaxing slightly now. That particular encounter hadn't been too bad, all things considered, and it wasn't likely he'd reappear during the course of this session. Matheson smiled at me encouragingly and went to speak.

There is one textbook question, appropriate given the circumstances, with which any such conversation must begin. I'd rehearsed the answer a million times, knowing full well what he was about to say. I'd almost started answering before he'd asked.

"When did this all start?"

I'd had a full-time job then, back in the days when I wasn't a bag of nerves, wondering where he'd appear next, what sinister or loaded utterances he'd make in that gravitas-laden voice of his. In actuality, it was just a few months back, but it felt like years now. A lifetime ago.

"There are things we all take for granted. A normal life, a house, a well-paid job, friends."

I remembered it word for word. The first things he'd ever said – all delivered whilst I was queueing at the post office to pick up a parcel I'd missed. I'd thought it to be a joke at first, an impersonator who'd painted himself in varying shades of grey, attempting to get a rise out of us. I ignored him, not wanting to encourage the prankster, waiting for a reaction from somebody else in the queue.

But nobody else batted an eyelid. He sparked up a cigarette and not a soul reacted. Staring right through me, he continued.

"But what is normal? What if normality was just a fragile concept, something to be tossed aside like so much detritus? Baggage to shrug off as we prepare for our voyage to... The Twilight Zone."

I did what any Englishman would have done when confronted with such an absurdity. I kept my head down, picked up my parcel and did my best to ignore it hoping that he'd go away. I swear he'd winked at me as I made my way out of the Post Office.

And from that date onwards, he'd just appear. Sitting on the edge of my desk or the corner of my bed, on the seat behind me on the bus or next to me in the cinema. No introduction, just... talking. In that way that made everything just... scary.

"Scary? Do explain," said Matheson, his right hand a blur as he scribbled down copious notes.

"Try to picture the scene," I said, shrugging, "You're just about to tuck into your Sunday Dinner you've spent the last two hours making. Up pops Rod bloody Serling with a 'A Sunday roast. That most quintessential of English weekend traditions. But traditions come with their own high cost... in the Twilight Zone'. And then he just sits back, looking smug. And your appetite is suddenly gone and there's nothing you can except to scrape your roast dinner into the kitchen bin, suddenly terrified by the ill-omened nature of roast beef and Yorkshire puddings."

"I could see how that could be distracting when..."

"And another one. You're on a date with that girl from Procurement who you've fancied for weeks and have finally summoned up the courage to ask out. You're getting a bit cosy on the sofa and she goes to the bathroom to freshen up. Then Rod Bastard Serling is suddenly there in the doorway with a 'Love can be as sticky as a vat of molasses, as unpalatable as a hunk of spoiled yeast. Exhibit One: a case history of a lover-boy who should never have entered... The Twilight Zone'. There are few things capable of ridding one of an amorous mood so quickly."

"Do you think it *is* Rod Serling?"

"What? Do you think I'm mad?", I barked, suddenly very aware of both of our roles, "Rod Serling died in the mid-seventies, a good half a decade before I was even born. And it's not just Rod Serling – it's like a black and white telly version of him. I swear if you look at him long enough you can see grains of static there."

David Court

"So, if you accept that it's just a figment of your imagination, then that is half the battle. Acceptance is..."

"It's not as simple as that," I interrupted, "Some of the things he says... they're prophetic. Thanks to some of his omen-laden speeches, I've avoided a works dinner that gave everybody else who went food poisoning, avoided getting in a mate's car which got into an accident that left him crippled, all sorts of things."

"So, this... version... of Serling is actively *helpful*?"

"Yes, but that doesn't necessarily mean *anything*. That could be the luck of the draw, because he's pretty much warning me about *everything* these days. Even a stopped clock is right twice a day. He's pretty one note, to be honest. I'm having to ignore him because If I didn't, I simply couldn't function as a human being. I just want rid of him, Doctor Matheson."

"You have to appreciate that this kind of therapy can take a very long time. With no guarantee of results. I suspect you sometimes *appreciate* his company."

"With all due respect, that's nonsense. You try living for a single day with that man constantly appearing in your life as the voice of impending doom. I've got the money, Doctor Matheson, if that's the issue."

"Calm down. I assure you; I'm trying to help."

I sunk my face into my hands, suddenly aware that my breathing was rapid and panicked. I was *safe* here, at least for the time being. I concentrated on the loud rhythmic *tick-tock tick-tock* from the grandfather clock that stood next to the door, gradually relaxing my breathing into following the same pattern. Slowly and surely, I eased myself away from the impending panic attack.

"If you will, Imagine the complex mechanisms of a clock..." came the voice from in front of you. I pulled my hands away from my face to be confronted by Rod Serling, sitting there in the place of Doctor Matheson. Of the Doctor himself, there was no sign.

Shadow and Substance

"An intricate arrangement of cogs and dials, all working together towards a unified purpose..."

I staggered to my feet, holding on to the chair for support as I felt my limbs buckling beneath me. Serling stood up as well, tapping an unlit cigarette on the back of his hand.

"...that purpose being to chart one of the oldest mysteries to mankind..."

He was up and to his feet by the time I'd made it to the door. Unable to wrest my eyes away from him, my shaking hands struggled blindly with the door handle. Eventually, it turned in my hand and I fell through the door, running straight into somebody who'd been in the unfortunate position of standing right outside. They didn't budge, as solid and unmoving as a rock.

It was Rod Serling staring down at me, an all-knowing smirk etched on those homochromous features.

"...the mysteries of time itself."

I turned and ran, carried forward by sheer momentum. My legs stumbled but thankfully I remained upright, arms flailing wildly for balance. The receptionist - undoubtedly roused by my shrieks of alarm - managed to drag herself away from her beauty regime long enough to step out into the corridor to see what all the fuss was about.

As she stood in front of me, perfectly lip-sticked mouth agape, her form shifted and wavered. Edges warped and morphed, white-noise static shadows gaining substance. Where there had once stood an attractive twenty-something dressed in bold primary colours was now a black and white woman dressed in nineteen-fifties fashions; pleated skirt and an angora sweater hiding those conical breasts that only women of that era ever seemed to have. All sanity-wrenchingly topped off with the bizarre anatopistic features of Rod Serling.

David Court

"Mankind travels through the pre-determined route map of his existence..."

Something inside me finally snapped. Without slowing, I reached forward and grabbed his head, slamming it violently into the receptionist's desk. The body fell limp as I pushed past it, now falling through the doors that led out onto the street.

It had stopped raining now, the newly emerged sun shining off the glistening tar of the roads. An expensive sports car drove slowly past, an overly loud radio booming out what at first sounded like a profanity filled rap track but turned out to be anything but – they were the carefully enunciated words of Rod Serling.

"...mostly unaware of the forks in the road, the eddies, gyres and currents that carry us along..."

As it slowly passed me by, the car shimmered and mutated from an expensive boy racer penis-replacement into a nineteen-fifties Ford Fairlane. I staggered back away from the road, stumbling into a group of people and losing my balance.

My back hit the pavement and I lay there for what felt like an age, my eyes screwed tightly shut. I knew what I'd see if I opened them, and I clung on to that fragile gristle of sanity for as long as I could. The voices of the crowd – complaining and concerned at first – were beginning to speak in chorus. Female voices deepened and children's voices slowed as they all began to carefully synchronise with one another, a dozen voices eventually speaking as one.

"...but we're about to find that all paths, regardless of the traveller, the length or course, eventually all end up..."

Don't say it. Don't say it. Don't say it.

"...in the..."

I threw myself onto my feet and barged through them, human bodies scattering like bowling pins. With my eyes tightly shut, I hurled myself away from them in desperation, screaming at the top of my lungs so I didn't have to hear *those words*.

Shadow and Substance

When I finally did open my eyes, it was too late to do anything about it. The black cab (driven by Rod Serling, obviously) didn't have time to avoid me. The first thing I noticed with the collision was that all of the wind had been knocked out of me, and I only had time for a single thought when the back of my head connected with the concrete kerb, a thing that it was never really designed to do.

"A black cab, just like the one I'd pushed Rod under," I thought, blackness creeping in at the periphery of my vision.

"Nice twist."

I awoke to blackness. There was a loss of sensation, as though I were floating in a void. Was this what death felt like? Perhaps I was in a coma? I imagine the reaction of most people, if they found themselves in this situation, would be to panic.

Not I. I closed my eyes (for what little worth that was), breathed in deeply (again, a pointless act) and listened. Nothing. Absolutely nothing.

Beautiful.

Wonderful, blissful silence.

No dry delivery of portentous dread. No expository cautionary tales.

Just an infinite black void.

But then something appeared, right in the centre of my vision. A white dot of light accompanied by a shrill piercing tone. It wavered, blurring, and then becoming focused again.

A voice in the darkness, American, emotionless.

"There is nothing wrong with your television set."

What? Who was that? The voice seemed to be coming from everywhere, louder than God.

"Do not attempt to adjust the picture."

A dread realisation began to dawn.

"We are controlling transmission."

No. This can't be. Not after all this. I began to scream aloud in defiance, hoping to drown out the voice. But it drowned even that out.

"We will control the horizontal"

The wavering dot of light became a shaft of brilliance, exploding left and right, burning a line on my sight. With no physical form to speak of, I couldn't cover my ears. Couldn't cover my eyes. I had no choice but to witness it all.

"We will control the vertical"

The dot erupted from the top and bottom to become a solid line of illumination, burning with an inner energy. And then everything erupted into light, maddening vistas and impossible imagery dancing across my vision. Huge waves of energy pulsed and ebbed, and I could only watch and scream dementedly, my last tattered vestiges of sanity ripped away.

"You are about to participate in a great adventure. You are about to experience the awe and mystery which reaches from the inner mind to... The Outer Limits".

SCENE: We're standing behind two doctors who are peering through a window into a padded cell. The occupant is collapsed in one corner quite, quite still. A track of drool trails out of his lips, and his eyes are empty.

DOCTOR OSWALD: How long has he been like this?

DOCTOR HASKIN: For a few weeks now. He was ranting when we picked up from outside Matheson's office, but that didn't last long. He just went quiet. He's locked in that brain of his, and I don't we'll ever be able to get him out. We can just feed him and hope that one day… just one day…

Shadow and Substance

CAMERA PANS THROUGH THE WINDOW AND WE ZOOM IN ON THE PATIENT'S EYES. IN THE BLACKNESS OF HIS PUPIL, WE SEE SINE WAVES.

VOICEOVER: The human brain, the most complex mechanism in existence. And like all mechanisms, capable of being damaged, or broken beyond repair. And like an automobile, if you suffer a breakdown, just be sure you don't break down in…

David Court

The Thing from Another World

TOPPLING TOWARDS Earth,
    the place of our birth,
is something burning bright like a furnace.
It's an alien vessel,
Which at a rough guess will
plummet out of control to the surface.

There are few places parkier
than the depths of Antarctica,
where the landscape is nothing but snow.
But then something of note, a
loud helicopter rotor
of a chopper that's hovering low.

They are in hot pursuit
of a stray Malamute
but keep failing to hit with their gun.
The Norwegians are frustrated
and get quite agitated when
it reaches Outpost thirty-one.

The Thing from Another World

The chopper lands on a verge as
the gunner emerges
and pulls out a grenade which he'd stowed.
The throw is fucked up a treat
and it lands at his feet
and the pilot and chopper explode.

With reckless abandon
He keeps shooting at random,
Gibbering, clearly off his head.
As stray bullets fly by,
Bennings is caught in the thigh,
And Garry shoots the Norwegian stone dead.

MacReady and Doc. Copper
head off in their chopper
and find that the Norwegian base is
just a charred shell that's filled
with dead bodies, as well
as a humanoid corpse with two faces.

They bring it from there
for their biologist, Blair.
"This thing isn't human," he proposes.
And meanwhile the mutt
Confirms somethings afoot,
As the bloody thing metamorphoses.

Whilst their dogs buy the farm,
MacReady pulls the alarm
And Childs turns the dogs into toast
Blair checks out the corpse
"This is alien, of course,
and can perfectly mimic its host".

"It's from an alien race
come from deep outer space
and we can't let it get out of here.
If it reaches civilization,
It'll mean all our damnation.
Earth will be assimilated in just a few years."

David Court

Bennings dies by cremation,
caught mid-transformation.
And they're forced to lock Blair in the shed.
With an axe he went crazy, Oh,
And chopped up the radio
And killed all the sled dogs stone dead.

Copper says "With our blood,
A simple test should
Reveal the alien now rather than later"
But the blood stores are trashed,
All the samples left smashed.
It's clear now that there is a traitor.

The biologist Fuchs
says that he'll take a look
and that he'll continue Blair's studies
But later that night
Of him there's no sight
So venture outside, do his buddies.

They find Fuch's corpse burnt black,
And so Windows heads back
In order to raise the alert.
Nauls too, comes back deflated
Fearing his friend assimilated
When he finds a scrap of MacReady's torn shirt.

As the team congregate
to debate MacReady's fate,
he appears with explosives, quite stressed.
"I'll blow you to bits,
If you attack me, you shits."
(Norris suffers a cardiac arrest).

Without hesitation, they try
Defibrillation
The outcome for Norris looks bleak
But to their disbelief
His stomach sprouts teeth
And teaches Copper a hands-off technique.

The Thing from Another World

The mutated fellow
Is toasted like a marshmallow
Although one you wouldn't dare digest
"Windows, gather everyone round
and tie them all down.
We're going to try out a test."

Clark, who fears for his life,
Goes for him with a knife,
And MacReady just shoots him stone dead.
They're all stunned into silence
By this act of violence
Having seen their friend shot in the head.

"Guys" said MacReady,
"I think I've got a theory.
The alien just wants to survive.
If we can just determine,
who's a host to this vermin,
then we might just stay alive."

Everyone tied and seated,
A copper wire's heated
And placed into samples of blood.
But when the wire tip was probin'
Palmer's Hemoglobin
It leapt off as far as it could.

With little advance warning,
Palmer's now transforming
As tentacles sprout from his head
Windows hesitates to flame him,
And death comes to claim him
And MacReady has to burn them both dead.

Garry's been through the wringer,
He feels loathe to linger, so
It's only fair that he seems a grouch.
"You've been through a lot,
But I would rather not
Spend Winter tied to this fucking couch"

David Court

With Childs left to guard,
The others head out to the yard
In order to go and test Blair
They open his shed
And find they've all been misled.
The alien has tunneled out of there.

Though they thought him Mammalian,
Turns out Blair is an alien
And the blighter's given them the slip
He's been scavenging equipment
which is for his ship meant,
and has part-built a makeshift space ship.

Garry looks all forlorn.
"The Generator's gone"
"Is there any way we can fix it?",
MacReady asks with a frown.
Garry stares at the ground,
"No, I meant as in somebodies nicked it"

"Oh, bugger, shit, and damn,
I know the thing's plan."
MacReady states, with some consternation.
"We'll all freeze to death,
And we'll breathe our last breath -
It'll be safe whilst it's in hibernation"

The most hopeful prognosis
was to lay the explosives
agreed the remaining three guys
The dynamite was placed
(and Blair melts Garry's face)
But then came the biggest surprise.

A vast tentacled Blair
Burst out into the air
popping open like some vile hemorrhoid
But with some dynamite (the last),
MacReady triggered the blast
And the base and the beast were destroyed

The Thing from Another World

As the flames all burn higher,
MacReady sits by the fire
As Childs reappears with a wry smile.
They can do nothing but watch
as they both share some Scotch.
"Why don't we both just wait here a while."

David Court

12 Drummers Drumming

NOT ONLY AM I too late, but they'd had time to go to
work on him.
Solomon's wracked corpse has clearly been left for me to find,
hanging from a crooked lamppost with tinsel-wrapped rope, a
gruesome display of both gaud and gore. I shimmy up the pole
to cut him loose, and his body falls to the cracked tarmac with an
organic thud.

A casual onlooker might consider my actions merciful, as
though I were planning on giving my old companion a more
dignified resting place than the ones those monsters gave him –
my reasons are, however, altogether less than altruistic.

It's not the first time I've done this. Solomon's ruined face is
a bloodied labyrinth of scars and incisions. Sometimes it's easier
when they take the eyes, so you don't have them staring at you.

I begin to prise open his jaw, but from the feel of his gums
through his skin I suspect I'm wasting my time. His mouth is
empty and filled with blood, a leaking scarlet maw of crudely
mauled gums.

They've taken his teeth already. I'll have no luck there. I'll
just have to hope that the meagre collection of molars and
canines I've already amassed will be enough to barter my way
through The Dives.

12 Drummers Drumming

I sense the shift in the air moments before my pigeon band starts to vibrate against my wrist to inform me of the same. I've jumped to my feet and span around just in time to see him bearing down on me, his pace slowing from a sprint to a jog. Despite the madness wrapping its tendrils around his addled brain, there's still some reasoning there. Now he knows I'm aware of his presence, there's a certain reticence. He's weighing me up, considering his options.

Even at their most intelligent though, they're far from sophisticated creatures. His options consist of fighting or fleeing, and it's rare that a Drummer will choose the latter. Especially as, in this case, he must consider himself the superior combatant. I'm a female (easily a head shorter than him) and appear unarmed.

His mouth opens wide in a silent scream, spittle spraying out from his slathering jaws. He lifts his weapon aloft – an old rusted rake with a bent metal handle -and moves to close the gap between us. Even when I pull out my blade – a vicious serrated thing – he barely slows.

We circle, staring each other down. His mouth is moving, his lips twisting into barked words. He's trying to intimidate me, forgetting – or oblivious to the fact – that I can't hear him. Still, it's having its intended purpose – I can lip-read the odd word and none of them are pleasant. It's clear that he wants to either rape me or disfigure me, and he's not fussed about which order he does that in.

His ears are a blotched mess of tumours and inflamed growths. It's been a while since I've seen one this far along the infection lifecycle that could still operate semi-intelligently. They're usually vicious, subhuman creatures driven solely by instinct at this stage, past the point of using tools or weaponry.

It's only when the rusted spikes of the rake miss my head by inches that I realise I'm allowing myself to become distracted again. Regardless of how infected they are, it's idiocy to ever consider them not a very genuine threat.

David Court

Holding the handle of the rake in both hands, he swings it around in a vicious arc, and it's only by throwing myself to the ground that I avoid being hit. I jab upwards with the knife in the moments that he's recovering his balance, the blade sliding neatly into his left thigh. I'm rewarded with a torrent of blood spilling out over his tattered clothes, and he staggers backwards. With luck, I've hit his femoral artery, and he'll bleed out in minutes.

Another swipe from the rake, but one-handed this time and more desperate than the last. I throw myself at him – even with my comparatively small frame, the injury to his leg causes him to lose his footing and he falls backwards.

I don't give him the opportunity to get back up. By the time his flailing hands are at my throat, I've stabbed him a good half a dozen times about the neck, slicing through both his jugular and carotid arteries. He lurches up at the last moment to bite at me, and the last slice ends up severing one of the tumorous patches from the side of his head. It falls away, like a huge bloodied scab.

He dies twitching just as the odour from it hits me – it smells of rancid food left to rot, and the aroma is still something I'll never get used to. It's all I can do to stop myself from retching as I open the thing's mouth to stare despondently at a mouthful of worn out, worthless, diseased teeth and blackened gums. A last gasp of foul air belches out of the thing as a final silent death rattle as I push the corpse away.

An unkempt garden from a nearby house serves as the final resting place for Solomon. I've heard rumours that some of the bands of Drummers have taken to cannibalism, and the poor guy has suffered enough. The cold winter earth is tough and unforgiving, and its growing dark by the time I've finished the job and patted the ground flat. The house will have to serve as my shelter for the evening.

• •

12 Drummers Drumming

By the time I've attached pigeon sensors to all the ways into the building, I realise my stock of masking tape is dwindling fast and I'm forced to be sparing with the last couple, hoping they'll remain attached overnight. I do one last recce of the house and check that each of the sensors is synched to the band I wear, tiny green lights on the surface of the sensors matching the heartbeat of the thing that pulses against my wrist.

I prop myself in a corner behind the door in an upstairs room, my knife at hand. It's as I'm sitting there in the twilight, mulling over the events of the day, when I see it. Strands of red and green tinsel are clinging to my filthy cargo trousers, sparkling pieces of foil glittering in the fading light. It seemed remarkably cruel, yet novel, for the Drummers to present Solomon as such a festive trophy. I was sure it was December, but was it nearly Christmas? Had Christmas come and gone? Such traditions seemed frivolous now, a thing confined to history.

No, not ancient history – just a single year.

One single Christmas ago, the day when all the noises stopped. How terrifying it must have been in those initial few hours when the true horror dawned – when individuals who'd found themselves suddenly deaf realised that everybody else had been similarly affected.

You know that expression, "In the kingdom of the blind, the one-eyed man is king?". Until that day, I'd never really contemplated its full meaning. I, however, had an advantage over all of those affected on that fateful day.

I was born deaf. I'd never known anything else. As society struggled, I was forced to lead, to teach.

Life staggered on, as normal as it could. The phenomenon was worldwide, and whereas science discovered a cause, it couldn't discover a *reason*. They nicknamed it *Shrike*, and it was a condition affecting the eardrums of every hearing human on the planet.

At that stage, it looked like society might adapt - but then things got much worse. Some of those affected, in increasing numbers, began to report their hearing returning. Some optimistically began to believe that all would similarly recover, but then those supposed lucky few began to hear other sounds – the sound of distant rhythmic drumming.

The drumming sound grew louder with each passing hour, ceaseless and maddening. Even in sleep, the rhythmic beats persisted, and those affected quickly went insane.

Drummers, the press called them. Angry, violent, and slowly becoming the majority. Physical signs became to mark them out – the infection that affected the eardrum became visible, tumours and lesions forming around the ear canal. Drummers would also jerk violently like yanked marionettes, each spasm accompanying the staccato rhythm that only they could hear inside their minds.

Society collapsed in weeks. Outnumbered by an enemy that they couldn't hear, mankind hid. The Powers That Be vanished from the scene, either seemingly all killed or cowering underground like rats.

• •

In my dreams, I feel the beat of the drums. In my subconscious though, I know I'm safe – for the time being. My restless mind is just interpreting the rhythmic pulse of the Pigeon band on my wrist.

The pigeon band is a bit of jury-rigged, commonplace technology – it hears *for* you. Noises – dependent on the volume and duration - register as anything from vibrations of varying strengths to small electric shocks through the band. The sensors I've dotted around are merely remote extensions of the same technology, relaying noises back to the receiver.

Simple, easy and cheap to manufacture, and critical to survival. Having been deaf for all my life, nearly forty years has seen my other senses improve to compensate and I'm trying not to rely on the band – but it's very easy to slip into habit.

12 Drummers Drumming

A sharp jolt wakes me from my half-sleep, letting me know that one of the sensors against a window has been triggered. I've trained myself enough that I'm wide awake in seconds, my hand around the hilt of the knife I've already grabbed by instinct.

The Drummers tend to have a tell-tale smell, the reek of the infection lingering in the air around them – the acrid aroma of decay. There's none of that, only the faint trace of Sulphur in the air, which in my experience, is typically associated with guns and cheap ammunition.

The door to my room slowly opens and I stay put in my corner, watching the long-barrel silencer tip of a handgun emerge into the room. A survivor then, but I'm just as likely to meet my end from a panicked shot if I startle them. For a moment, it looks as though the weapon's wielder isn't going to approach any further, but then they suddenly step inside, gun trained on the room's empty far corner.

I put my hands in the air just as the intruder trains their gun upon me. Even though my actions confirm I'm not a Drummer, they're not stupid enough to relax quite yet – there are plenty of survivors out there in the wildlands between settlements who are only looking out for themselves. You can't trust *anybody*.

I know the drill – I'm not stupid enough to think I stand a chance against a loaded pistol. The knife falls from my grip and I feel the thud as it lands on the wooden floor beside me. With a push, I slide the knife across the floor where it lands against their thick leather boot. Without taking their eyes off me, the intruder crouches down and picks it up. They've done this before – the pistol remains trained on my body, not on my head. It presents a larger target and one that they'll have plenty of opportunity to shoot should I lunge at them. Chest or belly, even a glancing blow, I'm as good as dead out here without medical aid.

They point up with fingerless gloved hands, clearly indicating for me to stand. In the dim light, they're nothing more than a silhouette, and I think they're deliberately exaggerating their signing so I can see it in the darkness.

David Court

Alright, I nod and sign back with two thumbs up, sliding my back up against the wall.

Who are you? The pistol is slightly lowered now, but not enough that I dare make a move.

I fingerspell *Melody*, deliberately taking my time.

Paxton, they sign back. I have no idea whether that's a surname, or a boy or girl's forename. From the physique and build, I'm pretty sure it's a man I'm dealing with. It's followed by more signing, still slow and deliberate. I'm now concluding that their hesitance is due to their relative inexperience with signing and not that they're being slow on my account. I've taught enough signing (It's an invaluable skill now, and we're highly revered) to know a person's skill with it.

Why are you here?

I match their speed in my reply. I don't want to either confuse or intimidate them.

It got dark. Sheltering.

Where are you from?

Birmingham.

There's a slump in the silhouette's shoulders as they relax slightly. The lowering of tension in the room is almost palpable, and the gun lowers slightly as they step forward. He's a white male, well-built with a crude crewcut which it looks like he cut it himself. He's more boy than man though, another teen hurriedly recruited into a desperate army. I've been around enough military to recognise the type. He begins signing a reply, but a sudden jolt of electricity surges through my wrist.

I interrupt him and hurriedly sign directly in front of his face. *Alone?*

He nods, a confused expression forming across his rugged face. I point to the plastic band on my wrist and he seems to understand. They're a universal piece of kit these days, instantly recognisable. Far too trusting, he moves alongside me, both of us hiding in the shadows behind the door.

12 Drummers Drumming

If I *were* a scavenger, this'd be the point where I slid the blade into one of his vital organs, having faked the whole pigeon alarm thing. Luckily for him, I'm not.

This time, I can smell the Drummer. It's a smell that's drawing nearer, like something from Satan's own arse-crack. A foulness that reeks of long decaying meat, cloying at the back of my throat and causing us both to dry heave. I can feel the gentle vibrations in the walls as it thuds into them as it haphazardly stumbles across the landing.

Truth is, we don't know how they hunt. Some of them are plain stupid, barely capable of registering something right in front of their face. Others seem to have an unerring habit of tracking their victims. The terrifying thing is that there's no pattern.

The Drummer stumbles into our room and towards the broken window across from the door, a shaft of dull moonlight reflecting across his warped features. This one is pretty far gone, his ears reduced to tiny sphincter-like holes amongst a mass of blistered tissue on each side of his ravaged face. We haven't been spotted. *Yet*.

Shoot, I sign, agitated. Paxton brushes me away, brow furrowed. I sign it again, my gestures more exaggerated this time, registering my annoyance. Before I can insist for a third time, he's taken his own blade out and is creeping up behind the Drummer.

The Drummer's standing perfectly still, staring captivated at a perfect full moon that hangs outside the window. His head is swaying gently left to right, as though he's hypnotised by the sight of the fluorescent lunar orb. The light of the moon glints against Paxton's wicked-looking blade.

The Drummer, suddenly roused to our presence, spins around. A flailing arm catches Paxton, who's caught unawares and sent staggering back against the wall. The blade bounces noiselessly off the floor and lands by the filthy rat-holed skirting board beneath the window. The Drummer's beady black eyes look from Paxton to me, and then back to Paxton again.

David Court

The Drummer's thrown himself at the poor soldier before he can lunge for his blade. He's straddling the boy, raining blows down upon him. Holding my knife, I run over to them and yank back on the hood of the Drummer's jacket. I'm hoping to pull his head back so I can slide the blade into his throat, but he takes me by surprise when, rather than stumble back, he gets to his feet and arms raised, turns to face me.

He lunges at me and I'm sent floundering backwards, insufficient distance between us for me to get a decent stab in. He stops in the centre of the room just as an unsteady Paxton is getting back up to his feet, his eyes darting between the two of us as he considers which will be the easier target.

Shoot! I gesture.

The Drummer, to my astonishment, looks back towards the blade and, rather than take either of us on unarmed, staggers towards the window. I've never seen this level of reasoning exhibited from one quite so infected.

I'm not going to let him surprise me again by demonstrating the level of sense required to pick up the blade and stab one or both of us, and I lunge at him. The window frame is a muddle of wooden splinters with no glass, and my plan is to push him out of it and break the creature's neck or back with the fall.

This day is ending up full of surprises.

The Drummer grabs at me and my momentum carries us both out of the window. A grab at the window frame comes too late, and I close my eyes tightly shut as we plummet towards the hard earth and concrete outside.

I open my eyes to find myself lying on the wheezing and trembling body of the Drummer, who ended up cushioning my fall. I clamber up to my feet and it doesn't make any attempt to do the same.

I think I've broken it.

Paxton appears in the doorway, a little bruised and bloodied from the brief skirmish – and perhaps just a little humbled – but

12 Drummers Drumming

okay. I slide the tip of the blade in through the back of the things neck, and it falls still.

Why didn't you just shoot him? I sign.

I ran out of ammo back at Croydon, he replies, sheepishly.

Luckily, our relieved laughter doesn't disturb any Drummers hiding in the dark.

• •

We take it in turns to watch over the other, each of us getting some well-needed sleep. There's already enough trust between the two of us for that – formal introductions can wait until the next day.

My dreams are mostly abstract, fleeting images of Solomon, both alive and dead. In a few snapshots of our overlapping lives he's happy – in the majority, though, he's frustrated, anxious to move on from the temporary shelter we've found ourselves in. *The mission*, he keeps signing as a reminder, *the mission*. I can see his hands focus on the words, each in crystal clear definition – the whorls on his fingers, the pores on his skin, the callouses on his knuckles.

The sun was partly risen when Paxton wakes me. *I gave you an extra hour,* he signs, *you looked peaceful.* On his turn, the boy sleeps like a corpse, arms and legs perfectly straight, his chest barely moving.

• •

We eat a meagre breakfast, sharing elements of each other's for variety; A sachet of Apple & Cinnamon muesli from his day rations, a few oatmeal biscuits from my rucksack. Some bottled water added to his powdered chocolate milkshake is drinkable if not particularly pleasant, and we eat and drink in silence. In a manner of speaking.

I do the necessary step of breaking the ice.

Why are you alone?

David Court

Separated from my squadron.

What happened to them?

He pauses. I don't know if he's hesitating because he's struggling to remember the appropriate signing, or whether he's reluctant to tell me.

Don't know.

Where are you going now? I ask, secretly hoping he's going my way. I'd expected to have caught up with Solomon at this stage and to be travelling with him, but... best laid plans. It's always better to travel in numbers – the increased risk of being discovered is easily outweighed by the advantages of greater manpower. The ability to have a good night's sleep, for one.

Catterick Garrison, he fingerspells. That's good – I'm heading up to the Pennines, and with a minor detour, that's on the way. I sign as such, and he smiles. It looks like I have a travelling companion. One that won't be quite as good at philosophical discussions as poor Solomon, but he'll do.

• • • • • • • • • • • • • • • • • • • •

My motives for delivering the boy to his Garrison are not entirely philanthropic. I know that a few of my colleagues – before we lost contact - were due to establish a research base somewhere in North Yorkshire to research the *Shrike*, and it's entirely possible that they've set up there.

The boy and I travel off-road, keeping away from the towns and cities. The Drummers tend not to roam far, so population centres are best to be avoided. The ones in the wilds tend to congregate in smaller numbers, so present less of a threat.

There's a stroke of luck on the second day when we come across a delivery van at the edge of a farmer's field. Looks like the driver, of whom there is no sign, tried to take the vehicle off-road and quickly found that it wasn't designed for rough terrain. It's from a local snack manufacturer – Boarwell's – and the back of the van is laden with hundreds of bags of Pork Scratchings

12 Drummers Drumming

and Pork Crunch. We cheerfully grab all that our rucksack and backpacks will allow.

At times, Paxton seems a million miles away. He'll communicate, but only when prompted. It takes the best part of a day to find out that he was recruited with very little training and left out of his depth with an equally unskilled squadron. Oddly, not once does the boy ask me why I'm travelling to the Pennines. Either he's afraid to ask, or he simply doesn't care. Nor does he seem to want to talk about the circumstances in which he ended up alone. I don't press him.

• •

Even from our distant vantage point on a nearby hilltop, it's clear that Catterick has been abandoned. I go to comfort Paxton but think better of it when it's clear that he looks unaffected, as though he'd prepared himself for exactly this outcome. The vehicles from the motor pool have all gone, the deep tracks of tanks and armoured cars snaking randomly across the fields surrounding the base.

The outside of the base is, luckily, deserted. He follows me down towards the gates like a lost puppy, without aim. The first thing that strikes me as I walk between the huge metal doors and stare into the courtyard is that there are no bodies. I've seen bases fall in Molesworth, Invicta, Camberwell - and this isn't like any of those.

Looks like everybody just upped and left.

With the boy following silently, I walk through a succession of abandoned rooms. Nothing has been taken, and nothing is in disarray. The offices and some of the barracks are even decorated for Christmas, brightly coloured tinsel and garlands garishly dangling from plain coloured walls.

The boy's mood doesn't even improve when we come across the fully laden armoury, it's inventory barely touched. Without emotion, he selects a L85A2 Assault Rifle and bundles enough ammunition to start a small war into his rucksack. I'm not keen on guns but, not wishing to look a gift horse in the mouth, pick up a Glock 17 pistol and ammunition.

It's when we're scouring through the few remaining rooms in the base – confident enough to do so alone now – that he comes bounding into the locker room I'm exploring, looking more enthused than he has since we first arrived.

I've found something, he signs, hurriedly. Without pause, he's off.

He's standing outside the door to a room when I reach the corridor, gesturing at the contents.

I saw from the markings on your backpack that you're a scientist, he signs, *and this looks like it'll interest you.*

I'd forgotten the Science Division logo and serial number on my backpack. Goes some way to explaining why he didn't ask who *I* was. Perhaps he's sharper than I suspected.

The room looks like it was a library before it was made into a makeshift lab. Bookcases and their contents – books spanning the decades – have all been pushed into one corner to make room. Understandably, literature wasn't on the priority list after the apocalypse.

Two improvised workbenches hold a variety of pieces of equipment; A centrifuge, a bulky ruggedized laptop, and two portable refrigerator units are still powered up, the emergency generator of the base still providing enough juice to keep them going.

It's then I spy the cup perched on the edge of one of the tables, fractal growths of mould emerging from within to creep over the vessel's lip. I recognise it as a retirement present we'd got for Alice, the boss of our lab. We'd had it custom printed especially for her, finding it difficult to find any matching the unique theme we were going for. It was plain white, bearing the legend "*Environmental toxicologists do it quietly*". She'd planned to retire at the end of the year, but the *Shrike* had put paid to that.

12 Drummers Drumming

So, we'd missed each other. The old department password still works on her laptop though, so I can at least try to find out what she'd been working on – what had happened to her.

Alice never was the most organized in our department, and her desktop is filled with a variety of folders and documents of countless formats. This would take some time.

Paxton is hanging around in the room like a bad smell, peering at everything I can see.

I grab his attention.

Shall we stay here until tomorrow? I ask. *There are a lot of notes to go through.*

He shrugs, non-committal.

Is it okay If I have a look around? he asks, as though he needs permission. I nod and he slopes off.

• • • • • • • • • • • • • • • • • • • •

It's a dull and laborious job, but by trawling through file dates, I manage to piece together a chronology of her notes. It looks like our studies into the *Shrike* overlapped for a while but then – apparently at the behest of the military staff gracious and patient enough to house Alice and her team – they began to concentrate on finding a cure.

Despite her lackadaisical approach to computer housekeeping, Alice was a stickler for laboratory guidelines. It's clear from the timings that her and her team rushed or were pressured into getting results, clinical standards loosened or, in some cases, bypassed completely. Despite the first cure prototype not working on the Drummer they'd captured, they continued with human trials regardless.

Alice and her team, reluctantly, at first, followed by a handful of soldiers ordered to do so. And then everybody.

And what's more, it appeared to work. Damaged eardrums began to heal, and the experiment was deemed a complete success. I stared at the words at the footing of the last of her notes, the black-on-white words burning into my retina.

David Court

"To hear words again. To be able to speak, to communicate as we always did. It has taken a year of work, but we may finally see the end of this nightmare."

I walk over to one of the refrigerator units, staring through the frosted glass at the dull blue illumination within. A blast of icy air hits me as I lift the lid and look at the contents – a frosted metal housing, mostly empty except for a few unused glass vials.

I hold one up to the light, peering at the cold gel-like transparent fluid within. So, this innocuous looking liquid suspension is the cure. From her notes, it's clear that it would be wasted on me – my eardrums had died long before the *Shrike*, and I'm somewhat reluctant to take her at her word regarding its success with others.

Knowing what I know, it's best disregarded for now. My own research takes precedence. I take one last longing look at it before replacing it in the refrigerator.

I don't think I'd gotten more than an hour into catching up on my own research studies before I'd fallen asleep at the laptop, slumped back, snoring and drooling in my chair. I had no idea what time it was, other than darkness had begun creeping over as I'd been looking through Alice's notes, and my sleep was fitful and shallow.

I was woken by an agitated Paxton who, the very instant my eyes open, leaned in and silenced me with a *shush* gesture. The obvious panic in my expression meant I didn't need to sign my concern before he gave me a response.

I don't think we're alone, he signed, stumbling over the words in his urgency.

The room was in darkness, the only light coming from the dull humming luminescence of the open refrigerator and that which streamed in from the lit corridor. I got to my feet as he trained the rifle around the room, darting the weapon's barrel from shadow to shadow. There was sweat on the boy's brow and he looked more panicked than I'd ever seen him.

12 Drummers Drumming

I fumbled around for my own pistol before remembering I'd stupidly put it in my backpack which was hanging over the back of the room's door. I made to walk towards it but Paxton's hand on my shoulder stopped me in my tracks.

His mouth was moving, as though he were muttering away to himself with reassuring phrases.

What did you see? I sign, my eyes nervously darting between Paxton and the door.

He mouths the words as he signs them.

I can hear them in the base.

I sign the next word very carefully, right in front of his wide staring eyes.

Hear?

I know I'd closed the refrigerator. I look over to it, and there's an injection gun lying next to it, an empty vial attached. On my laptop, Alice's notes about her final successes at the base fills the screen.

You used the cure, I sign, panicked.

I need to hear, he replies, *so I can protect us both.*

He doesn't try to stop me again as I slowly walk towards the door.

What can you hear? I sign, but I already know the answer.

His hands are on his temples, the veins on his head threatening to push out through his skin. His eyes are wild, staring. He doesn't sign the response, but mouths it. It's enough.

They're DRUMMING.

He's pointing the gun at imaginary foes now, ones that lurk in the darkened corners of the room. His body jerks erratically at regular intervals, every few seconds or so, like a violent hiccup.

I know from my studies that his spasms match the beats he can hear. For every drumbeat, his body can't help but react – an involuntary mini-seizure for each. My research earlier confirmed my suspicions, that the beats have increased in pace over the last year and will continue to increase in intensity the closer we get to the source.

David Court

The rifle slumps at his side, dangling from its sling, as he tries to sign a sentence to me. He's mouthing the words to himself, his fingers moving randomly in front of him as he struggles with his coordination.

I take advantage of that moment, grabbing my rucksack and running out into the corridor. I don't need to know what he was trying to tell me.

I run blindly, without daring to look back. Without the ability to hear, I have no idea whether he's followed me at all, or whether he's fresh at my heels. The exhilaration, the *fear*, that any moment could be my last. As I ran down dim corridors, I realise I'm in a part of the base I haven't been in yet. I'm beginning to tire and am forced to slow down, but the occasional quick tentative glance behind me shows he's nowhere in sight.

I duck inside an alcove and rest for a few moments, rifling through the contents of my rucksack. It had been open when I'd grabbed it, and I'm sure I felt something fall out of it as I ran from Paxton. Not the pistol, luckily, the weapon's weight keeping it firmly at the bottom of the bag. In fact, everything looks in place.

There's a gentle vibration from my wrist as the pigeon band dutifully informs me of a sound coming from nearby. The pulse is subtle enough to let me know it's distant, but insistent enough to let me know that it's constant.

The problem is, I have no idea whether the noise is coming from one of the unexplored rooms that surrounds me, or from an approaching armed Paxton.

"You should take one of the v3 Pigeon Bands, Doctor Kearney," they'd helpfully suggested, "They give additional feedback now, so you know which direction any sounds are coming from."

"Oh no", I insisted, "I've only got used to the Pigeon Band that I've got. Thanks, but no thanks."

Melody, you Luddite idiot.

12 Drummers Drumming

Still, any room should suffice. The entire complex was spread across a single floor, so I only needed to find a window I could open and then I could make my getaway – Unless, of course, Paxton had lost the remainder of the few marbles he had left and found himself a decent vantage point where he could see all the surrounding grounds whilst armed with his high-powered rifle.

It could end up being one of the shortest getaways of all time.

As I step closer to the closed doorway, the pigeon band vibrates that little bit stronger. Confident that he can't have got to the room before me, I read that as him approaching from behind and step inside, hurriedly closing it behind me.

I realise my mistake as soon as I step in – from all the rooms I could have chosen, I've wound up in what appears to be a shower block. The only daylight comes from glass bricks set just below the ceiling, too high and too small a gap to escape through. There's a foul smell in here as well, something the room's inadequate ventilation has struggled to shift.

I turn to step out, but the pigeon band fires a small jolt of electricity across the nerve-endings in my wrist. That implies the noise is coming from inside – or directly outside – the room. The sensation freezes me on the spot, knowing that Paxton could be *right outside the door*, and I stand there helplessly waiting for my doom.

Then I feel it. A subtle shifting in the air, the slightest of vibrations rippling across my tensed skin. I step further into the room, cautiously peering around the wall of stained blue tiles that hides whatever is in here.

At first it looks like a pile of rubbish, a heap of old tattered clothes that's been left here to rot. But then it suddenly moves, jerking at the same time as the Pigeon band delivers me a painful zap, ripples passing across the bulks surface. A malformed hand extends from the thing, crooked and warped fingers clutching at the tiled floor. Some of the fingers are long and wire-thin, others bloated and stubby. With each pulse on my wrist, a part of it covered by a brown-streaked hood from a coat rises and falls. Whatever it is, it's alive.

David Court

Even as I approach it, an ignored part of me is screaming at me to run away. A morbid fascination sees my hand extend towards it, grabbing the fabric of the hood. The rest of my body is arched away from it and my face contorted into a horrified grimace as I prepare myself.

With a jerk of my wrist, I flick the gathered hood of the material away from me, an act that uncovers the foul thing writhing beneath the filthy cloth. I step back, almost falling against the tiles, and gasp in horror at the thing on the floor.

The cracked and misshapen dome used to be a head, of that much I'm sure. The sides of it still bear the tell-tale signs of *Shrike* infection, cancerous growths clinging like moss around where the ears would have been. The ears and nose have long gone, sealed organically shut and reduced to scarred ridges of muscle and tissue. The mouth is still there though, a gaping and hideous maw enlarged to monstrous proportions, with a purple larvae-like tongue lolling about in the bloodied cavernous recesses. The odd tooth hangs there, yellowing, cracked, and crooked.

With each pulse of the watch, I feel the foetid air burst forth from that foul orifice and polluting the air about me. The slug-like tongue extends to a point, and then relaxes. The pigeon band fires a vicious pinprick into my nervous system with each sustained burst of its ghastly din.

It's a small blessing that I can't hear that noise, the sound of it screaming.

The sight of the thing is so horrific – so out of my sphere of *normality* – that it's almost a relief when Paxton barges into the room. As he unsteadily levels the rifle at me, being threatened the old-fashioned way by a man with a gun almost seems mundane.

He's understandably distracted by the mockery to normality unfolding behind me, and he seems unsure what to focus his attention on. The barrel of the gun hastily moves from me to the thing on the ground.

12 Drummers Drumming

Paxton suddenly staggers back, visibly pained, his eyes bloodshot and wide. He's witnessed the full horror that I'm immune to – he's heard the things scream and he looks shaken. He barges past me, slamming me against the wall, and opens fire on the monstrosity spread-eagled across the floor, unleashing the rifles fully-automatic wrath.

I turn away from the strobing muzzle flash but feel every 45mm shot hit its mark, the vibrations rippling through the floor and walls. I feel the trembling of shattering tiles, of fragmented porcelain shards ricocheting against each other.

Splashes of a dark black ichor spatter against me, and I recoil from its touch and smell. Paxton has his back to me, the gun now lowered. He's breathing heavily, his shoulders raised and lowering exaggeratedly, and the floor is scattered with cracking tiling and black and gold shell casings.

The thing twitches at his feet, the shroud -like fabric covering torn away. It's reduced to so much pulped meat now, a mess of fragmented musculature and burst organs. The ruined mouth stretches and puckers and the remaining fingers on its one hand jerk in time to the spasms of Paxton as he stands there, now otherwise motionless.

Then it happens. With each pulse, with each convulsion from Paxton, the dying thing matches the beat. Like macabre stop-motion photography, bones click into life, stretching, knotting. Ruined skin stretches over vanishing wounds, and the thing begins to rise.

I've reached the door by the time its featureless head is level with the stunned Paxton. It resembles a crudely sculpted flesh marionette, asymmetrical and twisted. The skin of the thing is discoloured and bruised, patches of it stretched gossamer thin over still-healing organs. As the knotted trunk of muscle that it uses for an arm reaches out for Paxton's face, blackened barbed points bloodily piercing through the creatures calloused muscle, the door has opened and I'm stumbling out.

David Court

I feel the boy's scream through the walls. I run, plummeting down corridors and through doors. This time, I don't look back until I'm in the open air and safely away from the base.

•••••••••••••••••••••••

I spend twenty minutes tentatively approaching the gates of The Dives, the perpetually guarded man-made barrier of abandoned vehicles and Jenga-like stacked trailers, before I realise that it's been abandoned. I simply walk into the Pennines, unhindered.

After spending the best part of an hour scouting through the outskirts of the deserted nearby market town of Richmond, I find a building that will do as shelter for the evening. An intact stairwell serves as an adequate mount for a pigeon sensor, and there's a fire-escape that'll allow egress should I be trapped upstairs.

Hidden in the woods, it's remained miraculously un-looted. It was left in a hurry and the occupants sadly weren't the type to keep a full food cupboard, but there's some meagre bounty for the taking. A half decent thermos flask replaces the dented water bottle I've been carrying since Blackburn, and there are enough powdered soups and milkshakes to keep me fed for a fortnight.

A handful of still-wrapped presents sit beneath a threadbare artificial Christmas tree. For some reason, I leave them undisturbed – as though the occupants could return at any time and life would suddenly, like a re-wound clock, return to some semblance of normality.

I spend the evening handwriting copious notes by torchlight, finding myself in the oddest of moods. I'm elated that my half-a-year of research has been validated, but equally terrified by what that *means*.

The popular consensus amongst the scientific community was that the *Shrike* and deafness and the phenomenon of Drummers were inexorably linked, that one led to the other.

12 Drummers Drumming

During a frustrating evening of theorizing and heavy drinking, I'd formulated a counter-opinion – that it was in fact the deafness that had *saved* us, that it was the bodies mechanism of defending itself.

Whatever the beat was – that unstoppable, perpetual rhythm – it *destroyed*. To hear it, was to be doomed. To be deaf, was to be safe.

The original inspiration had come from the oddest sources – in the days and weeks immediately following that fateful Christmas day, the God squad had come out in force. American televangelists, blissfully ignorant to how little money would come to matter, milked the situation for all it was worth.

It was Mankind's own fault, scrolled the teleprompter text, its purveyor smiling through a mouthful of perfect pearlescent teeth set against a dark tan beneath an expensive wig. *For too long, Mankind had ignored the word of God. For only those that are righteous, shall hear His word.*

Perhaps the noise *was* the word of God, she'd joked with Solomon. A voice of condemnation, of chastisement. And to not hear it, was to be spared. Solomon had laughed about it then, only deserting her when he realised the level of her dedication to this theory. They'd fought that night, both their tempers fuelled by some reserves of alcohol they'd found secreted in their bungalow come makeshift laboratory.

He'd accused her of not taking him seriously, of laughing at his arguments. I *couldn't help it*, I'd said, *people signing swear words in anger is an inherently comical sight.*

He'd gone by the time I'd awoken to a God-awful hangover, presumably to head further North to prove me wrong – or to reinforce a more sensible and level-headed science team.

Poor Solomon.

It was the big revelation that he couldn't accept, one that countered every belief he had as a scientist. When you've been deaf all your life, you develop a certain knack for recognizing sounds through vibrations – couple that knack with some expensive monitoring equipment to "listen" to the beats ever-present in the air beyond normal frequencies, and you begin to realise something.

I'd insisted that they weren't simple drumbeats, some ambient percussive white noise.

It felt like *data*. It felt like data coming in bursts, the gaps of which were noticeably lessening over time. From a source that, I suspected, lay somewhere in the North of England.

But what *kind* of data? Certainly nothing that I could interpret – it was far more advanced than any protocol I'd ever encountered.

Was it human-made, an act of bio-terrorism the likes of which the world had never known? Little green men, getting their revenge for us corrupting their adolescents by sending them "Johnny B. Goode" through space on the Voyager Golden record?

The word of God, condemning his creation?

Whatever it was doing, to hear it was to be mutated. It was like a string of code, slowly rewriting genetic information. At the periphery, thus far, they'd only seen a minor impact – eardrums infected, spreading slowly around the head and shoulders, brains blighted.

Here, nearer the epicentre, I'd clearly just witnessed an extreme. It was a theory, but it matched my studies – Let's say you have something well along the road of infection, used to this slow drip-feed of ultrasonic data, suddenly "cured" by Alice and her team. The lucky patient gets to receive the previously filtered data in its their unfettered, raw glory. And what you end up with is the blasphemy from the shower block.

Would this be what happened to us all, in time?

• • • • • • • • • • • • • • • • • • • •

In my dreams, I'm visited by Paxton's ghost. He's a twisted corpse, limbs held together by the flimsiest of gristle and sinew, but we somehow manage to avoid discussing that awkward

12 Drummers Drumming

topic. As we open the presents beneath the tree, eagerly ripping red and golden paper away from board games, jumpers, and toiletries, he feels compelled to confess something to me. *I wasn't entirely honest about being separated from my squadron*, he signs – even in dreams, I remain resolutely deaf – *but I ran from them panicked when they were attacked by Drummers.*

I'm fully aware I'm dreaming, and my subconscious had obviously pieced that together from our brief interactions. I'm about to tell him that it's okay when he runs to the window, staring out through it.

Can you hear that? he signs, his words carefully chosen.
I can, I reply. Because I can.

• •

My eyes are barely even open by the time I'm awake and dragging pieces of equipment from my bag to confirm what I'm experiencing. I can feel it in the air; a paradigm shift, as though something incredible has happened - another chapter begun.

Three separate checks confirm my fears. It's either an incredible coincidence, or fate has chosen some particularly apt timing. It's Christmas morning, exactly one year since the beat started, and the graphs confirm that it's now a solid single noise, a stream of digital Morse code. The military tattoo has become a drum-roll.

So, to honour him, pa rum pum pun pum. When we come. Merry Christmas.

• •

Cross Fell, they call it. The highest mountain in the Pennine Hills, all eight hundred and ninety metres of it. It had eluded me for so long, but now it takes just some cursory triangulation to get the source, almost as though it doesn't feel the need to hide from me anymore. By now, it's practically shouting where it is.

David Court

Is it broadcasting to the world? Or are there more sites like this, dotted around the globe? And are they all, like this one, screaming?

The landscape leading up the ridge is a graveyard of abandoned vehicles. Smart cars, sports cars, family saloons, and larger vehicles like buses and coaches are the first casualties, stranded in ditches, sprawled across rocks, or stranded on terrain too steep to climb. As I draw closer, I pass hardier transport – jeeps, Land Rovers, 4 x 4's – they've all met their match on this barren wilderness. Lastly, at points where even I struggle to navigate, the final resting place of the last of the metal behemoths: armoured cars, military jeeps, and even a tank.

I see and keep my distance from the occasional Drummer, but they seem unconcerned by – and even oblivious to - my presence, or even the company of other infected around them. They're staring at that distant peak, relentlessly placing one foot in front of the other, one foot in front of the other, one foot in front of the other.

For the most part, they seem physically unaffected by the drums. From the dozen or so I see, only one is abnormally shaped, dragging a huge arm the length and thickness of an elephant's trunk behind it on its trek up to the summit. Their muscles jerk rhythmically in unison, spasming like poorly animated videogame characters.

A dense hill fog is settling over the grey earth, soaking me to the skin. I'm ill-prepared for this trek but something compels me to keep walking. Not the same thing that compels the Drummers, but we are admittedly equally driven.

As the afternoon turns into early evening, visibility becomes poorer. The mist thickens, whorls of languid grey vapour hugging the earth. Whilst distracted, I almost collide with a Drummer – with panicked breaths and cursing my stupidity, I rest and let it vanish into the murky haze ahead.

12 Drummers Drumming

I can feel vibrations in the earth beneath my feet, tiny seismic shifts from an ever-present humming, like the operations of some vast, foul, stygian machinery. I place both my palms on the damp earth and feel it undulate beneath me. I try to concentrate on it, and not on the clicking spidery thing that clatters past me into the void.

In ancient times, this region was known as Fiend's Fell and was believed to be the haunt of evil spirits. It now feels that Saint Augustine's blessings have long since faded.

It's as the dense smog clears that I realise I'm just part of a crowd. Now dozens of Drummers walk alongside me up the steep grass and stone embankment, all focused on the path ahead. Some falter and stumble, dashing themselves on the sharpened gravel, but their kin simply step on or over them in ignorance to their plight.

I pass two who must have toppled from much higher, a male and female lying intertwined, limbs at obscene angles and skulls part-caved in like eggshells. They twitch in desperation, strangers locked together until they rot, stranded on this remote hillside.

Jack fell down and broke his crown, and Jill came tumbling after.

The mutations are stronger now, more pronounced. Perhaps they're metamorphizing *en route* now, deforming and shifting with each leg of the journey. Some are crawling on all fours like apes, some dragging themselves along with hook like appendages, some scurrying on fresh barbed limbs.

There's a certain beauty to it, a uniqueness to every one of them. Simple symmetrical human shapes contorted to bizarre flesh sculptures, none the same. Like evolution, some have failed and are left abandoned – others flourish, hurrying to the snow-streaked peak.

There is no fear now, as I walk amongst them. They have a greater purpose now than confronting or ending me, and I'm disregarded in their new priorities. I look around myself, down

David Court

the peak, at the crowds that follow in my wake. Hordes of them, gathering in numbers, all with one singular purpose.

And then, in front of me, a wall of them. The crowd is mostly halted, bottlenecked by something ahead. Too late, I realise that the momentum of those behind me will sweep me into the amassed crowds, and I look about myself in a panic. They have, as of yet, remained oblivious to my presence – I don't know if that will remain the case should I come into contact with them though.

Their numbers are too great, and I struggle to find a gap to make my way to safety. The crowds behind me push against me, and I'm forced into the misshapen throng. My shoulder barges into one of the Drummers in front of me, and it briefly turns to face me.

It's a ghastly, tilted thing of skinless musculature, with only one small, single remaining patch of flesh set atop its red and glistening head – a single green eye that stares through me before glinting and blinking. I grimace and retreat, shuddering in grim recognition.

No, it can't be Paxton.

The crowd heaves, rippling like a disturbed pond, and I'm carried forward. Spider legs with tiny furred paws brush against my shoulders, and I recoil away. I'm pushed into a wall of flesh-mounted eyes atop stunted limbs barely capable of carrying the things weight, and they glare at me, accusingly.

I hear my laughter echoing inside my skull, the last vestiges of panicked sanity pouring from me like so much sweat. I can see a hole in the cliffside, a twisted rock scar, and realise the hordes ahead of me are in single file, slowly marching in.

I'm reminded of the legends of the children of Hamelin, pulled into the underworld by the rhythmic beats of the Pied Piper.

It's like a precise military march; feet, claws, and pincers moving in perfect synchronization. *One step, two step, one step, two step, one step, two step.*

12 Drummers Drumming

Staggering out into the open, my stumbling legs break the beat.

They all stop. One by one, as though instructed to do so by the conductor of an orchestra, they turn to face me. A Mexican wave of misshapen faces – and things that once *were* faces. An array of eyes, antennae, proboscises turn their focus away from the cliff and to me.

There's nowhere to run, and they're upon me. There is no urgency – there's nowhere for me to run to, and they uniformly seem aware of that. They merely slowly advance and reach out for me. I'm briefly carried above their heads on a carpet of limbs of all textures, sizes, and shapes, and being slowly carried towards the jagged wound in the cliff.

I'm lowered down, exalted now at the lead of the queue. The crowds gather behind me, paused. They don't push against me – it feels like I have all the time in the world, but the wall of mangled and reworked flesh makes it obvious that I won't be leaving the way I came in.

The rhythm is more obvious here, thudding a snare drum heartbeat against the cave walls. I can feel the pulses travelling up through my feet and across my exhausted form. I'm struggling to formulate complete thoughts as even my teeth chatter from the dull yet insistent tempo.

It's coming from beneath me, that much is apparent now. It's like there's a drummer at the heart of the world, providing a percussive accompaniment to the end of times. A clarion call from the Earth itself.

I look ahead of me, a luminescent pool laps lazily against the rock at my feet. It fills the cave with a rare humidity, and sections of it bubble and steam as though it's oozing out from the planet's core. It's thick and gelatinous, and feels ancient – primordial, even. Like the chemical-laden soup from where we all sprung, here again at the end.

One of the Drummers is in front of me, staring down at the lapping waters that gather around his cloven ankles. His skin is coated with a vibrant sheen of reflective scales, the light emanating from below him glinting off the surface, refracting as he steps deeper in.

He seems to stumble, falling to one side. At first, I think he's lost his balance but then it becomes clear as I see the effect on the rest of him. He's being absorbed into it, dissolving painlessly into the primal broth. Flesh slides from his form, congealing about him. He remains calm, unmoved. The thick lumps and islands of detritus that drift lazily across the surface of the gelatinous pool are *biological matter*.

It's then, at the end, that my resolve leaves me, and I turn to run. The Drummers move as one, flooding into the cave as an impenetrable wall.

There is no pain. The same cruelly curved barbs that take my eyes act with an almost surgical precision, cauterizing damaged flesh. The ravages that surge across the geography of my twitching form are quick and total, slowly overwhelming my senses.

There is no pain. No sense at all, as I simply continue, blind, deaf, and without touch.

I feel the warmth of the fluid against my dying nerves, the last vestige of my senses telling me that they're lowering me into the pool. The warmth claims not only my form, but also my soul. That mankind should briefly burst out into a myriad of complex, beautiful and horrific forms at the very end before settling into this fate, this parliament of total harmony.

I hear their voices, and I feel their heartbeats. One rhythm shared by all, and then the most extraordinary sense of relief. They – we - have but one shared thought.

If I had words, I would tell of it.

● ● ● ● ● ● ● ● ● ● ● ● ● ● ● ● ● ● ● ●

"12 Drummers Drumming" was first published in "12 Days of Christmas", the second volume of the Christmas themed horror anthology from Burdizzo Books.

To Mnemosyne, a Daughter

AT NIGHT, the house breathed. Maxime had been lying there for a few hours now, listening to it. As the night had drawn in and the temperature had dropped, the blackened wooden beams that spanned the ceilings of the old house had begun quietly creaking and shifting. Almost as an accompaniment, air was filtering through windows left ajar and holes in the ancient brickwork. As it passed through the building, curtains fluttered in its wake. In Maxime's half-awake torpor, the faint whispering sounded like the sigh of a lover.

If you listened especially hard, past the ambient noises of the Château itself, you could hear the gentle rippling of the nearby Dordogne River. Maxime had spent much of the previous day sitting on its banks, enjoying the sights and sounds and yet failing to put a single word to paper.

Eventually lulled into a gentle sleep, Maxime dreamt that he was wandering the empty rooms and corridors of the Château de Amorette. Despite a cursory resemblance though, the Château in his dreams possessed a bizarre geometry. Doors that didn't – that *couldn't* – exist in the real one opened before him, and overly long corridors separated rooms that Maxime recognised as being directly adjacent to one another. A circuitous route that should have led him back to where he started from instead found him heading deeper into the heart of the old building. As with his dream the night before, he found himself in front of a single unmarked door. He pressed his face against the cool wood, the gentle sound of rhythmic breathing coming from behind it. Again, as with the night before, he awoke the moment that his hand touched the ice-cold of the door's metal handle.

Maxime held the packet of cigarettes in his hand, turning the box over and over like a magician preparing to perform a trick. He contemplated the boxes weight, thinking of each of the little, nicotine-laden, cancerous cylinders nestled within.

He hadn't smoked in nearly six years – a fact that, given his usual lack of self-control, he was proud of – and had no idea what had compelled him to buy them at the nearby village. He hadn't even remembered asking for them, but there they were when he emptied the shopping bag, innocently sitting next to the bread, wine, cheese, and milk.

What would one hurt? It might even help him relax; anything to put a halt to this hideous writer's block. Every time he stared at that first blank page on his laptop, it seemed to grow before his eyes – a terrifying vacant vista. Glacial, vast, *impenetrable*.

Like the possibly apocryphal nuclear launch sequence that involved two people of suitable authority turning two special keys at the same time, there were numerous barriers that lay between Maxime and the act of smoking a cigarette. First, the cellophane shroud that surrounded the packet would need to be peeled away. Secondly, the lid of the packet lifted before the layer of silver foil between him and his prize could be ripped away. The cigarette would need to be removed from the packet, lit, and then placed into his mouth and inhaled. It was a multi-stage ritual, one that Maxime's hardy willpower could easily abandon at any time.

To Mnemosyne, a Daughter

Three sentences. One hundred and fifteen words. The result of five hours sitting at the laptop. He'd deleted four times as many words as he'd ended up with.

With a complete lack of conscious effort, the cigarette was already lit and in his hands. Maxime closed his eyes and took a deep drag from it, savouring the flavour. The nicotine rush was almost overwhelming, a hazy light-headedness filling his senses. If he'd been standing, it would have knocked him off his feet. The ringing in his ears was an unfamiliar feeling though, and a not altogether pleasant one.

It took a good few moments until Maxime realised the ringing was coming from somewhere in the house, and wasn't an after-effect of the cigarette. He leapt to his feet – rather too quickly, as it happened, and he swayed unsteadily for a few seconds like a drunkard. He followed the sound – now identifiable as the ringing of an old telephone – to one of the small rooms adjacent to the kitchen. The phone sat next to a notepad on a cloth draped over a small circular table. It was old, all sharp Art Deco angles of dull black Bakelite, and dotted with dust.

He answered it, lifting the earpiece towards him.

"Maxime?"

The signal was weak, the voice on the other end of the line sounding like somebody trying to speak underwater, but even through the distortion, he recognised it.

"Murray!" replied Maxime, trying – and mostly succeeding – in appearing enthusiastic. Truth be told, he'd picked this location because he didn't think it even *had* a phone. That's what the letting agent had confidently informed him.

Murray Whale had been Maxime's publishing agent for the best part of a decade now. He'd been good to Murray, but the guy was an acquired taste. Many writers simply couldn't get on with him. He had that horrible habit that some Brits had of never actually getting to the point. What did they call it? "Beating around the bush."

David Court

"How's it going, my Number One writer?"

Even against the bed of white noise, Maxime could make out the nervousness in Murray's voice. What he *wanted* to ask is how much of the new book had Maxime written. To give him a word count he could placate the publishers with. Anything to prove to them that their golden goose was still capable of producing the magic when it was needed, even if this new book was now several years overdue.

"It'll come, Murray. I just need a couple of days away from everything."

"That's what you said the last time the publisher sent you on an all-expenses holiday, Maxime. I think they're running out of patience."

"I've said I'll get it written, and I will."

"Look - I'll just come out with it, Maxime."

That'll make a change, he thought. It was never good news whenever Murray got to the point. His agent stuttered before continuing.

"You're not going to like this, but they've insisted."

"The publishers? What have they done, Murray?"

"They're concerned you're getting distracted. That you'll do anything rather than just sit down and write the bloody thing."

"For somebody getting to the point, Murray, you're doing a bloody remarkable job of skirting around it."

"If you just let me finish... They're sending you an assistant. Somebody who'll do your shopping, cooking, cleaning, stuff like that. So, you can get on with what they're paying you for."

"I don't need a bloody PA, Murray. I'm forty-three years old and more than capable of wiping my own arse, thank you very much."

"Maxime, Maxime... let's just see how it goes. They didn't give me any choice."

Great. First, the phone-less house turns out to have a bloody phone after all, and now there'd be a bloody butler wandering around and distracting him.

To Mnemosyne, a Daughter

"Ok. How long have I got before my solitude gets interrupted?"

"They've flown her out this morning. She should be with you this evening."

No, not a butler. A nanny. *Merde*.

Maxime was half an hour into tidying up the few rooms he'd occupied in the Château when he realised the insanity of what he was doing. That was going to be Mrs. Doubtfire's job.

Maxime had often joked that he could be an expert in procrastination if he put his mind to it, but that wasn't far from the truth. For the past couple of days, he'd literally done everything he could do in the house to occupy himself other than do exactly what he was here for. The already beautiful gardens now looked even better, condiments and herbs had been alphabetically arranged in the well-stocked pantry, and he'd never smelled more fragrant or been more clean-shaven. He'd just stopped himself before arranging his stationery into chronological order of purchase.

It wasn't writer's block. Oh, he'd had his fair share of that to recognise that hazard of the trade rearing its ugly little head. This was down to *apathy*. He'd written the first book of the *Nightghast* trilogy – *The Nightghast Awakens* – back when he was a no-name, desperately scrabbling to get his stories published in any anthology that would have him. It was a cliché, but it had almost written itself. Truth be told, he'd been holding - and rewriting – the story in his head for the best part of the previous decade, so it was *easy*.

It did well. Maxime had never intended it as such – clearly his tastes in horror were tamer than most – but a publisher picked it up for their Young Adult market. His sassy heroine Lady Carina Delafont was a hit amongst teenage girls, and Maxime enjoyed his new-found popularity. They gave him an advance for the second book in the series, and that had been a success too.

The gestation of the second book – *The Maudlin Undead* - wasn't *quite* as simple as its prequel – Maxime had to admit that he'd begun to run out of ideas by the last third of that weighty tome– but it, again, did well.

Film companies starting bidding for the rights, and the names of actors and actresses that Maxime had *heard* of started appearing in various conversations.

And then the publisher had requested – nay, *demanded* – that Maxime finish the trilogy.

Truth be told, that's when the difficulties started. Despite the plot having lingered in the dim recesses of Maxime's consciousness for so long, there was very little left of it. The story of Carina had been told in the first two books, and he struggled to think of where to take her story next.

Still struggled. Damn him for throwing the word trilogy into the mix in the first place. Who determined that series of books nearly always come in threes?

And it wasn't just that, either. Despite large sums of money at stake, the enthusiasm just wasn't there. Writing for fun and to entertain himself was one thing, writing to order was quite another.

And it took less than a year for the publisher to go from, *"There's no rush. You can't hurry genius, right?"* all the way to, *"We've invested a lot of money into this property, and we're getting a little frustrated at your failure to give us anything"*. They were probably one piece of bad news away from, *"Maxime, we've thought about getting a ghost writer in."*

Property. That's what it was now. A franchise. Something to pin posters, T-shirts, spin off graphic-novel adaptations, novelty scented candles, bobble-headed plastic figures, and fan fiction from. It all felt out of his control and, as such, his heart wasn't in it.

To Mnemosyne, a Daughter

He was making his *own* rules with the first two books, but the third already had firmly established parameters set by the publishing company. The worst of these was that he wasn't allowed to kill off Carina, as they'd sold the videogame rights for stories that'd take place *after* the trilogy. The plot of the third was always just a series of vague ideas, but Maxime knew the series was always supposed to end with Lady Carina's noble sacrifice.

Still, at least the place was tidy and would stay that way. He picked up a clean glass and a fresh bottle of Sauvignon Blanc and strode purposefully towards the laptop, in much the same stoic, yet futile, manner that a soldier might march towards the front line.

The empty white screen was his battlefield. This was his moment. Time to go to war.

Maxime had no idea how much time had passed when the doorbell rang. Even though the skies outside the château had darkened, the brilliant rectangle of white on the laptop screen stared back at him defiantly. White, one should never forget, was also the colour of *surrender*. The doorbell buzzed again, the fading battery giving it the drawn-out timbre of a giant dying wasp.

As he abruptly stood up and was forced to steady himself against the desk, it was obvious that he'd made better progress through the bottle of white wine than he had the novel. The buzz of the doorbell sounded again, persistent, annoying.

The combination of frayed carpet and a loose doorplate saw him stumble out of the room, narrowly catching his balance at the last minute. How much wine had he *had*? As he stood there, his head swimming and eyes blurred, he could hear heeled footsteps approaching him from across the tiled floor. A woman's voice said his name.

David Court

He awoke from deep, vivid dreams that faded the moment he realised he was awake. He lay there for the longest time, bewildered. It was a limbo of sorts, and one he could remain a part of as long as he kept his eyes closed. Even the slightest movement caused uncomfortable pangs of nausea. He hadn't had a hangover like this since he was a *teenager*. How many bottles had Maxime drank?

"You were about two thirds of the way into your fourth bottle" said a female voice. English, her tone vaguely condescending.

"How did-" Maxime spat out, eyes still clenched shut.

"You've been chattered away to yourself for about half an hour now. You seem to struggle with internal monologue. Do you often feel the need to narrate what you're thinking and doing?"

"I wasn't aware that I was," said Maxime, slightly embarrassed. She didn't respond. Maxime pushed his face deeper into his pillows, still exhausted, and drifted off again.

Despite being very well-versed in the practical aspect of it, Maxime would never have considered himself an expert in the science of sleeping. However, there was one thing he was damn sure of – Nightmares should happen at night, not between lunchtime and early afternoon. Pour l'amour de Dieu, the clue was in the name!

*Night*mares.

However, wherever Maxime was, he was quite definitively in the middle of one.

The breathing of the house had, at the height of his imagination, resembled a sigh. The wind that presently whistled through the twilight corridors of the Château, each of them crooked and of an alien geometry that defied even the hazy logic of dreams, had never called his name before.

Maxime.

There it was again. It hissed with a chilling malevolence, taunting him. Each corner he turned; it was behind him. Every door he passed through and slammed shut behind him, it crashed against and scratched upon.

Whatever it was, he *knew* it. He recognised the shadow each time it fell against him, the very sensation of its presence. He'd mistakenly thought it long gone, evaded years back.

As he pressed his back against the only door in that final windowless room, hearing the wood splinter as his blighted nemesis slammed against it, he screamed for consciousness. He longed for the warmth of the sun on his face, the coolness of the crisp white blankets against his skin.

Maxime closed his eyes and tried to fight the dream, to force his consciousness into being awake, but the lurid surroundings persisted. The very wood he leant against began to warp and crack, tentacle-like wooden shards *click-clacking* out from the stripped surface and wrapping around his neck and wrists.

Bones strained and crushed beyond mortal limits, he screamed in agony as his wrists snapped – right first, quickly followed by the left. A rough, fragmented, scarlet shard jutted from both arms, blood pooling around his feet.

The screaming stopped as a fist of knotted wood slammed into his mouth, forcing its way past his shattered teeth and down his throat. A final act of futility as he fought for breath, his vision fading. A moonlit silhouette stood in front of him now, offering a hand to him far too late.

It was late afternoon when he sat bolt upright in his bed, a nightmare transformed to ethereal tranquillity. Lazy shafts of sunlight were filtering through the thin white curtains, illuminating the tens of thousands of dust motes that hung suspended in the air. Maxime briefly felt as though he were sitting at the heart of a perfectly scaled down nebula, the gravitic cosmic centre of a thousand tiny bright stars.

That was *bad*. He hadn't had a nightmare like that, since...

There were noises from downstairs, the sound of chinking cutlery and plates against tunes coming from a monotone radio only *mostly* tuned into a station. The signal would occasionally drop out, the gap filled by short bursts of white noise. There was a melodious whistling over the top of it.

His hangover seemed to clear with every step he took towards the kitchen, the scent of baking bread and the harsh tang of fresh coffee revitalising his senses. She was in the kitchen washing up some of the various plates and pieces of cutlery that Maxime had scattered about the house. She gave a terse, "Good morning" as he stepped into the room.

"I'm sorry," said Maxime, seating himself at the small wooden table that took up most of the room. "Murray never told me your name."

There was no immediate response. The only sound was that of a rhythmic squeaking of cloth against damp glass. The awkward silence hung in the air like a shroud.

After slowly and carefully placing the now gleaming glass on the counter, she turned around to face him.

"Beatrice," she smiled.

She was younger than Maxime had imagined her to be. He'd half-expected them to send an old nanny type, someone to both mother and mither him. Beatrice was far from that.

The first thing that struck him about her appearance was how unnaturally pale she was. Her skin was almost alabaster white, gossamer thin. He'd had a brief fling with a lass from Dublin a quarter of a century ago with a similar complexion – she'd often joked how she was one of those unlucky Irish with transparent skin who shouldn't be allowed out into the sun.

To Mnemosyne, a Daughter

She was short, but dainty. Her auburn hair was in a short bob, her left eye obscured by a perfectly coiffured lock. Her sky-blue summer dress was dotted with red flowers and green leaves, a look of fragility harshly contrasted by the thick, workmanlike purple boots she wore. At a guess, she was either in her late twenties, or somebody in her early thirties who'd taken *very* good care of herself. She reminded him of somebody he'd once dated, a Californian New-Age type who'd introduced him to the tedium of veganism and tantric sex. He'd broken it off with a convincing, "It's not you, it's me," but it was *categorically* her.

"There's some... *breakfast* in the oven for you. It's probably dried to black lumps of carbon by now, but you never know."

She glanced at the kitchen clock as she derisively intoned the word breakfast. Maxime moved away from the door as she stepped towards him.

"There's fresh coffee in the pot. I have to pop into the village for a few things, so I'll see you later."

Before he could reply, she'd brushed past him and, with the brief smell of Patchouli, was gone. As he picked up one of the chipped earthenware mugs that sat on the work surface, he saw the note she'd left for him.

"Write something. Anything. Just write.
B x"

She'd brewed a good coffee, and a decent quantity of it. It was strong enough to mask the charcoal coating on the once-perfectly-reasonable-but-now-cremated breakfast, and the remainder of his hangover was dissipating with every bitter sip.

The terrifying expanse of the blank white page stretched out before him, a seemingly unconquerable glacial landscape on a par with anything Sir Edmund Hillary had faced. His two index fingers hovered tentatively above the laptop keyboard.

Write something. Anything. Just *write*.

A title at least – that'd be a start. He tapped the Enter key until the cursor sat about halfway down the page. It blinked, taunting him.

Tap tap tap tap. Some words. Centre justified. Make the font bigger – a statement of intent. *Something*.

NIGHTGHAST III

WRAITHBANE

What was a wraithbane? Maxime had no idea. It sounded good though, so he could run with it. In this book Lady Carina Delafont would meet her nemesis, her equal in both mind and body. Wraithbane was a good as name as any for this foe, even if sounded like something from a Circa-1970's Dungeons and Dragons scenario.

Some scene setting pre-amble next, to remind the readers what had happened in the last two books. And then he'd do the Bond Cliché of dumping his heroine right in the climax of *another* adventure, which had always worked for him in the past.

Hit the ground running.

Some tentative keystrokes, words nervously and reluctantly joining their predecessors. And then more confidence, the *tap-tap* sound in the room audibly changing from the gentle pitter-patter of summer showers to a deluge of rain.

Within an hour, he'd written more than he'd written in the last week. Not as productive as some of his better days in the past, but in comparison to the complete lack of inspiration he'd been encountering, his neurons were now firing like a twenty-one-gun salute.

It was only when he stopped for his first cigarette break several hours later that he realised he'd already managed a four-digit word count. It was a rough first draft of which he'd probably strip out most of, but Maxime was smugly pleased with his progress, nonetheless.

The cigarette now reduced to a stubbed-out butt in an otherwise empty ashtray, Maxime got to his feet to stretch his tired limbs. As he stood staring out of the veranda window at the gentle flowing waters of the Dordogne, he heard clattering from the kitchen.

"Beatrice?"

No reply, but no further noise from the kitchen either. The clattering had stopped.

"Beatrice?" Maxime repeated, slightly unnerved. He suddenly felt very conscious of the fact that, since he'd moved in here, he'd happily left all the doors unlocked and many of the windows open. Where he was staying was so remote, so out-of-the-way, he'd never considered that an issue.

Until now. With the potential of a knife-wielding psychopath in his temporary home.

Maxime crept slowly towards the kitchen, listening for any sound. He was now at the closed kitchen door, armed with nothing more than a half-empty packet of cigarettes and a lighter. He'd *lung cancer* them to death.

Clichéd as it seemed, he breathed a visible sigh of relief when the next noise that he heard was Beatrice's whistling. He pushed open the door and she looked up at him, smiling. The counter in front of her was covered with un-bagged shopping – bread, milk, wine – the essentials. She'd changed since earlier, looking vintage *chic* with a faded pink Led Zeppelin vest that was adorably too large for her, a short black hemmed skirt with a repeat red heart outline motif and sheer white over-the-knee socks. She turned to place the bag of bread on one of the high shelves in the kitchen and his eyes were drawn to her figure, a flash of the curvature of a breast of pale freckled skin visible through the overly baggy arm-holes of the vest. She was quite beautiful.

David Court

Her eyes flickered back to his. Embarrassed at being caught staring, he made that his attention had been lingering over the impressive selection of multi-coloured wines.

"No writing, no drinking."

Maxime leaned against the door frame, suddenly quite pleased with himself.

"I've actually managed something. It's not great, but it's a start."

She raised an eyebrow, half-smiling, before going back to placing the shopping into cupboards, unimpressed. His mood deflated almost instantly.

"I thought you'd be happy. That's why you're *here*, isn't it?"

She didn't even turn to face him as she replied, more concerned with sliding each of the wine bottles into the appropriate receptacle in the wine-rack.

"You're a writer. That's what you're *supposed* to do. When you've finished, then I'll be impressed. If it's any good."

Maxime slunk back to his keyboard, thoroughly put into his place.

The words didn't flow quite as easily in the writing session that afternoon and early evening. Whereas, earlier in the day he'd been lost in thought - his mind a whirlwind of ideas – he was now finding himself reflecting more. Not only in being overly critical of his own writing, in which almost as many words were deleted as written, but in speculation regarding why he felt as such. Had he been writing to impress *her?* Her lack of interest had certainly caused a significant diminishment in both his mood *and* verbosity.

And Beatrice, Beatrice was quite the distraction also. As his thoughts should have been turning to Lady Carina, they'd turned to her instead. A scene of Carina donning her battle armour – some enchanted leather that she'd won in a card game from a

To Mnemosyne, a Daughter

character whose name he had to look through his notes to recall – it became a floral summer dress in his minds-eye, the soft curve of a delicate thigh framed by skirt and sock.

Still, the turn of phrase it had forced from him worked. Criticisms of his earlier work accused Carina of merely being a reworked male character - subject to a gender find-and-replace for political correctness - and it was interesting to write her as an actual *woman*.

He'd been sitting there in the dwindling light of the evening, staring at the last sentence he'd half written and pondering this new slight shift of direction, when the chink of glasses roused him from his reverie. He turned around to see Beatrice in the doorway. She was holding two glasses by the stem in one hand and a bottle in the other.

"This is a one-off," she said, smiling, "and we're not going to make a habit of this."

He closed the laptop lid and smiled back.

"You say that, but I hadn't really considered that my career in publishing would end up entailing looking after over-the-hill authors with writer's block," she said, staring him straight in the eye as she took a sip from her third glass of wine.

If there was a "present company excepted" on the way, she was certainly taking her damn time. He despondently considered the contents of his own glass as she carried on, either unaware or simply uncaring about the harshness of that hurtful statement.

"So, tell me about your books, Maxime."

Harsh or brutally honest? Perhaps she had a point.

"Maxime?"

He'd taken the last sip from the glass before he'd realised she was talking to him. He looked at her, surprised.

David Court

"Oh, sorry. I was miles away. My books? Murray hadn't told you anything?"

"I never asked. Or ask, for that matter."

"I write the Nightghast series."

She stared back at him blankly, waiting for him to explain. It hadn't dawned on Maxime that there might be somebody who had never heard of them – his usual encounters with women of Beatrice's age was when they were flirting with him in bookshops as he signed something for them.

"It's for my daughter," they'd lie, giggling. He'd dutifully ask their name, to be presented with a forename that no parents had given any daughter of theirs in the last two decades.

"Sorry, Maxime. I tend to only read *proper* books."

This time even she looked genuinely horrified when she saw the expression on Maxime's face. He'd tried to hide it, but never was terribly hide at disguising his emotions.

"Oh God," she spluttered, placing down the glass and pressing a reassuring hand on his shoulder, "That came out way worse that I'd intended. I mean I only tend to read the classics. What I'm trying to say is – bloody hell. I'm sure your stuff is great."

Her hand slid off him as he abruptly stood up. His attempt to look offended was somewhat offset by the fact that the wine had gone straight to his head and he was forced to stand there for a few moments, wobbling unsteadily. When his balance returned, he strode over to the kitchen as quickly and as confidently as his drunkenness permitted.

The neon of the kitchen light *plink-plink-plinked* into luminescence as he slumped across the kitchen counter, visibly shaken. His shaking hands fumbled for the packet of cigarettes in his shirt pocket before suddenly removing one, lighting it and placing it to his lips with the subconscious muscle memory of a thirty-a-day man.

He heard Beatrice's slow footsteps make their way up the creaking château stairs and listened as her bedroom door clicked

To Mnemosyne, a Daughter

shut. A tinny metallic click sounded as a latch slid into place, locking the door.

The prospect of another drink was forgotten as he flicked the ashes from his cigarette into his empty wine glass. Disappointment had turned into anger as he inhaled deeply, breathing angry fire into his lungs.

He was a New York Times bestseller, for God's sake. Who was she, this glorified temp, to put him in his place? Feminists had written *essays* on how good a role model his heroine Carina Delafont was – what had Beatrice ever done of worth?

He was still angry three cigarettes later as he stumbled up the stairs. He made no attempt to muffle his noisy footsteps as he stomped past the door to Beatrice's room, still muttering angrily under his breath.

Maxime thought his anger would keep him awake all night and that he'd be staring wide-eyed at the ceiling until dawn. In truth, that fire could only burn for so long – within moments of placing his head on the pillow, his body had resigned, and he'd drifted off into a fitful sleep.

At night, the house breathed. As Maxime wandered the twilight corridors of the château, it breathed with him. The creaking of the floorboards echoed the creaking of his limbs, the gusts of air drifting languorously through the passages matching his own slow inhalations and exhalations.

Something crept with him. It kept its distance this time, but he could feel it there. The alien angles of the thing shared the shadows with him, touching the walls that he'd touched. It was *stalking* him, hiding its footsteps in the sound of those of Maxime.

But, even hidden from him, it was a formidable and terrifying presence.

David Court

Suddenly a new sound dripped into the ambience – new breaths, more rapid than his own. They grew louder with every step he took, faster too.

He felt the presence behind him slink away, as though temporarily thwarted or reticent to show itself.

Beatrice's door was ajar as he found himself standing in front of it, the latch undone. Moonlight flickered through the shifting curtains of her room, bathing it in a rippling blue glow that evoked the shimmering surface of the Dordogne.

The door pushed open noiselessly, any sound it made drowned out by the noises from within that grew louder with every passing moment. The air was filled with short breathless gasps and Maxime looked over to the source of the noise.

Beatrice was lying there on the bare bed, thin white bedcovers pushed aside and draped across the floor like a shroud. Her back was arched, her head thrown back. Strands of her short auburn hair clung to the sweat on her forehead. Her mouth was slightly agape, the moisture on the tip of her tongue glistening in the moonlight. Her eyes were screwed tightly shut as her naked body writhed and contorted, her kneading fingers flickering in the dull blue luminescence. Maxime felt compelled to say her name, but she was a galaxy away.

With each breath, it was as though the room itself moved. The walls pulsed, the Fleur-De-Lis patterned surface appearing to undulate to her rhythm, pulsing and swelling as her fingers moved faster and faster. No, not *appeared* – the room *was* moving, the wooden floor creaking unsteadily beneath Maxime's feet, rolling and heaving like the gentle swell of the ocean.

Maxime wondered whether she was aware of his presence at all, until her eyes flickered open and she stared straight into his, each pupil dark and without reflection. Rather than shy away, her eyes locked on his and her pace increased. He felt ashamed, emasculated by her brazenness, but couldn't bring himself to look away. Beads of sweat began to gather on her forehead and

To Mnemosyne, a Daughter

breasts as her slender fingers frenziedly worked themselves between her glistening thighs.

He stepped slowly towards her, the clothes dissolving away from him like vapour the closer he got.

Convenient, he smiled, allowing himself to be swept up by the rules of this dream reality now. It was when he neared the bed, close enough to feel the warmth from her body, that he found himself unable to move further – an invisible barrier between the two of them, a glass wall of complete transparency.

This was maddening, yet utterly intoxicating. He longed to be the dominant one, to satisfy the cravings of both her and the stiff cock he was nursing. It was clear from the expression on her face, her eyes still locked like a missile onto his, that she was the way she wanted it. To be forced to watch.

Teasing him, she raised one hand to a breast, a perfectly manicured finger circling an already erect nipple. Maxime pressed against the barrier, the tip of his cock twitching in the cold air of the room. To be with her – to be *in* her now.

The room was in chaos now, furniture toppling over as the walls pushed against it, gravity itself feeling displaced amidst the miasma of wanton sexuality. Windowpanes, unable to bear the pressure of the walls shifting seismically against them, cracked noisily, glass exploding into the room in slowly spiralling splinters.

Beatrice's back arched violently, and Maxime realised she was floating above the bed, a trellis of bedsheets knotted into fingers holding her aloft. Her fingers shuddered and froze as she opened her mouth in a silent scream of satisfaction.

Maxime awoke to find himself masturbating, his right hand gripped tightly round his cock. At first, he was surprised at this cheeky betrayal by his brain – finding himself in the midst of a nocturnal act he hadn't done subconsciously since he was a hormone-ridden horny teenager – but then the fugue in his mind cleared and the memories of his dream were there, clear as day, ultra-vivid high resolution etched across the surface of his brain. She could have been there in the room with him, the rivulets of sweat dotted across her pale skin, the perfect curve of her breasts. His grip tightened as he remembered every detail of her, every aspect, and every contour.

She was suddenly abstract, jagged lines and vivid colours. His senses – now risen to the heights of ecstasy – struggled to formulate thoughts, his neurons short-circuited as he rode the downward spiral.

He held onto the one image his minds-eye could envisage, his body shaking at he rode that moment for as long as he was able. To hold on for just one more second...

A guttural lengthy sigh left him as he came, months of frustration escaping his body in one freeing motion and involuntary expulsion of air.

He slept a deeper sleep than he'd managed in years, dreamless.

The images of her still clung to him the next morning as he showered, wrapping pervasive tendrils around his still-buzzing brain. He felt strangely invigorated, a renewed need to write putting a spring in his step, urgency to his actions.

But those *dreams*. So lifelike – so *overwhelming*. Despite the torrent of cold water spraying down over him, even just remembering fragmented pieces caused his cock to twitch and harden. He could smell her now – the sweat on her body, the perfume on her neck. He had to steady himself against the shower cubicle wall to stop himself from falling over, such were the power of these thoughts – false memories from that wonderful dream.

To Mnemosyne, a Daughter

Fuck, he hadn't felt like this in the best part of twenty years. Libido was pretty much the driving force of the seventeen-year-old Maxime, and he must easily have worked his way through at least a rainforests-worth of tissue paper in youthful abandonment, but that wasn't the Maxime of today.

He turned the shower off and stood there for a while, letting the water drip from him. Now the bathroom was silent, he could hear the radio playing from downstairs in the kitchen – some tinny euro-pop that he didn't recognise. He could hear Beatrice as well, humming a quite different tune to the one playing.

Back in his room, he dried himself off and got dressed – it was a pleasant day, one warm enough to write with the patio doors open, so he chose a plain white T-shirt and some three-quarter length cargo-shorts that he rarely wore. He'd bought them – and often carried them around – on a whim but frankly felt self-conscious in them, like an old man pretending to be a teenager. Not today, though. Today he felt *young*.

There was a coffee waiting for him as he stepped into the kitchen, but no sign of Beatrice. Maxime picked it up to take a sip and thought he heard a noise from outdoors – the sound of footsteps. He pulled open the kitchen door – already ajar – and stepped out into the garden.

It looked like it was going to be a glorious day – even though it wasn't yet mid-morning, the sun was already high in the sky and beaming down on the Château and its grounds. The bees from the neighbour's hives were awake and busy, lazily flitting in amongst the flowers that bordered the garden.

He could see Beatrice now, standing at the very foot of the garden that overlooked the banks of the Dordogne. She was by the waist-height dry stone wall that stood before a steep muddy slope overwhelmed by thick vegetation and had her back to him, staring wistfully into the distance. Puffs of cigarette smoke hovered over her head like lazy smoke signals.

She was wearing a plain, white, knee-length dress, the fold of the fabric conjuring thoughts of her naked form draped in sweat-soaked bedsheets. Distracting images came flooding back from last night's dreams. He stood in the kitchen watching, reluctant to join her – for the stupidest reason he felt embarrassed, foolishly ashamed that she'd somehow know what he'd dreamt about. It took a few moments of that before he cursed his stupidity and strode purposefully out into the garden.

She was so lost in thought that he inadvertently startled her as he approached. Looking visibly shaken, her first instinct was to hide the cigarette – like a pupil being caught behind the bike sheds by the teacher. As she caught his eyes, Maxime felt ashamed too – suddenly reminded of the dream of last night, as though she could read his mind and know exactly what he'd *seen*.

"I didn't know you smoked," smiled Maxime, trying to hide the stupid nervousness in his voice.

"I... I haven't. Not for the longest time. But you'd left your cigarettes out on the kitchen counter. I didn't think you'd mind if ..."

She halted, but it was clear to him she wasn't going to finish the sentence – that she'd leave it hanging there, waiting for Maxime to step in.

"Not at all," he smiled. He'd subconsciously picked up the packet himself as he'd walked into the garden. He took one out and lit it, hoping that this act of solidarity would clear the air of this ridiculous awkwardness that clung there. "I hadn't myself until the other day, either. Thought I'd given up for good."

She raised an eyebrow, as though privy to some secret she wouldn't say. Without another word, she briefly looked at the lapping waters and flicked her cigarette towards them. The tiny white cylinder spiralled a few times before landing and being sucked beneath the churning waters.

To Mnemosyne, a Daughter

"Did you sleep well?" she asked, a playful smile at the corner of her lips.

"I've slept better," he replied, convinced by the warm flush that swept over him that his skin must be resembling the red of the rhubarb that grew in the château's greenhouse.

"What are your plans?"

"I'm thinking of popping into the village. Just a walk to clear my head. Might pick up a paper."

"Oh," she said, looking almost disappointed.

"I won't be long. I've got a book to write, remember?"

Despite reminding himself (out loud, at times) to not buy any more cigarettes, Maxime knew that that was his primary reason for venturing into the village. That, and he felt somewhat awkward in Beatrice's presence.

The walk up the hill away from the château was more tiring than he remembered. His ankles and thighs were protesting angrily by the end of the relatively small trek, but the view was worth it. From this height, you had an unimpeded view of *everything*; the majestic sight of the château and its grounds, the few tiny grey roads that snaked away from it and around it like the arches, loops, and whorls on a fingerprint. Nature (helped by man) had seen fit to dot forests and woods as far as the eye could see, and there it was in the distance – the clifftop village of *Rocamadour*, a random patchwork of light grey and beige medieval buildings set against rich vibrant green hills and cliffs.

It was a bright day, but with enough of a breeze to make walking pleasant. Despite forgetting which side of the narrow winding road you were supposed to walk on - and therefore offending a ruddy faced holidaying Parisian in a beat-up Citroen - he'd made it to the village in one piece.

Truth be told, he'd been daydreaming when the angry impending heart-attackee had startled him with three firm beeps of his horn. Despite coming on this walk to take his mind off Beatrice and to concentrate on thinking about the book, he'd been able to think of little else. Thoughts of her had wandered into every piece of plot-line musing, blundered haplessly into every piece of dialogue he'd been fermenting.

Aimlessly, he'd found himself wandering into one of those pubs reserved almost exclusively for locals. They were common across the world; the old one-eyed man and his dog who made a single drink last a day, the two old gents playing a game of chess they'd probably been playing since the late fifties, the old barman perpetually cleaning the same glass with a cloth. All four-and-a-half sets of eyes were on him as he walked towards the bar, only relaxing and carrying on with what they were doing before when he sat on the worn and threadbare stool that was there.

Despite the fact he was the only person at the bar, the barman clearly wasn't in any rush. It took a few moments of some precision glass-cleaning before he towered over Maxime and shrugged.

Maxime gestured to the nearest pump, a lager with a German name that he wasn't even going to attempt to pronounce. The image on the pump resembled one of those pretty airbrushed ladies they painted on the side of bombers back in World War 2, and Maxime could have sworn that the scantily-clad buxom ginger lady that leaned forward to emphasise her copious cleavage had Beatrice's eyes.

He was halfway down his drink before the Barman relaxed, clearly convinced now that Maxime wasn't here to trash the joint. Finally placing the never-cleaner wine glass back on the holder, he leaned in towards Maxime.

"Where have you travelled from?"

To Mnemosyne, a Daughter

Maxime leaned back on the stool and pointed in the approximate direction he'd come from.

"The Château."

"The Château de Amorette?" the barman asked, an eyebrow raised. The way he'd said it, you'd think you couldn't move for Chateaus around these parts. Maxime nodded.

The barman, fat jowls dangling like a thick polo-neck collar, leaned in closer. His thick-accented voice was now reduced to a low conspiratorial murmur.

"You a writer?"

"I am," smiled Maxime, leaning back and taking a sip of the lager. His attempt to come across as nonchalant was instantly diminished by the huge foam moustache that stuck to his top lip.

"A lot of writers gone through the château," he remarked, turning his attention to cleaning down the surfaces of the bar now, "A *lot* of writers."

"It's a writer's retreat," sputtered Maxime, suddenly feeling the need to justify himself, "I think a lot of famous people have..."

"Written anything I've heard of?" the barman asked, his back to Maxime and stretching up to pick up a photograph that sat next to some wine bottles from one of the top shelves.

"I wrote the Nightgaunt series?" Maxime prompted, already suspecting the answer. He didn't expect they read a lot around these parts, especially not YA horror novels.

Placing the dusty-framed, faded black and white photograph on the bar in front of Maxime, the barman shrugged.

"Grover Holness," he said, wiping the dust from the glass with a fat sausage-like finger. Maxime recognised the man – the great poet from the nineteen-thirties. Maxime owned a couple of his collections.

"What, Holness stayed at the château?"

The barman was now cleaning the glass of the photograph with the same cloth he'd used on the bar, the picture was revealed little by little. The photograph answered his question –

it had clearly been taken on the château grounds, the elegant topiaries of the garden as the backdrop."

"I've heard of *his* stuff. Read some too," the barman continued, mockingly. It took a while for what he said to register, as Maxime was focusing on the slowly revealed photograph. The pretty woman arm in arm with Holness, short bobbed hair and a narrow skirt that stopped mid-calf, the Greta Garbo-imitating style of the day.

Before the dust from the face was even wiped off with a single swipe of cloth, Maxime knew who the girl would resemble, as though he'd dreamt it.

Yes, there it was. As he'd suspected. As he'd known from the moment the picture had come down from the shelf.

He staggered off to the toilets in a daze.

The pouring taps and swirling waters of the basin did little to drown out the laughter that sounded from the bar. From the occasional word he picked up, they were openly mocking him in their mother tongue, blissfully unaware that Maxime spoke fluent French. It was a point of great humour that they'd never heard of him, one of the patrons saying, "I wrote the Nightgaunt series" in a sing-song humiliating tone, a poor imitation of Maxime that had the rest of the bar in hysterics.

It *couldn't* have been her. The picture was taken nearly ninety years ago. He'd been seeing her face everywhere – *that* must have been it. Merely an effect of an overly long and tiring walk, heady sunshine and overly strong lager.

Splashing some water over his face, he resolved to storm back into the bar and confront them – tell them his sales figures, tell him the A list stars who'd been attached to the film – but his confidence faded as quickly as the water down the cracked basins plughole.

To Mnemosyne, a Daughter

Who'd remember Maxime after he'd gone? YA authors were ten a penny, and his only legacy would be a group of fan girls who'd move on to the next thing. Lady Carina would be forgotten as quickly as Maxime.

He'd just leave. Only a little beer left in his glass. That'd be mostly sediment, so best just to be off. Not worth making a scene.

A guttural hiss sounded from behind him, from the light-shunned corner of the bathroom. Even in the midst of the afternoon, the light from the windows looked like it didn't dare venture there. A toilet cubicle, graffitied on its few pieces of non-cracked and splintered wood.

The sound again, clearly coming from inside it.

As Maxime stared at the room's corner, it felt as though the shadows were growing – expanding from it as blackened barbed tendrils of anti-light. As they fell across Maxime, a shiver traced an icy finger down his back. Besmirched fractals of pitch clambered across the floors, ceilings, and walls.

The hiss had Maxime's name on it, long, drawn out – like a death rattle.

The door flew open, the wood noisily splintering away from rusted hinges. A corpse with Maxime's face lunged forth, obscenely angled limbs clawing towards him. The eyes were empty pits, black holes that stared hollowly at him.

"Forgotten!" it hissed, awkward limbs flailing.

Maxime threw himself back into the bar, falling to the floor. He dragged himself backwards, trying – and failing – to get back to his feet. The laughter from the bar stopped as this shrieking stranger remerged into their midst, pointing at the toilet door with a shaking finger.

Maxime waited for the thing to burst into the room in pursuit, but it didn't come. He got to his feet, steadied by one of the now silent patrons. He didn't take his eyes from the toilet door until he'd ran, heart pounding, from the bar.

The laughter started again as soon as he'd left.

David Court

Cigarettes were *essential* now, to steady his nerves. The kindly old lady in the shop seemed very concerned as his trembling fingers fumbled with the correct change, but he'd assured her that he was okay.

Despite the fact he'd assured himself that he wouldn't be one of those people who came up with a rational explanation for the unexplainable, he'd already started doing so by the time he was on his second cigarette and at the outskirts of the village.

Sleep deprivation. That, or they'd spiked his drink. Even, potentially, an elaborate prank.

All of those were easily to come to terms with than the alternative.

As he descended the final hill to the Château, he felt himself calm down. His stiff shoulders relaxed, his staccato heartbeat settling to a normal rhythm. All the bad thoughts went away when he saw Beatrice sunbathing in the garden, the last of them evaporating into the ether when she looked back at him smiling, grateful for his return.

All was well with the world as he sat back at the keyboard. This was where he was supposed to be, and this was what he was supposed to be doing.

In the old days, he'd measure progress by *cigarettes*. Word count was never an issue – with the first book the sentences poured out in a deluge, the only bottleneck in the process being the time it took to ferry them 'twixt mind and keyboard and monitor. Maxime's internal clock, however, would mentally countdown the fifty or so minutes between each cigarette. Like clockwork, he'd sprung up from his keyboard and light up.

To Mnemosyne, a Daughter

Therefore, anything upwards of a pack of ten exhausted during a writing session was considered a good result.

That was what he'd missed most when he gave them up. Not the aroma, the nicotine, but that handy internal clock. Without cigarettes, his writing had become more intermittent. He'd have bursts of productivity coupled with equally long periods of procrastination – it had fucked with his *patterns.*

Today, however, was different. He didn't want to get back into the habit of regularly smoking again, so they sat on his desk as a warning – a deterrent. He'd try and write as much as he possibly could before indulging in another one from the packet.

"You could just destroy them," he thought to himself. *"Throw the packet into the bin and forget they were ever there."*

That wouldn't work. What if he *did* need one? It'd take him out of valuable writing time if he had to have another trip to the local shops.

Maxime stood the cigarette packet on end, feeling the weight as he shifted it. Probably a good six cigarettes rattled around in the half-empty paper packaging. He leaned in towards the packet.

"This is the deal," he whispered to it, jabbing a finger at the dull labelled packaging, "you're going to stay there, and leave me to my writing."

He leaned back in his chair and cracked his knuckles. With one last look at the cigarette packet, his fingers moved to the keyboard and started to type.

Maxime had once watched a documentary about fanatics of old-school arcade games. Not this new breed of videogame where you needed either eight hands or a degree to play them, but the classic ones that used to emerge like sprouting vegetation in the local arcade down on Hudson Street; Space Invaders, Galaxians, Frogger, Donkey Kong, Defender.

David Court

Some of the guys in that show were in their late forties or early fifties, but they all had one thing in common – when you watched them gaming, it was all about instinct. Their eyes would all but glaze over when you watched them, their hands twitching and jerking like they were afflicted with St. Vitus's dance.

They called it being in the *zone.*

On the best days, Maxime's writing was like that. It was almost clichéd to say it, but some of his best works had virtually written themselves. Today's writing session had been *phenomenal* – Beatrice had been on point, never interrupting him, but always making sure there was a fresh cup of coffee for him every time he'd instinctively reach towards it. Her presence was almost ethereal; just a brief wisp of floral fragrance wafting past to mark her passing.

Snacks would magically appear in much the same manner; sandwiches of thick wedges of cheese and thinly sliced tomato on brick-like slabs of rustic bread appearing by his side at lunchtime, and a bowl perched high with smoked almonds and shelled pistachios mid-afternoon.

Like in the old days, it was as Maxime became more aware of his surroundings and the passage of time that the magic began to fade. He'd find himself slowing, deliberating more and more over the sentences that, just a few minutes before, were flowing from him effortlessly. His eyes were drawn to the packet of cigarettes that stood there, taunting him.

He leaned back in his chair and looked up at the clock. It was early evening, the last rays of sunlight vanishing behind the hills of the Périgord Blanc. The sky was a brilliant fading oil-spill of vibrant reds, oranges, and yellows.

Glancing back at the glaring monitor, Maxime was genuinely taken aback by the word count. He'd written as much in a single day as would normally take him three or four. A cursory glance at the last few pages looked it'd require a bare minimum of editing as well – it looked like good, clean copy.

To Mnemosyne, a Daughter

One word stood out though – he remembered typing it and highlighting in yellow so he wouldn't miss it on his first round of edits. It was a new supernatural foe for his heroine Lady Carina Delafont – a minion of the main villain, it was a water monster known as the *Afanc*. If memory served, it was a creature from British folklore, but Maxime couldn't remember the exact origins or nature of the beast.

It would have been just as easy to make up something new, but Maxime loved to dot his stories with genuine – for want of a better word – creatures of myth. He felt it added a level of authenticity to his work. Also, as he'd learned, if genre fans suspect you've ripped something off, they will *not* let it lie – they'll round on you like a pack of rabid hound dogs. Or give your book a one-star review. Both were equally awful fates.

Instinctively, and not for the first time this break, he pulled his mobile phone from his jeans pocket and went to scour for the answer online. It was only when he saw the familiar NO SIGNAL legend boldly emblazoned across the phone display, he remembered the lack of phone and internet reception in this entire region, let alone here at the bottom of the hill.

It was one of the reasons he'd chosen this place, to be fair, asking that his agent find him somewhere where he wouldn't be interrupted. The only means of contacting the outside world was the landline in the small room adjacent to the kitchen.

He got to his feet, his relaxed bones and muscles protesting from the sudden activity. Now physically *and* mentally pulled back to the real world, his bodily urges became apparent. He'd sate them one at a time. First, the toilet. Secondly, a cigarette. Lastly, food and drink.

Especially drink. He'd earned it.

The pressure on his bladder abated, he grabbed the pack of cigarettes and headed towards the garden in a half-jog. The sky was, if anything, even more beautiful than before. Reds and oranges had darkened into vibrant purples and deep blues, pinprick stars beginning to peer out from the darkest patches. A few birds were singing themselves to sleep in the boughs of the trees that bordered the Dordogne, the only sound audible over the gentle trickling of its waters.

This place truly was magical.

"Good day?" a voice said from behind him. He turned to face Beatrice; her smiling face lit by the glow of the waning sun. Her hair was wet as though she'd just gotten out of the shower, and she was dressed in an oversized T-shirt with a faded indeterminable cartoon character on it and pyjama bottoms. She was as relaxed as Maxime had ever seen her, and still effortlessly beautiful.

"A *very* good day," he grinned, taking a cigarette from the packet and offering the packet to her. After a moment of hesitation, she took one.

The two stood there in silence for the longest time watching the sun continue its slow decline over the horizon, as though the act of speaking would break the spell and freeze it in place.

"It's still early," he announced, confidently. "I'm sure I saw a nice restaurant in the village. It'd only be a short walk, and I could treat you to a meal."

The restaurant in question was on the other side of the village from the bar, as far away as humanly possible and to still be in the same postal region.

She broke eye-contact, staring down at her feet. She looked torn, indecisive.

"If we're in luck," he continued, "it might be one of those places that serve you your dinner on planks or big chunks of slate instead of actual plates. They're always fun."

She smiled and looked back at him.

"It's late and I'm settled. Maybe tomorrow?"

"Okay, no biggie. You'll join me in seeing off some of that wine though, eh?"

To Mnemosyne, a Daughter

"It's a date."

Again, the discarded remnants of her cigarette arced though the air, a scaled-down Catherine wheel of orange spiralling sparks landing with a *hiss* in the river. Like the cigarette, she was suddenly gone.

The word 'date' hung in the air; a simple word charged with possibility.

The fridge contained one full bottle and the remains of the one he'd ambitiously begun last night – duly recorked by Beatrice, no doubt. He carried the half a bottle and two clean glasses into the living room. She had her back to him, flicking through a neat collection of vinyl albums that sat alongside a record player on the wooden cabinet that sat beneath the main bay windows.

"Anything good?" asked Maxime, sitting down and pouring the remnants of the half-bottle into the two glasses. Taking any small victory where he could, he allowed himself a moment of internal celebration that both glasses were as close to equal as could be measured.

"Every time I come here," she said, still concentrating on her record selection. "I keep saying I'll bring more records along, but I never remember. It's just the same old, same old. Let's see; We've got Charles Aznavour, Serge Gainsbourg..."

"Edith Piaf?" asked Maxime, strongly suspecting he knew the answer.

"Of course. It's a regular French Who's-who. All it's missing is some Maurice Chevalier."

Maxime suddenly sat bolt upright, as though struck by electricity.

"Ooh, ooh. What's the name of that one with the chorus that goes rat-tat-tat-tat-tat?"

Beatrice finally turned to face him.

David Court

"That could be pretty much any track on any album there."

Maxime tried to remember it as best he could but was far from a singer. Still, his tuneless rendition of what he remembered of the chorus seemed to be enough to cause Beatrice to nod excitedly.

"Chanson D'Amour!"

The mere mention of the name of the track was enough for the two of them to launch into a vague approximation of the song, every other forgotten word mumbled.

"Each... time... we... "

Muffled unintelligible words from both.

"Rat-tat-tat-tat-tat! Chanson, Chanson... D'Amoooourrrrr!"

Chucking, Maxime passed her the glass. They hadn't even started drinking yet.

It's only when you're stranded in a château that's a lengthy walk or taxi journey away from civilisation and listening to a stranger's album collection, Maxime mused, that you truly realise how many Sacha Distel songs you know the words to.

The last dregs of the full bottle of wine had been poured, and it felt as though the night was still young. They hadn't even yet – a slightly drunk Beatrice exclaimed – gotten to Distel's glorious rendition of "Raindrops Keep Fallin' on My Head" yet.

"This place has to have a cellar. It's a French château – there's probably some kind of law," a determined Maxime mumbled to himself, getting up onto his slightly unsteady feet. Three quarters of a bottle of wine felt like slightly more than that on a – mostly – empty stomach.

A likely looking keychain from a hook in the kitchen was grabbed and Maxime set about walking between all the various doors on the ground floor that he hadn't explored yet.

Beatrice was busy building up the playlist for the remainder of the evening and paying little attention to him as he blundered

To Mnemosyne, a Daughter

about the ground floor trying keys in every unusual door he found. It did seem as though the French were incredibly keen on building anterooms for midgets - every small door led to a room barely large enough to step into.

One, however, locked by a large matte-black metal key which dwarfed the others, opened to a staircase leading down into darkness. Maxime fumbled around on the wall inside the door and his fingers connected with a small switch. Flicking it, a dull orange light at the bottom of the stairwell sputtered briefly before flaring into life.

As Maxime carefully made his way down the narrow staircase, he noted the musty smell that emanated from the space below. With a few careful steps, he walked onto the concrete floor of the basement and looked about himself.

His heart leapt upon spying a wooden wine rack – more importantly, an *occupied* wine rack – but he found himself immediately distracted by something else down in the dry and musty basement of the château.

There were several bookcases that took up the majority of one of the chipped white brick walls of the basement, criss-crossed thick, ancient, black wooden beams heaving with a variety of books of varying ages and thicknesses. He stepped closer, his shoes tip-tapping against the bare concrete.

The arrangement was seemingly random; ancient tomes with torn leather bindings rubbed spines with assorted pulp novels from the thirties, and nineteen-seventy science fiction vied for shelf space with biographies, cookbooks, horror novels, and encyclopaedias. Maxime found himself walking up and down its length, staring in incredulity at some of the shelves' contents. Occasionally he'd allow himself the pleasure of sliding one out from the shelf and admiring it for a few moments; signed first editions, books that had been out of print for as long as he could remember, obscure novels he'd never heard of by writers that he *had* heard of. Maxime was in his absolute element.

It was Beatrice's voice that yanked him from the trance. Her silhouette was at the top of the stairs, the bright light of the kitchen behind her outlining the shape of her body through the thin fabric of her cotton pyjamas. Maxime had to force himself to look away.

"Any luck with that wine? A lady could die of thirst."

"Yeah, sure. Just coming up now."

The books weren't going anywhere – they could wait until tomorrow. Maxime, being far from a connoisseur in such matters, picked two bottles from the rack simply because they had the prettiest label. Wine's just wine, right?

At first, they were happy listening to the music that Beatrice had curated, a playlist that couldn't have been any more French if it had ridden through the living room on a bicycle wearing a striped jersey and beret with a string of onions draped around its neck. Maxime had started the evening sprawled back on a *Chaise Longue* that needed some serious reupholstering, and Beatrice was sitting on a long red leather sofa that took up most of the room.

As more wine flowed though, the music became less and less important than the conversation. Beatrice was now lying on her front and Maxime had somehow ended up sitting on the floor, leaning against her sofa.

"I'm not sure we should be drinking this," she smiled, taking another sip of the red, "That bottle might be worth a fortune. Each sip of this might cost *millions*."

Maxime shuffled on the spot, making himself comfortable against the firm leather.

"I'm particularly impressed by how you waited until we'd drunk two thirds of it before raising your concerns. We'd better not have that other one then – minimise the risk."

"Fuck that for a game of soldiers," she protested, shifting into a sitting position. She stood up and wobbled for a few moments,

To Mnemosyne, a Daughter

steadying herself. They were both getting quite drunk, and Maxime felt safer and more stable here on the floor.

She staggered off towards the stairs.

"If they *are* valuable collector's items, I'm potentially off for the most expensive piss of my life. So, get that other one opened."

Make yourself at home, Murray had said. He surely wouldn't mind a few bottles of plonk being downed as part of the creative process.

Even as he was opening the second bottle, his mind went back to the book collection in the basement. If there were a good few reference books down there, the lack of internet in the grounds of the château wouldn't matter. Just a book of British or European Folklore would give him the information he needed about the *Afanc*, and it'd settle that nagging doubt so writing could resume.

Beatrice emerged again at the top of the stairs, her T-shirt and pyjama combo replaced by a silk gown the same shade of red as the sofa. She smiled upon seeing that Maxime had opened the other bottle.

"So, you're upgrading our crimes from larceny to *grand* larceny? I'll drink to that."

With the contents of the second bottle from the cellar barely capable of half-filling a single glass, Maxime wondered whether it'd be a terrible idea getting another one. He could write off tomorrow as a research day, something more than achievable even when nursing a hangover.

"Is there anything higher than grand larceny?" he asked, peering back over his shoulder at her. Beatrice had nearly finished her glass as well. Her forehead screwed up in intense concentration, as though trying to weight up the good and bad points of such a decision.

David Court

"One more bottle. And we don't have to finish the whole thing – just another glass for the road."

Don't have to finish the whole thing. The drinker's classic lie, one that almost burnt his tongue as it spilled out over his lips. He could barely convince himself, let alone Beatrice.

"Sure thing. One more glass. But no getting lost in the cellar this time."

One book had caught his eye on his earlier visit, and Maxime afforded himself another quick look on the way past. It looked newer than the others, brand new in fact, and there was something familiar about it. He carefully slid it out from between two hefty tomes.

The title glared at him in a large white plain font – *The Path of Least Resistance* by Mike Ripley.

He *did* recognise it. Maxime shared an agent with Mike. The book, a crime thriller, was the final part of a successful trilogy he'd finished last year. They'd met at the last two of Murray's notorious Christmas parties for his clients. The first time they'd met they'd gotten along surprisingly well, half-heartedly promising – and never managing – to stay in touch. They'd met at last year's Christmas party as well, but Mike was almost a different man – he looked ill, distracted. Maxime, shallow as he was, didn't fancy getting caught up in a lengthy discussion about ailments, and so had done little more than say a "hello" in passing.

He emerged back into the living room, the book in one hand and a fresh bottle of red in the other. She stared at him, an eyebrow raised, a half-smile carved into her narrow lips.

"What have you got there?"

There was mock disappointment in her tone, but Maxime still couldn't help but feel embarrassed, like a naughty child caught doing something he shouldn't.

"It's just one book," he said, feeling suitably admonished. "I know – or rather, I've *met* this guy."

To Mnemosyne, a Daughter

He placed it on the kitchen surface, planning to at least give it a polite perusal over the next couple of days. He'd told Mike he would do as such at their first meeting, so it'd feel rude not to do so now the opportunity had properly arisen.

She held out her glass for him, and he filled two-thirds of it with the deep red liquid, the rich smells of which filled the room the very instant the cork was removed. Having done the same with his own glass, he placed the bottle back on the table in the centre of the room, placing the cork purposefully next to it.

"So it's there for later," he said, attempting to justify his actions, "If we want any more, of course. Or we could just cork it back up again, see how it goes."

She was still giggling at him as he resumed his place, back leant against the sofa. As he took the first sip from this fresh glass, he felt her shifting behind him.

"I'm supposed to be here to stop you indulging in these bad habits," she spoke softly, her mouth inches away from his ear.

He turned to her, their faces now almost touching. She was lying face-down on the sofa, her head propped up in her hands. Her wine glass – already bereft of half of what he'd poured – was resting on the arm of the chair.

"You *are* helping," he smiled, "Without you, I'd have to have all this wine for myself. You're sharing the burden."

Their eyes were locked, unblinking. Christ, she was perfect. Her complexion was like unblemished porcelain, her eyes shimmering cyan. Maxime must have looked like a dishevelled wreck in his crumpled two-days-of-wear shirt and random stubble, but Beatrice looked flawless. Even her auburn hair that had fallen out of place looked perfectly arranged.

"It's a dirty job, but someone's got to do it," she whispered, leaning in closer. Her scent was easily as intoxicating as the wine, and he closed his eyes expectantly. Every one of his senses seemed heightened as he felt her lips faintly brush against his own, the very tip of her tongue reaching out to touch his.

David Court

When it all became too much bear, the anticipation driving him wild, he pressed back. His eyes flickered open as he found his face pressed against the still warm leather of the sofa.

Beatrice had gone, the sofa now vacant. The indentations in the leather, slowly creaking and shifting back to normal, were the only sign she'd been there at all. The lights in the room had been dimmed, and the bottle on the table was now empty, as was the glass sitting next to it. Maxime's glass was still next to him, barely touched.

Had he fallen asleep, the wine having finally got the better of him? Had he been sitting there, unconscious, as Beatrice had finished her wine and made her way off to bed? Bizarre - his skin still tingled at even that faint touch, and the sheer quantities of adrenaline coursing through his system made him feel like he wouldn't sleep in a *week*.

As embarrassed as he was confused, Maxime dragged himself to his feet. He glanced up at the clock – it was the early hours of the morning, but that didn't tell him anything. He hadn't had any idea what time it was anyway.

He picked up his glass of wine, intending to take it upstairs and finish it as he read Mike's book, Thing was, though, the book wasn't where he'd left it. At least he didn't *think* it was. He felt comparatively sober now, but it could have been that he'd misplaced it earlier in the evening.

Thinking that drinking any more was probably not the best idea, he carefully poured the rest of his wine back into the bottle.

Beatrice's room was shut as he walked past it on the landing, a thin snake of light coming from the gap at the bottom of the door. With the general background noise of the house – the creaking of floors and beams, curtains shifting in the wind – it was impossible to tell if there was any activity from within the room, whether Beatrice was awake or not.

To Mnemosyne, a Daughter

Maxime stepped into his room, slowly closing the door behind him. The room was pleasantly cool, the windows having been opened mid-afternoon to remove the musty aroma that seemed to seep into everything in the old house. He stripped naked and climbed into the old bed, enjoying the sensation of the cool sheets against his skin.

He'd find Mike's book tomorrow. Could well have been he'd moved it, or it had fallen somewhere. Beatrice may well have tidied it up, returning it to one of the shelves.

He lay there in the darkness, listening to the reassuring ambience of the Château de Amorette. Funny how he hadn't thought of Mike for ages, but now he'd been reminded the thoughts began to slowly seep back from the periphery of his consciousness.

Murray's Christmas Parties were the thing of great legend, typically descending into debauched affairs. Cocaine use seemed to be quite prolific amongst Murray's retinue, but Class A drugs had never been Maxime's thing. He'd been introduced to Mike earlier in the evening, and they'd later gravitated towards each other in that they were the only two not snorting white powder up their noses in the other room.

"Not a fan of cocaine, then?" Mike asked, eyeing up the selection of unopened wine bottles against the wall.

"Not really. I hear it's very moreish, though."

Mike laughed. That was good. Anybody willing to listen to and laugh at Maxime's recycled jokes was clearly a reasonable person. Mike grabbed hold of a bottle of Sauvignon Blanc and, with an approving nod from Maxime, filled both of their glasses.

"I read your first Nightgaunt book, you know."

"I'm ashamed to say that I haven't read yours, yet. It's on my 'to read' pile," lied Maxime, "What did you think?"

David Court

"I'll be straight with you – I didn't think it would be my cup of tea. It was my daughter's recommendation. Your heroine Clara…"

"Carina"

"Your heroine *Carina*. I thought her a bit of a Mary Sue at first. She's beautiful, super-smart, *hyper*-sexual and a master of every weapon – I thought for the first fifty pages or so it was just the wish-fulfilment of a man old enough to know better. But you did something smart with her – little by little, you started to introduce the flaws. You added chinks to her armour, and she became properly fleshed out. And I couldn't put it down once I got that. Really clever."

The spectre of that phrase was haunting him now, though. *Wish-fulfilment*. A little like a middle-aged writer becoming slowly obsessed with someone a decade his junior, almost definitely misinterpreting her friendliness as flirtation. Maxime should really have known better.

There must have been a subtle pattern to the noises of the house, a regular repeating rhythm as the beams contracted and expanded. This much was apparent when Maxime's attention was instantly aroused by a tonal shift, an unexpected emergent instrument in the nocturnal concerto. Creaking over and above the expected tempos, footsteps on the wooden rafters. They soon stopped, to be replaced by another noise – the faint metal clicking of metal against metal as the handle to his room was slowly turned, of an ancient bolt turning against a rusted tumbler.

Maxime sat up, trying to focus through the darkness. He was used to living in the city, where the evening was forever lit – where streetlights stood as eternal nocturnal sentinels and car lights illuminated the darkest of streets. Here, bar the beams of moonlight that swept through the shifting curtains like searchlights, darkness clung to everything.

The door creaked slowly as it was pushed open, a restraining handheld against it. Maxime squinted at the shape that appeared in the doorway, the shoulders and head of a female silhouette framed by silver moonlight.

Maxime sat up further, pulling the covers about himself.

"Beatrice?"

"Shush" came the response. As she approached, Maxime could see that the moonlight shone off hair longer than Beatrice's, hair that fell over naked shoulders, but both the voice and figure were clearly hers.

Maxime sat there in silence, pulling the covers tighter about himself.

"I need you to lie flat," she instructed in a low whisper, stepping closer to the bed. The moonlight gleamed off her shoulders, the flickering of beams resting across the gentle curve of her breasts.

Apprehensively, he did as he was told, lowering himself down onto the bed, flattening the sheets about himself. Despite his nerves, he was at least relieved twofold to confirm that this visitor was Beatrice and that she hadn't sleepwalked into his room.

"Beatrice, what are you d-"

A shush again, louder this time, a finger raised to her face.

He lay there, frozen. Legs together, arms by his side. Truth be told, although he wouldn't admit it to himself, he felt a little emasculated by this bold show of brazenness from her. He was the one used to performing the seduction, the one making the first move.

She slowly moved to the foot of the bed before crouching down and lifting the cool white sheets. Maxime suddenly realised what she was doing – she was under the covers on all fours at the bottom of the bed, and slowly making her way towards him.

David Court

Her long hair brushed against him, trailing against his legs and across his thighs. He could feel the warmth radiating from her as she passed over him, deliberately avoiding contact where she could. Every moment of skin contact was quite deliberate on her part, each causing him to shudder involuntarily, his arousal mounting every time. For one thrilling moment, it felt as though she was running the tip of her tongue against the length of his dick, but the moment lasted just an instant. When her face was level with his, she straddled him, but only gently lowered her weight onto him. It felt as though she were hovering there, suspended a fraction of an inch away.

Her hair was much longer than before, the long strands of it cascading about his face – a tunnel in which the only thing he could see was her. She stared down at him, her tongue licking her lips, her eyes half-closed. He went to lift his hand, to stroke her face, but her own arm snapped out with a strength defying her slender frame and held his down by the wrist.

She lowered her face over his, the pair's eyes now firmly locked. Maxime didn't dare move, not even to blink. Her hips began to move, slowly rocking. With each move, her legs gripped tighter against his own legs. It was like a pulse, her legs tightening and loosening. The ripples of movement travelled up the length of her body, her breasts pressing against his chest as her breathing increased in pace. He could only watch as her eyes closed and lips parted, her movements increasing in speed and strength.

She rose as he did, carefully – and frustratingly – altering her position so the tip of his erection would rarely touch her. Each time it brushed against her skin, he trembled at the sensation and was convinced he'd seen the hint of a smile in those parted, gasping lips. This was maddening but utterly *intoxicating*, an experience threatening to overwhelm all his senses; the smell of her sweat and the feel of it as each tiny drip landed on him, the electric touch of her skin, the tiny involuntary gasps that burst out of her, rising in crescendo and increasing in pace.

To Mnemosyne, a Daughter

He wanted nothing more than to grab her grinding hips and ease into her, but the expression on her face – that *determination* – told him he was mostly unnecessary to this whole sexual equation. She just wanted him to *watch*.

There was a certain liberation in the frustration though – even without actual *coitus*, he'd never felt as turned on. There was no pressure to perform, no responsibility to do anything other than simply enjoy the sensations. To be in the presence of such a sexual being was almost reward enough, her arousal only fuelling his.

Her movements were increasing in pace, and the rhythmic rubbing of her hips against his cock was almost too much to bear.

With one final violent spasm, a sigh struggled to escape through her gritted teeth. She squeezed his wrists tighter as she came, pinning him further onto the bed with a preternatural strength. His cock jerked one final time as he came too, exploding over his belly and chest. As he lay there trembling, his neurons dancing as though at a party at the end of the world, she lifted herself off the bed and, without a word, left the room.

Maxime had no idea how long he'd lain there, the cool, drying cum on his chest, the sheets scattered about him like broken wings. The act of ejaculation was usually a soporific one, but he felt charged, as though every muscle and synapse was aflame. Whereas his brain should have been mulling over what just happened, the bizarre relationship – if you could *refer* to it as that – between Maxime and Beatrice, it was ticking over with story ideas and concepts. He could see solutions for ideas that had been abandoned or he'd considered unworkable.

This final book could be more than a placeholder.

This final book could genuinely be his fucking *masterwork*.

David Court

A potential awkward situation the next morning was – temporarily – averted. Maxime had procrastinated in his room for a good thirty minutes wondering how to broach the subject of last night with Beatrice – indeed, whether to mention it at *all*. However, there was no sign of her as he crept down the stairs – just as simple note scrawled on the wipe-clean board on the larder fridge.

> *"Gone for a few days... get writing!"*
> *B x"*

Friendly with a kiss at the end, as though nothing out of the ordinary had happened at all. He hoped she hadn't left on his account, but the impulsive forceful woman who'd shared his bed last night didn't strike him as the type to have regrets or to be ashamed.

Fixing himself the first coffee of the morning, Maxime noted that she'd filled the fridge with provisions – milk, cheese, cured meats. A freshly baked loaf of bread sat wrapped in brown paper on the windowsill next to large sealed jar of peanuts, almonds, and cashews. Funny – he'd lain awake for most of the night, and hadn't heard any movements from the house, let alone her leaving and returning with shopping.

The formidable challenge of the Chapter header followed by an endless wasteland of empty pages; once a challenge, now a space to be conquered.

The usual frustrations of trying to find the right word to use had been neatly reversed – if anything, Maxime found himself cursing his keyboard. What a primitive way to commit words to a story – Oh, for a faster means than this mechanical bottleneck. The words – the *perfect* words, crystalline in form and structure

To Mnemosyne, a Daughter

– were all dying to escape him, and his fingers were slowing him down.

By the time he reached for his cup of coffee, it had already gone tepid. This had *never* happened, in all his years of writing. There was typically never *enough* coffee.

Reluctantly, he dragged himself away from the keyboard to make a fresh batch of caffeine. The kitchen clock showed that it was already mid-afternoon, the sun now at its very height. As he stood in the kitchen waiting for the kettle to boil, he found himself absent-mindedly looking out of the window.

He was looking for her. Or for any sign of her.

Smiling to himself and now armed with coffee, he sat back down at the keyboard. Taking a few sips and enjoying the heady effect of the caffeine on his already buzzing brain, he glanced at the word count.

He had an idea of how long the book was going to be – the publisher had insisted that it be the thickest volume yet, ("The last book is *always* a good third thicker than the others") although that was his plan all along.

In one single writing session, he'd written a good fifth of the book. The word count was now just a few thousand words shy of that of Book Two of the trilogy, and that had been thicker than the first.

He glanced at what he'd written. Despite the fact it felt as though he'd written it on automatic pilot, the words he found himself staring at weren't simple a stream of consciousness to be edited and refined later. Although it felt somewhat like he was reading them for the first time, this was good, clean copy.

No, *more* than clean copy.

This was as damn close to proper literature as he'd ever written. The sentences sung to him, the words ebbing and flowing with a rhythm and pace that had him on the verge of tears. Traditional sentence structures merged into experimental prose, but never in a way that seemed pretentious or out of anything that the story required, nay, *demanded.*

David Court

If he hadn't known otherwise, he'd have been convinced that these were the words of a far better writer than himself.

At the height of his art, when he felt barely conscious of his surroundings, when the words flowed out like blood from a freshly sliced jugular, he thought of her.

Sometimes as abstract fragments – her eyes, her moist lips, a summer dress fallen from a bare shoulder.

At other times, as scenes – a microcosm of their brief encounters. Some were real; the way she closed her eyes when she inhaled her cigarette, as though projecting herself a million miles away, her moonlight-framed naked silhouette in his doorway with the fullness and curve of her hips, the way she pursed her lips when sipping her wine.

Others were fictional, events that never were, but as strong and as real as any thought; Lying in the sunlit garden and naming clouds, sitting on the banks of the Dordogne, their naked toes idly splashing in the waters. Skinny dipping in the waters, holding her close as she mounted his dick, no words or sounds save a short and pleasured gasp.

He'd hear her voice, and the typing would stop as he focussed – before realising he was imagining it. Each creak of the house a plimsoll footstep, each curtain flap, the flutter of her dress.

The house was in darkness when he sat back, exhausted. The only light was the diode glow from the monitor that, riddled with a labyrinth of words, cast a muddy grey half-light across the room.

Afanc.

The thought came to him like a prod to the forehead. The mythical beast from earlier on, the one he needed to research. It was like a loose thread in a perfect tapestry, a flaw that could unravel the whole piece.

To Mnemosyne, a Daughter

His legs protested the moment he stood up, followed by equal dissent from his bladder. He'd been that devoted – obsessed – with putting word to page that his soul was sated at the neglect of his physical frame.

Perhaps it *was* about time to stop for the day. A glass of wine, a bit of research and a relatively early night would wind him down nicely, all ready to start afresh tomorrow. A visit to the bathroom – and a few splashes of cold water across his face – revived him somewhat, and he stared in triumph at the man in the mirror.

"You," he said, genuinely pleased with himself, "are about to put the finishing touches to a fucking great book."

Beatrice had picked two reasonable bottles of red from the village, perhaps somewhat reluctant to let Maxime loose again on the potentially priceless collection in the cellar. But, venture into the cellar he had to – in the absence of the internet, it was the only potential source of research material that he had.

The cellar door had been locked. Not unusual, but the keychain was missing from the bare hook in the kitchen as well. He was sure that he hadn't locked it himself, so set about looking for the keys. They weren't in any of the usual spots that lost things find themselves. He scoured tables, down the side of or back of chairs, and window sills but to no avail.

No sign of it in his own room, although searching in that untidy pit took longer than he'd have liked. Could Beatrice have taken it?

He cursed himself for his nervousness as he stepped into her room, fumbling in the dark for the light switch. Flicking it, the room was suddenly lit by a dull under-powered bulb that flickered into life. The room was tidy, the bed neatly made, looking as though it hadn't been slept it for an age. In fact, there was no sign she'd been here at all – drawers were empty, as was the wardrobe that took up most of one wall.

A thin layer of unmarked dust clung to many of the surfaces, none of which housed the key or its keyring.

In the end, stubbornness and brute force won out over patience. The lock was old. and the metal worn, and a hefty push from Maxime loosened the mechanism with a broken click. He fixed himself a glass of wine and carefully made his way down the narrow wooden steps into the cold confines of the poorly-lit basement.

Even with the haphazard ordering and the barely legible text on a few of the more worn out spines, a few relevant books were identified and carefully removed from their bookshelves. Books on Folklore, myth, and legend from both Europe and the British Isles – some relatively new and intact, some older than he was that were barely held together by unstitched and decaying binding.

The book from Mike was here as well, slid neatly back from where he'd removed it. He placed that on the pile as well, determined to at least make a start on it in whatever time he had left here.

Despite the balmy summer evening above, thin wisps of cold air hung in patches around the basement. The warm air from the château above seemed reluctant to venture down here. Ideal conditions for wine, but the change in temperature made Maxime uncomfortable. He gathered his small curated selection of books and retreated to the muggy warmth of the lounge. The lock now broken; the door could only be partly closed behind him.

The mythological creature he'd picked turned out to be more obscure than he'd envisaged – it was only as he came to the last reference that he could find any evidence at all that he hadn't just made the thing up.

To Mnemosyne, a Daughter

The *Afranc*, a lake monster from Welsh folklore; a demon who will devour any unwary or foolhardy enough to swim in its waters.

It was a description close enough to satisfy the pedants. He'd expected more text than the paragraph he'd been presented with, so this intense level of dedicated research would have to suffice.

Just time to make a start on Mike's book and wind down with just the one glass of wine. Maxime, never quite content with his own cover biography, had the habit of comparing his to others. Mike was no exception – he had a better photograph *and* blurb as well. In the photograph Mike looked healthy and happy, a far cry from the version he'd met last. So sad that he probably couldn't appreciate the overwhelming and unexpected success of his last book due to his illness. The man looked gaunt and frail – not quite at Death's door, but certainly in the neighbourhood and asking for directions.

He opened the book proper. The novel had an impressive "Also by the same author" as well. Maxime wondered what happened to Mike – was he still writing? Was he even still *alive*?

And there, on the first page, crisp black Garamond text on an off-white background:

To Beatrice
With all my love.

It's not an uncommon name, thought Maxime, pacing the floor. *You're in a château in the heart of France – you probably couldn't wave a baguette without hitting the odd Beatrice or two*. Still, something unnerved him, and he found himself once again within the dry cold walls of the basement, pulling books at random from out of their cases.

The collection grew at the same rate as his sense of impending dread. It became to form around him, a rough halo of scattered papers and torn pages.

David Court

Dedications from a dozen books, professing thanks or love to Beatrice, Bea, B. Sometimes going as far as terms of affection; Honey-Bee, Bumble. Handwritten or typed into the leading pages of manuscripts and books and in the margins of sheet music and poems.

Anthologies, pieces of academic text, biographies and autobiographies, every conceivable type of factual or fictional work – some probably as old as the château itself, the newest being Mike's.

And not simply dedications; Hand-written love-letters and poems, and photographs. Oh, the photographs – sketchy black and white shots pre-dating both World Wars, a faded Polaroid with seventies décor and dress, snapshots of every decade of this century and the last – of happy strangers with one familiar enduring component.

Beatrice – unchanging, never aging.

Love and thanks from a myriad of men and women, the countless names and pseudonyms of a libraries worth of long-gone writers.

And Maxime had heard of almost *every single one of them*. Names taught on syllabi across the globe, names that featured at the top of so many 'best of' lists that they might well be virtually carved into place there.

Maxime slumped back against the wall, holding a sketch on faded yellowing paper. It's a charcoal study of Beatrice, the lacquer sheen protecting it from the elements and ravages of time now patchy at best. She's looking coquettishly at the artist, her hair the same length it was that last night she visited him. Despite the crude medium, the gleam in her eye is apparent. It's Beatrice, in a sketch dated May the ninth, nineteen-twelve.

As he staggered upstairs, Maxime was clutching at the hastily gathered pile of documents with such force that a few became torn, ragged growing rips in the paper threatening to tear fragments away from the whole.

He was muttering Murray's name as he stumbled towards the kitchen, throwing the papers down on the kitchen counter. The black, seventies Bakelite phone still sat where he'd last used it on the table and he picked up the handset, flicking through his own reception-less mobile phone to find his agent's number. Murray would know what was going on – he'd arranged for Beatrice to visit him, after all.

The handset was dead as he lifted it to his ear. Overwrought now, he yanked at the cable which cracked up towards him like a whip, unconnected. He looked around the small room at where to insert the cable – the bare concrete walls didn't *have* any sockets. The phone could *never have worked*.

Reality was unravelling. Grabbing the papers again as though they offered some manner of protective ward, he stormed towards the kitchen door and some way out of this damnable building.

He felt it before he heard it, the same presence that had been haunting him. A shift in the air – not just a lowering of temperature, but as though the house had undergone a paradigm shift. Corridors felt narrower, lights dimmer, ceilings lower. Windows were dirtied or cracked, Rorschach patched stains blotting out the view from outside. It was as though Maxime had wandered into the beast's lair, a distorted and damaged version of reality.

It was clear to him now – the beast *was* Beatrice. All this time, they'd both been tormenting him in different ways, and now the game was up, he'd wandered headlong into this cruellest of final betrayals.

The corridor to the kitchen stretched out before him, a short passage rendered into a stretched labyrinth. Tendrilous shadows crept from the distance like cracks in glass, the thing forming in front of him like blackened smoke forming a shape.

The *other* Maxime emerged from the corrupting black smog, a perverse reflection of himself. It scurried towards him like a broken-stringed marionette, fingertips extended to raking claws, mouth extended to jaw-breaking proportions. Spider leg fingers wrapped around Maxime's throat as the two of them tumbled to the floor, the hideous blasphemy leering over him.

A foul-smelling acrid fluid dripped biliously from the things slathering mouth, burning the skin where it landed. It was laughing, a hollow guttural noise that turned Maxime's stomach as much as the thing's appearance and foul stench.

For a moment, their eyes met. Well, whatever the thing had where there *should* have been eyes. Two dark pits, portals into some stygian abyss – a dark void in which Maxime could see his own reflection.

Curling up watching the bad reviews pour in like so much raw effluence. "The last time I saw so few stars", jokes an ex-friend, "it was at one of Scott Baio's showbiz parties." Identifying the mocking tone of the interviewer far too late, the last to get the joke. Languishing under pen names, terrified to stick his head above the parapet again. A needle in one hand, a bottle of bourbon in the other – an experiment to see which would end him first.

The reflection was fading as quickly as Maxime's last vestiges of oxygen. There seemed to be little purpose in resisting.

No, *bullshit*. What he'd written – that was his legacy and it was *good. Fuck this noise.*

The skin puppet's hands fell away from Maxime's neck, and it staggered back, stunned. Time enough for Maxime to get to his feet and push his way past the foul thing, throwing himself into the kitchen and out the door.

He could see the twinkling lights of far off Rocamadour in the shadow of the hills. There would be solace there, *normality.*

Each step towards the boundaries of the château grounds was more leaden than the last, as though the air itself were thickening up to conspire against him. His pace slowed down to a crawl, the very act of placing one foot in front of the other a test of endurance. The breath was sucked from his lungs as the

To Mnemosyne, a Daughter

resistance increased, the exhaustion he felt as though he were wading through congealed and hardening molasses.

Maxime's heart threatened to burst out of his chest as his hands stretched towards the gate at the edge of the property. Every inch of movement was a fresh triumph, every further inch a new goal. His legs began to buckle, and there was no energy left within him to halt the inexorable fall. *This must be what falling in zero gravity feels like*, he thought, as the droplets of his sweat tumbled slowly with him like tiny pearlescent beads.

He was barely conscious, all vestiges of strength drained from him, when she helped him to his feet. He remembered - at her soft instruction - dragging one foot in front of the other. Nausea would threaten to overwhelm him when, on occasion, the fight left him, and he fell – but she was always there to catch him, to hold him and whisper kindnesses into his ear.

When the cold touch on his skin had gone – when they were inside the confines of the house – the grip around him strengthened, increased in confidence. He could smell the familiar aroma of his sheets, of his own room, and then drifted off into the deepest of sleeps.

A myriad of thoughts coursed through his addled brain as he awoke, and the first thing he saw was her. He was under the covers, she on top in that summer dress, slowly and gently rubbing the backs of her fingers against his cheeks.

Anger. Betrayal. All these thoughts were vivid and raw, ready to explode to the surface.

"You came back," he found himself saying, the relief obvious. He had no anger left in him.

"I never left," she whispered, planting a kiss on his forehead as gentle as a breeze.

Maxime had no idea how long he'd lain there but knew from her lingering touch that she'd never left his side. The light faded and returned, like time-lapse photography marking the passage of time, but Maxime didn't know whether the waxing and waning light came from outside the window or from his own lapsing into and out of unconsciousness.

David Court

With rest, came strength. Eventually, strength enough to push himself away and awkwardly sit up, back pressed against the soft velour headboard. Determination enough to shy away from her touch, turn his eyes away from her own. And in turn, the strength to speak. To ask the only question of any value.

"Who *are* you?"

She was honest, at least. Even for a man whose primary tool was his imagination, what she said was incredible – but her matter-of-fact manner and that which he had already witnessed gave her words credibility. Her softly spoken words were part confession, part history lesson.

The house had always been a Writer's retreat, of sorts. Owned and built by an author of some repute and bequeathed as a dying gasp on her deathbed to benefit others. Before her death, she'd written and boasted at length about the magic in the place, never believing for one moment that her words could ever have been literal.

Beatrice had no idea how she'd came to be, what had come before, or how long she had *been*. Perhaps she'd always been here, waiting to be summoned. Perhaps she'd been written to life by a writer's vivid imagination. Perhaps, in a way, she *was* the house.

For some – the mundane, the dull – those whose writings would never amount to anything – writers in name but not in deed, she'd watch from doorways. She'd flit by, ethereal, her face pressed against windows, but they'd *never* see her.

For others, she'd just be a voice. A muse of sorts, a spark of inspiration – the whispered thought in the dead of night that smashes like a sledgehammer through a wall of writer's block, a missing sentence to turn sentences into verse and song.

To Mnemosyne, a Daughter

For others, those possessing their *own* magic ... oh, she could be *so* much more. Friend, lover, confidant. For those willing to submit, she could *tease* the words out of them.

"So, were the words I wrote my own?"

Absolutely, she insisted. They were always there – they just needed encouragement. There just needed to be the desire to tempt the words out - and one thing she had mastered was the act of intensifying desire.

"And the... thing? That fucking monster that's been trying to kill me?"

Only what you carried into the château with you, she said. *The magic in the château just gave it life.*

"Gave what life?" he asked. There was so much to take in, his head was spinning.

Self-doubt. Your fears and worries, those nagging doubts that lessen you. But, to your words.

The relationship is reciprocal, she insisted, placing the unfinished manuscript on his lap. He picked it up as though it were delicate china, as though at any moment the magic would be lost, and the pages would disintegrate into ash.

Read, she asked.

The words were clearly his own – his sentence structure, his turn of phrase – but it felt as though he were reading them properly for the first time. It was effortless, an enhancement wound through the core of the syntax and semantics. The characters sprang to life, more real than they'd ever felt. One, in particular.

He carefully placed the manuscript back onto the bed, beside himself.

"It's you, isn't it?"

She smiled back at him, relieved that he understood.

"Lady Carina," he continued, "She... she's the same character as in the preceding two books, but she's become *you*. Your mannerisms, your words – I've written her as *you*."

"I'm in all them *all*," she said, standing up to stare out of the window. "I'm the heroine, the love interest *and* rival. I'm the villain, I'm the one they declare their love to in the songs and poems."

She sat back down on the bed, placing each hand onto Maxime's. Her touch was warm, electric. With each beat of her heart, Maxime felt envigored, renewed.

"If they write about me, I live on."

Her hands gripped his now, tightly, tenderly.

"And as long as your works are remembered, *you* live on."

He gripped her hands back, for comfort as much as anything.

"You saw what happened when I tried to leave."

"There's an *arrangement,* Maxime. You're not a prisoner. You're free to leave at any time."

"There's a *but*, isn't there? I can tell from your tone."

"If you go, you take what you've written. You'll never finish it – you'll never be able to hit those notes again, to feel that *longing*. Oh, you'll try. But it will always, frustratingly, remain as your unfinished masterwork."

"And the alternative?"

"You stay here and finish it, and it gets unleashed on the world. And it will be *glorious*. Your name will be on the tip of the tongue of every scholar, on the shelf – or the thoughts – of your peers."

"But..?"

"As I said, you *stay here*."

"But I'll be missed. People know I'm here – they'll come looking."

"They won't. You'll return to the normal world – a fragment of you, at least. A *shade* of Maxime, you in all but most of your spirit. A diminished You. Soulless. A husk. And the *beast*? That leaves too."

Mike... That was what happened to Mike. Gaunt, half a man. Nervously looking about himself, as though haunted.

"Mike is here, in a way. They all are. But they are *remembered*."

She stood up, her hands lingering over his as she did.

To Mnemosyne, a Daughter

"The decision has to be yours. I'll see you downstairs."

He was alone, just him and the unfinished manuscript. What he'd read – it was wonderful. He'd never better it, even in a lifetime.

Outside of the writing, what was there? The aches and pains that came with middle age, the pained attempts to recapture youth. This was a chance at *legacy*. But, at what cost?

Clutching at the manuscript, renewed, he made his way towards the stairs.

Maxime's pace increased the further he stepped away from the house, and he never looked back. The sun was lower in the sky today, clouds gathering on the horizon, and the walk into Rocamadour was therefore still long, but not unpleasant.

Warned that any taxi would take at least an hour to arrive, he ordered a wine. It was unpleasant, a sour note clinging to his taste-buds that didn't shift until he was seated on the plane.

He felt nothing as the plane lurched skywards, the wheels retracting as they ascended into the golden tinged clouds. He felt drained, *numb*.

At times, he'd feel a presence behind him. A voice, whispering his name – a cold shadow falling across him. He'd turn around to both a vacant seat and silence.

It was a feeling he'd learn to live with, but one he would never get used to.

"It's done," he smiled. He didn't even need to read what he'd written – it felt right.

"If you're sure," said Beatrice, standing behind him in the glow of the monitor. She wrapped her arms around him and perched her head on his shoulder.

David Court

With a practiced flourish, the finished manuscript was dragged onto the email. With barely a pause, Maxime clicked the "Send" button, and his final story began to soar across the gulf of the North Atlantic Ocean.

Ironic – the story was such a big part of him, and a *literal* part of him was on a plane flying over that same stretch of ocean now.

Maxime stood up and stepped over to the window, staring at the moonlit grounds of the Château de Amorette. Everything out there was bathed in an ethereal silver glow, and Maxime stared at his own hands, flexing and relaxing his fingers in the light.

"Am I still real?" he asked, "What happens next?"

He felt her behind him, pressing against him.

"I think you know," she whispered, the tip of her tongue flicking gently against his earlobe. One of her hands slowly moved down his chest before snaking its way inside the waist of his jeans. He shuddered at the cold of her skin; his cock already rock-hard before her fingers had even touched it. The tips of her fingers brushed against it delicately before her eager hand grabbed its length and began to softly knead the erect organ.

He could feel her warmth against his back as her other hand moved round his chest as though to hold him in place. Without turning, eyes half-closed, he moved his left hand around himself to her left thigh that was currently pressed against him. He began grabbing folds of her dress, pulling it slowly up. She moaned contentedly each time his fingers brushed against her skin. It was her turn to gasp with surprise as, when enough of her dress had been lifted, he slid two fingers into her panties.

The room sank into the distance, and with it, the world. There was no house, no future, no past – just the two of them. His fingers slid inside her and neatly matched her rhythm – with each tiny thrust of his penis in her grip, his finger slid deeper inside her.

She suddenly pulled herself away from him, stepping backwards to the bed. Moments before, they were still in the

To Mnemosyne, a Daughter

study, but that barely mattered. Maxime pulled his shirt over his head as he approached her, throwing it into the corner of the room. Beatrice, never once taking her eyes off him, sat on the edge of the bed. She lay back, hoisting her dress up to her waist.

He didn't need instruction. In a single move, he was on his knees and tracing the tip of his tongue across her thighs. Now it was *his* turn to tease – they had all the time in the world. He could tell from the excitable noises she was making – heightening in volume and pitch every time the tip of his tongue snaked near her pussy – that she was lost in the moment.

As Maxime finally slid his tongue inside her, it was all she could do not to yell out. It felt good for him to be in control – he rejoiced in each tiny spasm she made as his tongue worked its magic. Her hands moved to his head, her fingers stroking his hair – stopping and shuddering when his tongue worked deeper.

When neither of them could take any more, it took just two words – a plea – for him to stand up and unbuckle his jeans. She stood up to undress as well, the two of them almost falling over themselves with excitement as their clothes scattered on the floor.

They lay next to each, naked now, Maxime's erection pressing hard into the deep of her thigh. Despite their eagerness, they simply stared at each for the longest time. None of this still felt quite real to Maxime – with such an incredible amount to take in, reality had taken on somewhat of a dreamlike state.

But what a dream.

Her hand moved to his cock, gently stroking it with the back of her hand. He lowered his head to her right breast, his tongue circling her areola and spiralling before zeroing in and gently flicking her erect nipple.

"I want you, Maxime," she whispered, breathing gently into his ear.

Maxime, traditionally, had never been the sharpest on the uptake. He was far from slow-witted, but he had an over-tendency to overthink things, a trait that would sometimes see him lose out.

291

David Court

However, when a beautiful woman in your bed tells you that she wants you, there's no avenue for ambiguity. He gently shifted his body until he was on top of her. With a single thrust – and a silent open-mouthed gasp from Beatrice – he was inside her.

They kissed, drinking deep of each other. Her mouth went to her neck to plant gentle kisses across it, before tracing down to the nipple he'd neglected earlier.

She looked so fragile beneath him, her pale, almost translucent skin and delicate features. However, he was a fool to underestimate her strength. She began to grind her hips to match the increasing speed and strength of his thrusts, wrapping her legs around him to pull him deeper inside her.

His breathing increased, as did hers. Her moans matched the guttural noises he couldn't help but make with each thrust, their sounds hiding the noisy splintering from the walls, bricks noisily rolling against each other.

Hairline cracks appeared at the edge the glass of the window, spider-webbing across the surface until they met in the centre of the pane.

The resultant sound of the shattering glass didn't bother them. They could only see and hear each other, and they were all that mattered now. Furniture began to buckle, wood warping and melting. Books fell from dripping shelves, cups from a bedside cabinet that could no longer support their weight.

She was on top of him now, his hands cupping and kneading at her breasts and nipples as she rode his cock. Beatrice's fingertips raked across Maxime's chest before she grabbed his wrists and guided his hands to her hips.

The bed was the last thing to go, the surrounding room now fallen into the void that lay beyond the fractured walls. They were locked together as it crumpled away from them, spiralling sheets and broken metal struts tumbling into nothingness.

To Mnemosyne, a Daughter

They were now literally all there was, no up, no down – nothingness surrounded them, this instance of the house now crumbled into the void.

She clung onto him as he came, pushing him deeper inside her – an act that caused her to do the same, spasming violently and crying tears of joy.

He hugged her tight to him, their tears mingling.

"Is this it?" he asked.

She smiled at him, stroking his hair.

Moments in time; a newcomer gets her first Oscar, just as the third newly released book of a trilogy receives critical acclaim. Screenwriters win an Oscar too, passing thanks to a tired and ill-looking author in the audience. A book with a handwritten note is pushed onto a dusty bookshelf. Film makers ask for a fourth book, but it never comes. A couple love, age, and die, never to leave the place they call home. They are prisoners there, of sorts, but are prisoners who don't want to leave truly prisoners at all? Instances die and are reborn. Existing in solidary, and yet simultaneously. For a heartbeat as much as for eternity. A writer with writer's block desperately seeks assistance.

Ins and outs, shifting and pulsing.

At night, a house breathes.

David Court

You Only Live Thrice

"**W**ELL, FUCK ME.**"

The pilot, convinced that Ernst was trying to get his attention, turned around to look at him. This unnerved Ernst, as, all things considered, he'd rather the man concentrated on flying towards the island and not into the ocean. He gestured for him to get back on what he was paying him for, trying to make an apology heard over the sound of the rotors. Eventually, he took the hint.

A somewhat relieved Ernst turned his attention back to the source of his astonishment. He'd long since had to give up owning cats at his doctor's recommendation when he'd developed asthma, but there it was, sitting atop the newly dry-cleaned trousers of his grey Mao suit.

A thin, long white cat hair.

Cat-hair was *ubiquitous*. He remembered the good old days when you'd always find the same three things in the desk drawer in his lair: his treasured confiscated Walther PPK, a remote control for the meeting room trapdoor, and a series of lint-rollers.

He'd always swore to every new generation of henchmen that Fleming Charteris III was the same cat, and that he was just particularly blessed with health and feline longevity. He never dared admit the truth to them, that there had been six of them.

You Only Live Thrice

This particular family of pedigree cats just didn't live that long, sadly. He missed every one of those fluffy white bastards dearly. Like a phantom limb, he could occasionally still feel the weight of Charteris on his lap, rumbling with that familiar gentle and contented purr.

Ernst stared out of the window, the sun beautifully reflected in the calm copper and bronze waters of the Atlantic. The island loomed closer, the dormant volcanic crater that dominated much of it a familiar sight. The sea grew angrier the closer it got to the volcano, explosions of white spray from where it clashed with the harsh rocky outcrops that bordered the island.

The pilot gestured at Ernst to replace his headphones, and reluctantly he did so. He didn't like to wear them as a rule, the bulky cans sitting painfully across the scar tissue criss-crossing the right side of his face.

"I land you on the bitch, yes?" came the crackling voice through the intercom.

"I beg your pardon?"

"The *bitch*. The sandy bitch."

"Oh, the *beach*. No, you need to land me inside that volcano."

As rather a futile gesture, all things considered, given the size of the thing, Ernst found himself pointing at the volcano. As though that made everything clear.

They squabbled for a few minutes, the helicopter pilot not backward in coming forward about how he wasn't feeling particularly comfortable navigating his helicopter into the mouth of a once-active volcano. Ernst tried to convince the man that it was perfectly safe, and that the last pilot had happily done it, but he'd had to agree to pay the man a few hundred more euros for the privilege.

He missed *henchmen*. The days when you could order some orange jump-suited minions to lay down their lives for the cause at the drop of a hat. They would have happily flown into the mouth of a volcano, and they'd have been bloody grateful for the opportunity to do so. That was before they unionised, anyway,

David Court

and it all became a little complicated. Pilots like this were just hired hands in comparison.

Ernst looked around at the dilapidated interior of the volcano as the terrified pilot gripped onto the joystick, his knuckles white with fear. He remembered the good old days, when this would have been a hive of activity. You wouldn't have been able to move for buggies whizzing back and forth, and squadrons of henchmen in formation jogging with rifles.

Now, it was a shadow of its former self; rusted scaffolding that looked fit to collapse, and walkways overgrown with vegetation. That was the thing about your hollowed-out volcano bases – they were fuckers to maintain.

The chopper touched down on one of the few patches of floor that wasn't dotted with empty crates or dismantled computer equipment, and Ernst stepped out into the cool air of the gigantic cavern. He turned to face the pilot, who was already waving goodbye and preparing to depart.

Not so fast, Pedro.

Ernst reached inside his pocket and pressed hard on the remote control connected to the electrical pulse generator he'd secreted on the pilot's neck just as they'd left the mainland.

The pilot jerked and flailed like a marionette and slumped forward, unconscious. Ernst stepped back to the helicopter, switching off the engines whilst smiling at the slumbering form of his pilot. He closed his eyes, enjoying the blessed silence. He'd wake him when it was time for them to go.

It looked as though he was the first to arrive.

There was a chill in the air, the first hints of autumn. They usually came here in the summer, when the inability to heat a complex the size of it didn't matter as much. But, a change this year, at Auric's insistence. Ernst didn't like the cold – it made his scars tighten and ache, made those creeping tendrils of arthritis just that little bit more difficult to evade.

He walked up to one of the huge computer consoles that lined the wall, a long-dead wall of dead lights coated in an inch-thick layer of dust. To think, these were all the rage back in the day. They were always trying to impress each other, Ernst and his friends, always bragging about the number of flashing lights or spinning-tape reels that theirs had.

There was probably more processing power in his mobile phone than every computer in this whole facility had. Thinking back, he couldn't even remember what they really used these huge computer banks for.

Decoration, mostly.

The dust suddenly began to vibrate, huge plumes of grey powder filling the air, dust become smoke. The ground itself was shaking as a violent grinding and rumbling noise grew louder. Suddenly, a patch of rocky ground in a corner of the cavern burst open, rocks and pebbles sent flying and ricocheting off each other. Something was emerging from the rocks beneath them, all vicious-looking spinning blades and drill bits. The caterpillar-tracked thing reared into the air before crashing down to earth, the array of drills on the vehicle's nose slowing to a halt.

He always did know how to make an entrance.

A panel in the vehicles side hissed open, and Auric stepped out. Well, hobbled more than stepped, slowly edging down the ramp on his solid gold walking frame.

"Auric! My old friend! It's so good to see you!" said Ernst, genuinely buoyed to be reacquainted with his old friend.

"Age has treated you well, Mr. B" came that old familiar Slavic accent, as the old bugger smiled through the winces of pain that came with each movement.

"You too," lied Ernst. He looked back at the beast of a machine that Auric had arrived in. Realisation suddenly dawned, and he smiled with glee.

"Is that-?"

"It is," grinned Auric, now finally close enough to Ernst for the two to shake hands heartily. "The FBI sold it on, and I found it in the hands of a private seller. I couldn't resist."

David Court

Ernst stepped over to the mighty contraption, sliding a finger along the thing's scratched steel frame. Oh, he missed those glory days. Riding out in ridiculously impractical vehicles; huge tunnelling machines like this, submarines, cargo ships capable of *swallowing* submarines.

Something inside the vehicle caught his eye; a familiar embossed crate.

"I thought we said no alcohol this year? We've all been told by our doctors to keep off the stuff."

"Oh, it's only a few bottles of cinnamon schnapps. It won't hurt. We barely meet. And I think we've got *ages* until he arrives."

"Cinnamon schnapps?"

"Oh yes, Goldschläger."

"Ha, of course! What else?"

Hugo and Julius arrived together, surfacing in a midget submarine that emerged in a frenzy of bubbles into the algae encrusted pool in the adjacent cavern. Hugo's skin was as white as his beard as he staggered onto the quay, shaking his head in disbelief. He looked like he'd been through quite the ordeal. He appeared to be fishing in his pocket for something, but by the time Ernst had offered to assist, he'd found his inhaler and was panting into it like a distressed pufferfish.

"I tried to warn him. Tried to tell him it would be safer by air, that the waterways under the base would be way too poorly maintained to navigate..."

Julius stepped from the submarine, as confident as ever. He smiled at Ernst and Auric, peeling the driving gloves from his metal hands as he stepped towards them.

"You know me, gentlemen. I never can say no to a challenge."

He held out his hand, and Ernst shook it. He could never quite get used to the icy touch of Julius's metal grip. From the

You Only Live Thrice

look of discomfort on Auric's face as they shook hands, he was clear he felt much the same.

"I've had some wine delivered in advance, gentleman" announced Julius as he headed towards the meeting room, "and I'm having a helicopter deliver us some lunch in about an hour or so."

"Oh great," muttered Hugo, "The fucker insists on driving *us* here at top speed through green murk with no visibility, but he'll let them safely airdrop our *dinner*."

"No, I expect you to *die,* I said. Should have seen the look on his face," bellowed Ernst, spilling most of the glass of Château Latour 2009 as he gesticulated wildly.

"Bullshit", interjected Hugo. "Francisco said it was *him* who said that."

"Where is Francisco, anyway?" asked Julius, pouring himself another glass of wine. "He's usually a stickler for punctuality. Always the first here."

Auric took his eyes from his phone for a moment, slowly stepping over to the assembled group.

"They put him in a home, I heard. Alzheimer's."

They all went silent. There were fewer of them left each year now, mused Ernst. Rosa had died in her care-home, and The Cypher was on his last legs (no pun intended), cancer-ridden and wheelchair-bound. All of them except Auric raised a glass to their fallen colleague. Nobody there was all that surprised - Auric and Francisco had never really seen eye to eye, despite their shared hobbies.

David Court

"Whyte told me he put him to the test at the bar at his casino, you know" said Hugo, leaning in conspiratorially, as though he were the bearer of a dreadful secret.

"What, *him?* What test?"

The bait was taken. Hugo re-joined them, ushering them all to move closer as though the entire place were bugged.

"His insistence on how he took his Martini. Remember? He'd raise one eyebrow in that way that he did, and smugly announce he wanted it *shaken, not stirred*. Whyte thought he'd put it to the test when he came to the bar back in the seventies. Whyte got his barman to stir the fuck out of it when he wasn't looking, whilst Jimmy was distracted by some blonde or other – you know how he was with the ladies."

Ernst took a moment to pay attention to how excited Hugo was, how invigorated he was at this moment. The sad truth was, he told this story every single time. He was getting noticeably more senile every time they met, and with every meeting, they all suspected it'd be the last time they saw him.

But it was worth playing along, just to humour the old boy. Ernst feigned eagerness and stared at Hugo.

"Really? What did he do when he took the first sip?"

Hugo smiled and sat back, the lower half of his face now a gleaming mass of white beard, moustache, and dentures.

"Not a thing," he smirked. "Whyte said the bastard didn't even *notice*. He couldn't even tell the difference, the smug shit."

"I never saw the point of having it like that, anyway" announced Julius, always eager to have the last word. It didn't help that his obnoxiousness increased with every sip of drink that he imbibed. "It's supposed to be stirred so it doesn't break the ice. He was being precious about a piss-weak martini. The man was full of bullshit."

Ernst went to speak, but then thought better of it. However, having poured himself another glass of this delicious wine, he decided to have his say after all.

You Only Live Thrice

"You say that, Julius, but we owe our lives to that bullshit. If it wasn't for him, we'd all be dead or locked up in Federal prison by now. It was only by him telling his superiors we were dead that we're all around now, able to enjoy this fine repast."

Ernst moved a jabbing finger around all his colleagues at the table.

"Hugo, your frozen corpse is supposed to be floating in deep space somewhere. Auric, you were allegedly sucked out of a plane window to your death, and he told his paymasters that he dropped *me* down a fucking chimney, for Christ's sake."

He turned to face Julius, who was staring down into his glass, refusing eye contact. Ernst waited until he looked up, and their eyes were locked.

"And you, Julius. What was your supposed fate again? Boiled to death like a lobster."

Julius gave a snort of derision and slowly placed his empty wine glass back on the table.

"You say it like he did it out of the goodness of his heart, Ernst. He bankrupted us all, you included. Our freedom came at a *price*."

"Come on, Julius. You know his lifestyle. You think his Secret Intelligence Service paycheque covered the way he lived? I doubt his expense claims even covered his tuxedo dry-cleaning bill. You can't blame him for wanting to make a little on the side. Civil servant pensions are pretty dismal these days. It's not rocket science, Julius."

Julius sneered in disgust, wounded by Ernst's closing gambit.

"Oops," said Ernst, completely devoid of any sincerity, secretly pleased to get one over on his old cohort. The ex-rocket scientist.

"Poor choice of words."

David Court

The best part of six bottles downed between them, accompanied by a seemingly never-ending stream of Schnapps chasers, and even Julius seemed to have cheered up. They'd all gotten through the typical arguments they had whenever they got together – primarily rants about who'd owned the most powerful laser weapon – and now they'd settled into the typical quieter, maudlin stage of the night.

Auric had been quiet for some time now, seemingly lost in thought. He smiled whenever they caught his eye but seemed distracted, a thousand-yard stare boring into the walls with a force as powerful as any of the weaponised lasers they'd ever owned.

"What's up, Auric?" asked Ernst. "You're uncharacteristically quiet."

"He loves only *gooooooold*," Hugo half-mocked in a sing-song voice. Ernst waved him away, concerned for his old cohort and his dwindling mood.

"I'm okay, my old friend," Auric replied, taking a deep breath and looking around at his friends. "It's just that..."

Ernst shuffled along the sofa, placing his arm on Auric's shoulder.

"Just what?"

"I'm just being a silly old man, Ernst. Ignore me."

"Tell me what's on your mind."

"Do you ever feel you've wasted your lives, my friends?"

Julius muttered something condescending beneath his breath, before lighting a cigarette and wandering towards the balcony.

"I can't complain, Auric. He was good enough to let us get away with a fair fortune, and I myself have lived a life of considerable luxury. Never quite as rich as I'd like – I don't think any of us achieved that – but, all things considered, I've always had enough to get by. Always wine and champagne in the fridge, nice cars in the garage, a beautiful woman on my arm."

You Only Live Thrice

"Ernst, it's just that – we seemed to spend so much time threatening people or trying to steal from them. Some of the things that we invented to try and achieve that – If we'd patented some of that technology, given it away to benefit the world – we would have been made men. Financially *or* spiritually. Maybe both."

Auric was just voicing the thoughts that Ernst had had in the night, on those evenings when you just can't sleep and the dark thoughts creep in. There were way many more days behind any of them than lay ahead, and it's not unreasonable for a man to take stock of his life towards the end of it.

Without a word, Ernst stood up. He made his way to the dining table, now an array of picked-clean golden serving platters, and picked up the bottle of Krug Private Cuvée that sat at its centre. Filling four glasses with the expensive champagne, he took one glass to each man.

"That's one reason we're here tonight, Auric. Balance, Friendship. Let's drink to absent friends."

All of them, even Julius – typically not fond of schmaltz or ceremony – raised a toast. Each of them remembered the halcyon days of giants with steel teeth, obscenely code-named women, and eccentric assassins with surplus nipples and henchmen with lethal razor-edged bowler-hats. The glorious days when you could buy sharks and killer whales, keep them in a tank in your lair, and not have the humane society coming down on you like a ton of bricks.

His glass of champagne downed with way more haste than one should honour a two-thousand-pound bottle with, Julius looked to his watch.

"This is all very nice, but let's not forget the reason we are all here this evening, the reason that we're all eschewing our normal summer visit. I'll remind you all that our visitor will be with us shortly."

David Court

James was in Argentina when he got the call from Felix, busy trying to rustle up sufficient resistance to confront an imminent invasion coming from northern Peru and Brazil.

They took their games of Risk seriously at the Bide-a-Wee home for retired secret agents.

In all honesty, he'd rather hoped that retirement for spies would have been more like how it was in the television show *The Prisoner*. Admittedly, you had to contend on occasion with being pursued by a giant white ball if you fancied a walk along the beach, but at least you had the sea air.

Swings and roundabouts.

Felix had fared somewhat better than James. As a rule, they didn't stick senile secret agents past their prime into care homes over there in the States – they tended to give them positions in Congress or give them meaty book deals.

Felix couldn't talk at any length – he was about to be interviewed by Oprah – but warned James he was going to send an important email that needed his immediate and utmost attention.

Some three hours later, when another ~~inmate~~ retiree had finally bankrupted himself on online poker on the home's solitary shared computer, James opened the email.

It was brief – a date and time, a set of coordinates (latitude and longitude) and four sets of initials.

EB, HD, AG, JN.

The co-ordinates looked familiar, but didn't ring any bells, and the date was much the same. The initials however – they were a different matter.

After some fiddling around trying to find where he was going to go – he'd gotten the latitude and longitude the wrong way around, so had nearly ended up travelling to the Isle of Man – he realised he had to be prepared.

You Only Live Thrice

He had a deadline, a volcano base, and four retired super-villains. No doubt Felix had gotten wind of some diabolical scheme of theirs and was requiring the help of James.

One last job. For Queen and Country, chap. Still powerful words now, even for a country that had done its damned best to forget him.

The Major had never been the most stable of individuals even back in his prime, but now, in his twilight years, the term 'eccentric' didn't do him justice.

His room was a mess of contraptions, all seemingly constructed to make the simplest of activities more complicated. Why stir your tea in moments when you could drag a weighty machine the size of a shoebox over to do it for you - which would take so long to perform the aforementioned action that your tea would be cold by the time it had finished?

The remote control for his television had a remote control of its own – a bulky thing made from an old manual typewriter that spat sparks and the occasional bout of flame.

"I don't care how much of the money you kept hidden in your mattress, James," The Major spluttered, exasperated. "They're all using Euros now. It's all worthless. You should have exchanged it *years* back."

The Major couldn't help but feel guilty, seeing James's poor, beleaguered expression.

"You silly sod. Though I might be able to help."

The Major wheeled slowly towards his wardrobe, his motorised walking frame coughing out plumes of grey smoke. After three attempts and much cursing, he found the section of wardrobe to press to open a secret panel and handed the revealed package within to James.

"Should be everything you need in there, chap."

David Court

James placed the contents of the package on the only part of the bed not covered with half-constructed devices and, as he looked at each, The Major proudly described them.

"Six thousand Euros, enough to charter a trip to the island from the mainland and purchase a weapon on the black market."

"Bulletproof girdle. Armoured, and capable of reducing four inches from your waist size."

"Advanced colostomy bag. Self-regulating, and able to be discretely hidden under any clothing."

James held up a tiny unlabelled plastic vial to the light, staring at the three tiny tablets within.

"And what are these?" he asked, "Poison capsules, I presume, for if I get captured?"

"No, James. Viagra."

Admittedly, it had been some years since James had travelled the world, but when did it all become so *complicated*? There was a time that nobody would bat an eyelid at James carrying his Walther PPK, a briefcase explosive, and pens laden with poison darts onto any flight, but now you weren't even allowed to carry *shampoo* on unless it was in a clear container.

There'd been a moment of embarrassment where he'd kept setting off the scanners, but he'd explained that was just his artificial hip. And knee joints. And shoulder joints. He suspected the security guard had let him on the flight because he was bored of him, to be fair.

They couldn't even sell him a Martini on the flight – or even Gin and Vermouth so he could mix his own. In its stead, he had to tolerate an overly priced cup of powdery, luke-warm Hot Chocolate and a packet of dry roasted peanuts.

He tried to watch *The Bourne Identity* on the flight, but it annoyed him too much. The film makers didn't have a *clue*. The fella in the film reminded him of his successor – just an angry man who liked beating up people with any implements to hand. Chap hadn't even prepared a witty line to quote for each baddie he brutally dispatched – a schoolboy error. Where was the wit? The charm?

At one stage, this young upstart Bourne fella had used a fat dead chap to cushion his fall from a great height. It was an ideal opportunity for a pun – perhaps an eyebrow raise and a wry announcement of "What a waist!" as he'd walked away from the corpse, something like that. Not a word.

He and Alex had tried to outdo each other in the early days, and no pun had been out of limits. James had to be honest, in that there were times when he'd deliberately engineered the death of a henchman to suit a pun he was desperate to use. Electricity, that was always a good one. "Shocking" or "He blew a fuse" were always favourites.

It didn't look much like fun being a spy *these* days.

With the flight to the island chartered and the reassuring weight of a pistol back against his waist, he looked at himself in the hotel mirror. With the girdle on – sterling work from The Major – the suit still fit. A little tighter around the belly and a bit tighter around the hips (and breathing when walking was a struggle) but it still fit, nonetheless. The top button on his shirt didn't fit around the expanse of skin that was his neck, but it was the style to have it undone these days, he'd heard.

Truth be told though, he was nervous. His eyesight and reactions weren't what they were, so he didn't fancy his chances in a gunfight. He'd lost his last fistfight – a struggle over the remote control at the home when he'd been desperate to watch the new *Homes Under the Hammer* – so he didn't have much confidence in that regard, either.

David Court

The only thing he had going for him is that *they* were all ancient as well. But he'd only ever confronted one of them at a time – never four of them before.

He smiled at visions of a myopic gunfight in the volcano lair – all of them exhausting their ammunition trying and failing to shoot each other, all desperately squinting in an attempt to draw a bead on their targets.

He was half-tempted to settle his nerves in the hotel casino, but his skill with cards had departed him, too. He struggled to win a game of Happy Families these days – many a care home dessert had been gambled away – *no pun intended* – fruitlessly.

Back in the day, he had another way of de-stressing before a job. However, as the only sniff of skirt he'd had was a doddery old dear on the slot machines in the foyer who'd confused him for her son, that was an avenue best left unexplored.

Probably for the best, mind. Erectile dysfunction was a terrible cross to bear. And he hadn't had the heart to tell the poor old Major that if he popped one of those little blue pills to help with his quandary, his heart would probably pack in. The old fella, unbeknownst to him, *had* given him suicide pills after all.

Every wave they bounced across or straddled sent paroxysms of pain across James's taut nerve-endings and worn out bones. The surge of adrenaline – the thrill of the job – used to mask out the pain, but now it wasn't enough.

It seemed so unfair. You work your whole life and by the time you're finally ready to rest up, your body doesn't behave any more. The best bits of you have already gone. You're simply in no position to *enjoy* it.

It was part way through the journey - brain cells jogged into activity by the bumpiness of the journey, no doubt – when he realised why he'd remembered the date. It was the day he'd last been at this island, on one of his first ever cases. He couldn't quite remember why he'd been here, though. Probably to stop the firing of an orbital laser, or the launching of a nuke. That was typically the case.

But, that date - coincidence, or fate? Time would tell. And, given a temporary new lease of life by this unexpected and long overdue adventure, he felt that he had all the time in the world.

It was dark when they arrived, and the boat captain was forced to circle the island a few times, looking for somewhere to land. Eventually, it pulled up to the rusting remnants of a quay, and James was helped off the boat. The captain offered to wait – for the cost of a few hundred more Euros, naturally – but James told him to leave.

"But how will you get off the island?" the captain asked, clearly more concerned for his own pocket than the old man's welfare.

"I'll make my own way," James replied. The captain shrugged, and the boat sped off. James watched it leave, the lights vanishing into the low fog of the sea.

The last time he was here, he'd arrived by one of The Major's miniature submersibles, removing his wetsuit on the beach to reveal a perfectly tailored, double-breasted Victorian morning suit. The next few hours had been spent tentatively approaching the volcano via the cover of thick vegetation, avoiding patrols, or dispatching lone minions with either karate or a well-aimed bullet.

This time would be way more straightforward. He'd simply wander up the path, knock on the front door, and see what happened.

Julius stood on the balcony, watching James approach through a pair of old binoculars. He wasn't making the slightest attempt to disguise himself, slowly advancing towards the base.

David Court

He noted that the man was walking with a slight limp and having to stop for a short rest every few dozen paces.

Julius picked up the walkie-talkie, flicking the button on its side.

"Are you all in position?" he whispered.

Three whispered voices replied in the affirmative.

"Is he nearly here?" asked Hugo.

Julius looked down at the path, which was empty. However, an orange glow appeared in the darkness and he saw his old nemesis leaning against a palm tree. Moments later, he expelled a few mouthfuls of grey smoke from an e-cigarette that had seemed to appear from nowhere.

"Errmm.. Nearly," came the reply.

"And you have the laser controls?" asked Ernst for the third time in as many minutes. Julius had never known him as keen. Julius looked in his pocket and pulled out an innocuous looking silver box with a single red button.

"Primed and ready."

An e-cigarette for the condemned man didn't sound nearly as romantic as a proper *actual* cigarette but needs must. Embarrassed that he was out of breath from such a short walk – breath that now smelled of Peach Passion – he steadied himself before knocking on the door. Three heavy raps, reverberating across thick steel.

No answer. He tried the handle, which clicked satisfyingly. Unlocked.

He slowly pushed open the door and stepped into the cavernous chamber.

You Only Live Thrice

From their positions on the balcony, they all watched him enter. Julius came down to join them. It looked to them all as though he were about to say something, but upon seeing James, he froze. It was as though seeing him again had stunned him into silence, a rare feat with the normally overly-verbose Julius.

He was unaware of their presence, stepping further into the cavern with his gun drawn. His eyes scanned the corners and shadows of the room, never thinking once to look up.

Each man was lost in his own thoughts, briefly, confronted with the sight of their nemesis. He'd once seemed invincible -- resourceful, suave to the point of arrogance. And now, here he was, this bewildered and confused old man, wandering the unknown.

I was never convinced that hair was his own, thought Hugo.

He always seemed taller, thought Auric.

I always envied his eyebrows, mused Julius.

He used to seem more... Scottish, thought Ernst.

Not all of his talents had left him – James knew he was being watched; that much was for certain. It was a skill he'd honed well over the years – it never hurt to know that your enemies were studying you, or that you'd gotten a lady's attention.

The room was dimly lit, all rolling shadows and blind corners. It could have been worse – at least he wasn't being pursued by a psychotic extra-nippled assassin through a hall of fairground mirrors.

Floodlights burst into life one by one as he stepped into the centre of the cavern, each firing into life with a dull metallic *kchink*. James heard noises from above him and, lifting his hands to shield him from the light, stared at the four individuals standing on the balcony. Julius, Ernst, Hugo and Auric. The only time he'd ever seen them together was as four mugshots lined up in a mission briefing, and it had been a lifetime since he'd been face to face with any of them.

They appeared to be squabbling with each other, arguing over who should get to speak first.

In the end, it was Ernst who pushed his way forward, leaning over the balcony and shouting.

"We've been expecting you!"

They turned to Julius, all of them encouraging him to do something. The wily old villain leaned over the balcony, holding out a remote control. Without a word, he jabbed forcefully at the button with a thin, wiry finger.

James span on the spot, aiming the gun desperately in search of any movement. All about him, motors were springing into life, and a dull bass sound began to fill the cavern.

The lights dimmed, and a series of lasers fired into life. Bright reds, yellows, and greens – all fired out from projectors set around the room, an array of geometric patterns flashing out and dancing across the walls, ceiling, and floors.

The sound increased, the strains of *Agadoo* by Black Lace now recognisable and increasing in volume. A banner was unfurled from the balcony, draped from one side to the other.

Happy Anniversary.

The party went on until the early hours. Felix had sent his apologies, booked to appear on *Ellen* that same night. *Life's too short* was an oft-mumbled phrase that lolled across the drunken tongues of all present at some stage during the festivities. A compromise was reached by the end of it, in which it was agreed that James was indeed a jolly good fellow. And so said all of them.

Even Julius, reluctantly.

The Ghastly
Glittergrieve

AT THE SAME precise time, every year,
Come dark on Christmas eve,
A blighted spirit springs to life,
The ghastly GLITTERGRIEVE.

As children try to fall asleep,
it scurries 'cross your ceiling,
A shadowy nook it'll find itself,
(One prime for self-concealing).

No bigger than a walnut yet,
this crooked little shade.
Observing from his darkened perch,
to watch festive tables laid.

Invisible at first, he is,
for his acts of misfeasance.
But before the day's events are done,
you'll feel his Christmas presence.

David Court

He's there for every opened gift,
For all wrapping ripped away,
For every garish Cracker pulled
On each fateful Christmas day.

He's watching, in the shadows hid,
for each present you reveal.
(This is a task he undertakes
With fervour and with zeal).

In small black claws, he holds his book
with your name etched within.
A black mark will be noted down
For every spotted sin.

For every time you grimace
at your gift of aftershave,
the demons sat there thinking,
"That is no way to behave."

With each half-hearted "Thank you"
that trickles from your lips,
Against your name, he's glad to see,
Another black mark slips.

Each cardigan you toss aside,
each pair of socks rejected;
To the scrutiny of the Glittergrieve,
you're silently subjected.

The demon's purpose is laid bare,
once revelries have ceased.
For every black mark in the book,
The Glittergrieve' s size increased.

The Ghastly Glittergrieve

It's midnight now, on Christmas day.
And everybody's resting.
But you're awake from too much beer,
Your bladder is protesting.

The tap's turned on, to wash your hands -
Your bladder now relieved.
But in the mirror, there it stands.
The ghastly GLITTERGRIEVE.

Dark eyes poke out through masks of skin,
All evil, black and hateful
The faces from which it peers behind
peeled away from the ungrateful.

Atop his face of ruined flesh,
a faded paper crown.
A tinsel wreath hangs round his neck,
cracked baubles draped around.

It rises up, towering o'er you now,
a weird and twisted shape.
Red, Green and Gold and shimmering,
a crude wrapping-paper cape.

With practiced claws it steals your soul,
Your watcher, now your killer.
In one fell swoop, you're destined to be
A demons stocking filler.

The lesson here? Be thankful for
your gifts, which are meant well.
And if you're good, you will receive
Good tidings and No Hell.

David Court

Red Sky at Night

ANYTIME YOU'D ever speak to Old Ma Waldron, no
matter whether she was behind the counter at the Shop n
Stop or just sittin' out on her front porch looking cranky, she'd
remind you how she was dying. Every Summer would see her
red as a beet complaining about how she was fixin' to die of
heatstroke, and every Winter would see her as white as a Klan
hood and the fella inside it, moaning that she'd be dead by
Spring.

For someone who'd been nigh-on-dead for so long, she was
doing a terrible job at meeting her maker. Mind you, if the Grim
Reaper ever did visit the Shop n Stop, he'd have found himself
standing outside with an empty wallet and a handful of stale
candy afore he knew what was happening.

That said, she was deader than most. Ma Waldron was one of
those women who was *born* old. Even those of us who'd been
living here for goin' on thirty years can't remember her being
anything *but* old. "She's got one of them faces," Father Wakeford
had always insisted, "that naturally falls to frownin'". She'd
always spoke about how in her youth, she was pretty as a
picture, but truth be told, that must have been an oil paintin' left
out to blister and warp in the sun. Her eyes were too close
together, and she had a big old bulbous nose that was as red as
her moods. Each ear looked like it had been pinned on by a kid
in a blindfold at a party like the tail on a donkey. A cleverer man

Red Sky at Night

would say she looked like a Picasso picture brought to live, but as far as we were all concerned, she was the spittin' image of the Potato Head figure from the yellowin' sun-faded box that was a permanent fixture in the Shop n Stop window, and had a nickname to match.

She didn't walk much these days, seemingly just appearin' in precisely the place she could cause the most aggravation, or get the biggest audience for her complaining. Woe betide anybody younger than her (which was pretty much everybody south of Methuselah) who got within the range of Ma Waldron and that damnable stick of hers. She'd shuffle slowly up and down the street with her tiny feet kicking up plumes of sand and dust bigger than she was, constantly chattering away to herself or cursing at others. Where most of us had a heart, Old Ma Waldron had an over-developed bile duct.

Up until about a week ago, that is. The rumours started when the weather started to turn fine, with Father Wakeford sayin' that he'd sworn he'd seen Old Ma Waldron smilin' away to herself. That seemed about as unlikely as Dan Abrams puttin' up a Black Lives Matter flag in his backyard, but then a few others said they'd seen the same.

Me? I guessed something was up when I was browsin' through the Stop n Shop looking for some new rolls of twine when I heard a noise that no human being has heard since Neil Armstrong took his giant leap – it was an alien noise, like nothing I'd never heard. "Beyond the realms of mortal ken", whoever *he* is.

Old Ma Waldron was wishin' me a good morning.

There was a shelf to support myself against, which was lucky, because it got stranger still. She started engaging me in what I can only define as *conversation*. There was an excitement to her tone I hadn't heard since she was caught bragging about poisoning Dan Abram's Rottweilers, Sturm and Drang. Not about her comin' death for once, but the weather.

"It'll be glorious in a week or so. You mark my words, Tom Bastow," she chuckled, rocking in that old chair so hard it was

David Court

squeakin' like a horny mouse. News travelled fast, and Old Ma Waldron's personality shifting from grumpy old curmudgeon to optimist was all anybody in the town could talk about.

That was until the evenin' of the red sky just six days later, anyroads.

In a farming community like ours, there's an excitement in the air when there's a red sky in the evening. Goes back to Bible times, that one. Matthew wrote about it. "When it is evening, ye say, fair weather: for the heaven is red.". What it means in fancy science terms is pressure movin' in from the west, making it more than likely the next day will be perfect for us out in the fields.

And golly, were those heavens red that night. It was a July evening, with the sweet perfumed smell of the Alfalfa drifting over the hills. Usually, there'd be a tad of variety to the shade – gorgeous oranges, reds, and purples – but this evening there was none of that. Just a thick blood-red scarlet, horizon to horizon, pierced by a flesh pink moon.

I was puttin' the world to rights in O'Malley's with a cold beer when Hickox came bargin' in, as ruddy faced as one of Doc Quince's underfed pigs. He was agitated, spluttering over the words as he tried to spit them out. Took a beer to calm him down, which I suspect was his plan all along.

"It's Mrs. Potato Head," he coughed out through his beer-foam moustache, "you need to see this for yourself". And instead of insisting the damn fool tell us all rather than waste our time, that evening saw half a dozen of us traipsing up the hill towards Hickox's farm and across his potato field.

We heard her before we saw her, that raspy voice of hers singin' "Johnny Appleseed" as loud as her tiny lungs would allow. Then Hickox stopped, and pointed down.

There was Old Ma Waldron, in a shallow hole she'd dug herself, just lying there amongst the roots and the tubers. We looked down at her, and she looked back at us with a huge

Red Sky at Night

cracked yellow-toothed smile, as though lyin' with the potatoes in the dry dirt was the most natural thing in the world.

Hickox stepped in to try and lift her out, but she whipped out with that stick of hers like an ornery rattlesnake. He fell backwards on his ass, and we couldn't help but laugh. But as we're laughing, Waldron just starts singing louder to drown us out.

It'd repeat for anybody who went near. Anybody went to pull her foolish hide out of that hole got a crack of the stick, and anybody who leaned in trying to convince her to come out was drowned out by verses of that damnable folk song.

I knew exactly what Hickox was going to suggest when he sidled over to me with that sneaky look in those monobrowed eyes of his, and damned if I was right.

"You keep her distracted, Bastow," he said shiftily, "and me 'n the boys will grab her."

There was quite a gathering of us now, a good dozen or so standing around the hole. I waved my arms in the air until they were all looking at me.

"Now, fellas," I implored, trying to bring some sense back into this crazy evenin' in which we'd found ourselves, "if Old Ma Waldron wants to lie with the potatoes singin', I don't see why any of us should stop her."

Hickox looked dejected, but the other boys just looked relieved. That stick *hurt*, and nobody looked that desperate to be its next victim. Only advantage of the blood red glow that filled the heavens was that it hid their bruises.

"Anyways," I proclaimed, already beginning to slowly stroll back, "there's time at the bar for another two or three drinks yet this evening. Who's with me?"

And so, it was that we left Old Ma Waldron in the hole, bellowing as loudly as she could. She was still singing when we got back to the bar and even though it was a damned warm evening, we closed the doors and windows to drown her out.

I will swear on my grave that when I emerged out into that blood red night, staggering out of that bar back to my bed with four glasses of cold beer swillin' inside of me, she was *still* singin'.

It weren't just my eyes that were bloodshot next morning. When I woke up, I was worried I hadn't slept at all - even now, the sky was still that persistent brilliant scarlet. Looking at my bedside clock though, it was morning. Just that the sky hadn't changed, is all.

Red skies in morning? They ain't so good. Especially when there ain't even no sun.

Waldron had stopped singin' though; that was some small blessing. I was convinced I'd heard her in my sleep, half-tempted to storm out to Hickox's potato field and bury the damned witch.

Despite the fact the skies looked like something from a child's drawing of hell, life carried on as normal. The rain clouds the dawn's red haze suggested never appeared, and the whole day passed by in a weird, balmy haze.

Nobody saw Mrs. Potato Head that whole day, but nobody was daring to bring it up. The Stop n Shop had been left open all night, so it was clear she hadn't gone back to her bed. It would have taken any of us just a few minutes to walk back to that hole right now to check up on her – hell, Hickox must have taken a damned detour on his farm to get into town and *not* walk past her. Old dear like that, left alone for the evening lying in a damned ditch? Truth was, nobody wanted to be the one to find her in her ready-made *grave*.

We sat there in that bar that evening, still under that damned red sky, nobody wanting to make eye contact with anybody. All of us sat in silence, staring into our beers. In the end, I couldn't stand the guilty quiet anymore.

"I'll go," I said, slamming my empty glass onto the table and standing up. A few eyes looked at me. "I know what you're all

Red Sky at Night

thinking," I shouted, pointing my finger at every one of them. "It was Tom Bastow said to leave her, so it's Tom Barstow's fault."

I went to leave.

"Old witch was nearly dead anyway. Ain't a man here who wouldn't wish it, neither," I muttered, slamming the door behind me.

As an aside, there ain't no point in slamming a saloon door shut. Truth be told, it just swings in and out without a noise, which damn sure diminished the dramatic impact of the exit I attempted.

As I drew closer to Hickox's farm, I could hear the whispering behind me. They'd followed me out of the bar, but at enough of a distance that when I snapped around, they all made out they was just loiterin' and not trailing behind me at all. It was only when I reached the field and was walking to that hole that I felt I had to say something.

"Goddamnit," I shouted, spinning on my heels to turn to face them. They all started concentrating on each other or paying attention to the dirt beneath their feet, but I damn knew they were listenin'. "Anybody who wants to see what's in that accursed hole, come join me. Tarnation, Bill Hickox, this is *your* blasted farm so quite why you're being so sheepish back there, I don't know."

If I'd embarrassed him, this red hue we were all immersed in hid it damn well.

With hindsight, I don't know why I was quite so nervous and what I expected to see down there in the dirt. Waldron had looked like a decayin' corpse at the very best of times, so there wouldn't be any surprises.

Through squinted eyes and with a beating heart, I stood on that crimson-soaked soil and stared into that similarly crimson soaked hole.

David Court

Empty. Nothing but a whole tangled bunch of roots, potatoes, and tubers.

I climbed in, looking for any sign of her, anything she might have dropped or left. The soil was damp, and everything down there was covered in a layer of moisture and a sweet sap that stuck to my arms and hands. A thick metallic smell filled the air, even noticeable over the earthy scent of the alfalfa.

Two dozen anxious real eyes and one glass eye stared down at me.

Like the Lord above flicking a light switch, the redness faded, and the evening sky was restored to its rightful pin-pricked inky blackness. The moon suddenly shone into life like a bulb, lighting up the field and all who occupied it.

And like a searchlight, it shone into the hole in which I was kneeling. Like you'd see at a fancy theatre, marking me as the center of attention. Only now could I see the ground around me was specked with clots of a thick coat of bright glistening scarlet, the same deep crimson that coated the skin on my hands and arms. The same blood which coated those thirsty potato roots clung to me, dotted in parts with thicker congealed lumps of gunk; gristle, clumps of matted hair, tiny chunks of wizened stripped flesh, and strips of flayed skin that was once wrapped loosely around a haggard and grisly old potato-faced coot.

"You ask me, we're wastin' our damn time," said Dan Abrams for the fifth time that hour, as he half-heartedly prodded the long grass in which we were walking.

"We don't need to ask you, Dan, you just keep on tellin' us, regardless," I snapped, tired of his incessant complaining. Damn my luck for being paired with that old bigot. He looked ready to whine again, so I said something I knew would shut him up.

"What are we keeping you from anyway, Dan? You got some choir practice planned at home, maybe some singin' of those

Red Sky at Night

Fatherland songs with your boys? Deutschland, *Deutschland über alles...*"

"Tom Bastow, you've been riling me for too damn long now," he stopped, waving that gnarled old stick in my direction, "I ain't no Nazi. I just like the memorabilia is all. I *inherited* that coat and medals."

"And you just wear 'em round your house for fun, right?"

"Ain't no point in medals if you can't wear 'em every now and again. Much as how you're wearin' most of that Waldron hag on your hands and arms. Ain't no chance we're finding anything else of her tonight."

Truth be told, it pained me to say, he was probably right. If we did find her, there wasn't much of her that she hadn't left in that potato hole.

Bears, it was decided. That, or coyotes. People seemed to forget we'd seen neither round these parts in the best part of twenty years, but people will often look for a simple explanation rather than struggle to think of an alternative.

So, in his infinite ursine wisdom, some bear (or pack of bears) had wandered to Hickox's farm – possibly in league with some conspiratorial coyotes – and had snatched up Old Ma Waldron from her hole. The more optimistic amongst us liked to think she'd tried to fight 'em up, maybe cracked a few of 'em with her stick, before being dragged away to their lair.

Any relatives she had either openly despised her, had been disowned by her, or both, so her funeral was a quiet ceremony. I'd washed off as much of her as they'd found in that hole, so her coffin ended up as empty as those cheap knock-off, stale fortune cookies she used to try to sell.

We buried it facing Father Wakeford's chapel.

She'd have *hated* that.

David Court

You know when you have a toothache – one that's just a nagging pain, not yet agony, so you tolerate it? And then one day, ages later, you get it sorted by the dentist or it just vanishes by itself? That was what life without Old Ma Waldron was like. You didn't like her grumpiness, but you'd gotten *used* to it.

It didn't seem right going into the Shop n Stop without being stared at by somebody convinced you were going to rob her blind, same as it didn't seem right when you weren't screamed at when you got to the counter for not having the exact change.

But times goes on. We were all extra cautious about looking out for bears and coyotes for a while, but that passed. Old Ma Waldron was forgotten about, same as we stopped talkin' about the day of the red sky.

The extraordinary gets explained away, or simply passes on. The sheer volume of the mundanity of small-town life drowns everything else out, eventually.

Until Hickox and his damn potatoes.

"Are you sure this is a potato?" I asked, holding the withered, gnarled thing up to the light. It was weird and malformed, with a thick red skin that resembled bark. Stems protruded from it, looking more like matted, dried hair than vegetation. The twisted little thing I held between my thumb and forefinger looked more like discoloured root ginger than it did a potato.

"Yup. Whole damn field came out just like this 'un," said Hickox. "They taste fine. They just look a little odd, is all."

I looked from him to the potato, and then back to him. I had to ask.

"Hickox, you didn't use of the potatoes that grew in the..."

He screwed up his face, offended by my line of questioning.

Red Sky at Night

"What do you take me for, Tom Bastow? I fenced off that part of my field. I ain't using any part of it that went anywhere near that damned hole."

"And they taste okay, you say?"

"As good as any I've ever grown. Only reason they cost less is because they don't look all that appetizin'."

"I'll take a bag then. And you still owe me four beers from the weekend, so we'll call it quits."

You could almost see the cogs whirring and grinding behind his eyes as he tried to do the calculations, an effort his brain decided was just too much. He smiled and handed me one of the bumpy burlap sacks.

These things weren't only ugly, they were *heavy*. I was out of breath by the time I'd hauled that misshapen bag into my pantry, resting it against the wall. Hickox certainly had packed 'em in – the sack was full to overflowing and a few of them had fallen out. They didn't roll though, like a potato should – being so knobbly and warped, they just stopped where they landed.

I picked one of them up and took it into the kitchen, studying it on the way. Now I was lumbered with a bag of them, I was wonderin' what the hell to do with 'em. You couldn't peel 'em – they were so awkwardly shaped, it'll be like trying to bathe a cat, as in you'd end up bleeding with the skin scraped from your fingers. Like the other one, it was shaped like a stumpy and hairy five-pointed star. Had a stink to it too, that I hadn't noticed before – a whiff of staleness to 'em, like they'd gone bad already.

Hickox had better not have sold me a bag of rotten potatoes.

The thing was dry to the touch, not even a hint of moisture to it. I placed it on my kitchen counter and took the penknife from my keyring, hoping to cut open the thing to find out what state it was in. Admittedly, the blade was dull and hadn't been sharpened for some time, but it barely made a mark on the thing. The outside was so thick, it was like trying to slice into the gnarled bark of a tree.

David Court

I spent a few minutes sharpenin' one of my kitchen knives, determined that little bugger wouldn't the better of me. I held the potato in place and, the tip of the blade already on the table, sliced down with the quickest motion I could.

Damn thing shot across the room, bouncing off my kitchen window and landing in the sink. Ordinarily, that wouldn't have been too bad, but there was three days of washing in there and I had to reach into the stagnant gravy, oil, and coffee soup to fish it out. As I held the soaked thing to the light, I could see I'd carved a shallow neat line across it, little more.

Next time, it wasn't so lucky. I sliced across the same line against, holding it stronger this time, and sheared it neatly in two. A pungent liquid trickled from the heart of it, released from a hollow at the heart of that yellowy-white flesh. It made me gag, bringing back memories of the coppery scent in that potato pit. Only now I'd cut the thing in half, did the skin strike me as a mite odd – it was as thick as the shell of a coconut, and nearly as coarse.

The smell was vile. Even just this tiny thumb-sized quantity of liquid had a pungency that filled the room, forcing me to open the windows to get some damned air in. The paint on the kitchen surface had already faded to a bleached pale stain from where it had pooled. Ain't no way I was cooking with these malodorous little starchy fuckers.

I hoisted the sack, which I could have sworn was heavier still, out into the garden and poured the contents into the compost tumbler. They mightn't be good for cooking, but they'd decay into adequate fertiliser. Seeing them all lying there in that deep metal drum, it struck me how alike they all were. I'd imagined them all to be random little collections of lumps, but no, they were all very similar – only slight variations amongst 'em in size or shape. All were bloated, five-pointed stars, one tip of each bristling with wiry stems. My thoughts went to the little pool of bilious toxic shit brewin' in the heart of every single one of the little buggers.

Red Sky at Night

Hickox needed to be told, before he went and damn poisoned somebody. I set off later that evenin'. Being public spirited is one thing, but nothing says you can't have a nap first.

The walk to Hickox's place takes you past O'Malley's, so I took the opportunity of peering through the windows to see if he was there. Unusually for this time of the evening, he wasn't. The bar looked quieter than usual but still provided an awful temptation, yet my urge to do the right thing presently outweighed my need for a cold beer. The fact that Hickox owed me a few free beers to compensate me had nothin' to do with the bearin' on that decision.

There was a dull red hue settling across the sky as I walked up the path to Hickox, and the cold was creepin' in. I briefly glimpsed over to the fenced-off patch of field where Waldron had been taken from us, remembering that fateful night those few months back.

Bill Hickox looked after his house and farm alone, after his good lady Annie had passed on two winters back. Time was, you'd find every kind of vegetable in his fields, but now it was just taters. It was easier, and people would always need 'em.

His front door was ajar when I got there, a thin smattering of soil leading from the path into his house. Annie Hickox would have had his guts for garters in the old days, insistin' he takes off his filthy work boots before coming into their humble abode. In her absence, standards had long slipped. Still, I ain't one to speak – times have been where'd I'd be drinkin' coffee from a bowl rather than make the effort of washin' a cup.

"You about, Bill?" I yelled. The man had a shotgun, so it was best to make my presence known. No answer. This wasn't unusual; many a time I'd come in here to find him passed out drunk on some under-fermented Poteen. I'd have to carry the fella to his bed, with him breathing whisky fumes over me and callin' me Annie.

Truth be told? I'd rather have found him like that.

As I walked towards the door to his living room, I heard a weird sound – like the scurrying of rats with a whole mess of tiny footsteps followed by silence. I called out Bill's name one more time before pushing the door open.

Whether the things working on Bill's face hadn't heard me approach and scampered away with the others, or were simply too engrossed or brave to care, I'll never know. He was lying back on his fully reclined La-Z-Boy chair, one of those things perched on his shoulders and another one balancin' on his chin.

The protuberances on the two little blasphemies weren't the tips of stars – they were limbs. Two little potatoes, neither more than four inches or so in height, balancing on two little stumpy legs while busily working away with their squat little arms. They were both doing something with Hickox's face, and I stood there for a few moments in horrified silence watching the frenzy of movement from the pair of them.

I'd often wondered how I'd cope with being exposed to something so out of the ordinary that it'd make me question my very existence in this fragile plane I laughably call reality. Turns out my first reaction'd be to piss my pants and cuss.

"Shit," I found myself sayin', rather louder than I'd intended.

Almost comically, the two little potatoes slowly turned to face me, their little stem buds winkin' where their eyes would have ordinarily been. Figures. As one, they both hopped down, each onto an arm of the reclining chair.

I could now see Hickox's face.

His skin, ordinarily wrinkled like one of those tortoises from National Geographic, was smooth, but bunched in all the wrong places, like it was modelling clay that had been worked on. Despite the two little taters staring at me accusingly, I couldn't stop staring at that face.

I'm not ashamed to say, I pissed myself again.

The pink clay was stained dark red in places wherever there were features. His two eyes were set at different heights on that lop-sided face, each possessing different sized dark pupils. The nose that sat beneath them wasn't his – it was dainty and feminine and hanging at an awkward angle. The mouth was the

Red Sky at Night

worst – two lips attached to a patch of flesh of a different shade, pressed into the soft pliable skin, and drooping at both sides.

I could see Hickox trembling, a muffled moan coming from behind those closed alien lips.

It was then I saw the scattered bodies on the floor, all with similarly crudely assembled faces. Eyes, noses, ears, and lips had been forcibly pulled from each and transplanted on another body. Some of those bodies were still, and some writhed like they's partially paralysed but still conscious. A few of them had even been scalped, the tops of their heads glistening domes of bleeding crimson flesh. There was Father Wakeford, his bald pate topped off with Widow Davis's blood-streaked, blonde curls. Abrams was wearing Old Man Stockley's glass eye like a cyclops, the glass orb crudely pressed into malleable flesh.

Like the Potato Head in Waldron's window.

They emerged from the shadowy recesses and the darkness in the room like a flood, a thundering of tiny feet as hundreds of the tiny little taters charged towards me. A chorus of cackling shrieks came from each, the familiar bilious tones of Ma Waldron reverberatin' around the room.

That noise alone is enough to rouse me from my piss-stained torpor and my thick work-boots get to stampin' on the first wave. My own defiant screams drown out that incessant noise as I make short work of that first batch.

The thick skin on 'em counts for little as I'm stamping down on the little buggers. I've hammered nails in with these boots. With each of the little shits I tread to a lumpy paste, the smell in the room gets worse, that acid at the heart of each of 'em filling the air with an acrid burning odor. I can feel myself start to go faint, but seemingly shocked by my frenzied retaliation, the next wave backs off. They stand there watching me as I stare down at my handiwork.

A few dozen of the things litter the ground beneath me, pulped potato skin and flesh coating both the carpet and the soles of my boots.

A monster mash.

David Court

I turn to run and am out that door quicker than you could holler "sentient potato". Turns out though, these spuds are *smart*. It would only take a clumsy or panicking man not looking where he's goin' with a few of those taters underfoot and lyin' in wait, and such a soul could find himself plummeting face first onto the path, leaving himself a mite vulnerable.

They're on me like a plague, tearing and gouging. Before I realise what's happening, a few of 'em are holding my mouth open and another is clamberin' right on in. I bite down as hard as I can and then realise that's exactly what they wanted – that damned acid fills my throat, hurtin' all the way down. I can smell it too – they're leaking it from their skins and rubbing it into mine, and all I can smell, or taste is burnt flesh. I can hear Old Ma Waldron cacklin' from a hundred tiny mouths and I find I ain't even capable of fightin' back no more. All I can do is stare up at that damnable red sky, and now I can't tell the sky apart from the blood in my eyes, and then even they're gone.

"Red Sky at Night" was first published in "Under the Weather", the weather themed horror anthology from Burdizzo Books.

Par

CAREY LEARNED from a very early age not to tell anybody else about the voices. They'd tolerated it when she was tiny, laughing at her flights of fancy with her imaginary friend, but had endured it less as she'd gotten older.

The adults had once thought it funny that she'd be forever blaming the disappearance of the last biscuit, or bottle of juice, on her invisible playmate – but she'd noticed how it had begun to anger them. *Stop making stuff up*, she'd be told. *Stop lying*. It became easier to just take the blame herself, rather than shift it.

And then, as she entered her teens, she'd all but mastered the subtle art of subterfuge. *Hide any evidence*, she'd realised, *and there won't be any blame*. This was easy at first, as the requirements of her from the voice were straightforward, stealing food, cheating on tests. Later, it became more demanding – bullying money from her schoolmates, stealing from her mother's purse - things which forced her to become even more resourceful and secretive.

And then, on the morning of Carey's sixteenth birthday, the voice asked her to kill.

This was the first time that Carey had ever dared deny the voice. All its previous requests had been beneficial to her, but this was the first of its requests that seemed to serve no purpose. At first, she'd even laughed, convinced that it must be joking.

David Court

When it had repeated its demand, she realised the sincerity behind it. *No,* she'd said.

Kill for me, it had insisted.

Carey ignored it. It asked again as she got into bed that night, whispered it as she tried to sleep. It was the first voice she heard when she woke, and it grew louder and more insistent as she ate her breakfast. It distracted her at school, bellowing the request into her ears when the teacher asked her a question, so loud that she couldn't hear.

That evening, at the school bus stop, it asked again. Frustrated and tired, she took it out on the ants that flitted across the sun-drenched pavement – a trivial massacre that she hoped would sate the demanding voice. Two dozen tiny lives were snuffed out under the treaded grip of her Converse trainers, wiped clean on a grassy verge while she waited for the verdict.

They don't count, it declared. *It must be bigger.*

●●●●●●●●●●●●●●●●●●●●●

This troubled Carey, an animal lover. She'd never really considered ants to be *proper* animals anyway, just mindless little creepy-crawly automatons, but the prospect of ending the life of anything larger bothered her. Here was the girl with more farm animal stuffed toys than could comfortably fit on the windowsill they called home.

It became a battle of wills. The voice would scream at her long into the night, insisting she carry out its dark will, and Carey would eventually fall asleep through sheer exhaustion. After a few days of that with no result, the voice changed tack. It allowed Carey to forget about it, remaining silent, bar an occasional frustrated murmur. This would continue for days at a time, until it abruptly reminded her of its noisy presence.

Carey didn't want to admit it, but that tactic had nearly worked. It was impossible to relax or concentrate, knowing the voice could erupt at any time – typically when most inconvenient. She wasn't quite at her wits' end, but she was certainly in spitting distance of it, when the voice tried a quite different strategy.

It asked her nicely.

If you don't want to do it, it said politely, its calm tone one of convincing sincerity, *you don't have to. I'll go somewhere else.*

Even though it frustrated her when it acted like a petulant child, the thought of not having it in her life terrified her. Even though she didn't even know its name (despite asking on multiple occasions), the voice was a constant, as much a part of her as her own arms and legs.

To be bereft of it, would be unbearable.

Like the old lady who swallowed a fly, she'd work her way up in size until the voice was satisfied.

Trying to forget about the anthropomorphic jolly bumblebee that adorned her bedroom curtains and bedspread, she slowly crept towards the kitchen window and her prey with a rolled-up comic. The pollen-drunk bee, too laden to escape, was quickly dispatched by Carey's makeshift weapon. She winced and shrieked as she carried out the crime, anything to dull her senses to the grim reality of her act.

As she looked at the flattened remains of the insect, spread equally between window and comic, she hoped that would be enough. The voice wasted no time in calmly informing her that it wasn't.

With her pocket-money, she bought a humane mousetrap from the local store, leaving it hidden in the dark recesses of the yard, a tempting prize of Pepper Jack cheese lurking within. If she had to kill, she'd at least make sure that the condemned had a decent last meal. She'd originally intended to buy a normal mousetrap and let that do the work, but the voice made it clear in no uncertain terms that that wasn't the deal. *Carey* needed to be the instrument of death, not just its conductor.

David Court

She rushed down the next morning, picking up and shaking the tiny plastic box. The weight of it and the sound of scurrying tiny footsteps confirmed that the trap had been effective.

She peered through the tiny airholes set into the traps side, and two tiny dull black orbs stared haplessly back. It was a tiny grey-brown mouse, whiskers and pink nose quivering in fear. With a readied brick in one hand, she flicked the metal catch to spring the traps door open.

As expected, it bolted for daylight and freedom. It fled the humane trap to meet its fate on the flat edge of an altogether less humane slammed-down brick. Trying to hold back the tears, Carey waited for the voice, dismayed to hear that the mouse also failed to meet its exacting murderous requirements.

I can't do it, she admitted, as much to herself as to the voice. She was about to resign herself to the voice departing her for good when she saw it, or more precisely *him*.

Chester.

The mangy old cat was perched on the top of the fence, staring down at her with its single remaining narrowed slit of a green eye. Who knew how long it had been sitting there, watching her? Either it had smelled the fear of the trapped mouse or had smelled the fresh pre-prepared bloodied remains. Either way, she had its total undivided attention.

Rather than clear away her handiwork as she'd intended, she slowly placed the brick down. Chester's eye was locked on her and, for each step backwards she made, it drew closer, silent padded footfalls across the top of the fence.

Silently, it dropped to the ground and turned its attention away from Carey towards the mouse carcass. Despite the creatures age and stained, matted fur, it still intimidated her with its calm, nonchalant demeanour.

She watched it eat for a while, listening to the crunching of tooth against tiny bone. Old fangs mauled and ripped through flesh as it relished every part of the tiny morsel. It lay down, its noisy throaty purrs echoing around the garden as it concentrated fully on finishing this freshly prepared meal.

It was too distracted to notice her approach, too startled to stop itself being grabbed by the filthy scruff of its sinewy neck. He was carried and thrown in the garden's water butt, the lid slammed down to both prevent his escape, and partially drown out the sound of his desperate flailing. He'd instinctively clawed her *en-route* though, carving two long bloody gouges across Carey's flushed tear-streaked cheeks.

The voice thanked her.

Chester's muffled, plaintive and desperate meows became less and less frequent, more and more waterlogged. After a few minutes, Chester meowed his last.

She'd fished his corpse out an hour later, hiding the bedraggled lifeless bag of clicking bones and scabbed fur under bags of rubbish in the garden bin.

Friends forever? the voice had whispered.

Friends forever, Carey replied.

• •

He appeared for the first time, that night. At first, she'd thought herself to be dreaming, watching the face on the Justin Bieber poster contort and writhe, until he'd stepped out of it and into the room. In the subdued glow of her decade old Miffy nightlight, he shimmered with an unreal quality, looking like a superimposed image, something that didn't belong here. A crude cardboard mannequin of her favourite pop star (for that week, at least), given jerky, erratic life.

It hurt to look at him, making her eyes feel like she'd been staring for too long without blinking. As she turned away, she felt him draw close.

I am Par, he said, the first thing he'd ever spoke that wasn't a request or a demand. His voice was calming, as soporific as the soothing warmth he projected. She closed her eyes and dreamt of him.

David Court

With each tiny murder, with every tiny soul snuffed out, Par grew. His movements became less unnatural and his form developed, texture and contours emerging from his iridescent form. She found she could look on him longer each time, before being forced to avert her gaze.

With Par there in person to urge her on, and the tangible benefits of each victim, she found it easier to kill. And she was finding that each kill made the next easier, numbing her.

She'd had, however, been forced to become more resourceful in her pursuit of prey. She'd had to stop luring cats to their doom when the police had become suspicious and she'd been forced to resort to travelling further afield in search of fresh victims.

A stray dog, a skinny saggy-titted mongrel that had recently given birth, had been a rare find. Exhausted and hungry, it had barely struggled as she'd smothered it. She'd hoped to find its puppies as a bonus, scouring the local back alleys and wasteland, but to no avail. Still, that satiated Par more than the cats had - his form appeared more solid, more *tangible*.

They'd talk into the night, Par and Carey. He was *so* grateful for her assistance, and she was grateful for his company. She had no friends her own age, singled out – not unfairly – as the weird kid. She was *happy* to be an outsider – Par was all she needed.

We'll be together forever, she'd smiled, resting her shoulder against his warmth.

Par agreed.

When she'd moved out of home three years later, Par had moved with her. They'd joke about which poster to put up next –

Par

whether she'd like him to appear as David Boreanaz, Adam Levine, or Norman Reedus. If she was ever feeling playful, she'd threaten him with a Barney the Dinosaur poster, a mockery of a warning that caused the two of them to collapse in paroxysms of laughter.

With a moderate wage from waitressing, it was easier to get hold of animals. She'd calculated a route of pet shops and animal shelters she could use, anything to avoid going to the same one twice within as short a time as to arouse suspicion. She'd got the art of killing the innocent little things down to a fine art; a snapped neck for the bigger ones, drowning or smothering for the smaller ones.

As she became immune to the deaths, she was changing too. Her skin grew pallid, her hair now lank and hanging from her shoulders like dried straw. She gave up looking in the mirror after a while, content with gazing at Par's own ethereal countenance. But in that, she'd noticed that Par's development had slowed to a crawl. It still hurt to look at him for prolonged periods of time, and there was still something unnatural about his appearance – and it was still impossible for him to remain out of the poster for long.

Par hadn't asked anything of her in an age, but she knew what he'd ask the next time he did. It was the only possible course of action. The day was coming, and she dreaded it.

And then it came, casually, as she ate her breakfast of leftover burritos from the evening before. Spoken matter-of-factly with a complete lack of reverence, but each word he said slammed into her like a controlled explosion.

You need to kill for me, Par asked. She turned to face him, squinting at his unfathomable beauty.

Bigger, this time.

And then? she'd asked.

Immortality, he said.

●●●●●●●●●●●●●●●●●●●●●

David Court

Par had never criticised Carey's appearance, never told her to comb her hair, wash her face, or dress nice. *You're perfect as you are*, he'd said. Her bosses at the diner had criticised her looks, complaining that she smelled like she hadn't washed herself, her hair, or her clothes in a month, but she'd reacted to that by simply quitting. She didn't need the job anymore.

The boys, though. If she didn't look nice, they wouldn't notice her.

Par, reminding her that this act was for their mutual benefit, had told her how to make herself pretty. He'd talked her through how to cut and style her hair just right and had told her which clothes to buy and wear. Carey stared at herself in the mirror, realising that she hadn't done so for the longest time. An unrecognizable woman stared back at her; make-up hid the bags under her eyes but couldn't mask the tiredness within the eyes themselves.

I can't do this, she said. *Animals are one thing, but people...*

You just bring a boy home, he'd chuckled. *You don't even need to kill this one. I'll do it.*

In her addled brain, this was all the justification she needed, absolving her – in a warped way – of all responsibility. One thing she'd become very good at was justifying her actions, however extreme.

Despite that, he could tell she was still uneasy. He could read her like a book, and she needed support.

Forever, he'd whispered.

Forever, she'd replied.

• • • • • • • • • • • • • • • • • • • •

The cacophony of deafening percussion and discordant guitars that poured out into the street outside the bar were like sounds from an alien landscape, like nothing she'd ever heard. She felt awkward in these tight clothes, the cold autumnal hair

Par

raising the goose bumps on her bare short-skirted legs like tiny motes of braille.

Par had told her to come here, had reassured her that she was beautiful and that all eyes would be on her and only her, when she walked into the bar.

She stumbled on her never-before-worn-heels as she walked down the beer-streaked concrete steps that led into the basement that served as a bar, straightening herself up before anybody had spotted. Par had told her that she needed to look confident, like she'd been here a million times before. He'd gone through her instructions in considerable detail, emphasising every step as though he'd been rehearsing it from his home in the *other place* beyond the poster.

As she stepped into the gaudy neon lights that struggled to light the room, the handful of patrons all turned to stare. Her only competition was a woman old enough to be Carey's grandmother, plastered with inch-thick make-up on a face locked in a permanent blood-red lipped smirk.

Bar stools were shifted across stained floors as she approached the bar, and as the barman approached, she could feel a dozen eyes locked on her. Trying to hide the fear in her voice, she asked for a drink with all the confidence she could muster.

They never asked her for ID. Either she'd made a convincing job of looking old enough, or this was the kind of place where that didn't matter.

• • • • • • • • • • • • • • • • • • • •

In the end, he was as easy to lure as Chester had been, way back then. In the same way Chester had been lured by the promise of an easy meal, the same logic had applied here. She'd sat there for the evening listening to the trucker's crappy jokes, pretending to be enthralled by his dull cliched tales and outright lies. She'd watched with some amusement as, instinctively, his

David Court

right hand nervously rubbed the pale patch on his finger from where he'd recently removed his wedding ring.

The hungry look in his eyes made it clear that he thought she was *his* prize for the evening. He had no idea.

It was all she could do to wriggle from his eager grasp to find her key and unlock her flat. He was at least ten years her senior, an old drunk who'd probably looked half-decent back in the day. He'd told her how he loved her a good two dozen times since they'd left the bar, his fat tongue slobbering hollow Jack Daniels soaked platitudes into her ear.

She'd hoped that Par would have been waiting for them then, as they fell inside, but there was no sign of him. When she'd stumbled towards her bedroom and the poster, the man had followed, panting like an excited mutt. Within moments, he was pushing against her, rubbing her through her dress, breathing clouds of bourbon fumes all over her pretty washed hair. His own limp long dark hair was in her eyes and her mouth, and she squirmed and writhed against him, desperate to escape. She kept glancing over to the poster, anxious for Par to emerge and intervene.

She heard a belt buckle being undone, a zip opening. His right hand was inside her dress, squeezing her nipple between thumb and forefinger with a clumsy inelegance that made her retch.

Abruptly though, she relaxed against his grip. She could feel that Par was near, the familiar sense of comfort that came from being in his presence. The man jerked briefly, and lurched back, his grasping hands returning to his side – a puppet left to dangle, enervated.

The man's eyes flicked open, and she saw her crystal-clear reflection in the brief struggle that took place there. In the literal blink of an eye, she saw Par staring back at her through those eyes. He smiled, and he was on her again - *no, not again – for the first time.*

Par

They fucked, there and then, her eyes closed tight through the entire act. It hurt her almost as much to look into those eyes, as it did to look at the empty shell that they used to belong to.

Forever, he'd whispered, Par's own voice present even when played across the stranger's vocal cords.

Forever, she'd replied, falling into a peaceful sleep.

• •

She gave up trying to move after the third day, when the cramps got so bad it was like somebody was grabbing at her guts with a spiked glove and trying to twist them like dough. Her limbs burning like wildfire, she'd crawled to the bedroom. Her muscles felt like they were peeling from her body as she'd clambered onto the bed and collapsed there, her skin temporarily cooled by the softness of the sheets.

She'd had a fever, as a child. The days and nights had flickered by like a slideshow, all sense of time and space subverted. This was the same, the only solid anchor that existed between all states being the immense pain she felt.

Par was with her, speaking soothing words which ended mid-sentence after which, she'd awake in the dark, abandoned. He'd return, just to vanish again.

She tried not to think of the room, the web-like strands that hung like drapes from wall to wall, of the damp things that slid from the walls. She merely had to look at him, her eyes welling up with the sight of his unearthly beauty.

The smell of the room had shifted from stale to foul; the odorous taint of acidic fumes that caused her throat to burn. To sate her occasional fits of delirious hunger, Par would leave her offerings on the bed. Rotten soil and rain-soaked meat parcels freshly dug from the garden; her tiny countless crimes exhumed.

She tried to not think of the contents as she pushed each of them into her desperate maw through a patchwork of bloodied stained teeth, all ground to flattened knolls of dentine.

David Court

. . . .

On the third week, the pain stopped. Carey was numb, her senses dulled through the multitude of tortures against her flesh. Her eyes were unable to focus, stinging mists of ammonia half-blinding them. She couldn't see herself, and none of her that remained could feel.

That was, thought Par, some small blessing.

He leant in close to her, pressing a hand against her distended stomach. He could feel them moving beneath the flesh, tiny barbed hands reaching up to press against his.

You'll be a wonderful mother, he whispered, leaning into what remained of her face. He noted that the two gouges from that first victim had reappeared on her pale skin, a roadmap of tiny murders. *They'll be here soon, and they'll need to feed.*

She went to lift a hand to him, but her muscles failed at even that. A single fingertip was raised, quivering.

Immortality, you said.

Her voice struggled to emerge from her cracked dry throat through her parched bleached lips. It barely registered as a whisper.

Par, sensing the time was due, stepped back. She struggled just a little as they emerged, feeding from blood, muscle and bone as they burst forth; messily, noisily, angrily. Born from blood and born *to* blood. Her body went limp, her duties complete.

Of a sort, he smiled as they scurried from the bed and across him, cooing and purring as they warmed themselves against his welcoming, iridescent form.

Your sacrifice will never be forgotten.

Par stepped back into the poster, taking his children with him.

Blare the Bright Fanfares

IN THE END, it was Sergeant Lodge who said what they were all thinking, miserable old Lodge who rarely spoke other than to scream obscenities or orders.

"So, I'm saying this with genuinely no offence meant," he muttered, stepping away from the assembled troops and towards the Major, "but wouldn't it make more sense to send *him* as reconnaissance?"

A calloused and nicotine-stained finger pointed towards the hovering form of Sovereign, who simply stared back at the Sergeant, a perfectly sculpted eyebrow raised. The superhero stood out from the battlefield like a clean patch on a muddy face, the green-trimmed yellow cape on his pristine costume fluttering gently in the mid-morning German breeze.

Faint murmurings of approval from the amassed soldiers grew louder and more confident, and it took three appeals from the Major – each louder than the one before - to finally silence them.

"Sergeant Lodge, I can appreciate your position, but we have no idea what's out there. We're not going to be sending our primary asset out onto the front lines until we have an idea of what we'll be facing."

Without taking his eyes from the Major, Lodge spat a chunk of tobacco into a shallow puddle at his feet. He spoke quietly and calmly, but every syllable was clearly soaked with vitriol.

David Court

"I've seen tank shells flattening against your boy's chest. We've seen him punching a Messerschmitt out from the sky, and turn barbed wire into molten puddles. The boys from 11th Armoured said they saw him breathing in a battlefield full of poison gas and blowing it out as harmless snow. I've also seen -"

The Major stepped forward, meeting Lodge's glare with a look equally as defiant.

"You know your orders, Sergeant."

Lodge continued, undeterred.

"I've *also* seen brave men ripped to shit by mines. I've had good pals barbequed by German *Flammenwerfer* teams. I've had young, scared, and dying boys crying in my arms asking where their legs have gone after a round or two of Nazi artillery fire."

The Major took another step forward, visibly breathing in enough air to deliver one of those trademark bellowing rants he did when he'd properly lost his temper.

Sovereign, finally breaking his silence with an attention-seeking cough, placated them all. He simply stopped hovering, landing on the muddy battlefield floor with the grace of a ballet dancer. His wheat-yellow boots sank into the mud dirtying them for the first time, but he seemed unfazed.

"The Sergeant wields a cogent point," said Sovereign, turning to face the soldiers. All had now fallen silent. To hear Sovereign, the first of the heroes, was like hearing *God*. That was if God had the kind of Received Pronunciation you tended to only hear on the BBC World Service.

His cape dragged through the mud as he walked towards them, now stained with encroaching veins of sodden earthen brown, each step weighing it down further. Like Moses and the Red Sea, the crowd parted before him and he stepped into the heart of them. Lodge was as cynical a New Yorker as you'd find, but even he found himself awestruck as Sovereign brushed past him.

Blare the Bright Fanfares

"Enough valiant men have died in this accursed theatre of war, whereas I've mostly just stood around and observed. It was Merlin himself who bequeathed me my magical belt with the strict rule that it could only be used for the purposes of *good*, and what's more honorable and decent than punching Nazis, eh, lads?"

An enthusiastic "hip-hip-hooray" went up from the soldiers. The Major spoke up, his voice frail and apprehensive. He was as red through embarrassment now as he had been with rage earlier.

"But, Sovereign, Sir – I'm under strict instruction from Prime Minister Churchill himself to –"

"I'm not scared of Churchill, Major – and more to the point, I'm not scared of the Germans either. What I *am* fearful of, is another one of these brave chaps dying for a patch of muddy soil so that my uniform remains *Rinso* clean for your damned propaganda photos."

Sovereign slowly lifted into the air, his muddied cape dangling heavily down. Cheers went up and fists were pumped into the air, Lodge's amongst them.

"So," he concluded, staring down at the shrinking form of the impotent Major, "Let Churchill and the Germans do their very worst!"

Sovereign opened his one working eye - the other bruised and battered, closed and filled with blood - to see a vague humanoid-shaped hole in the church ceiling. He was lying on his back in a fragmented *pick-up-sticks* tangle of collapsed flooring and broken pews, sharp wooden shards piercing his tough skin.

He'd never felt *anything* like the first punch that had landed on him and had been as stunned by that revelation as he was from the resultant concussive force. And yet, from that moment, every punch had been stronger and faster than the one before.

David Court

Sovereign had been trying to take the fight away from the battlefront, trying to lure his foe to the lower stratosphere. His foe had taken the bait, but it was short-lived – he'd attacked from above, delivering a punch that had sent Sovereign plummeting from the heavens to land here in this abandoned church.

He staggered unsteadily to his feet, exhausted muscles protesting as he pushed the pews aside. His once beautiful, primary-coloured costume was scorched and shredded, victim of dozens of well-aimed throws, punches and heat-beams. Even the belt of Merlin which once gleamed with an inner magic, energized with the arcane powers of the Grand Magus himself, now hung dully from his waist.

The musty, shadow-filled church was suddenly filled with light, and Sovereign looked up to see his foe casually peeling the roof from above him, rolling it up as though it were the lid from a tin of sardines.

Sovereign balled his fists as his foe descended towards him, steadying his feet on the uneven ground. His enemy landed without a sound, brushing fragments of brickwork and rubble from his shoulders.

His uniform was a dark wine-red, a white and black Iron Cross logo across his muscular broad chest. His cape, boots, belt, and gloves were the same black as that logo, each of them trimmed with fine braided lines of gold. His hair – blonde, of course – was cropped and streaked with darkened smears of soot.

"Still got some fight in you, eh, *Miststück*?" he asked in a broad Germanic accent, copying the fighting stance (and accent) of Sovereign in a mocking manner, "Queensberry rules, eh, *what-what*?"

Who *was* this man? They'd heard rumours that the Nazis had persisted in their Übermensch experiments, but the only examples of it Sovereign had fought so far had all been failures. The only fallouts of it that he'd witnessed – and easily beaten -

Blare the Bright Fanfares

had been gargantuan strongmen with the wits and smarts of a three-year-old child, or masterminds with a combination of singularly useless powers and glass jaws. This one was different – he was smart, and he was tough, and neither British nor American intelligence had given Sovereign any warning of his existence.

Sovereign, realising that he was fighting a losing battle against the nausea that threatened to overwhelm him, stared at his oppressor. He went to deliver a line that would cut the Nazi to his quick – something about Hitler's rumored mono-testicular qualities – but the words were drowned in a throat-full of blood, lessening the impact somewhat.

The German leaned closer, a hand behind an ear.

"I'm sorry, Sovereign. I didn't catch that – would you like to repeat it?"

Sovereign spat out a mouthful of blood, feeling a tooth or two leaving his mouth at the same time. The German took a step back, feigning repulsion at the sight. The plucky Brit lunged forward with a sudden left uppercut, sending his adversary staggering backwards. Steadying himself, the German gave a grin, flecks of blood dotted across his otherwise perfectly white teeth.

"Nice one, Englander!" he beamed. "Now it is *my* turn."

A fist with the force of a sledgehammer smashed against Sovereign's temple and threw him backwards. He felt his skull crack, a painful reverberation that rippled through his jaw. A volley of punches thudded into him as he stumbled back – he'd barely flinched from one blow before another hit him, all raining against him like a hail of bullet fire.

It had been the longest time since anything had truly surprised Sovereign. A lifetime ago, when as an archaeologist he'd stumbled into the secret underground chamber at Glastonbury Tor and been deemed worthy by the Wizard Merlin, he'd learned of the existence of magic and the supernatural. Since that fateful day, he'd battled with demons and fought a multitude of both human and superhuman menaces – but never anything like this.

This new foe had countered everything that Sovereign had thrown at him, and with ease. It was as though he were being toyed with, and Sovereign was feeling an emotion he hadn't felt since that day he'd first put on the magic belt.

Fear.

Sovereign was still standing, but barely. He hadn't even witnessed his opponent *moving*.

"Super-speed," mused the German, smiling. He looked genuinely surprised. "That's a new one."

The German was suddenly right in front of him, index finger tensed against his thumb and posed to flick. It was as though Sovereign were watching a reel of film with frames missing, the German in front of him, seemingly without motion.

"Who are you?" coughed Sovereign, the strength fading from his legs.

The German's eyes gleamed with malice, a rictus smile carving its way across his perfectly chiseled Aryan features.

"You will go to your death at my hands, and never know," he cursed. "Besides, you're not even fit to speak my name."

The index finger flicked against Sovereign's forehead, the force easily matching any of the German's punches. Sovereign's vision filled with a dull oily red, the sounds of the outside world replaced with the torrential rushing of water. He felt his back collide with the church wall behind him, but there was no pain, only a warm, all-encompassing numbness. He felt something inside him burst open as he lay on the floor, the last vestiges of his strength now leaking out and pooling beneath him.

He could only watch as the German crouched down and picked up a piece of black twisted metal from the detritus littering the floor, smiling as he did so. As he stepped closer, he started to rub the tip of his finger against it. It moved in a blur, sparks flying as the once flattened edge of the metal was sharpened into a point with every passing moment. He stepped over to Sovereign, testing the weight of his rudimentary weapon, swinging it like a baseball bat for effect.

"Any last words?" he mouthed, standing over the downed superhero. The arm holding the makeshift metal spear was drawn back, the tip aimed at Sovereign's forehead.

This is it, thought Sovereign. It dawned on him in those deliberately drawn out final few seconds that it had been an age since he'd contemplated his own mortality. Other soldiers may have had heroic imaginings about how they'd like to meet their final fate on the battlefield – perhaps sacrificing themselves heroically to save the platoon or a colleague – but Sovereign, with his extra-ordinary powers, hadn't considered dying *at all*.

Like a puppet with its strings cut, his limbs failed to respond. All he could do was glare defiantly at his foe, try to meet his maker with all the dignity that he could muster.

Merlin, I tried. I hope I did you proud.

Their eyes met, Sovereign and his nemesis. The German's teeth were gritted in anger as he cruelly lingered over that final killing blow.

The tip of the makeshift spear – once locked on, unfalteringly began to quiver, the hand holding it suddenly shaking nervously, uncertain. The wide glaring eyes that moments before had glinted with hate began to dull, blinking as they filled with water.

The German's grip relaxed, and the metal fell from his hands, bouncing twice against the stone floor before coming to rest. The empty hand fell to his side, and he staggered back. He appeared distracted, his eyes darting from one wall of the church to another. The emerging look on his face was as though he'd just suddenly been let onto the world's greatest secret. His mouth formed an "Oh" as he looked mournfully towards the prone form of Sovereign, tears carving a clean path down his mud-spattered face.

His eyes moved skywards, and he was gone. The walls shook from the sonic boom, clouds of dispersed rubble coughing into the deserted church. Sovereign's eyes closed, and he slumped into a deep unconsciousness.

It was a few minutes shy of midnight when the staff car containing Doctor König pulled into the compound. It was the squeaking of the brakes of the Mercedes Benz as it pulled in that had eventually roused him from his slumber, thankfully settling the argument between the two soldiers over who'd have to wake him up. He was very tired, and truth be told, more than a little drunk. He'd made his way through the best part of a bottle of fine Port when they'd come for him, and – despite his protestations – they'd refused to leave without him. One of them seemed keen on reminding König that he had a gun, which had somewhat influenced the good Doctor's final decision.

"Military business" was all they'd replied when questioned. The combination of the dull un-talkative company, alcohol flowing through his veins, and the warmth of the black leather seats had done little to keep him awake, and he imagined he'd slept for most of the journey from Berlin. Probably snored noisily for much of it, too.

Handed his old Military Pass, identical from when he'd handed it in, other than a refresh of the expiry date, he was led through endless slate grey corridors. The lights would occasionally flicker, the brief bursts of unexpected darkness disturbing König yet not his unblinking silent military escorts.

The walk led him away from any offices and into darker, less used chambers and rooms. A draughty motor pool now lay empty, a firing range equally deserted. He was guided through three thick bulkheads, each more secure than the last. He stood in bewildered silence as the soldiers turned levers and slid bolts and locks aside.

There was another man waiting for them in the last room, a man who commanded a greater authority than his small stature

Blare the Bright Fanfares

would have suggested. The soldiers went pale, hurriedly and awkwardly saluting as he told them to leave the room. The man leaned in conspiratorially close to Doctor König, emphasising the importance of his being here. He spoke of duty, of honour, of The Fatherland. König nodded nervously as he listened, terrified that the man could hear his heart beating in his chest, smell the stale drink on his breath.

The last door was wooden, un-windowed and more mundane than the previous bulkheads. At the man's bidding, König stepped towards it, turned the handle, and stepped inside.

The room, previously in darkness, lit up as he stepped in, dull strips of lights *plink-plink-plinking* into life, one after the other.

A figure cocooned in thick battleship chains sat at the room's centre, head turning to face König as he stepped inside. There was a single vacant chair in front of and facing the burdened captive.

"Werner Hartmann," exclaimed König, remembering those Aryan poster-boy features that had made him the most popular candidate. If there was any emotion there upon seeing him, König concealed it well.

The figure smiled back at the Doctor, craning and stretching his neck. The colossal chains rattled and clanged against one another as he shifted in his seat.

"They call me *Überlegen* now, Otto."

Otto shifted uncomfortably on the metal seat. It was as cold as the damp room, and this wouldn't do his hemorrhoids any good at *all*. He stared down at the blank sheet of paper in front of him, feeling the cold weight of the fountain pen in his grip.

"They told me you asked for me in person, Werner."

"You were there at the start, Doctor König. It only seems fair that you be here at the end."

David Court

Otto remembered the selection process. Despite his
protestations, his superiors were more concerned with the
appearance of the chosen candidate than their worthiness
through other criteria. The Ministry of Propaganda had drawn
up the posters before the first needle had punctured skin; bold
striking symbolism of a blonde-haired sculpted superhuman
carving a swathe single-handedly through the amassed Allied
forces.

Hartmann and several other German youths had fit the bill
perfectly, all matching the supposed Aryan ideal. The
Übermensch formula itself – Doctor Ambros's chemical soup
that would supposedly awaken the latent powers dormant in the
Master Race – had been refined for human application through
the vile experimentation in Mengele's laboratories.

There had been five of them, at the start. They'd all sworn an
oath to the Fatherland and then, moments later, were injected
with the Übermensch compound.

Becker, the youngest of them, had died not only first, but also
nigh-on immediately. He'd bled to death in front of them,
drowning in his own un-clotting blood. Schulze was next,
rendered blind within moments and dying from a massive
aneurism within the hour. Vogel had complained of feeling
nauseous within moments of the injection but survived nearly
twenty-four hours before spontaneously combusting whilst
asleep. Kuhn, the only female in the group, simply vanished
from her locked dorm never to reappear, leaving only a glowing
faintly radioactive silhouette on the wall. Her screams though,
lingered for hours – an awful disembodied shriek that curdled
the blood and echoed through the walls.

But Hartmann, to the amazement – and relief – of König and
his team, survived for the day. And then a second day, and then
a week.

And on the eighth day, his first power emerged. Without
realising it, Hartmann had walked to the canteen without his
feet touching the ground, levitating for the entire duration. With

Blare the Bright Fanfares

training, that developed into flight. Otto marveled at the sight of the boy loop-the-looping in the skies above the compound.

And on the eleventh day, Hitler's inner circle came to visit – and the day after, Otto and his team were unceremoniously removed from the project. They paid him enough to keep him in expensive Port until the end of his days, forced him to sign an array of terrifyingly worded non-disclosure documents, and then drove him home.

And now, months later, as quickly as he'd been forced to leave, he'd been driven back.

"At the end, you say?" enquired König, scribbling some notes onto his pad. The boy looked agitated, and it was noted.

"Where did you go, Otto?" asked the boy. "You promised you would be the one who completed my training."

"The decision was taken away from me, Werner. I guess they considered care of such a highly strategic asset too important for a lowly psychologist and his team of doctors. And from what I hear, that was the correct decision."

"What you *heard*?"

"I didn't work here for years without making some friends. They kept me updated with your progress. I know about the rate at which your new powers developed, about them preparing you for your first battlefront trial."

"My first battlefront trial," the boy repeated, contemplating the words as he mouthed each one.

Otto stood up and stretched his tired arms. He took a step towards the boy and brushed his fingertips against one of the huge chains that bound him.

"And from what I've heard, *this* won't make any difference."

"You're right, Doctor. I could shrug them off at any moment, but it makes *them* feel safe if I keep them on." He nodded towards the door, to the soldiers beyond.

Otto sat back down, once again picking up his notepad.

"They tell me you've decided to be a conscientious objector."

"I've decided not to fight, if that means the same thing."

David Court

"You've been seen now, out there, on the battlefield. Every ally will be having nightmares about you tonight, and every front page will have a picture of you tomorrow, and every editorial in the days to come will be an article about you nearly killing Sovereign. They've invested too much in you; They won't let you *stop* fighting."

Überlegen became a blur of motion, the chains spinning around him like a tornado. Otto could feel the movement of them, the air being noisily displaced. The chains were suddenly all collapsed in a pile in the corner of the room, noisily clanking and rattling as they settled. The boy stood in front of the doctor, staring at him, defiant.

"They can't make me fight. They can execute me or lock me up, like they do with all the other *verweigerer*."

"That's not going to happen, Werner. They won't put on a firing squad for a man immune to bullets – nor will they lock him up somewhere he can escape from at will. They'll threaten your friends, your family. And you will fight."

Werner placed his hands onto Otto's shoulders, resigned.

"How did this happen, Otto? How did it all go so wrong? You promised me that I would be a Propaganda poster-boy, nothing more. I am not a soldier."

"But they made you a soldier, Werner. And from what I've heard about your battle with Sovereign, they made you a damn good one. What happened out there?"

The power was *addictive*. To use it just made you want to use it more. In the forty-minute battle with Sovereign, he'd established that he was by far the better fighter. Sovereign was losing, and he knew it, but that British stiff upper lip wouldn't let him quit.

He'd had to fight every instinct he had to lower his guard enough for the Brit to get his free punch in. It was obvious that the weakened hero had ploughed every ounce of strength he'd had into that uppercut, but Überlegen had barely felt it.

"Nice one, Englander!" Überlegen beamed. "Now it is my turn."

Sovereign was punch-drunk, barely reacting as Überlegen's fist smashed into his head. As the hero tumbled backwards, time seemed to slow, his flailing body floating as though underwater. Beads of Sovereign's sweat and blood hung in the air like Christmas baubles, and Überlegen realised he'd just obtained another super-power.

His body was moving at super-fast speeds, and his perception had altered accordingly. Amused by this new-found gift, he stepped over to the suspended hero and delivered a hefty volley of punches to his ribs. Sovereign's skin rippled from each fresh blow, and Überlegen stepped back to where he'd originally stood.

"Super-speed," he said aloud, overjoyed. "That's a new one."

The unstable Übermensch compound churning around in his bloodstream was gifting him with new powers or evolving his present ones at a terrifying rate, and Überlegen wondered if it would *ever* stabilize. He hoped not – becoming more Godlike with every passing moment was nothing if not intoxicating.

Time returned to normal, the beads of sweat and blood splashing onto the floor beneath Sovereign's unsteady feet. Überlegen flexed and relaxed his new power, marveling at the pace at which the world moved around him and how easily he could control it.

He was in front of Sovereign in an instant, his hand ready to flick at the Brit's forehead. How much damage could he do with just a single thumb and forefinger?

"Who are you?" coughed Sovereign, the words barely audible through shattered teeth and lungs pooling with blood.

"You will go to your death at my hands, and never know," smiled Überlegen. "Besides, you're not even fit to speak my name."

David Court

The single flick sent Sovereign cartwheeling across the ruined church, crashing into the far wall. It was time to end this. He'd fly Sovereign's defiled corpse to the front, dropping his ruined body at the Allies front door. Überlegen leant down to pick up a metal pole, sharpening the blunt tip with a hyper-velocitized finger as he stepped towards his ineffective nemesis.

"Any last words?"

Sovereign was already beaten. His mouth opened and closed like a landed fish, attempting to make one last statement of defiance. Überlegen was in no doubt that if that man had any strength left, he'd still be fighting.

"So, you had him at your mercy," asked Otto, continuing to note down the boy's story. "What happened?"

"Another super-power, Doctor. One that only allowed one course of action."

"Yes?"

"I could hear his thoughts, Doctor. And not just his – the ones of all his platoon I hadn't killed yet, the ones I was saving until later. But those ones from Sovereign – they weren't what I expected. They weren't of anger or hate towards me – but of regret. Of having failed. And in that moment, I think I understood what they were fighting for. I felt Sovereign's pain."

"*Empathy*. You gained the power of empathy."

"I've been thinking about that a great deal since, Otto, but I believe it was something more than that. I think in that moment I gained a greater understanding – an expansion of consciousness, if you will. I realised the futility of all of this – that men from both sides are dying in a struggle that could be ended. Armed with that, how could I continue as I had? I panicked, and I came back here. And I needed to see you."

"Why me?"

Blare the Bright Fanfares

"I've been here for nearly a day now, and in that time, I've gained another super-power. A variation of that *empathy*, perhaps. Perhaps something completely new."

Otto could taste blood on his lips, and a sharp metallic tang filled his nose. A carefully placed fingertip told him what he needed to know; that his nose was bleeding.

"Mind-reading," announced Werner, "but I'm not terribly good at it yet. I needed to know whether you could be trusted, whether your intentions were pure when you first brought me here."

"And?" asked Otto, confident of the answer.

"Your intentions were good. I'm picking up a lot of that – good men, led – or leading others - down uncomfortable paths. Perhaps for tradition, perhaps through obligation, perhaps misguided. The guards out there; good men, wrong choices."

"But that doesn't alter the fact that you –"

"The man you were with earlier – he was not a good man. And he surrounds himself with equally bad men."

Überlegen ripped the Iron Cross symbol from his chest, letting the black and white fabric flutter to the floor.

"What was it you called me earlier, Otto? A conscientious objector?"

"Yes, Werner. That's how they see you."

"They're not quite right. A conscientious objector will not kill, and they'll find out how wrong that label is. I'm just very conscientious about *who* I'll kill. As I said, it's a struggle that can be ended. By the right man. Or the right *super* man."

With a leap and a bound, Überlegen was gone.

"Blare the Bright Fanfares" was originally published by Local Hero Press in "Fight the Good Fight 5"

David Court
About the Author

David Court was born and resides in Coventry, UK, with his patient wife Tara and three less patient cats. When not reading, blogging angrily on www.davidjcourt.co.uk, drinking real ale, being immune to explosions, writing software for a living, or practicing his poorly developed telekinetic skills, he can be found writing fiction. David has had several short stories printed in various anthologies, including *Fear's Accomplice*, *The Voices Within*, *Sparks*, *Visions from the Void*, *Weird Ales* and *Hydrophobia*. Including this current book, he has four collections of short stories – *The Shadow Cast by the World*, *Forever and Ever, Armageddon* and *Scenes of Mild Peril*.

David's wife once asked him if he'd write about how great she was. David replied that he would, because he specialized in short fiction. Despite that, they are still married.

About the Author

Hi there.

So, here we are at the end of the book. I hope that means you enjoyed it. Whether or not you did, I would just like to thank you for giving me your valuable time to try and entertain you. I am truly blessed to have such an opportunity, people kind enough to give my books a chance and spend their hard-earned money buying them. For that, I am eternally grateful.

If you would like to find out more about my other books or forthcoming projects, then please visit my website for full details. Also, feel free to contact me on Facebook, Twitter, or email, as I would love to hear from you; all necessary details are below.

If you enjoyed this book and would like to help, then you could think about leaving a review on Amazon, Goodreads, or anywhere else readers visit. The most important part of how well a book sells is how many positive reviews it has, so if you leave me one then you are directly helping me to continue on this journey as a writer.

With love and genuine thanks,

David Court

Twitter: @DavidJCourt
Facebook: https://www.facebook.com/DavidJCourt
Website: www.davidjcourt.co.uk
Email: davidjcourt@googlemail.com

Printed in Great Britain
by Amazon